"COLLUSION ON THE FELT"

A Novel by

Michael Philip Pernatozzi

iUniverse, Inc.
New York Bloomington

Collusion on the Felt

Copyright © 2008 by Michael Philip Pernatozzi

All rights reserved. No part of this book may be used or reproduced by any means, graphic, electronic, or mechanical, including photocopying, recording, taping or by any information storage retrieval system without the written permission of the publisher except in the case of brief quotations embodied in critical articles and reviews.

This is a work of fiction. All of the characters, names, incidents, organizations, and dialogue in this novel are either the products of the author's imagination or are used fictitiously.

iUniverse books may be ordered through booksellers or by contacting:

iUniverse
1663 Liberty Drive
Bloomington, IN 47403
www.iuniverse.com
1-800-Authors (1-800-288-4677)

Because of the dynamic nature of the Internet, any Web addresses or links contained in this book may have changed since publication and may no longer be valid. The views expressed in this work are solely those of the author and do not necessarily reflect the views of the publisher, and the publisher hereby disclaims any responsibility for them.

ISBN: 978-0-595-52505-8 (pbk)
ISBN: 978-0-595-51254-6 (cloth)
ISBN: 978-0-595-62558-1 (ebk)

Printed in the United States of America

Chapter One

In the face of seeming unbeatable odds, those societal combatants summoned the adrenaline to make a left turn where the rules dictated a right one.

The taxi driver had been shot point blank in the face, the article said. It was the fourth such murder in three weeks. These were senseless, meaningless crimes during which a few hundred dollars at best could hope to be gained. Detectives were split over whether the shootings were the signature of the same killer, or whether one or more copycats were swooping down to take advantage of a frustrated police department. Nevertheless, more and louder rumblings from an increasingly panicking taxi driver force could be expected tomorrow morning on the steps of Las Vegas Metropolitan Police Headquarters.

Sal Mooring Jr. continued to scan the local section of the Sunday edition of the *Review Journal*. There were no further developments in the seven million-dollar Wells Fargo heist. Officials were still convinced it was an inside job, though. Mooring chuckled. Of course it was an inside job – the third taking of an armored vehicle in two years. You put seven million dollars in cash in a truck, give some college dropout the keys and a gun, and then gasp when they all vanish.

He glanced at his watch. It was ten minutes after two. He had just enough time to put on his starched white tuxedo shirt and black string bow tie and begin the dreaded drive to the strip. Although today was

Sunday — it was his Thursday. But the usual bumper-to-bumper traffic of California weekenders crawling through the desert for yet another crack at fortune was predictably waiting to take its toll on Sal's nerves. They did tip well, though — *if* they were winning. And therein lies the Sal Mooring paradox of Vegas. Like nearly all strip dealers, Mooring's hourly wages barely hovered above the legal minimum. His bread and butter were the tokes, painted clay chips usually tossed toward the dealer during the hasty exodus of ecstatic players whose personal wealth has temporarily increased. The bigger the booty, the bigger and more frequent the tips. The problem, however, was that the casino doesn't want the players to win. They don't like it when dealers deal house-losing hands. On the one hand, dealers work for peanuts for the chance at the generous tokes. On the other hand, when they get those tokes from winning players, casino management leers at them.

Sal hoped they'd do a lot of leering tonight. It wasn't enough that the mortgage, the car payments, and literally the food on the table were dependent upon the good luck of the players, but the dealers had to pool their tips for all three shifts and divide the total evenly among all of them. So, it didn't matter that Sal turned on the charm for his guests and ran a lively, friendly table. All of his tokes went into the shift's tip bin like everybody else's for a later divvy. He often wondered how many rude and unfriendly cronies he was carrying.

He folded the newspaper section in half and lofted it onto the coffee table in front of him. It landed on the pile of folded sections he'd read earlier. Sharon would be home from the day shift shortly after he left and would probably spend the evening sifting through the colorful advertising inserts.

Sal and Sharon had met in the dealers' lounge two years earlier while working the graveyard shift at Harrah's. When they announced their plans to marry, the casino quickly reminded them of the rules prohibiting nepotism. One of them would have to leave. They agreed it would be Sal.

As he buttoned his shirt in front of the living room mirror, Sal thought about their lives today. The past two years had been difficult, largely due to their differing work schedules. Not even their days off coincided. Except for a couple of short vacations and those few days when one of them called in sick, they hardly saw each other awake.

Both were successful dealers at major strip casinos with their combined annual income topping six figures. They both wanted to raise children, but agreed they would wait until they could survive on just Sal's income. Although they weren't extravagant, they found it difficult to save much. When they were able to get out together, they did it all - casino hopping, fine restaurants, showroom entertainment. When they weren't out together, each was out alone. Both enjoyed gambling. He favored twenty-one; she preferred video poker.

The more they played, the more evident it became that Las Vegas hadn't been built on the winnings of players. They infiltrated the flourishing job market, set up housekeeping and invariably joined the ranks of some sixty-seven percent of locals who gambled, patronizing the neighborhood establishments to the tune of one point eight billion dollars a year. Even as legalized casino gambling was capturing election-day trophies throughout the country, Vegas visitors continued to increase by the tens of thousands every year.

Mega-resorts responded, adding thousands of new rooms to the town's already burgeoning slate. Football fields of casino space, themed by cultures, countries, futures, and pasts blanketed the sun-drenched Mecca. They grew and continued to grow until their seams began to rupture, and then they renovated. The more popular gaming became around the country, the more Las Vegas continued to prosper and the more hope-filled Easterners and Californians flocked to the palm-treed neighborhoods. Paychecks in one hand, slot handles in the other, the workers of Las Vegas were also the city's most frequent customers – and losers.

And so it was with the Moorings. Since they couldn't spend a lot of time together, each found company among the many locals' establishments during their separate off times. Sal was a better than average blackjack player, thoroughly familiar with basic strategy and able to walk away a winner perhaps a quarter of the time. Sharon caught the video poker bug a few years ago when she won a couple of thousand dollar jackpots early in her Vegas experience. The rush associated with a flashing screen, blinking light and ringing bell of a just beaten video poker machine is often enough to addict the occasional player and pull her across the moderation line in the sand. Sal and Sharon had found plenty of company there. Consequently, a savings account that could have blossomed, lay nearly dormant except for the monthly plucking of maintenance charges penalizing below minimum balance accounts.

They had little to show for their long hours, tedious work and inconvenient work schedules. The occasional windfall quickly found its way back into the casino coffers. They hadn't talked much about their out-of-control finances, but lately Sal was growing weary of their financial treadmill.

The black string tie dangled beneath the unbuttoned collar as Sal patted his glistening temples. He was fortunate to have held on to his full head of thick brown hair, an enviable standout among his thinning, receding peers. Although he hadn't worked out at the gym since he and Sharon married, his six-foot frame deceivingly displayed a well-toned body. He was considered handsome by many, mostly because of his chiseled facial structure, highlighted at the angles set off by his chin and cheekbones. He liked to boast he'd inherited his father's work ethic and his mother's good looks. They were both gone now, having died far too young. First his father, Salvatore Sr., five years ago; then his mother, Anna, three years later. He remembered recoiling on each of those occasions, searching in vain for reasons why hideous cancers had lain in wait during otherwise healthy lives, only to creep up and snatch away what should have been the best years of their lives. Neither had ever smoked nor excessively drank. They had boasted about having avoided the temptations of illicit drugs all their lives. Sadly, Salvatore Sr. had never met his would-be daughter-in-law and Anna passed away only two months after Sal and Sharon wed. Neither had ever visited Las Vegas, opting instead to homestead in eastern Ohio where the seasons were distinct and the family roots dense. Sal missed them both and was learning to live with the remorse that they would have loved the twenty-four hour excitement of this over-the-top town.

As he meticulously cinched his tie, he reflected on the newspaper stories, admiring the enormous courage it must have taken to pull off those daring armored truck heists. In the face of seeming unbeatable odds, those societal combatants summoned the adrenaline to make a left turn where the rules dictated a right one. They conjured up the audacity to make what wasn't theirs, theirs. They blew into the trumpet one last powerful bellow and hit that evasive high note. Those daylight renegades were indeed models of defiance, brave enough to elbow their way to a life of life's pleasures. Sal Mooring Jr. aspired to be counted among them.

For all his twenty-nine years, Mooring had hugged the middle road, working hard, doing without, hoping and dreaming that all would pay off just like his dad promised. Now, a few months on this side of the big 3-0, it occurs to Sal how imperfectly average his dad's life had been in the wake of living *by the book*. The time was here for Sal to re-write that book.

Scribbling an "I love you" followed by a happy face on the notepad by the answering machine, he pressed the automatic garage door opener and winced at the bright sunlight. He tossed a cold water bottle on the front seat of the simmering Plymouth Voyager and eased it out of the garage into the 108-degree August sunshine. The strip was buzzing as expected. Mile long traffic lines crawled, stopped and crawled some more as first time visitors rubbing elbows with Vegas veterans gawked and pointed at the architectural upmanship evident on Las Vegas Boulevard. Where once single story ranch style stucco buildings dotted the strip's dry, sandy landscape, thirty story replicas of European and Middle Eastern icons have sprung up among the miniature versions of New York, New York and Monte Carlo. Italy is well represented both with its touch of Venice at The Venetian and the most expensive hotel ever built, MGM/Mirage Resorts' Bellagio with its breathtaking frontage lake featuring the dancing fountains. If that weren't enough, the view across the boulevard features Paris's Eiffel Tower, built by Park Place Entertainment, the corporate spin-off of Hilton Hotels' former gaming division.

The town, whose gridlocked traffic had long ago outgrown the streets' capacities, had in recent years opted to construct pedestrian walkways over the busy streets at the famed Flamingo-Strip and the Tropicana-Strip intersections.

As the twenty-first century dawned, the once famous desert stretch of single-level flash and neon had erupted into a world of themed high-rises and digital motion marquees, one more ostentatious than the other. And the next is already in production on the mental palette of independently wealthy architects. The question on everyone's mind: when and where will it all end? When will one more extravagant world replica be just one too many?

Similar questions had been asked since the mid 1950s when The Desert Empire became the fourth property erected in the shadow of Bugsy Siegel's Flamingo. And the same curiosity continued to weave its way into locals' conversations now, some fifty years later. When will one more be too many?

This day, on the second floor of the Desert Empire Resort and Casino, in that area accessible only to a privileged few, Charlie Palermo sifted through the previous week's correspondence. Among them were a memo from Human Resources: something about enforcing the employee parking lot issue; the Hotel Vice President announcing the appointment of a new front desk assistant manager; and the usual assortment of unsolicited publications specializing in news of the gaming industry. Palermo kept the paperwork moving from his in-basket to the trash basket while his quick, alert eyes riveted in on the essentials. Actually, it was only one eye. The other darted like a rabbit from one black and white monitor to the other in the mass of jerky zooms and racking focuses looming floor to ceiling just outside his glass enclosed office. The Video Surveillance Director was celebrating his fifteenth year as chief of this "eye in the sky" and prided himself in his highly regarded and disciplined observation techniques. Nothing escaped his gaze and scrutiny. He and his crew of seven surveillance agents were among the most informed and talented on the strip. And something had just caught his eye.

Without loosening his visual grip on monitor eighteen, Palermo's right hand found and lifted the telephone handset.

"Palermo. Put Reno on."

On the wider shot of monitor twenty-six, Palermo watched as the Pit Clerk placed him on hold and looked around the pit for Stan Reno, the Pit Manager on this shift. From his vantage, Palermo could see Reno talking to an Asian player at BJ table 114. As the Pit Clerk also discovered Reno, Palermo whispered into the office mic that spoke to his surveillance crew.

"Hold steady on eighteen, Colonel. Did you catch it?"

Through the glass, Palermo could see the cameo of a back-lighted "thumbs up" from the Colonel whose own eyes were glued to monitor eighteen.

"Yeah, this is Reno."

"Palermo."

"Shoot."

"BJ 119, third base."

Reno turned in the direction of Blackjack Table number 119 and sized up the player sitting to the dealer's farthest right. "Yeah?"

"He just hit on sixteen against the dealer's six up and drew a four. Recognize him?"

Reno slowly shook his head. "No. Never saw him before. What'd Mooring do?"

"Pulled a ten to his sixteen."

"Shit happens."

"Watch this guy's play. He's either counting or stupid."

"It's an eight deck shoe, Charlie."

"Okay, then – he's stupid! Just keep an eye on his play. What'd he buy in for?"

"Couldn't tell you. He sat down with a short stack of green. Might have come from the other pit."

"All right, keep an eye."

Palermo pressed the intercom button on the phone. "Colonel, how long has he been sitting there?"

"About ten minutes."

"Did he buy in?"

"Yeah, I think it was two Franklins."

"He didn't just sit down carrying a stack of green?"

"Not while I've been here."

Palermo looked at the clock on his wall, one of very few on the entire property. It was three-fifty PM.

"Rewind VCR eighteen to about three-thirty, Colonel. Verify that guy's buy-in."

"Roger that."

The Colonel reached for his walking stick. At a time and in a town where youthful appearance seemed preferred to competence, the Colonel knew he was lucky to be employed. Being tucked away in the surveillance department where few knew he was alive, let alone working, was a blessing, he often thought. He'd never really been a Colonel. In fact, during his six years with the Army, he never got above Staff Sergeant. He earned his Colonel title with each added wrinkle on his worn, experienced face, a face that has stared at surveillance monitors and before that through binoculars from catwalks back to the days when all casino managers' names ended in vowels. Very few knew the Colonel's real name. That's the way he liked it.

So far, the Colonel had survived the rash of corporate takeovers that seemed to endear Las Vegas Boulevard to Wall Street. And the takeovers were briskly followed by downsizings, restructurings, mergers, consolidations, and the erection of what have become known as mega-resorts. The catchy desert-suggesting names of the fifties and sixties like Dunes, Sands, Sahara, Desert Empire, were being modified or replaced by international destinations like Paris, New York, New York, Orleans and Venice. The Colonel knew he and his forty-five years of experience were teetering on borrowed time. The lower the profile he could keep, the better. And the more sophisticated human resources technology became, the better his chances of hiding in the depths of the computer database. He felt safe and secure up here in the dark. Besides, he knew that of all the surveillance agents up and down the sprawling Strip, there were no eyes or minds sharper than his own. His boss, Palermo, knew that and made every effort to keep the Colonel conveniently out of sight of the company brass.

"Tape's cued, CP. When you're ready."

Palermo acknowledged with a nod to the intercom on his way out onto the surveillance floor.

"Break time," whispered Tanya Lee as she tapped Sal Mooring's right shoulder. It startled Sal because it hadn't seemed like he'd spent forty minutes at the table yet. With eyebrows raised and a slight tilt of the head, Sal pulled the shoe to the center of the table. He up-clapped his hands showing the cameras he wasn't leaving with any of the casino's money, politely thanked his players, and wished them good luck.

"See Reno," Tanya whispered in Sal's direction, then she smiled, removed the next card from the shoe, and slid it across the table to the discard point. "Good luck, everyone."

Sal glanced at his watch and noted he'd only been dealing twenty-five minutes. Then his eyes shot over in Stan Reno's direction. Reno motioned that he wanted to see him.

"What's up, Stan?"

Reno gestured with his head toward the black bubble peeking down from the ceiling above him. "Sherlock Palermo."

"Yeah? What did he see?"

"Your third baseman. He took a card with your six up."

"Oh, yeah. He pulled a four. The little shit."

"I've never seen him in here before. What's his story? "

"No story. He's in town for the Westinghouse Convention. I don't remember seeing him before either."

"You think it's a fluke?"

"I just think he got lucky."

"What was his buy-in?"

"I called it out, Stan. Two hundred."

Following a brief, awkward stare, Reno said, "I told Palermo he came to the table with a short stack of green."

Mooring looked up at the decorative black bubble, one of hundreds throughout the property behind which leering lenses panned, zoomed and focused on the hands of players and dealers alike, expecting to catch someone doing something underhanded. Management views the surveillance group as kind of a double check, one of many in a long hierarchy of game protection elements.

First, are the house rules. Although they vary somewhat from property to property, they're designed to accomplish the same thing - house protection. On those games where cards are pitched by the dealers and the players are allowed to pick them up, house rules prohibit touching the cards with two hands, reducing opportunity to sneak a card into or out of the game. When held, the cards may not be pulled any closer to the player than the inner rim of the table, insuring that the cards remain in camera view at all times.

On a majority of table games, shoes are used. The shoes contain sometimes six, more often eight decks of cards. With these card delivery systems, players never touch the cards. They signal their intentions with their hands, thus virtually eliminating any opportunity to mark the cards. And, due to the sheer volume, making it nearly impossible for card counters to keep track of those all-important ten-value cards. Over the years, casino bosses have uncovered myriad ways enterprising players have developed to shift the edge away from the house. A well-placed fingernail etch on a card's corner; a dot of dye visible only with specially treated sunglasses; even amateur magicians using slight-of-hand techniques are among the limitless attempts at equalizing that have historically widened the canyon of mutual distrust in casinos.

Introduced in the early nineties, mechanization made its way to the tables in the form of automatic shufflers. At first they were rudimentary, able to shuffle only single decks. But as the decade progressed, so did the technology increase. Now there were several generations of shufflers at work in virtually every casino, some capable of handling six or eight decks. Not only had game security increased by bewildering card counters and handcuffing would-be dealer-cheaters, time spent making money significantly increased. There were no more long unprofitable re-shuffling breaks.

Beyond the house rules and the technologies, are the dealers, drilled in all the local dealing schools to protect the bank, protect the game, protect the house. The anatomically perfect dealer would actually have four eyes: two where they are now, and another two near the ears. The job requires physical coordination and agility, an acute sense of mathematic concentration, a customer relations personality, an almost numbness to wafting cigarette smoke, and an uncanny ability to bring luck to the house. If that weren't enough, dealers must also strain peripherally for visible or audible clues of player cheating. They remain alert to the almost smothered clink of clay against clay emanating from their far left or right as a player daringly sneaks a past posting, attempting to add one or more chips to their wager once the outcome of the cards is known.

Next up the pecking order are the floor supervisors: "the "suits," tasked with watching not one game, but several, perhaps four to six. They're always former dealers, usually burned out, who accept the promotion and accompanying responsibilities as a welcome change of pace only to end up with less take-home pay than the dealers they supervise. They're experienced in multiple games and have the ability to size up situations quickly and identify less than absolute accuracy at a considerable distance. In addition to guarding the hen house, they keep track of the large currency called out by the dealers when they change cash to various colored cheques.

You'll hear the dealer call out "Change one-hundred," as the hundred-dollar bill lay beside the neatly stacked chips. The floor supervisor will quickly eyeball the layout and call out, "Go ahead." Then they indicate on a notepad or computer that a particular table just dropped another hundred-dollar bill. At the end of the shift, the paper money in the drop and their personal running total better be pretty darned close.

The Pit Boss is in charge of all the floor supervisors and dealers in the pit. The larger casinos could have several pits active at any given time.

The Shift Supervisor is in charge of all the pits.

And charged with all casino action is the Casino Manager. That title, in today's corporate environment has given way to more appropriate nameplates like director or vice president of casino operations. And you can walk into any of their offices and you'll see a huge video monitor connected to a multi-camera switcher with remote zoom and focus capability. They, too, are eyes in the skies of the casino.

The telephone rang.

"Shit, Mooring, that's Palermo no doubt," said Reno. "He's gonna ream me about the stack of green."

"You want me to stay on break or go back to the table?"

"Go ahead take your break now. You go back to the table so soon, it'll look goofy."

Reno answered the phone.

"Reno. It's Palermo again. I just looked at the tape of that clown on 119."

"Yeah?"

"He bought in for two-hundred dollars – at that table."

"And your point?"

"My point? You told me he joined the table with green already."

"What difference does it make? I talked with Mooring. The guy's in town for the convention. Mooring thinks he took the card out of ignorance and got lucky. I'll keep an eye on him, okay?"

"I've got to put this in my report, Reno."

"Do what you gotta do." Reno hung up the phone fighting the temptation to wave one particular finger at the dome and walked over to table 119 instead.

Chapter Two

...when you walk into the Baccarat Salons to deal the "game of kings," you leave many of the house rules behind.

Of all the table games in the casino, there is one which offers the highest potential for reward to the lucky player. Baccarat. Known as "the game of kings," Baccarat is also one of the most mispronounced names in the casino. French, it's pronounced "Bock'-a-raw," not "Back'-a-rat."

It's a simple game with three possible betting circles: Banker, Player, and Tie. Two cards each are dealt to the Banker and to the Player spots from an eight-deck shoe. The first and third cards are dealt to the "player"; the second and fourth cards to the "banker."

The highest hand in baccarat is nine. The "Player's" hand is acted upon first. The hand whose card values total nine or is closer to nine wins. Since nine is the highest hand you can have in Baccarat, ten is deducted from any total exceeding nine. For example a total of fourteen would actually be a total of four. If a bettor places a wager on "Player" and "Player's" cards total closer to nine, that bettor along with all other bettors who wagered on "Player" wins even money. Face cards and tens have a value of zero. Aces are worth one. All other cards are face value. Once wagers are placed, bettors have no decisions to make. The dealer does all the work and the card values and rules dictate whether a third card is added to the betting positions. It's a game where fortunes are won and lost, yet whose mainstream appeal is rather limited. Less than one percent of gamblers play baccarat.

One reason the average Vegas tourist meanders past the Baccarat Pit is its somewhat intimidating appearance. It's usually off to the side of the casino, up or down a couple of richly carpeted steps, surrounded by gold railings, and lighted with expensive crystal chandeliers. If that weren't enough, the crisp black tuxedos worn by the Baccarat staff, or the large percentage of Asian players serve as unintentional deterrents to the casual visitor.

If there is a class society among dealers in the casino, the upper crust can certainly be found in the Baccarat Pit. And the cream of the upper crust, those very specially chosen few, would be located in the *salons* of the Baccarat Pit. Salons are the very elite private gambling rooms set aside for only the highest of high rollers, known in casino parlance as whales, whose minimum lines of casino credit top one million dollars. And for the privilege of dealing to these sometimes arrogant, demanding, often contemptuous gamers, baccarat dealers in the salons can bank on annual wages and tips exceeding one-hundred-thousand dollars.

And at high-rolling resorts like the Desert Empire, when you walk into the Baccarat Salons to deal the "game of kings," you leave many of the house rules behind. Sheiks from the Middle East, wealthy Asian businessmen, eccentric show business producers, super sports celebrities – these are the patrons of Baccarat Salons. And they don't like a lot of rules. Millions of dollars can change hands every few minutes. The level of stress shouldered by the dealers and their floor supervisors is stratospheric. One wayward joker, overlooked during the purging of new cards, flipped from the shoe and landing defiantly face-up, meaningless, has cost the casino hundreds of thousands of dollars and floor supervisors their careers.

Rolly Hutchins wears his distinctive salt and pepper hair proudly. At fifty-seven, he is among the oldest dealers at the Empire, and one of the most revered by his co-workers. His tenure in the Baccarat Pit is legendary. On breaks, it's not unusual to see Rolly at the center of a group of admiring younger dealers whose riveted eyes and gaping mouths telltale their absorption in one of Rolly's personal stories of Las Vegas's steamy Seventies. Remembered by many as the winding down of the "good old days," the post Howard Hughes era provided the break-in for many of today's senior dealers and casino middle management. Many of the corporate collegiate upper management, on the other hand, were barely potty trained when the likes of Tony Spilatro were barking orders at dealers to "dummy up and deal." Those were the days when the number of hands dealt per hour were everything in the eyes of the bosses. Idle cards and dice, sidelined during superfluous bullshit with the players, couldn't make the house any money. How things have changed over the years. Today, bullshit rules!

Rolly was one of a scant minority of Vegas veterans who successfully made the transition from yesterday's robotic card shuffler to today's charming goodwill ambassador. Others, many of them Rolly's former comrades, fell from corporate grace under the pressure of trying to look and sound like they cared about the gamblers' social lives behind a forced, teeth-gritting smile. And at least once a year, normally during performance reviews, upper management tries in vain to recruit Rolly into the ranks of the suits. The ritual has been ceremoniously carried out since the mid 1980s. Rolly's response was always the same. He expresses his gratitude, makes believe it's a tough decision, and offers his regrets in choosing to remain a dealer.

Sal Mooring and Rolly Hutchins hit it off immediately. Meeting in the dealers' lounge during breaks shortly after Sal was hired at the property, the two took an immediate liking to each other. Sal was drawn to Rolly's affable style. He was particularly taken with the ease with which Rolly mixed with the other dealers, even those not members of the elite Baccarat "society." Similarly, Rolly was impressed with Sal's apparent maturity and professionalism, qualities not readily found among a majority of the other complacent veterans of the industry.

But more than that, Rolly and Sal's relationship was developing more toward one of family. It was the kind of father-son relationship that Rolly had always missed in his personal life. His wife Beatrice had never been able to bear children and they had long since resigned themselves to it. From Sal's perspective, Rolly was a lot like a big brother, a seasoned professional who generously shared his time, advice and experiences to mentor anyone who needed them.

As Sal passed by the Baccarat Pit on his way to the break room, he glanced over toward Rolly's table. As usual, Asian players, five this time, occupied the table. They were obviously whales. Stacks of pink and lavender chips denoting value denominations unfamiliar to the average gambler and convertible into more money than many people make in a lifetime were opaquely visible through the curtain of cigarette smoke billowing above the players' heads. One of the five, cigarette clenched in his crooked teeth, was ceremoniously, yet superstitiously, peeling over the second of two cards dealt face down at his position. Watching intently, behind and on either side of Rolly, were two stone-faced supervisors. The player was taking his time, as many do, in uncovering the value of the facedown card. The other players at the table were peering through their spectacles and mumbling in their native tongue.

Sal stopped alongside the Baccarat Pit railing to witness the outcome of the card turn. He noticed the familiar hint of a smile on Rolly's face – a sort of smirk – as he soaked up the tremendous tension of the high level action. Each of the gamblers had huge stacks of lavender chips piled on their respective "Player" spots. At stake for each was three hundred and fifty thousand dollars, the maximum individual wager permitted in the Desert Empire Baccarat Pit without approval from higher up. Authority to accept wagers up to a million dollars was delegated only two weeks ago to the Baccarat Shift Managers. It hadn't come easy. Corporate authority regarding money risk never does. And the accompanying admonishments to use the authority judiciously or face career-altering consequences had resulted in a solemn refusal to grant such requests thus far.

At stake for the casino was one point seventy five million dollars, the sum of all five players' bets. It was a critical situation, indeed - one that admittedly came with the territory. With the exception of members of the executive committee, few were aware that the Desert Empire's daily break even point was nine hundred thousand dollars. It was a tough nut to crack for sure, but there were other properties in town with a significantly higher daily revenue challenge. The Bellagio, for one, needed three point five million dollars a day to pay the bills. But, here and now for the Desert Empire, the bottom line was on the line.

The first card revealed for "Player" had been a two of hearts. The "Bank" already showed a total score of "eight." As the white-knuckled player eased a peek at the top corner of the now nearly mutilated card, he and his fellow players could make out what appeared to be a horizontal line. Only the three and seven offered such possibility. And only the seven would mate with the "Player's" deuce to form a natural nine and tilt the table toward the Asians to the tune of three point five million dollars. Once the horizontal line was revealed, the slim Asian slapped the card back facedown to the glee of his teased countrymen. With the outcome still not absolutely certain, the group burst into hurried Mandarin punctuated with laughter and accompanied by a frenzied swapping of pink chips back and forth in front of each other.

"Jesus! Flip the goddamned card, you stupid bastard!" Charlie Palermo screamed at the video monitor. "They're making these fucking' side bets with each other on the turn of the card!"

"From what I could see, CP, we're about to lose big," offered the Colonel. "I think it's a seven."

"We should never have started allowing these nitwits to handle the cards. I *told* Mesmer it was a huge mistake. Turn the goddamned card, asshole!"

Palermo's reference to Mesmer was not totally out of character to anyone within earshot. Nathan Mesmer, the most recent bundle of joy delivered by the parent corporation, Monarch Resorts, had assumed the role of Vice President of Casino Operations just six months earlier. Palermo was known to say that Mesmer had packed all of his casino experience in a strand of linguine. That slur was said to have launched the "hate Nate" campaign that began to simmer on the casino floor.

Palermo's eyes shifted from the monitor down to the VCR beneath it, verified that the digits were changing and that the tape was indeed recording, and immediately refocused on the debasing in the baccarat pit.

Sal smiled and slowly shook his head. From the boisterous confusion, it looked like the players were about to have a big takedown. Sitting on that green felt was enough money for him and Sharon to raise and educate several children, live out their lives in luxury and still have enough left over for their grandchildren. Even with all the attention being drawn to the table by the slaphappy group, Sal noticed that Rolly's eyes were locked on the facedown card and his trademark smirk hadn't wavered one crow's foot.

The two supervisors standing on either side of Rolly, however, were beginning to sweat the game - supervisory behavior that shows they're upset with the house losing, or, as in this case, the extremely high probability of house loss. Sal could see their jaws tightening while they unconsciously shifted their weight from one foot to the other. One's eyes rolled ever so slightly. The laughter and alien murmuring abruptly stopped as the apparent elder of the group gestured to the card handler to get on with the game. Following a few guttural sounds, the player slapped his hand on the facedown card, lifted it in the air and bellowing like a sumo wrestler bounced the "7 of diamonds" face-up on the green felt.

"Lucky bastards!" said Palermo, scowling.

The whales roared! Sal's eyebrows rose, his eyes closed and his head fell in solemn reverence. He caught the irony, too. This new one point seven-five million dollars won by the collective group could change generations of lives forever. But he knew, when the dust from this solo victory settled, the new one point seven-five million dollars would likely perch alongside the original one point seven-five million dollars forming a burgeoning three point five million dollar ride for the next turn of the cards. To these wealthy high roller businessmen, it was merely a game.

To Rolly, it was just another day at the office. He cut the cheques at each of their betting circles, matching their wagered stacks with payoff stacks. As far as Sal could tell, Rolly hadn't noticed him watching. Sal headed for the Dealers' Lounge.

Arthur Kaiser had been watching Baccarat Table Six for the past few minutes from his position at the entrance to the room. As Baccarat Shift Manager, Kaiser knew only too well that the heavy action going on in his room had now reached an alert level. Nathan Mesmer had made it very clear at his initial Casino Staff Meeting that whenever the baccarat bank won or lost two million dollars or more on one hand, he must be notified and kept abreast of the continuing situation.

One of the Asian players slid his winnings into the Player's wagering circle next to his original bet and waved his hand in a circular motion, indicating to Rolly that everyone at the table intended to let it ride. Rolly smiled and held up one finger. He looked over at Arthur Kaiser. This would have to be Kaiser's call.

Kaiser patted the moisture from above his upper lip. All eyes were on him. Three and a half million dollars rested on his consent. Since each player's individual bet would total seven hundred thousand dollars, he would be well within his new authority to approve the wagers. But three and a half million, if lost, would be his worst nightmare tomorrow when Mesmer's sneer met him nose to nose. It would be great if the casino won, though. The game was designed to favor the house. And, if the house lost this hand, any further decisions on granting wagering waivers would have to come from Mesmer. Kaiser forced a weak smile and nodded his approval. Then he whispered to one of the floor supervisors that he'd be back in a couple of minutes.

Double checking that his suit jacket was buttoned, a recent Mesmer image standard added to the many others, Kaiser exited the Baccarat Room and headed upstairs to the shared managers' office. His fingers trembled as he shuffled through the Rolodex in search of Mesmer's home phone number. Finding it, he quickly punched the numbers into the phone. If he were allowed to smoke in the office, this would be the perfect time. A male child answered the phone.

"Hello, this is Arthur Kaiser at the Desert Empire. Is your father at home?"

"He's outside," came the youthful reply.

"Can you ask him to come to the phone? It's important."

Kaiser could hear the boy shouting in the background to his father. Mesmer was probably lying out by the pool. Kaiser stretched the phone to the cord's limits out near the office entrance. He could hear the eruption of yet another Chinese earthquake from the Baccarat Room below. The company had just lost another 3.5 million dollars.

"This is Nathan Mesmer."

"It's Art, Nathan. I'm sorry to trouble you at ... "

"What is it, Kaiser?"

"We just turned over five million in two hands."

"Five?"

"Yeah, first one-point-seven-five and then the three-point-five rode."

"Who's dealing?"

"Hutchins."

"How long till the cut card?"

Kaiser hadn't looked. He should have known that Mesmer always wants to know how much longer the shoe has to go. The cut card is placed about one and a half decks from the end of the shoe after the shuffle. Its presence on the table signals the final hand from the shoe.

"I'm sorry, sir, I didn't look."

Mesmer's calculated pause made the intended point.

"Relieve Hutchins now. Keep me posted. Get that five million back – and then some!"

Kaiser hung up the phone. As if to punctuate the termination of the call, a huge roar of laughter and screams emanated from the room below. Kaiser shook his head. Was it possible the five million rode and won? He grabbed the Rolodex card with Mesmer's phone number and trotted down the balcony stairs, instinctively checking the button on his suit jacket. As he turned toward the Baccarat Room, he could see that a large crowd had gathered alongside the railing. The whooping and hollering from inside hadn't subsided a decibel.

When he reached the room, he politely excused his way through the impromptu gallery and hurried inside. The stacks and stacks of lavender cheques on the layout spoke volumes about just how big this last loss was for the casino. He caught the eye of one of the floor supervisors, Harry Fetters, standing behind Rolly and gave a quick cutthroat gesture signaling a change in dealers. As Fetters moved away to tap a new dealer, Kaiser approached the other supervisor, Dale Bouviet and whispered, "How much?"

Bouviet brought his hand up to his mouth feigning a nose rub and mumbled "Five and a quarter mil. We're down ten and a half."

"Jesus Christ! Who okayed the wager?"

"What do you mean? You did," stammered Bouviet.

"I shit. I was upstairs."

"You okayed the wager before, we just …"

"I must okay EVERY fucking wager EVERY fucking time, fuck face! I'll deal with you later!"

Kaiser surveyed the layout and noticed the red cut card was lying on the table. Finally, that shoe was over. With a new dealer and a new shuffle, it was possible to begin to even the score.

When the group of Asians noticed that Rolly was being relieved, their mouths dropped and they began shouting in rapid fire Chinese. One of the players pulled his many stacks of lavender cheques toward him and stood up. The others quickly followed. In a universal language they were saying, "He goes, we go!"

The prospect of these guys walking with the casino's ten and half million dollars drained the blood from Kaiser's face. He managed a crooked smile, held up his hands motioning to the players to please wait a minute, and barked to Dale Bouviet, "Get me a Chinese Host now!"

Hosts in the casino world are revered members of the management team, and their pay reflects their tremendous value to the company. Casino hosts are the point of contact for the casino's most highly valued clientele. It's the host that the high rollers call when they're planning a trip to Las Vegas. It's the host who makes it a point to know, and store in computers, the player's favorite cigar, drink, candy, flowers, sleeping accommodations, preferred tee time. It's the host who knows how the player likes his eggs, when he likes his eggs, and where on the plate he likes his eggs.

When a hard working host decides to leave a property, it's a smart casino that realizes that where the host goes, so go that host's players. Small wonder why a host's compensation increases by leaps and bounds as his or her following swells in number. When you factor in today's necessity for multi-lingual hosts to cater to the international high rollers and the invaluable awareness by the hosts of the fine points of diversity, cultural etiquette and the many varied superstitions particularly among the Asian players, the value of a good, sharp host skyrockets.

Sue Min Wong, age twenty nine, Vice President of International Marketing, had been with the Desert Empire for eight years. Born in Taipei to affluent parents, she moved to San Francisco at age nine when her father's import/export business established a division there. She was well educated at the University of California at Sacramento, majoring in Business and Economics. Her father's dream of Sue Min working in the family business was almost realized until he brought her to Las Vegas as a twenty-first birthday present. Like many both before and since, she was immediately smitten by the apparent glamour and excitement of the twenty-four hour city named paradoxically "The Meadows." Although she returned home with him following their visit, her life's ambition had taken a new turn. Days after she graduated from UCS, she moved to Vegas to begin her new career. Her moist-eyed father paid for the one-way ticket.

Young, beautiful and fashionably Asian, she breezed through Dealers' School getting placed at the Golden Nugget Casino, downtown. Her dealing skills at the tables were surpassed only by her charm and personality. Within six months, a visiting casino boss from the Desert Empire who was playing at her table, left his business card tucked under a twenty-dollar toke. It's an event dreamed of by every break-in dealer – an invitation to come in for an audition. She did. Not surprisingly, she was offered an extra-board position immediately. Extra-board is a scheme dreamed up by the casinos to swell their ranks with willing, albeit desperate employees, who accept the opportunity to work whatever hours are offered to them, sometimes, but not often, less than forty a week. Employees on the extra-board save the casinos money because they're ineligible for the benefits accorded their full-time counterparts.

The opportunity to deal to the high rollers at the Desert Empire, however, was more than enough incentive for Sue Min to accept the extra-board offer. She was confidant that in due time, her success would win her a permanent position. She wasted no time creating a demand for her services, flashing her bright white smile and gently shuffling with her beautifully manicured, creamy perfect hands. All who placed wagers on her table felt as though they were on a date with her. When they won, they stayed and gave it all back. When they lost, they kept pulling out those crisp hundred dollar bills. And win or lose, they were always sure to leave a generous tip. Within a year, and during a brief era when dealers kept their own tips rather than pool them, Sue Min was the highest compensated dealer in the twenty-one pit. Her annual wages exceeded seventy-five thousand dollars, a remarkable achievement considering her base hourly wage was only four dollars and fifty cents.

The one drawback noted by the casino was that, as a dealer, Sue Min could only display her obvious charms to a full table of seven players at a time. The then Casino Manager, Herb Dennis, suggested an idea to her that she consider moving into the Casino Hosts' Office where she could optimize her contributions to the company. Her starting salary of eighty-four thousand dollars made it an easy decision for her. That was five years ago.

One of her first blockbuster ideas was to invite a group of twelve wealthy Chinese businessmen from Taiwan with whom she was acquainted through her father, to stay at the Desert Empire as her guests. The group occupied the top floor of the famed Olympic Building in the three 4,000 square foot high roller suites for three days and two nights. She had found these gentlemen listed in the Casino's VIP database where they were identified as twenty-one players who had not visited the Desert Empire in three years. She had a very focused objective for this particular junket.

One day into their visit, she telephoned the three suites and invited the group to join her for gourmet Chinese food in the Palace of Palms Restaurant at seven PM. When they had assembled that evening, Sue Min entered the restaurant looking like the proverbial China Doll. She was breathtaking in her good luck red dress, tight fitting where it counted, hanging loosely six inches above her knees, and flashing that brilliant white smile. Her long, shiny black hair enveloped her face with a glowing radiance.

During the lengthy traditional Chinese meal, she cleverly introduced the subject of Baccarat into the social chitchat. To these novices, Baccarat was a strange, boring looking game for high society Europeans. Sue Min lured them into her confidence and quietly apprised them of the significantly better odds of winning as contrasted with their usual game of Twenty One. She added that it was the easiest game in the casino to play, too. The only decision Baccarat players had to make was on which of two circles to place their wager - three if they wished to bet on a tie. She offered to take them into the Baccarat pit after dinner and have one of the dealers show them the particulars. She even offered to provide each of them with a hundred dollars in chips to use during a practice shoe so that they'd have no risk first time out. She also let it slip that Baccarat has been catching on with more and more of their fellow countrymen and this would be an excellent opportunity for them to "get up to speed" on the game.

Whether it was the prospect of spending more time in her company or of basking in the wake of her perfume, the group accepted her invitation and that night Baccarat at the Desert Empire became the game of choice for Chinese high rollers. And Sue Min Wong secured her name on the list of Desert Empire legends.

Sue Min was browsing the computer database in the Host's Office this night, working her usual sixth day. Although her International Marketing Office is upstairs among the Executive Offices, she often settles in the hosts' office just off the casino floor. Immediate access to her invited guests is very important to her.

"Sue Min!" The abrupt entrance by Dale Bouviet startled her. "We need you in the Baccarat Salon right way!" Bouviet was nearly out of breath.

"What is it?"

"We just lost ten and a half million and these Chinese guys are ready to walk because we changed dealers. Kaiser sent me to get you."

All she had to hear were the words "ten and a half million" and "walk" in the same sentence.

"*Nobody* walks, Bouviet!" And the speed with which she moved more than made the point.

When she arrived at the Baccarat Salon, she waved off Arthur Kaiser and his lame attempt at explanation and immediately approached the angry players. She smiled that gorgeous smile and politely bowed. Their furrowed brows and tense frowns softened as they returned the customary greeting. As in a huddle, she spoke soothingly in Chinese with full knowledge that as she leaned forward her full cleavage was seductively up for review by their inspecting eyes.

She told them she understands they are upset because it was time for their lucky dealer to take a break. One of them shook his head and accused the casino of wanting to change their luck by bringing in a different dealer 'maybe more lucky for the house.'

"If they can change dealers when they want, then we can leave with our money when we want," another said.

"What would you like for me to arrange?" asked Sue Min, leaning forward ever more slightly.

"Bring back our dealer or we take our money to Caesars Palace," the eldest gentlemen declared.

Kaiser's ears perked when he made out the words 'Caesars Palace.' Mesmer would have his head if these guys left for the Palace.

Sue Min turned toward Kaiser. "Arthur, they're adamant about leaving if they don't have their dealer back. They said...."

"I heard," said Kaiser. "Caesars."

"Well, the cards are on the table. Can we bring back the dealer? Who was it?"

"Hutchins. He's down in the break room. He really does deserve a break, you know."

Sue Min turned toward the group of players and spoke to them in whispered Mandarin. When she was finished, the gentlemen exchanged curious glances. She'd said something they hadn't expected. Apparently awaiting a response from them, she prompted with another whisper.

Several of the men made that uniquely Asian "thinking" sound of sucking saliva through closed teeth and puckered lips. Then they convened in a huddle, mumbling sounds that even Sue Min could not make out. Finally, the eldest of the group gestured for Sue Min to lean in his direction. He whispered their response.

She nodded, taking care to avoid any facial expression. She turned and walked over to Arthur Kaiser. As she leaned in toward him, he turned his ear to her, making eye contact with the group of staring players.

"They'll stay," she whispered, "under two conditions. They want Hutchins back immediately and...."

"That's a 'can do', what else?"

"They want me to place the bets for them. One big bet for the entire table, each hand."

"That's impossible," snorted Kaiser. "You know the rules here."

"With all due respect, Mr. Kaiser, may I suggest you allow Mr. Mesmer to make that call? After all there are ten and a half million dollars at stake here."

"Tell them I'll see what I can do."

As she walked over to the group, Kaiser reached inside his jacket and removed the Rolodex card, motioning to Bouviet and Fetters to approach.

To Bouviet, he said, "Take this to Ernestine in the pit and have her get Mesmer on the phone. Let him know it's urgent that I speak with him."

To Fetters: "Go on down to the break room and get Hutchins. Tell him I'll make it up to him later." Then Kaiser walked out to the Pit, clearing his throat for a bout with Mesmer.

Chapter Three

Reminiscent of a similar gesture by a rotund American baseball player three-quarters of a century earlier, the Chinese player pointed to the stack of twenty-one million-dollar chips.

As the Sunday sun melted into the majestic Spring Mountains, twilight settled over the Las Vegas valley. The temperature variance at this time of day in the August desert is negligible at best. It might be described as slipping from impossible to unbearable. However preferable over the bright daylight sun, hot summer evenings, dry heat or not, can be extremely uncomfortable. On the other hand, there are few places on the planet where the color drenched sun-streaks pierce the white billowy cloud puffs with more prism splendor than on Vegas's west horizon. Travelers headed east on one of the city's many surface streets at this precise time of day absorb the breathtaking mating of humanity and nature as the day's final splashes of sun ricochet off the emeralds, the golds, the oranges and the reds of the impressive Las Vegas skyline.

The driver of the sleek yellow Viper convertible, however, wasn't the least bit interested in the beauty of the moment. Nathan Mesmer had only twenty-one million dollars on his mind. Most of that twenty-one million dollars had moments ago belonged to the Desert Empire. On his own approval less than three minutes ago, Sue Min Wong pushed stacks of chips equaling ten and half million dollars into the "Player's" wagering circle on behalf of the Chinese delegation.

'Bank shows five, Player shows … six,' gasped the telephonic relay from Kaiser. 'Christ, Nathan, we're down twenty-one million!'

At that, Mesmer actually jumped into the Viper, vaulting over the closed door and pivoting in mid air, still grasping the cellular phone.

"Stall, Kaiser! Stall! Do you hear me?" Mesmer huffed and wheezed. "After Hutchins pays them, get a fill to the table. Just stall! I'm on my way."

A fill at the table meant that a security officer would go to the Casino Cashier and pick up more chips to refill the depleting bank at the table. Aside from being an excellent time killer, this particular table was in desperate need of a fill. The next bet was sure to be twenty-one million. There weren't enough chips in the table bank to match it in the event they won again.

The group at the table was so lost in celebrating their most recent win, they weren't even aware that the fill was underway. Kaiser whispered to Hutchins to take a little more time in paying off the ten and a half million dollars. Rolly nodded knowingly. The game sweating was in full swing.

Sue Min allowed the group to kiss and paw her and did her best to look like she was happy about this most recent, embarrassing turn of events. Her strategy was to keep them at the table knowing they would continue to let the winnings ride, eventually balancing the scales. Tradition and odds were both in the house's favor.

Sal Mooring glanced at his watch. His break was coming to an end. He thought he'd try one more time to reach Sharon. The two previous attempts met with the answering machine. She hadn't mentioned having had any plans for this evening, but then she was famous for being impulsive. No answer again. This time, unlike the others, Sal left a brief 'I love you' followed by a kiss.

He checked his watch. Something seemed strange there in the Dealers' Lounge. Usually, at this time of evening, the room would be at least seventy-five percent filled with dealers and smoke. But there were only three other dealers in the room right now, two of them were dozing sitting straight up. The third, Josh Keaton, had just entered the room.

"Where is everybody?" Sal asked Josh.

"They're watching the show."

"What show?"

"You don't know? There's a group of Asians busting Baccarat's balls."

"Must be that same group I was watching on the way down here," Sal said.

"So far they're up 21 mill and word is they're letting it ride."

"Up 21? Is Rolly dealing?"

"Yeah. They insisted! Threatened to walk!"

"That explains why he only had a three minute break."

"That's nothing," Keaton continued. "Guess who's placing the bets for these guys."

"Who?"

"Wong, that chick from Marketing. They actually have her placing their bets! Can you believe it?"

"Kaiser's got to be livid," said Sal smiling.

"You kidding? He's been glued to the phone with Mesmer. Everyone expects Mesmer to come storming in any minute."

Sal stole a final look at the mirror, straightened his string tie and walked quickly out of the downstairs lounge and up the employee access stairs to the hallway behind the Race and Sports Book. As he entered, he was surprised to see only eight or nine bettors scattered throughout the book. The noisy crowd just outside Baccarat, he figured, had lured the rest into the main casino. In a moment Sal would know just how huge that crowd had swelled since he had gone on break.

As he rounded the corner from the Dice Pit, he was stunned at how sparsely the twenty-one tables were populated. The dealers presiding over the dead games were standing at the required parade rest, while their entire upper bodies ached to turn around and witness the Baccarat debacle. Sal noticed a singular live game with two Asian blackjack players still involved in deep concentration, apparently totally unaware of their stark surroundings. Adam Arnold, their dealer, seemed equally oblivious. Stan Reno, standing post at the twenty-one pit podium, allowed his attention to sneak toward Baccarat. Sal approached.

"Stan, where do you want me?"

"What?" Reno didn't even turn around.

"What table do you want me at?"

Reno turned toward Sal. "Oh, Mooring. Go ahead and tap out Tanya on 116. There's no action here, anyway. Those bastards over there are wiping us out."

Sal looked over at table 116. There were no players.

"Mind if I take a peek at what's going on before I relieve?"

"No, go ahead. Just keep it brief."

As Sal was making his way toward Baccarat, Nathan Mesmer exploded through the doors at the hotel valet entrance and was double-timing it toward Baccarat. He hadn't taken time to change clothes. Here came the Vice President of Casino Operations in red shorts, shower clogs, and a blue muscle shirt. As if to reduce the attention drawn to himself, he slowed down his stride. He need not have worried, though. Every eye in the casino was locked on the Baccarat table. Sue Min had just pushed a stack of chips worth twenty-one million dollars into the Banker's betting circle.

Another nuance of Baccarat is that when money is won in the Banker's circle, a five percent commission, called a "vig" is paid to the house from the winnings. There's no rhyme or reason for this particular rule, except that it gives the house a little advantage. Even when the house loses to a Banker wager, it picks up five percent. That "vig" is sometimes enough to discourage bettors from wagering on the Banker's circle. And in a game that is nearly fifty-fifty, to avoid betting on one of the two circles for fear of paying a five percent commission on winnings creates a psychological edge for the house. If the house were to lose this next hand, it would take five percent of the twenty-one million dollar payoff, which translates to one million fifty thousand dollars. That's a substantial sum, but not an appreciable reason for the house to break out the champagne.

Mesmer excused his way through the crowd of onlookers and approached the entrance to the Baccarat Pit. Kaiser's polite greeting was abruptly interrupted.

"Talk fast," Mesmer whispered. "Where are we?"

"She just put it all on Banker," Kaiser wheezed.

"Twenty one million?" Mesmer clarified.

"That's right, sir."

Rolly Hutchins surveyed the layout. All was ready. The twenty-one million dollar wager stood defiantly perched on the Banker's circle. The table bank had been freshly replenished and could afford to pay this and several more hands, if that nightmarish necessity arose. There was nothing left to do but slide the cards out of the shoe. The same player who squeezed the winning cards before Sal went on his break motioned that he wanted the cards pushed over in his direction. After all, it was he who had mustered all of the wins so far. This was not a time for the group to tamper with Lady Luck. That would not be the Chinese way. Up on the second floor, Charlie Palermo stood behind the Colonel watching the full shot monitor. He had just instructed the Colonel to focus two cameras on close-ups of the two card positions. Only the soft, amplified music piped into the casino could be heard. The crowd of onlookers was silent. And everyone in the crowd could hear the barely audible sound of new cards meeting green felt as Rolly began the deal.

Carefully, he slid two cards face down onto the card area labeled Player. Just as carefully, he pushed the other two face down cards in the direction of the Chinese player who would turn those cards in the order and at a pace to be determined solely by him. With the two pairs of face down cards now positioned, Rolly's eyes met with the Chinese player's eyes. The player ever so slowly turned his head toward his betting partners looking for a sign from them whether he should turn the cards first or let the dealer turn the other pair first. All he got back from them were cold return stares. He would have to make his own decisions. He whispered to Sue Min as he gestured toward Rolly.

"He wants you to turn one of the cards," she said to Rolly.

Rolly bowed toward the player and quickly revealed a King of Hearts, worthless in Baccarat point value.

"Player shows zero," Rolly announced.

Immediately a murmur emanated from the onlookers.

"Mother of God," Mesmer sighed. "Where will it end?"

"It's a King, CP," the Colonel announced, forgetting that Palermo was literally breathing down his neck.

The Chinese player placed one hand on top of each of his face down cards and began rubbing the cards into the felt, slowly at first, then picking up force, gritting his teeth. After a ten second eternity, he threw back his head, squeezed his eyes closed and lifted the right hand card up over his head and flung it back onto the felt, face-up.

"Bank shows nine," said Rolly.

"CP, it's a fucking nine!"

"Christ, you know he's got a picture card under there, Colonel. I'm sick."

Mesmer neither heard Rolly nor could he make out the card.

"What the hell is it?" he attempted a whisper.

Hutchins heard him and mouthed "nine."

"Did he say 'nine'?" Mesmer grabbed Kaiser's wrist and squeezed it.

"Yes," moaned Kaiser, "nine! Please let go of my wrist. You're breaking it!"

"It's not your wrist I'm interested in breaking, you idiot."

Word quickly spread through the crowd that the bettor had just revealed a nine and the murmuring escalated.

When the anxious commotion began to subside at the table, Rolly once again looked over at the Chinese player for his cue. The player leaned over toward Sue Min and whispered.

"He would like you to turn over your second card," she relayed to Rolly.

Rolly again bowed to the player and quickly turned over the second card for the Player.

It was a four.

"Player shows a total of four," announced Rolly.

In a game where twenty-one million dollars goes to the player whose cards total closest to nine, four was not a good position for the casino. Mesmer just stood there at the baccarat podium, wincing from the burning sweat in his eyes. His lower lip was beginning to spasm. Sal had worked his way from the rear of the group to the front. In all his years working in a casino, he could never remember anything quite like this. Virtually all action in the gambling hall had ceased, but for this one hand of Baccarat. The usually boisterous crap games lie silenced, as the shooters made their way to where the real action was. The few remaining blackjack players had now joined the throng outside the Baccarat Pit. Every eye was screwed to the one remaining face down card in front of the Chinese player.

Reminiscent of a similar gesture by a rotund American baseball player three-quarters of a century earlier, the Chinese player pointed to the stack of twenty-one million-dollar chips. He rubbed his hands together as if starting a friction fire. Letting out a karate scream, he slapped his hand onto the card. With his now familiar fanfare, he tossed back his head, squeezed his eyes closed, picked up the card and flailed it face-up on the table.

Everyone gasped whether they could see the card or not. Instantly Rolly sized up the card's value and calculated the two-card score.

"I can't look, Kaiser, what the fuck is it?" asked Mesmer trembling. Kaiser's own vision was blurred from the perspiration in his eyes. "I'm not sure ... "

"It looks like a deuce, CP," the Colonel bellowed, "an outstandingly gorgeous little motherfucking deuce!"

"Banker shows one," declared Rolly. The throaty gasps of disappointed realization by the Chinese group, however, all but drowned out his announcement.

"Did he say 'Banker shows one?" Mesmer panted to anyone who could hear him.

The best reply he could hope for came next, however, as Rolly extended his hands and began to pull the twenty-one million dollars toward the house coffer.

As if awakening from a coma, Kaiser shook his head briskly, blinked repeatedly and moved toward the crowd gathered outside the pit.

"It's over," he said. "Please continue to enjoy your stay at the Desert Empire."

More than anything else, his announcement was intended to get the employees back to their workstations.

"It's *not* over," interrupted Sue Min. "Mr. Nim has informed me that he and his associates will be back to the Desert Empire another time when the outcome will most assuredly be substantially different," she said smiling.

The group of players smiled and nodded. As Mr. Nim rose, so rose the others. They spoke quietly to Sue Min as the rest of the casino slowly began to resume its business as usual.

Mesmer, in his beach attire, looked and felt terribly out of place.

"All right, back to work," he ordered to no one in particular. He pulled up the front of his muscle shirt and buried his face in it, blotting the flowing perspiration from his eyes and forehead. "I'm going home to enjoy the final moments of my weekend."

As he passed Kaiser by the Baccarat Pit railing, Mesmer mumbled, "Good job, Art. Keep me posted."

Kaiser responded only with a sneer to the back of Mesmer's head.

With the action in the Baccarat Salon at an end for the time being, Rolly Hutchins covered the table bank with the plastic cover, locked it and placed the key in Kaiser's hand. Now it was break time.

Chapter Four

*... the fresh deal delivered four clubs to the royal,
all in ascending position, lacking only the ten.*

The ritual of tie removal and neck emancipation was especially welcome this late night as Sal made the long, dark lonely walk from the main property building to the employee parking lot. The Sunday tradition would continue as he would soon pull into the one Taco Bell in town whose drive-thru dared to keep weekend hours to one AM. He couldn't shake the indelible feeling of knots tightening like vices inside his chest at the realization that twenty-one million dollars could actually change hands on the turn of a card. He's seen action before, plenty of it. He dealt with gargantuan fortunes daily, some going away with the players, most however returning like swallows to their Capistrano table banks. He had long ago come to grips with the fact that but for one instant of Lady Luck, there goes several college educations, a home, new cars and a retirement nest egg. He had learned to accept the players' stares of hatred which punctuate lip quivering prayer when he pulls a five to a killer sixteen making the dreaded twenty-one.

But this night, this action, he would never forget. So unbelievable were the casual smiles of resignation by this group of sinfully wealthy icons of Asian business when ... oops, it's a deuce. We lose. So what. We'll be back. Tsai Chen. What the fuck!

As he approached his car, he could see what appeared to be a small piece of paper tucked under the left windshield wiper. On closer review, however, he could make out more clearly that it was Art Kaiser's business card. Scribbled on the back were the words: *Had a pretty good shift. Let's celebrate at The Neon Lantern. My Treat! Rolly.*

So Rolly wanted to celebrate? Celebrate what? Sal started up the car. He would call Sharon on the way to the Neon Lantern.

The post midnight cruise south on Las Vegas Boulevard hadn't lost any of its original allure, thought Sal, admiring the glittering lights, the picture-perfect palm trees, the slick, colorful electronic signs. And even at this late hour, when most towns are curled up and fast asleep, the tourists in Vegas continued gawking. Camera in one hand, plastic cup in the other, they are lured into a beckoning maze of pyrotechnic flare-ups, synchronized dancing fountains, and amplified pre-recorded outdoor sound-tracks, trying desperately to capture the moment on film or tape to relive back home when the inevitable boring reality sets in.

The street traffic, though still heavy with pedestrians, was relatively manageable now and the windows-down ride was a soothing change of pace for Sal. This was definitely time for unwinding. If he weren't going to meet with Rolly, he'd be taking his bag full of Taco Bell treats into the living room for a few hours of digital cable surfing.

He made the right turn onto Flamingo and reached into the door pocket for the cell phone. Sharon would probably be sleeping, but she'd want to know that he wasn't coming straight home. Two rings. A third ring. Why wouldn't she answer? After the fourth ring, the answering machine picked up. Rather than leave a message, Sal touched one-six to retrieve any messages that had been left. There was one from Sharon's mother, " ... *nothing important, call when you can."* Then came Sal's own message from the Dealers' Lounge when he threw a kiss and said he loved her. Now there was Sharon's voice.

"Hi, love. I heard your message. Love you, too. Listen, I'm out with Missy. We're over at the Rio. I've adopted this cute little Double-Double Poker machine and it's been teasing me all evening. I feel lucky, Sweetie. So, Missy and me decided we can't leave until one of us wins a jackpot ... which we'll split with the other. So I got two chances!" she said giggling. "See you when you get home. I'm on cell. Love you."

Sal was passing the Rio now. Could she and Missy still be there? As usual the parking lots were packed. Here was one property in town which couldn't make up its mind whether it was for tourists or for locals. An all suites hotel, it managed to sustain unparalleled appeal among visitors *and* residents. As a result, the Rio, owned by the Harrah's Corporation, kept adding hotel towers, restaurants, casino floor space, parking garages, and more attractions.

The fact that Sharon was with Missy bothered Sal. Missy was one of Sharon's co-workers at Harrah's, divorced, mid-twenties, very attractive and rather wild. The two women had been out gambling together several times before, and each of those times Sal and Sharon ended up in an argument. When she was around Missy, Sharon drank and gambled far too much. The last time the two were out, Sharon had sunk over four hundred dollars in the slots, winning nothing but a hangover and too few hours sleep before work the next morning. He didn't need another one of those episodes.

'I'm on cell,' she had said. Sal sent out the speed dial call. After one ring, the annoying message from the phone company apologized that the cellular member is either unavailable or out of the cellular area. Bullshit, thought Sal. She's turned it off. He quickly called their home and left a message on the answering machine for Sharon to call him on his cell as soon as she came in. He let her know that he was stopping off at the Neon Lantern to have a drink with Rolly and would be home soon. After a brief hesitation, he blew her a kiss and whispered, "I love you."

The Neon Lantern had the kind of atmosphere that appealed to people who just wanted to sit in the dark, talk, munch and sip. There were no live bands, no loud crowds. Any music was nearly imperceptible. Places like this were few and far between. But for those who counted themselves among this targeted market, it was a great place to begin the unwinding process after a late shift.

Rolly loved to come here. And at this time of night, there were only three or four other couples cuddling in scattered booths as Sal stepped in the door. Rolly motioned for him, although Sal had no problem locating his lone friend.

"Unfucking believable, Rolly," Sal said, in a breathy whisper.

"What's that, kid?" Rolly feigned curiosity.

"You know damn well!" Sal slid down in his seat, smiling and shaking his head.

"All in a day's work, my friend."

"Right. There are *countries* with less cash flow in a day's work!"

"What are you drinking?"

"They got any food here?"

"Like what?"

"I don't know. Tacos. They got anything like tacos?"

"There's nothing *like* tacos, Slick. Either its tacos or it's something else."

"Is that a menu? Toss it over."

"Why don't you eat in the employee cafeteria? It's fast and free?"

"Just toss me a menu, please. You are buying, right?"

"Why not?" Rolly shrugged and tossed the menu to Sal.

"By the way, what did you mean by 'had a good shift?'"

"One of the best, kid. Didn't you see the action on that table?"

"Hell, yes, I saw the action. So did everybody else in the casino. But we also saw something else."

"Yeah, what's that?"

"If you had a good shift, that means you pulled in some good tokes. Those Chinamen didn't throw you a *kiss*!"

"They never do."

"Yeah, I know. You've told me that before. They're cheap sons-of-bitches."

"Yeah. It's a half-assed custom or something. They don't tip."

"Yet, you call that a good shift?"

"Oh, it was terrific."

The waitress approached the table.

"Debbie, darlin'," Rolly said pointing to his Bud Light, "let me have another of these, and my buddy here thinks he's in Mexico."

Sal smiled. "He means I have a taste for tacos, but I see you don't have them on the menu. Let me have a ham and cheese omelet, hash browns and rye toast. And a Diet Pepsi."

"Perhaps I could get the cook to put together a Spanish omelet for you?"

Sal was visibly moved. He smiled broadly at the flirt.

"I appreciate that, Debbie, but I'll stay with the ham and cheese."

"I'll be right back with your drinks," she said smiling. Sal watched her walk away.

"Easy boy. Let's not forget what you've got waitin' for you back at the ranch."

"No harm in looking, right?"

"I guess that depends on what you're lookin' for, now don't it?"

"Hell, I don't even know where Sharon is right now to tell you the truth. Her last message said the she was out with her friend Missy at the Rio. That had to be several hours ago."

"Sharon's a big girl. She knows her way around this town."

Sal took his cellular phone out of his pocket and placed it on the table. He double-checked that it was powered up.

"I know she does. But when she's out with this Missy, she gets a little screwy. I've got a sick feeling this night is going to cost me a bundle before it's over."

"She gamble a lot?"

"Not usually. Once in a while we both belly up a hundred or so. But every time she gets out with Missy, she loses more and more."

Debbie returned with the drinks.

"I checked with the cook," she said to Sal, "and he said there'd be no problem with a Spanish Omelet." Her lips-only smile was warm and Sal felt the heat.

"You are rather persistent, aren't you?" He returned the smile.

She smiled and nodded.

Sal leaned intimately forward. "You know that Spanish Omelet sounds better and better every time you say it."

"Spanish Omelet," she whispered.

"Hell, I'll take a dozen," bellowed Rolly.

They all laughed.

"Sold, Miss Debbie. I'll have that Spanish Omelet. And thank you."

"My pleasure." That smile was unwavering.

This time as Sal watched her leave, it was more than obvious that she was relishing the attention.

"Hey, brother, let's toast the best customer service this side of the strip."

They clinked their beverages. But while Rolly sipped, Sal stole a glance in the direction of Debbie's last known whereabouts, the swinging kitchen door.

"Damn, boy, if I didn't know no better, I'd think you were bit."

"What's her deal, Rolly?"

"Can't say. All I know is she's always here when I come in. But I gotta tell you, I'm seein' sides of her I just ain't seen before. And I credit that to you, Slick."

Sal's cellular phone rang.

"That's Sharon!" He was startled.

"Be cool now. That's your baby."

"Hello?"

"Sal? Hi, sweetie!"

"What's going on?" asked Sal.

"You know."

"I *don't* know ... and *where* are you? Are you home?"

"Not yet. Me and Missy are still working on the machine I told you about."

"Sharon, how much have you lost?"

"Lost? I haven't *lost* anything."

"What are you talking about?"

"I'm *investing*. It's only a loss when you walk away a loser. I'm still an investor."

Sal shook his head. "All right. How much have you *invested?*"

"I'm not sure I want to go there just yet." Sharon's feel-no-pain voice began to quiver.

"How much have you invested, Sharon?" Sal could feel the fear in his voice.

"I knew I shouldn't have called you."

"Sharon! Please just tell me how much of an investment we have in this machine of yours right now. Please!"

Sal could hear a distancing of the sound, a ruffling noise, then Sharon's whimpering voice in the background, begging Missy to speak to Sal.

Missy lost the debate.

"Sal, this is Missy. What's going on here with you and Sharon?"

"Missy, please put my wife back on the phone. This is between the two of us."

"Listen, Sal. I don't know what you said to her, but she's hysterical. She's not getting on the phone with you again."

"Missy, all I want to know is how much has she lost so far?"

"The *investment*, if that's what you mean is only six hundred dollars for the both us."

"You mean she's lost three hundred dollars of our savings?"

"Not exactly, Sal. She advanced me my half, too, which I will pay back."

"She took six hundred dollars of our money!" Put her on! Put her on now!"

The phone went dead.

"Hello! Hello! She hung up!"

"That sounded way too serious for me, Cowboy. Here, take a sip of my beer and loosen up." Rolly slid his beer toward Sal. "Don't get yourself all tight and twisted up over money. Six hundred ain't gonna break you. Besides, she might even still win a jackpot. The night's still young."

Sal chucked a healthy swig of beer. "She's not going to win shit! Besides - she's not the only one losing our money. She gave three hundred dollars to Missy to gamble with! Not only that, but get this – if either one wins, *they split*! Have you ever heard of such an asinine plan in your life? What the hell kind of a dimwit am I married to?"

"I know it ain't my business," said Rolly, "but are you two having money problems?"

"Ah, it's not that. Not really. We're *making* pretty good money. We just can't seem to *save* much. If it's not one thing, it's another. And we both like to gamble."

"Is it gettin' out of control?"

"I don't know if it's out of control, but it seems like it's getting worse."

"How do you mean?"

"It's happened before, Rolly. A lot. Except now it happens more often and the stakes keep getting higher. I just don't know what to do."

"Have you talked?"

"Oh, we've talked. We make promises that we break and make all over again."

Debbie arrived with Sal's order. "Spanish Omelet, hash browns, rye toast," she said cheerfully. Both men looked up. "That does look good," said Sal.

"Can I get you another Diet?"

"Please."

Rolly leaned back and sipped his beer while his hungry friend dug in to his late night meal.

A few blocks east, a tearful Sharon Mooring sat at the "double double" video poker machine with her head buried in her arms. Sitting at the "double double" next to her was her friend Missy. From the size of the crowd at the Rio, one would think it was eight o'clock in the evening instead of two in the morning. The Rio's action just never seems to dwindle.

Missy was feverishly working on *their* machine. They had been taking shifts all evening trying to materialize the evasive Royal Flush along with a two thousand dollar pay out. This particular row of video poker machines also offered an alluring twelve thousand five hundred dollar jackpot for a royal flush that appeared in reversible sequence: ten through ace or ace through ten, suited. It was this "alternative" high-powered objective that was driving these ladies this night. And they had plenty of company at the machines around them.

The older, straggly-haired blonde lady with the perpetual cigarette dangling from her protruding lower lip sounded the jubilant jackpot bell and lit up the lights about an hour earlier when she hit a non-sequenced royal flush for two thousand dollars at the machine at the other end of the row. She had "held" the Jack, Queen, and King of Clubs. When the Ten and Ace of Clubs slid perfectly into place on the draw, she threw both skinny arms up in the air as if signaling a perfectly executed field goal. The longer that bell sounded before the technician turned it off, the more adrenaline pumped through Sharon and Missy.

"I told you he'd be pissed," said Sharon with her tilted head cocked in Missy's direction.

"He'll get over it in a hurry, honey, especially when we pop this thing." Her eyes never left the screen. Her fingers never slowed on the buttons. Missy's long freshly manicured designer nails crowned finger tips adorned with glistening rings, including a band on her left thumb. They hovered and danced, gliding over, yet tapping ever so quickly the hold buttons, as cards appeared and disappeared in fractions of seconds. With each dried up deal there went another dollar-twenty-five.

"What if we don't win? I can't get any more money out of the ATM. We're at our 24 hour limit."

"Come on, Sharon. Don't jinx us. This baby's ready to hit."

Just as Missy said that, the fresh deal delivered four clubs to the royal, all in ascending position, lacking only the ten. In the ten's position stood an eight of diamonds. Missy drew in a loud shrill inhale.

"Oh, God, Sharon. Look at this! It's in sequence, too!"

Sharon quickly raised her head and focused on the screen next to her. The red five of diamonds looked defiantly out of place alongside the most beautiful quartet of sequenced royal clubs Sharon thought she'd ever seen.

"Shit, Missy. It has to be! It has to be!"

"Pray hard. Here we go ... "

"No! Stop!"

"What?"

"Not yet. Give me a second. I don't know if I can handle getting this close and then missing."

"Sharon, we may have already waited too long. Maybe the machine won't hit now because we threw out the timing."

"That's not how it works."

Sharon was correct. That card value was pre-determined as soon as Missy had pressed deal. The two of them could wait three months and the card would be the same. It's just sitting there, inside, electronically, waiting to show itself.

"Think we'll live long enough to see it?" asked Missy.

"Okay. Go ahead. Come on ten of clubs!" Sharon squeezed her eyes closed.

Missy pressed the deal button. Up popped the meaningless seven of spades.

"Bastard," sighed Missy. "This really pisses me off."

"I'm dead meat. That was it; our last hope."

"No way, kiddo. We're just getting warmed up. Trust me."

Sharon zipped open her purse. She felt around inside for the lone crumpled twenty dollar bill. She carefully removed it and began smoothing out the wrinkles.

"What do you say I give this machine a try?"

"No way! We can't afford to lose our last twenty on a cold machine! We've been priming this one all night!"

"Well, it *is* my money. I say we give this machine a little ride. Don't worry, we'll still split."

Sharon fed the smoothed bill into the bill acceptor. The rollers inside locked onto the twenty and guided it on the one-way journey to the coffer. Eighty credits appeared on the lower right hand side of the video screen. Sharon lifted her eyes upward and pressed the max coin button. The payout table lit up in the far right column. Seventy five credits remained and the first five cards slammed against the inside of the video screen's glass, one at a time.

"You never answered me," said Sal, gulping down the final helping of Spanish Omelet.

"I never answered you about what?"

"Your note. You said you had a 'good shift.' How can you have a good shift when the jerks didn't toke you?"

Rolly just stared back at Sal. He looked furtively to the left, then to the right. Then he leaned over toward Sal.

"If I tell you, I'll have to kill you."

"All right, so you can kill me. What the hell are you talking about?"

Rolly reached back into his rear left pocket and pulled out his wallet. He tossed it on the table in front of Sal.

"What? Am I supposed to look in your wallet?"

"Go ahead," Rolly said.

Sal slowly reached for the worn wallet. Holding it close to his chest, he looked inside.

"Okay, so you've got three twenties, two fives and a couple of ones.
"Seventy-two bucks. Let me have it back."

Rolly reached for the wallet and tucked it safely in his pocket.

"That's what I've got till payday," said Rolly, smiling.

"If there's a point to this, I'm missing it."

"There was a time, my boy, when my life was a lot like yours – me and my wife playing by the rules, barely making ends meet. We didn't argue much, but when we did, it was always about money – or lack of it. But, those days will soon be coming to an end."

Sal deadpanned, "Yeah with that seventy-two bucks, security is just around the corner! Rolly, what the hell are you talking about?"

Rolly leaned forward and whispered, "Like I said, if I tell you, I'd have to kill you."

"Quit joking. Tell me for Christ's sake."

"Not here." Rolly looked around. "After we eat, we'll take a spin. Finish your meal, kid."

Chapter Five

You have no idea what awaits you after twenty or twenty-five years of loyalty. They chop off your gray hairs at the neck with a razor sharp ax.

It was nearly two-thirty AM. as the six-year old BMW negotiated a worm-like turn in the dark stucco walled neighborhood for no particular reason. The two had sat silently facing forward for the past ten minutes, motoring aimlessly and randomly through the back streets of the entertainment capital of the world. "What do you want to be doing in five years, Sal?" Rolly finally asked.

"Haven't a clue. Why?"

"You're what – around thirty now?"

"Yeah, twenty-nine."

"When you're thirty-five, forty, are you still going to be flipping cards to people who bet your unborn son's college education on each deal?"

"I don't know. Maybe I'll be in management by then. Why?"

"Oh, management? Excuse me! Don't you realize that given a decent year, you take home more than Stan Reno now?"

"Okay, then, I'll stay a dealer like you. What's the point?"

"The point is, Slick, after all the years of biting my tongue and smiling through gritting teeth, I've had it. I'm up to here with watching obscenely wealthy assholes bet the net worth of a small company on the turn of a card, snap their fingers for a drink and a Cuban cigar and all I have till payday is seventy-two fuckin' dollars!"

"You've done all right."

"It's never enough, Sal. You know that."

"No argument there. Where are we going with this?"

"I'm trusting you, kid, because I genuinely believe I know you. Don't let me down on this."

"Rolly, don't tell me anything you don't want to. I'm not sure I like this lump in my throat right now."

"Let's cut to the chase. I've been dealing a long fucking time. A lot of us at the Empire have. It's a shit life. Maybe for the first five years you're proud to be a hot shot dealer. But, I'm telling you, man, twenty goddamned years down the road - you've seen it, heard it, and smelled it all! You've had your fill living for your twenty-minute break away from the stench of cigarettes and cigars; the arrogance of rich, liquored-up widows whose dangling jewelry is worth more than my house; the snarls and scowls of foreigners who still believe luck stacks up against house-favoring odds."

The only motion Sal's bewildered face could muster was the slow increased deepening of the furrows on his brow. Here was a side of Rolly he had not seen before. Rolly, who had up till now spoke directly into the windshield, turned quickly to catch Sal's reaction. Instinctively, Sal quickly closed his mouth.

"Don't tell me you haven't thought about this stuff, Sal. I saw you watching that action tonight. One thing about you is you wear your feelings on your face. Probably a lousy poker player. One glance at you tonight and I knew instantly you were salivating. You're no different than any of us, kid. We all want the most out of our lives and we resent the fuck out of those assholes who already have what we want and who rub our noses in it."

Rolly was hitting home with Sal now and they both knew it.

"Then you got these corporate sons-of-bitches who are so full of college accounting courses that the bottom line wraps itself around the necks of employees until we're choking our eyeballs out. They don't give a rat's ass about us, our families, our feelings, or anything. They can say what they want about the Mafia when they had their hands on Vegas. I worked here then. At least they knew how to treat their employees. You always knew where you stood with the bosses. When business slowed down, they used their imaginations to increase their market share. Not like these guys today who just slice up people's careers with an ink pen in the name of downsizing, restructuring, or layoff. It's all the same!   Peoples' lives are just over. And do you think it matters how long you've been there? Hell no! As a matter of fact, the way they see it, the older you are the more of a liability you are. How many old farts have you seen terminated since you've been in the business?"

"I don't know." Sal was startled. "Quite a few, I guess."

"Quite a few, huh? You have no idea what awaits you after twenty or twenty-five years of loyalty. They chop off your gray hairs at the neck with a razor sharp ax."

Sal instinctively massaged his throat.

"I caught on to these bastards a long time ago and I've been preparing to even the score. But there's only so much I can do as a Baccarat dealer. Frankly, Sal, I've got some pretty amazing plans and I need more help. I'm hoping I wasn't wrong when I pegged you as the right guy to join up."

"You're not talking about ripping off the casino, are you?"

"Let's just say I'm talking about beating the casino at their own game. There's a lot of money in it for all of us. What I want to know is - are you interested?"

"Jesus, Rolly, you've got be shitting me!   Fuck yeah, I want to be rich. I don't like the crap you talked about any more than you do. But, come on! Do you think you're the first jacked-off dip shit who thought about stealing from the house? What do you plan to do about all that fucking security!"

Rolly smiled. He knew now he hadn't guessed wrong. Sal was definitely aboard. His concerns about security were not unexpected. But Sal had accepted the price of the car by pointing out the thinning tread on the tires.

"If I can convince you that I've got that totally covered. Can I count on you to jump in?"

Sal breathed deeply. All of a sudden *he* was the college dropout being handed the keys to an armored truck full of millions of dollars. Rolly's question was pinpoint. If Sal could be convinced – totally convinced – that Rolly's plans would defeat all the layers of house security, why would Sal have any reservations?

"If you can convince me – and that's a huge *if*, Rolly, I'm down for this."

The muffled ringing of Sal's cellular phone interrupted any reaction Rolly was about to experience. Sal lifted the car's center armrest, retrieved the phone, and flipped down the mouthpiece.

"Hello."

"Where are you, Sal?" It was Sharon.

"I'm out taking a ride with Rolly. I'll be home shortly. Are we rich?"

"Are you sitting down?"

"Yeah, this car has seats. Are we rich?"

"We're rich, baby!"

"No shit?"

"Missy hit the big one–twelve thousand five hundred dollars!

Sal shook his head and smiled.

"Well, *are* you rich?" asked Rolly.

Sal nodded quickly.

"So we're splitting that with her?"

"Already did, sweetie, sixty-two-fifty apiece."

"I hate to bring this up, but she ought to pay back what she borrowed from you from her half, don't you think?"

"I don't know what you mean."

"Sharon, she used *our* money to bet with. It was a loan...."

Rolly reached over and tapped Sal on the leg. When Sal looked over at him, Rolly closed his eyes and shook his head. He was saying, "don't worry about it."

"Never mind, Sharon. Congratulations! This is terrific news. I'll see you and your half of the jackpot at home in a little while, okay?"

"Okay, sweetie. Bye."

"This is turning out to be quite a day for you, isn't it?" asked Rolly.

"I don't remember one quite like it, to tell you the truth. Damn, I'm glad she won that."

"That doesn't change your mind now, does it?"

"You mean about letting you convince me? Hell no. Convince away."

"Okay. I'm going to have to go back in time a little, so that it makes sense."

"I'm six grand richer. I can afford the time."

"That group of Chinese guys who were playing in the salon last evening ... ?"

"Yeah?"

"I met the youngest guy last year over at Caesars Palace. My wife and I were playing tourist that weekend and were over at the Palace going through the Forum Shops. Beatrice loves that. Me, I was along for the walk. Halfway through, I convinced her to do some shopping while I tried my hand on the player's side of baccarat. It's one thing to deal the game. Playing it is a whole other trip. She agreed and we decided to get back together in about two hours. I bought in at a table for three hundred dollars and sat down next to this Mr. Yen, Archie Yen. He had about three-thousand in front of him. I figured he was doing pretty well, so I decided to bet whatever he bet."

"Now there's a strategy," chuckled Sal.

"Yeah, it's one of many. Anyway, we're winning like crazy. He bets banker. I bet banker. Boom, we win. He bets tie. I bet tie. Boom, we win. It didn't seem to matter what he bet, we were winning. After about five hands, this Mr. Yen notices that I'm placing my bet after he does and that I'm betting exactly what he does. Of course, the amounts of the bets were different because he was a hell of a lot better financed then me. So, once he notices this, he decides to test it. When the next hand was about to begin, he held back his bet, apparently waiting to see if I would bet first. I didn't know what he was doing, so I simply held back, too. When the dealer asked for all bets down, Mr. Yen slides a five hundred dollar chip onto the Player's circle. So I slid my three quarters onto the Player's circle. Immediately Mr. Yen moves his bet to the Banker's circle. I was caught off guard and left my bet on Player. I won. This Mr. Yen looks at me and mumbles something in Chinese. He pushes in his stack to color out. I was eight hundred dollars up, so I pushed in, too. He leans over to me and whispers in a gravely voice, "We must talk.""

"Was he angry?"

"I couldn't tell. When I colored out, I started walking toward the cage and he walks over to me."

"'I must thank you,'" he says.

"I go, 'What for?'"

"He says, 'Before you sat down, I lost ten-thousand dollars. After you sat down, I win back ten-thousand and another five-thousand. You good luck for me.'"

"No shit," said Sal, smiling.

"Then this guy, a total stranger, mind you, hands me a one thousand dollar chip and invites me to the bar to have a drink with him."

"Of course, you accepted."

"Naturally."

"How did it feel to be somebody's good luck charm?"

"It felt strange. Especially since I was following *his* bets. To me, he was *my* good luck charm."

"Did he ever know that?"

"I don't know. I never said anything. The Chinese are an interesting people. They're very superstitious. Once something is working for them, they're hell bent on keeping it. That's what he wanted to talk to me about over a drink. He told me that he and several of his friends made frequent trips to Vegas, maybe six or seven a year."

"All the way from Asia?" asked Sal.

"No. San Francisco. Anyway this guy says a couple of years ago, he and his cronies stumbled onto a surefire way to even up the odds with the casinos. And it's netted them a ton of money."

"Did he know you were a dealer?"

"No, to him I was just another tourist. So anyway, while he's telling me about all this money and stuff, he tells me the secret to their success. You'll never guess what it is and it's brilliantly simple."

"They count cards?" asked Sal.

"Hell no, that's much too complicated and way too easy for the pit bulls to catch."

"Okay, then what?"

"What time is it?"

Sal looked down at the radio's clock. Quarter to three, why?"

"Quarter to three," Rolly repeated. "Tell you what, let's go downtown. There's a buddy of mine who works at the Gold Mine Casino I want you to meet. We'll clue you in down there."

The BMW headed for Glitter Gulch.

Chapter Six

Balastrieri was now sitting in wait like an impatient starving lynx, ready to spring when his prey moved into the quiet dawn, down the path of vulnerability.

Ralph Tamhagen breathed in deeply, taking the final drag of the cigarette to the far corners of his lungs where he held it during the twisting and pressing of the smoldering butt. The exhale that followed was a cloudy sigh of resignation. Tamhagen lived alone in his single bedroom apartment. After a busy swing shift at the Desert Empire, he looked forward to his all night ritual of nicotine and caffeine . He spent most summer nights sitting on the cramped third story balcony, filtered cigarette in one hand, mug after mug of black coffee in the other. On this particular early morning, however, there was a temporary new addition. Charlie Palermo had passed along a memo from Human Resources at the end of Tamhagen's shift tonight.

"By the way, Colonel," Palermo had said nonchalantly, "Got a memo here from H.R. They want you to attend some sort of diversity training on Tuesday."

Tamhagen, plucked it from Palermo's hands as he ambled past him toward the exit door. He refused to let Palermo know how unnerving it was to hear anything from Human Resources. Now he'd have to go sit in a classroom and make small talk with people he neither knew nor cared to know.

And why diversity training? Tamhagen didn't need that. It was just him and his monitors and his VCRs. He'd been through similar sessions throughout his career. They were all pretty much the same. Introductions to tell who you were, where you worked, how long you'd been with the company, expectations of the training. Bullshit like that. Only now, being with the company a long time was such a liability. The worst part, thought the Colonel, was that he'd have to climb that long set of stairs outside the training room. The last time he did that the legs wanted to shut down half way up. It would be so embarrassing on Tuesday if he needed help to make it all the way. The mere thought brought a numbness to his knees.

The crickets were singing their early morning tune and the moon was parked proudly in the distant eastern sky. The Colonel would have liked to just roll over onto a cooler part of a pillow and doze, but that would require rising up out of his comfortable folding chair, reaching for his walking stick, and limping his way toward the bedroom. The mere thought of that chore often resulted in the Colonel's remaining on the balcony, asleep in the chair until the sweat on his brow began to simmer from the morning sun. He folded the Human Resources memo and slid it in his shirt pocket behind his pack of cigarettes. He'd get up in just a couple of minutes. For now, he wanted to contemplate.

Nicholas Balastrieri looked up from the video poker screen. The two attractive women were still seated in the patio-like section of the coffee shop, giggling, smoking, and talking. They'd been there more than half-an-hour since they won their jackpot. He'd never heard more noise from two human beings.

Balastrieri, thirty six years old, unemployed, divorced father of two boys, tipped the scales at 144 pounds. At six foot three, he appeared somewhat ungainly. A black mustache of which he was once attentive had been allowed to distend untamed, surrounded by varying days of unshaven beard growth. He viewed daily hygiene as an inconvenience directed at people with full time jobs. Recently, he'd begun wearing a grimy old ball cap to hide his thinning crown and neutralize the need for hair grooming. His worn jeans, faded dark Vegas promotional T-shirt and black running shoes rounded out the portrait of a workforce dropout who loves his alcohol.

He'd been working the aisle nearby where the women were playing when their screams mixed with the piercing slot machine bell and flashing light broadcast their newfound fortune. It was his jackpot, too. He'd earned it weaving in and out of the slot machine aisles for several hours, looking for the occasional spilled or dropped coin on the floor amidst the loud carpet design. He was hoping his excursion would uncover some uncollected credits, perhaps a half-full cup of coins, maybe even a forgotten purse or wallet.

But, when the bells and lights signaled the women's jackpot, his heart, too, began pounding. Ever since he lost his job as a slot floor person at the Highway Ninety-Five Casino on the outskirts of the valley, life had been one miserable, stress-filled day after another. That was four months ago. At termination, they said it was poor performance. But, it was his partnership with hard liquor that led him down this road. He knew it. And the Human Resources people at Highway Ninety-Five Casino knew it. Getting a new job was not among his current options. They would always check his background. And admit it or not, he was sure these companies shared codes with other companies, thus blackballing known losers.

Having spent nearly six years in and around slot machines, he naturally gravitated to them now. He'd learned some of the ruses slot cheats practiced to relieve slot players and casinos of their money.

There were tricks like stuffing paper towels or a handkerchief up the pay out mechanism, preventing coins from falling out. Then when an unsuspecting player hits the cash-out button, the coins are prevented from falling out. When the player goes to get help, the perpetrator simply walks by, reaches up into the mechanism, and pulls out the stuffing. The unobstructed coins then fall freely into the waiting cup.

Another artifice involves the use of static electricity. For some reason it works best with video keno machines. The player, wearing leather-soled shoes presses and rubs his foot repeatedly into the dry casino carpeting, building up static electricity. The player then touches the metal coin receptacle on the machine, zapping it with static.

Instantly, the hopper begins to pour its precious mother load into the collection tray.

Of course, there is always the diversionary tactic where one person walks up to an unsuspecting, usually elderly player and asks a question. A partner, simultaneously arrives on the other side of the player and picks up any cups of coin or a purse the player may have stored on the side of the machine.

As the technology involved with the video surveillance in the casinos improves, however, it becomes increasingly difficult to pull off these capers. In the sixties and seventies, black and white cameras were severely inferior. The contrast problems created by the bright lights on the casino floor signage and slot machines, coupled with the camera's automatic iris, caused the lens to shut down continually, leaving a dark, indistinguishable picture. Even when the contrast was somewhat normal, the distance between the non-zoomed, poorly focused camera and the subject made positive identification all but impossible. The picture merely confirmed that something happened. Beyond that, you'd need a confession.

There are lots of incidents where slugs are used, particularly in the dollar machines. As in all the machines, deposited coins must pass through a "comparator" which instantly compares the coin's size, thickness, make-up, and so forth with a coin stored in the comparator. If one of the compared characteristics fails the comparison test, the machine rejects the deposited coin or slug. Therefore, passing slugs is no easy task. Yet, bogus coins turn up daily somewhere in Las Vegas. The design of the hopper is such that coins are disbursed from the bottom of the hopper when players cash out. So until nearly all of the legitimate coins are disbursed, the hopper becomes re-filled with slugs. That's about the time the thief cashes out, gets up, and leaves the casino.

Balastrieri had been forced to dabble in some of these and other scams, but he'd never tried the big one. He'd thought about it often enough. He'd fantasized about reaching way down for the temerity it would take. But, up until now, when he reached down he found nothing but ground-up nerve. Tonight was different. Maybe it was because they were women, easy to strong arm. Maybe he was just getting more desperate, hungrier, angrier. For whatever reason,

Balastrieri was now sitting in wait like an impatient, starving lynx ready to spring when his prey moved into the quiet dawn down the path of vulnerability.

For the moment, however, the two women were still locked in giddy conversation under relentless clouds of cigarette smoke, unaware they were in such razor sharp focus. Confidently, Nicholas Balastrieri smoothed a wrinkled one dollar bill and fed it into the bill acceptor. Four credits appeared. He had no real interest in playing. It just looked better to the eye in the sky.

Rolly and Sal were making their way toward the elevator in the Gold Mine Casino parking garage downtown.

"These places give me the creeps," said Sal, talking about the downtown casinos. His words echoed in the nearly empty concrete shell.

"Hey, at one time this *was* Vegas, don't forget," reminded Rolly.

He pushed the lowest button, where the "C" had long ago worn away. "And to a lot of old timers, it still is."

"Yeah, maybe so. But the low-lifes seem to have discovered the charm of the downtown. Give me Boulder Highway, any day."

Sal was referring to the highway running north-south on the east side of town that extended from Lake Mead to Fremont Street. Boulder Highway was home to some of the valley's oldest and newest gaming properties, all of them targeting locals. The newer locals' establishments like those built by Station Casinos had made a significant impact on the local traffic to the downtown area. That left tourists looking for nostalgia or a very cheap room. Either choice required mingling with the dregs of society.

The elevator doors opened onto the casino floor. The carpeting was old, somewhat tattered, and stained with every liquid imaginable. The putrid odor of aged smoke slapped at the nostrils. Only a handful of players were evident in these very early morning hours.

"This place is dead," remarked Sal. "How do they stay in business?"

"It's early yet," smiled Rolly. "You ought to get down here some Saturday evening. It's hoppin'!"

They passed a "dead" craps game. The crew stared at them. It reminded Sal of a set-up that would be featured in Madame Tussaud's wax museum of casino scenes. The boxman was sitting in place with his chins hovering over a yellow and blue bow tie, wearing a frayed, wrinkled gray suit, his half-closed eyes peering through smudged bifocals at more money in the form of casino chips than he's made in his lifetime. Flanking him on the right and left were the dealers who, too, looked like they'd slept in their graying white shirts whose pleats were only a faded memory. Across from the boxman, with his back to Sal and Rolly, stood the stickman. He's the one who calls out the roll of the dice and who uses his stick, a thin version of a cane, to move and navigate the dice across the table and around the stacks of wagered chips. At the moment the stick, like the rest of the crew, was at rest. From the looks of them, it had to have been over an hour or so since the last player had dropped ashes on that table. "Check out the minimum," Rolly said as he nudged Sal, smiling.

"Dollar minimum," said Sal in a choked voice. "Shit, I didn't know they still had dollar minimum games in this town."

"See that table over there?" Rolly pointed to a craps table across the pit.

"Yeah?"

"Quarter minimum. And I don't mean green chips!" chuckled Rolly.

"Twenty-five cent craps! It's like a sixties time capsule!"

With Rolly in the lead, they headed toward a back wall. As they neared it, Sal could see a very sturdy looking door, with a low profile look. The words "No Entrance" were painted beneath a blacked-out window. Rolly pressed the button on the left doorjamb. Soon, the door was cracked open so that a pair of wide eyes could be seen peering out at them. As soon as those eyes recognized Rolly, they opened even wider, accompanied by an instant keyboard of white teeth.

"What do you say, Nappa, you ol' fuck?" Rolly extended his eager hand.

"Whassup, man?"

"Same old, you know."

"What the hell you doin' downtown?"

"Brought down a friend of mine to meet you. Sal Mooring, say hello to Nappa Jackson."

Sal extended his hand and Nappa wrapped both of his around it.

"How you doin', man. How long you known the Rollo?"

"Met him when I started at the Desert Empire couple of years ago," said Sal grinning.

"We go way back, man," said Nappa. "I think I've known Rolly longer than I've known my wife. Anyway, welcome to the Gold Mine."

"Thanks," said Sal.

"Nappa, what's the chance you could show me and Sal the ropes upstairs?" Asked Rolly.

"Very good chance, my man. Ain't nobody here but me. Come on up."

The three of them entered the door, pulling it locked behind them, and climbed the long, carpeted stairway to the Gold Mine's surveillance department.

"I'm glad you're the only one here," whispered Rolly. I hope we have a few minutes to talk. What time does the day shift start arriving?"

"Oh, we got about an hour, hour and fifteen. Whassup, man?"

"Nothing special. Sal here's never seen a surveillance operation. Since you're one of the best, I thought of you right away."

"Definitely came to the right place," said Nappa smiling.

Like Rolly, the affable black man's face displayed the measure of many years' experience in his craft. Graying temples and a thinning crown helped nudge his age appearance into the mid fifties, an accurate presumption. Jackson's gaming career spanned four decades, but had peaked more than a decade earlier. His persona as an eagle-eyed surveillance agent was now more nostalgia than gospel. And the Gold Mine Casino had added him to their surveillance team six years ago as a "juiced" favor to their then Surveillance Director. As soon as the director retired, the over forty, black minority, was shelved on the graveyard shift, and all but forgotten.

"Where do we start?"

"Let's take him to mission control," said Rolly. "That's always impressive."

"That's right over here," said Nappa gesturing. "This is where it all happens, man."

The three walked over to the main control console. There were television monitors of different sizes and ages stacked six high and there had to be ten rows lined side-by-side. On the screens were black and white live pictures from the casino. There were close-ups on individual player positions at blackjack tables; wide shots of entire craps tables, with and without players. There were close-ups of what appeared to be dealers' hands and the cards in front of them. At Nappa's invitation, Sal sat down in the pilot's seat. In front of him were rows and rows of buttons, some lighted, some dark. There were joy sticks for panning and tilting the camera lenses, controls for zooming in and out, switching devices where various cameras could be selected for closer scrutiny on the larger, color monitors. It was truly the "room of distrust."

As Sal looked around, he saw the rows and rows of VCRs lining the back walls of the room. Any wall space remaining was home to shelf after shelf of videotape cassettes, labeled by day of the week and week of the month. Except for the bluish light pouring forth from the banks of television monitors and the glow of the VCR LED displays, there were no overhead lights in use. The entire experience gave Sal a voyeuristic feeling.

"They actually pay you to work up here?" asked Sal.

"Hey, you know, it's a living, man. Somebody's got to do it," said Nappa laughing.

"You work up here by yourself?" asked Sal.

"On graveyard, yeah. It's that way a lot of places. Don't need but one guy up here overnight anyway. Believe it or not it gets awful boring."

"I'm sure," said Sal. "Got any interesting stories?"

"Hundreds of 'em, my man. What do you want to hear?"

"What do you mean?"

"Pick your topic: sex, attempted murder, collusion, inside job, out and out thievery…"

"Tell me about some thievery," said Sal.

"Better yet. I'll show you." Nappa hurried toward a file cabinet in the back of the room.

"Pretty incredible place, eh, Slick?" asked Rolly.

"Yeah, and Nappa's cool, too," said Sal.

"He's going to show you some shit, man. You won't believe the gonads on these guys trying this stuff in full view of the cameras."

Sal cleared his throat. "My point exactly. I'm still waiting to hear about this foolproof scheme of yours."

"It's not a scheme, it's more of a strategy."

Nappa returned carrying a couple of videotapes. "If I remember correctly, the man requested thievery. Right?"

"Right," said Sal.

Nappa pushed the tape labeled "Greatest Hits" into a VCR on the console. The large color monitor on the right scrambled to action. Nappa narrated.

"This is a craps game, man. Six months ago, swing shift. Keep your eye on that good-looking bitch in the blue outfit. That guy next to her is accumulating quite a few black chips. There's got to be two-thousand in his rack. Now notice where everybody's eyes go when he rolls the dice."

"They all follow the dice across the table," said Sal.

"That's right, man. Except the bitch's eyes. Where are they lookin'?"

"Damn, she's looking right at his chips."

"Check out what she does on the next roll. As you see, when the man rolled the dice, she reaches with her left hand and scoops two or three black chips from the man's rack. He never saw her."

"How did she get caught?" asked Sal.

"The camera, man. Alex was working that shift. He don't miss nothing."

"With all the action going on in the casino on swing shift, this guy Alex just happened to have the camera focused on that table and he happened to be looking at that monitor?"

"Yeah, that's right," said Nappa. "That's what we do. We get paid to know what to look for."

"I know that," said Sal, "but with so much going on, how do you know what to focus yourself on?"

"Comes with experience," said Nappa. "Hey, check this out."

Nappa pressed the fast forward button and the picture sprang into action.

"This one you're not going to believe," he promised. "Caught this dude myself."

The speeding picture slowed to normal. The camera was aimed at a twenty-one table and the lens was pulled back to reveal three players and a male dealer.

"Let's see how sharp you are there, Salvatore. Let me know when you see something suspicious."

They watched the action: dealer dealing, players signaling, combinations hit and busted, chips lifted to the dealer's bank. Sal could see nothing out of the ordinary so far. Out of Sal's vision, Nappa nudged Rolly. Rolly had seen this video before and knew what to look for. He smiled in anticipation.

"It already happened, my man," said Nappa. "Looks like you missed it."

"I didn't see anything. Play that back."

"You don't usually get a second chance, but what the hell."

Nappa reversed the tape a short way and hit play.

Sal studied every move.

"You missed it again, dude."

"All right, what was it?"

"Man, you're a dealer. You mean you can't tell?"

"It all looks legit to me," said Sal.

"Okay. Keep your eye on the dealer's right hand."

Sal watched as the dealer pitched a card to the player sitting at third base, his farthest right. He saw the player toss down the two cards he was holding, indicating that the eight of clubs busted him. He watched the dealer reach with his right hand and pick up the one hundred dollar black chip from the player's betting circle. His right hand then moved to the bank in front of him, presumably to deliver the black chip. With his left hand, he reached across his body to scoop up the three face-up cards. His right hand raised up to his mouth to cover what appeared to be a cough, after which it lowered to assist his right hand with the cards.

"Did you catch it," asked Nappa?

"You mean when he covered his mouth," asked Sal?

"Let me tell you, man, at this particular moment that dealer has been on the floor for 40 consecutive minutes. You saw him look to his right just before this deal. It was at that moment that he saw his relief dealer checking in to the pit. He feels very confident that this is his final hand before his break."

"Did he deposit that black chip in his mouth when he coughed, asked Sal?"

"I certainly thought so," said Nappa. "So I called down to the pit and told the pit boss to hold up the relief."

"Oh shit," muttered Sal. "That poor bastard."

They continued to watch the video as the dealer flipped over his hole card, played out the hand, paid first base, collected from the second position, and deposited the cards in the receptacle to his right. It was obvious from the hesitation that he expected to be tapped on the shoulder by his relief. That didn't occur. So he began another round of card pitching.

"So he's got that black chip in his mouth the whole time now, huh?"

"You see, my man. This guy may be dumb, but he's not totally stupid. I had been watching him set this scam up all during the previous 40 minutes. Every couple of minutes he would cough, bringing his right hand up to cover his mouth. That way, when he decided to actually cop a chip at the end of his hour, the hand lifting wouldn't appear out of the ordinary."

"Except he failed to factor in Nappa in the sky," Rolly said as he smacked his old chum on the back.

"What balls." Sal shook his head. "What did they do to him?"

"Exactly what you think," said Nappa. "And he had to leave town a couple of weeks later. Last I heard he was selling cars in St. George."

"Nappa, I had a long talk with Sal tonight. I wanted to bring him over to get a bird's eye view of what goes on up here."

Nappa's eyes connected with Rolly's. "He's in?"

"Let's say he's very interested."

"I don't know about the 'very'," said Sal. "I mean you just got done proving to me how impossible it is to hide from the cameras. A guy would have to be a pinhead to risk a career and prison with these piss ass odds. Frankly, I'm not sure I'm interested at all."

"Can't say as I blame you," said Rolly. "After all you're only playing with half a deck right now. There's so much more you need to know. There's no doubt in my mind that when you do know the whole story, you'll be begging us to let you in."

"All right. You've got the floor. Bring on the whole story," Sal said.

"Turn around," said Rolly. "Tell me what you see."

Sal turned in his wheeled, pedestal chair.

"Wall to wall VCRs," he said.

"How many?"

Sal sized them up. They went from floor to ceiling with heat escape air spaces in between them. There were twelve in each shelving unit and there were twelve shelving units.

"I'd say a hundred and forty-four," said Sal.

"A hundred and forty-four," repeated Rolly. "And how many eyes does Nappa have?"

Sal hesitated, then looked over at Nappa. "Two."

"Do you like those odds, Slick? A hundred and forty-four to two?"

"I don't get it," said Sal.

"My friend," said Rolly, "When those two eyes of Nappa's are looking at one monitor, shit is happening on the other hundred and forty-three."

Sal nodded in agreement.

"The only record of what's on those hundred and forty-four recorders is on the tapes, right?"

"Right," said Sal.

"We take away the tapes and there is no record. None!"

"How do you propose to get those tapes out of the recorders?" asked Sal.

"All part of the big plan, my friend," said Rolly with a smile. "All part of the big plan."

Chapter Seven

He glanced down at his mangled arm where moments ago that feisty bitch had dug in her manicured claws and harvested skin, blood and muscle.

The Monday morning sun was already heating up. Missy handed her valet check to the attendant.

"I can't believe we actually stayed out all night?" said Missy giggling.

"I don't even feel tired," said Sharon. "But, I bet I sleep like a baby all day."

"Not me," said Missy, "I've got some serious shopping to do. And I know just the place."

"The Fashion Show Mall?"

"You got it. Join me for lunch at Spago's?"

"No thanks. When I do wake up, I've got a week's worth of laundry waiting. I'm not free and clear like you, you know."

"Hey, we free and clear ones have laundry, too. Only difference is we have half as much laundry and twice as much fun."

The two walked across the eight lanes of the porte cochere to the valet pick-up area and sat on one of the benches. Behind them, staring through the casino's black tinted glass doors stood a befuddled Nicholas Balastrieri. He hadn't counted on the women having used valet. His mental rehearsal had centered around surprising them in the hotel parking garage. But, he'd invested nearly three hours in this development and was determined to cash in, no matter what the unexpected challenges. On the up side, it looked as though only one valet ticket had been turned in, indicating both women had apparently arrived in the same car. They probably left the other's at another location. That happens frequently, especially when co-workers go out together after work. In that case, they'd be returning to their place of work to retrieve the other's car. He pushed through the door and walked briskly to his car in the self-parking lot. He would need to be ready to follow them as soon as their car arrived.

He sat behind the wheel of the green three-year old Trans Am which he'd pulled into position at the far end of the valet delivery area to await his prey. His heart pressed into his throat as he saw the women rise to greet the white Toyota as it eased to a stop. He pulled his gearshift lever to drive and checked the rearview mirror. No one was behind him. No one was noticing him. No one cared. He pressed the accelerator and began to tail the target to a place or places yet unknown.

Sue Min Wong stirred as the flare of sunlight bathed her eyelids. In the cool comfort of the bedroom, the bright heat seemed oddly imposing. She blinked quickly trying to compose the situation. As she focused, she recognized the vertical blinds and the half-moon notch in one of the slats permitting this trespass of exterior brilliance. Her surroundings gradually began to make sense. It had been more than two months since she'd shared her bed with Archie Yen. She listened. His snore told her he had stayed, unlike their last time together. She'd remembered awakening alone that time and finding his handwritten note. Maybe he did mean some of those wonderful things he'd whispered to her a few hours ago.

She glanced at the clock radio. It was seven-twenty. They had slept less than four hours. And that's exactly how she felt. Nude, she turned onto her back and lay staring at the ceiling. She pulled the sheet up to her chin as the cold air conditioning breezed over her. Archie stirred, squirming for a more comfortable pillow position. Then the snoring resumed.

Sue Min began to mentally play back the highlights of yesterday's exploits in the Baccarat Pit. Archie had proven, once again, his uncanny knack of predicting the fine nuances of human behavior. Kaiser couldn't have followed Archie's script any closer if he'd studied it for a week. But then Kaiser, like most of his gaming cronies, behaved so transparently, so predictably. Any first year, C-average Psychology student could forge a plan that foresaw his actions and reactions. Yesterday's outcome had been so on target, Sue Min's initial reluctance to participate evaporated along with her moral footing. She'd spent months deflecting Archie's insistence that she join the growing group. Now, there could be no turning back. Whatever the plan, it had better work. The beautiful Asian, college educated, highly respected International Marketing Vice President had unearthed a new set of ethics. The collusion was maturing. She closed her eyes, soothed by the rhythm of Archie's heavy breathing and the warmth of his flesh against her. All would be perfect were it not for the very real possibility that her father may one day learn of his daughter's collapsed resolve. That thought, joined by a single wet trickle descending her firm cheekbone, guided her back to sleep.

Sal had not expected to find an empty house. All the way home from downtown, he practiced how he would discuss this night with Sharon. He came to the realization that as much as he thought he knew her, he really didn't. He was at a loss to predict how she would respond if she knew the kind of dialogue he and Rolly had shared all night. Rolly had made a strong, but futile case that he not tell her at all. Although Beatrice was fully aware of Rolly's involvement, her support had not come easily. Rolly had shared that with Sal on the way home and encouraged him to keep things uncomplicated, at least for the time being.

Sal, however, remained convinced that Sharon needed to be in on whatever he decided to do. He knew he needed her support. Besides, their relationship had not been built on lies to this point. Why start now? And if Sharon weren't included, she would view any changes in Sal's behavior suspiciously. Lies would lead to more lies. Neither of them needed that.

But where was she? Nothing in the house had been touched since Sal had left for work some eighteen hours ago. Why would she still be out? He knew they'd hit the big jackpot. She should have been home hours ago. He picked up the phone and pressed Missy's speed dial number. He got her answering machine.

"Missy, this is Sal. It's eight o'clock in the morning and Sharon isn't home yet. I'm worried about her. Please call me as soon as you can."

Knowing he had to leave for today's shift in six hours, Sal headed back to the bedroom. Today was Sharon's Saturday. She and Missy probably had breakfast together and were going to do some shopping to celebrate their winnings. But why hadn't she called? She has a cell phone. She has a cell phone!

He scrambled for the bedroom phone and punched in her cellular number. It rang the customary four times before a recorded message said she wasn't available. Damn her!

Certain she'd be home soon, Sal removed his clothes and flopped on the bed. The cool sheets felt good against his tired, strained body. He reached over and set the alarm. He pressed the sleep button joining the eight o'clock news. Stocks on New York's Wall Street were on another roller coaster today, starting up, but dipping during the past hour. Several economic indicators pointing toward recession were reportedly behind the fickle market's reaction. Before the announcer turned to local news, Sal's eyes were closed and his mind was painting the picture of his future financial freedom. Rolly was putting together a team meeting in a couple of weeks to announce the strategy. Both Rolly and Nappa expressed unremitting confidence in their ability to create the mother of all casino rip-offs. The snoring began, lightly at first, then heavier with each succeeding breath.

Had he remained awake, he would have heard on the radio news that two local women were found beaten and robbed in the hotel parking garage at Harrah's. They were both rushed to Sunrise Hospital, their conditions unknown. Neither of their identities was available for release.

Nathan Mesmer pressed the set button on his keyless entry pad summoning the high pitched chirp, confirming the Viper's security and began the short stroll from the executive parking area into the Desert Empire Resort. The instant he opened the glass door, the expected blast of chilled air enveloped him. Isolated and sporadic tones generated by the very few slot machines in use blended with scattered, echoed clinking of table game chips. The more prominent sound trickled from the ceiling speakers playing light, melodic music.

Monday mornings were always quiet at the Desert Empire. Even at this hour, a little after eight A.M., just a handful of diehard players could be found populating the casino. Only a quarter of the pit was activated. A majority of the tables were closed and cloaked in dust covers. Of the six open tables, all were of the twenty one variety and only two had players. The midway games, a term sarcastically used to describe the non-traditional casino games like Caribbean Stud Poker, Let It Ride, Pai Gow Poker, Three Card Poker, Casino War etc., were all closed. Those types of games irked Mesmer. To him, they took up valuable square footage failing to generate the income potential long relied on from blackjack. But, those midway games were necessary to stay competitive in game selection with the other houses on the strip. Some tourists, intimidated by the noisy, smoky, complicated craps game or the social scourges associated with making the wrong decision at blackjack, felt more comfortable at these fun games even though the possibility of winning the lofty multi-hundred-thousand dollar bonus jackpots was a stratospheric leap of faith. Additionally, casino moguls were hopeful once the novices got comfortable with pit play on the midway games, they might likely dabble in traditional games in the future. The jury was still out on that one.

As Mesmer strutted passed the four idle dealers standing guard on their dead games, he intentionally avoided eye contact, choosing instead to give the tables a once over visual cleanliness inspection. Break room scuttlebutt was rife with rumor over an account of one particular morning casino stroll a few days following Mesmer's arrival at the Empire. The recounting is nearly always the same.

Back then, few knew the name of the new casino boss and even fewer knew what he looked like. As the telling goes, Mesmer, wearing his trademark double-breasted, pin stripe suit, starched white shirt and power red necktie happened into the casino early on a Monday morning in February. To many, he looked like one of the guests in town for a corporate convention. Natalie Waynor, a black dealer in her early forties had been standing post at her dead twenty-one game, par for a Monday morning. She tells that this well-dressed man walked up to her table and looked her in the eye. He said nothing. After an awkward beat, Natalie gave him a closed lip smile, followed by, as she describes it, a warm greeting.

"Good morning."

"Is it?" Mesmer replied.

"I certainly hope it is," she said, adding after another pause "is there something I can do for you?"

"What's your last name?" Mesmer asked.

"I beg your pardon, sir?"

"Don't give me that. What's your last name?"

Fearing a dreaded confrontation with a guest, a death knell for strip dealers, Natalie looked to her left, hoping to make eye contact with the floor supervisor or the pit boss. Adam Fields, the floor supervisor was huddled with Jake Tipton, the pit manager around the pit bookkeeper, apparently processing a marker for another player. She couldn't get their attention.

"Young lady," Mesmer snarled, "I asked you a question."

"Sir," she pleaded, "I'm not permitted to tell my last name. Was there something I may have done to annoy you?"

"You don't know who I am, do you?" asked Mesmer.

"No, sir, I'm sorry I don't. Should I?"

"Take a good look at this face," Mesmer gestured with his thumb. "My name is Nathan Mesmer, Vice President of Casino Operations. You *work* for me."

"Mr. Mesmer. I'm sorry. I have heard you were coming, but I've not had the pleasure of meeting you, yet. Forgive me." She wasn't certain she was actually guilty of anything, but wanted out of this very uncomfortable situation post haste. "My name is Waynor, Natalie Waynor."

"Miss Waynor, do you have any idea why I approached your table?"

"No, sir, I don't."

Mesmer's eyes lowered as his head turned slightly to his right. "See that ash?"

Natalie's eyes locked onto the single cigarette ash sitting on the dark green felt.

"Yes, sir, I do."

"Why is that ash on your table?"

"I obviously didn't notice it, sir."

"Miss Waynor, have you any idea how many dealers in this city dream about getting hired by this property?"

"Hundreds, sir."

"Is there some particular reason the Desert Empire should keep you employed here instead of one of those other *hundreds* who realize the earning potential available to them here at the Desert Empire?"

"I'm an excellent dealer, sir, and I...."

Mesmer interrupted, "You're a pig, Miss Waynor. And I'll do the evaluating as to whether a dealer is excellent or not."

Natalie fought to control the quiver in her upper lip.

"Monkeys can be trained to do what you do," he continued. "I expect one-hundred percent commitment from my dealers."

Mesmer's voice had risen to a level now where Fields and Tipton had turned and looked in his direction. The other dealers, having overheard most of this confrontation began using their hands to comb the felt of all dust, lint, and ashes in sight. Tipton walked over to Waynor's table.

"Good morning, Nate," said Tipton. "Is there a problem?"

"Tipton, mind your own business." Mesmer growled, "If you'd done your job to begin with, I wouldn't need to do it for you."

Tipton looked into Waynor's eyes. Moisture had begun to collect.

"I left a cigarette ash on my table," she explained to Tipton. "Mr. Mesmer noticed it and was bringing it to my attention." She reached down and brushed the ash toward her, over the table's edge into her other hand, after which she let it fall into an ashtray at the corner of the table. She rubbed her hands together, clapped them for the cameras, and then wiped them on her black apron.

Tipton was speechless. He nodded weakly, and looked over at Mesmer.

"This won't happen again, Nate," he promised.

"Put the word out, Tipton. Dealers, and for that matter pit bosses at the Desert Empire are employed at my mercy. Nevada is an "at will" state meaning that you're employed here for as long or as short as I will it. From this point forward, housekeeping on these tables is a *major* issue. I don't want to see ashes or lint or empty glasses or ashtrays with more than two butts in them ever! Can I rely on that order to be understood?"

"Absolutely, Nate, and..."

"And where do you get off calling me Nate in the presence of your underlings?"

"I'm sorry, Mr. Mesmer."

Mesmer looked over at Natalie, whose tears were now very evident. He rolled his eyes, sneered, and walked away. As he passed the remaining dead games, the croupiers were busy polishing the red plastic card receptacles and futilely rubbing long-standing stains out of the felt. A new era at the Desert Empire was obviously underway.

On this Monday in August, Mesmer's scan of the tables revealed immaculate cleanliness. His morning pass-by had now become a ritual, likened to a military open-ranks inspection. The dealers despised him. He made no eye contact with them. They stared right through him, wearing half smiles one might find on a ventriloquist's dummy.

Mesmer strutted up the carpeted stairway to the executive mezzanine, checking for dust on the gold-plated railing. He rounded the corner and entered the outer administrative office which led to his. Rhonda Bethtold, his administrative assistant was busy clacking on the computer keypad. As she noticed his arrival, she turned and greeted him.

"Good morning," she said.

"Good morning," he returned. "Coffee on?"

"You bet," she said. "How was your weekend?"

"Great until yesterday," he muttered. "Those bastard Chinks in baccarat nearly bought this hotel last night."

"I hadn't heard," she said. "What happened?"

"More than I have time to talk about right now," he snapped. "Put the word out that I want a staff meeting at ten o'clock. Everybody."

'Everybody' she knew meant heads of all casino departments: the main casino, race and sports book, slot operations, keno, the poker room and baccarat.

"Got it," she said. "Meeting at ten."

"I'll have my coffee now," Mesmer announced over his shoulder as he entered his office.

She answered, "Right away," then whispered to herself, "asshole."

Chapter Eight

My ten o'clock meetings begin at ten o'clock!

Las Vegas metropolitan police officer Harve Dedman flipped back the cardboard cover of his tiny spiral tablet and pulled a ballpoint pen from the pocket of his beige uniformed shirt.

As he waited in the hallway outside emergency treatment room number two at Sunrise Hospital, he scribbled the words "Harrah's Garage Attack" at the top of the page, followed by the date. The nurse had assured him just moments ago that he would be able to talk with the young lady shortly. The door opened and Dedman rose.

"Officer, you may talk with her now. Please try to make it brief. She's very sore."

"Thank you," Dedman said. He pushed open the door. "Hi, ma'am," he said smiling, "I'm officer Dedman from Metro. How are you feeling?"

Missy managed a low moan and a slow shake of the head.

"We weren't able to find any identification, ma'am. Can you help me out?"

"He took our purses," she murmured. Her lips felt three inches thick and she sounded like her mouth was full of cotton.

"May I have your name?"

"Melissa Mangen," Missy said.

"Did you say Mangen?"

She nodded.

"What about your friend? What's her name?"

"How is she?"

"I haven't talked to her yet. She looks like she took some similar punishment. What's her name?"

"Sharon."

"Sharon?"

She nodded impatiently.

"Her last name?"

"Mooring."

"I'm sorry, I'm having difficulty...."

"Mooring. Ouch!" It was obviously difficult for her to talk and she was beginning to resent what she perceived as Dedman's lousy listening skills.

"Sorry, Ms. Mangen. That was Mooring, right?"

She rolled her eyes, closed them, and spelled the name slowly.

"Is she married?"

"Yeah."

"What's her husband's name?"

"Salvatore. He goes by Sal."

"Thank you."

"I understand from talking to the nurse, Ms. Mangen, that several thousand dollars were found on both you and Ms. Mooring...in your ah...in your brassieres. In fact, each of you had nearly identical amounts. Can you explain that?"

"We hit a jackpot at the Rio," she muttered. "We weren't about to stash all that loot in our purses with all the gooneys around here. Good thing we did. Look what happened."

"When was it you hit that jackpot, ma'am?"

"Last night. What do you think, we leave work every day with our bras full of money? We're not the criminals here, pal!" She writhed in pain from the outburst.

"No, no," Dedman apologized, "of course not. We just need to..."

"You just need to catch the bastard who did this. That's what you just need to do!"

"We intend to, ma'am. You say you hit the jackpot at the Rio?"

"That's right."

"You were attacked in the parking garage at Harrah's?"

"That's where we work. We're dealers. We left there last night. After we hit, I drove back so Sharon could get her car. The creep must have followed us from the Rio."

"Can you give us an approximate time when you hit the jackpot?"

"About three, I think."

"I hate to trouble you with these questions, but I think it's important. Can you describe the approximate location of the machine you were playing?"

"Yeah, it was across from the Carnival World Buffet."

"Uh huh." The scribbling filled the first page, which he flipped over. "Great buffet, isn't it?"

"Please, I'd like to go home."

"Of course. Just give me a description of your purse so we can have it for the record."

"It's black, about so big," she said gesturing with her hands. "It has a couple of zippered compartments. All my cards are gone. That really pisses me off!"

"Last question, I promise. What did this attacker look like?"

"He was creepy. Looked like he hadn't shaved for a couple of days. Hair was straggly, long and filthy."

"What was he wearing?"

"I have no idea, officer. We weren't on a fucking date! He pulled up behind us in the garage and jumped us!"

"Did you happen to notice what kind of car he was driving?"

Missy thought for a moment, trying to replay the scene in her mind. She did get a glimpse of the car and could recall its color.

"It was green," she said, "dark green. But I couldn't tell you what kind it was. Most cars today look too much alike."

"Of course. I think that's all for now. Can you give me a phone number where we can get in touch with you?"

"Yeah, 555-5958. There's one more thing you ought to know."

"What's that?"

"Before that asshole got away, I carved some skin with my nails. Look for a creep with long, deep gouges in his arm."

"Good for you. That's important for us to know. I'll leave you now and I'll keep in touch."

"Thanks, officer. What did you say your name was?"

"Officer Dedman…Harve Dedman."

"Thanks, Officer Harve." Missy managed a miniscule smile, but Dedman paid more attention to the wink.

"How's the other woman?" Dedman asked the nurse outside ER number two.

"Similar injuries with regard to the face, but she suffered a slight skull fracture when she fell."

"Can she talk?"

"Not yet. It may be a couple of hours."

"Has anyone notified her family?"

"We couldn't find any ID."

"I got her name from Melissa Mangen." He gestured toward ER number two.

"Can I have it? We need it for our records?"

"Mooring, Sharon. Husband is Sal. Mooring and Mangen both work at Harrah's as dealers. They hit a jackpot last night and stuffed the money in their bras for safekeeping. Smart move, don't you think?"

"I'll say."

"Listen, I'll see what I can do about notifying Mr. Mooring. You don't see any reason why his wife won't fully recover, do you?"

"No. She's already awakened briefly. The doctor feels after she rests for a couple of hours, she should be able to be released."

"Good. Oh, and do me a favor. Ms. Mangen put some rather deep nail scratches into their attacker. Would you see to it that any scrapings under her nails are safely preserved. DNA, you know."

"I'll take care of it right now."

"Thank you, ma'am."

"No problem, officer."

As Dedman reached the waiting area just inside the emergency entrance, he stopped at a bank of telephones and picked up a phone book. Only about half of the residents of Las Vegas included their address in the phone book, the remainder opting instead to reside anonymously. Sal and Sharon included their address with their listing. Dedman jotted it down along with the phone number, and exited the hospital. In a twenty-four hour town, there was the possibility that her husband would be at home, he thought. That would be a good place to start.

"Where's Dickerson?" demanded Mesmer, as he surveyed the nearly full table of casino managers. George Dickerson, the Poker Room Manager, had been late at Mesmer's last staff meeting two weeks earlier. Mesmer was not amused.

"I think he's on his way, Nate," volunteered Emma Jordan, Slot Operations Director. "He was on the phone when I passed the Poker Room and he held up one finger. I took it to mean he'd be here in a minute."

"That depends on which finger he held up," joked Hal Howard, Keno Manager.

Emma smiled and shook her head. No one laughed. Mesmer shot a dagger look at Howard. The silence was icy.

"My ten o'clock meetings begin at ten o'clock," Mesmer began. "Anyone whose schedule is busier than mine is permitted to be late. I haven't yet met anyone at this property who fits that description."

The group sneaked glances at each other; some adjusted themselves in their seats. Along with Emma Jordan from slots and Hal Howard from Keno were Vince Mateo from the Race and Sports Book, Charlie Palermo from Surveillance, Arthur Kaiser from Baccarat, Stan Reno from the Twenty-one pit, and Dale Brooker from the Dice pit. Rhonda Bethtold had taken her administrative post at her boss's immediate right. Missing, of course, was George Dickerson from the Poker Room.

"It's been about six months since I took over here," began Mesmer, "and during that time I've made some observations about the way this operation runs. You'll recall at our first meeting I promised I wouldn't make any sweeping changes until I had an opportunity to evaluate you and your methods of doing business with each other and with our customers. I've now had an opportunity to do both and I've drawn some conclusions."

Mesmer stopped and slowly panned his audience, locking eye contact with each person. During this half-minute, which seemed like ten, his unattractive under bite intensified, and the right side of his jaw pulsated with increasing rhythm. This behavior seemed odd to the participants, even for Mesmer. It made them uncomfortable and a few squirmed restlessly as his laser stare tracked on to the next person.

"Not one of you has picked up a pen and prepared yourselves to take notes. I just said I've drawn some goddam conclusions which are likely, by the way, to change your working careers and therefore your personal lives, and you just continue to stare at me with those empty eyes and expressionless faces!" His voice was now so loud that George Dickerson stopped fast in the outer office, declining to enter the conference room at this particular point. Instead, he elected to stand in earshot, but out of sight for the moment. He knew, too, that this tardiness was a felony from which he would probably never recover.

Everyone predictably scrambled for a pen or pencil from pockets, purses and from each other, and studiously braced themselves for Mesmer's next sacred pronouncement. Everyone, that is, except Charlie Palermo. The Surveillance Director was not a direct report to the Casino Vice President. That would be like the proverbial fox guarding the hen house. Instead, Palermo's loyalties shot directly to the resort's president Thomas Brolin. His presence at this *everyone* meeting was more tradition than a requirement – a tradition that Mesmer had never actually officially blessed. In fact when Palermo entered the room this morning, Mesmer became visibly annoyed, but lacked the chutzpa to send him away. This adversarial relationship between surveillance and casino has been long standing and perfectly reasonable. Surveillance is big brother and everyone in the casino is suspect. Anyone in Palermo's position needed absolute autonomy and Palermo relished in it. His refusal to cower to Mesmer's insulting demeanor was a welcome opportunity to demonstrate to the ogre that his reach had its boundaries. And Palermo was out of bounds. Out of spite and principle, he would take no notes.

In the outer office, Dickerson, aware of the momentary disruption of the meeting decided to make a hurried entrance now. He feigned the last few steps of a dead run and turned the corner into the conference room. Avoiding eye contact with Mesmer, he surveyed the table for an available seat. Finding one at the opposite end from Mesmer, he walked briskly toward it, mumbling a tardy apology to no one in particular. Mesmer wouldn't let him off the hook so easily.

"Dickerson, see me after this meeting," he barked.

"I'm sorry I'm late, Nate. I had a call from an unhappy..."

"After the meeting," Mesmer surly repeated. "And take out a pencil."

Dickerson instinctively patted the chest pocket of his shirt and searched his suit coat pockets in vain. He brought no pen or pencil.

Rhonda empathetically passed one down to him. Dickerson smiled in appreciation. The meeting could now resume.

"Conclusion number one ... " Mesmer snarled.

Chapter Nine

Ladies and gentlemen, that noise you just heard was the sound of shit hitting the fan.

"When can I see her?" Sal Mooring asked, his hair showing the ravage of a short-lived deep sleep. Wearing his dark blue cotton robe, he continued pacing frantically back and forth over the same five-foot area. Officer Harve Dedman had awakened him just moments earlier by pounding on the front door, following several futile attempts with the doorbell.

"Hopefully sometime this afternoon." He glanced at his watch. It was now ten-thirty.

"She *is* all right, though?"

"As I said, her face took a pounding and she has a slight concussion, but it's nothing life threatening," said Dedman.

"How's her friend Missy?"

"Melissa? I was able to speak to her. Her mouth is swollen making her speech a bit difficult to understand, but she's okay."

As things began coming into focus for Sal, the realization that Sharon could have just as easily been killed began setting in. He collapsed onto the sofa. "Did the bastards take everything?"

"According to Ms. Mangen, there was only one guy, and yes, he took their purses."

"Son of a bitch!" screamed Sal. "Sharon and Missy won a big jackpot last night!"

"The money's safe," said Dedman smiling. "They hid it in their bras before they left the casino. The guy got away with eye make-up and lipstick."

"Well, he got more than that, officer. I'm sure he got her cards! All of them."

"Fortunately, they're replaceable," Dedman said. Sal seemed a bit too upset over the wrong things. His wife was in the hospital, semi-conscious, badly bruised with a concussion, and this guy is concerned about 'the cards.' Get real, Dedman thought.

"Mr. Mooring, if there's nothing else I can do for you, I need to be going now. I want to get the guy's description out on the street and turn the case over to one of our detectives."

"Thanks, officer. I'm going to get dressed and get down to the hospital."

Sal walked Dedman to the door and opened it. Dedman turned to Sal.

"I hope you don't mind my asking, but what's Ms. Mangen's story? Is she seeing anyone?"

"Not that I know of," said Sal. "You interested?"

"I don't know. I just thought maybe there was something there, you know?"

"Hey, whatever," said Sal. "Missy is a character, I'll tell you that."

"Well, I hope all turns out well for you and your wife. See you."

"So long." Sal closed and locked the door. He looked at the clock and realized his shift began in a couple of hours. He'd have to call off. He picked up the phone and dialed the Desert Empire.

"Connect me to the twenty-one pit, please."

"Twenty-one, this is Ralph."

"Ralph, this is Sal. I need to speak to Stan Reno."

"He's in a meeting, Sal, with Mr. Big."

"Mesmer?"

"Do you know another Mr. Big?"

"Listen, Ralph, tell Stan I won't be in today. My wife was mugged this morning and she's in the hospital."

"My God! Is she all right?"

"She's got a concussion from what the police tell me. I haven't been able to see her yet."

"Well, you do what you gotta do, Sal. I'll let Stan know and I'll call the scheduler to bring in a replacement."

"Thanks, Ralph," Sal said, and hung up. As he hurried into the bedroom to change, he smiled to himself. "She hid the money in her bra! No shit! That's my baby!"

Nathan Mesmer's meeting adjourned at around eleven-thirty AM. and almost immediately word of the casino executive's mandates was spreading throughout the Desert Empire. A few employees watched the department heads vacate the conference room and couldn't help noticing their somber mood. George Dickerson had stayed behind at Mesmer's earlier request and Mesmer's screaming voice could be heard indiscernibly from the hallway outside the outer office berating him for his cavalier and insolent attitude toward tardiness.

Up close, Dickerson knew better than to let his body language proclaim his utter contempt for this repulsive bully. Instead, he struck a submissive pose, raised his eyebrows, and compressed his lips. His job and career carried far more magnitude than his desire for instant gratification. The finger pointing made his stomach churn, however, and for a flash he let his eyes focus on the waving digit, secretly vowing a vengeful payback. When Mesmer had blown off enough steam and decided to come up for air, Dickerson humbly apologized, promised never to repeat such brazen behavior and asked for the asshole's forgiveness. The behavior, tone, and words met with Mesmer's approval and he dismissed him with one last finger pointing toward the door.

At the bottom of the stairs leading from the mezzanine into the casino, Stan Reno was halted by Rich Domingo, a blackjack floor supervisor on his way to lunch.

"What the hell went on up there, Stan? Everyone coming down looks dead."

"You going to lunch?" asked Reno.

"Yeah, you?"

"May as well. It's the last day to eat in the coffee shop," said Reno.

Domingo clearly heard him, but opted to wait until they were alone at their table to get the full scoop. They walked the length of the casino to the coffee shop in silence, glancing periodically at what little action there was in the casino. Other participants from this morning's meeting could be seen in hushed circles scattered throughout the floor, obviously sharing some of Mesmer's dictums of doom. The looks on the faces of the listeners gave Domingo intimations of what was to come at lunch. He could see the concentration on Reno's face, punctuated by a pulsating cheekbone.

When they had signed in as executives at the hostess podium and been shown their seats, Reno picked up his menu, looked perfunctorily at it, and replaced it in front of him with a sigh.

"Something's wrong with that bastard, Rich. I don't know what it is, but something is definitely wrong with this guy," said Reno.

"So tell," pleaded Domingo.

"All right and whatever I tell you, you need to tell as many people as you can. This ain't one of those 'don't tell nobody' things."

"Whatever you say."

"Number one, as you heard me say, this is the last day for the executives to eat here in the coffee shop. Starting tomorrow, it's the employee dining room like everybody else."

"What for?"

"Oh, he threw out some ridiculous numbers about how much money this property loses by letting the suits eat in the coffee shop. I think he said hundreds of thousands a year. So pick something good from the menu. Tomorrow it's buffet leftovers."

"That sucks."

"Wait, I'm just getting started. Number two. Two weeks from today the dress code in the casino changes for those of us who wear suits. Sport coats are o-u-t. No more light colored suits. All we're allowed to wear is black, dark blue or dark gray. That's it."

"You've got to be shitting me! Who's going to pay for this new wardrobe?" Domingo fidgeted with his tie.

"Who do you think?"

"Did he say why?"

Collusion on the Felt

"Image. He says we got to raise the bar on our image. I don't know what the fuck he's talking about. You think our players give a shit what color our suits are? I don't know. Number three – and this don't affect us in twenty one like it does the dice pit – but starting next Monday, the players aren't allowed to bet table odds for the dealers. The most they can place behind their pass line bets is a measly five-dollar chip."

"That's unbelievable."

"Believe it."

"Why, Stan? Those guys are going to starve! They rely on those odds bets. And how does Mesmer suppose the Georges (industry term for generous tippers) are going to react to a house rule forbidding them from making odds bets for the dealers?"

"As to the 'why,' Mesmer was totally up front with that. When players bet heavy odds for the dealers, that's money the house may not see. It's that simple."

"But these guys work for tips, Stan. This is going to cut their take-home forty percent easy."

"I ain't done," Reno said as he held up his hand.

"This is making me sick," said Domingo.

"Number four. Effective immediately, if not sooner, there's no more smoking in and around the pit area, and that goes for drinking soft drinks and water. You want to smoke, you want to drink, you do it on your break in the employee dining room."

"Image again?"

Reno nodded.

"Where's this guy coming from?" asked Domingo.

"You should have seen him ream Dickerson when he walked in a couple minutes late. He made him stay after the meeting so he could humiliate him some more. I'm telling you, Rich, this guy is no good. I got a bad feeling about him."

A cheerful food server joined them at the table to take their order.

"How are you today, Mr. Reno?" she said with a smile.

"I'm going to miss you, kiddo," he said. "You're going to be a lot less busy in here for lunch starting tomorrow."

"I heard," she said. "It's all over the place."

"Let me have the usual. No use changing now, huh?"

"One club and crispy fries. And you, sir?"

"Sounds good. Make it two," said Domingo.

"Thank you, gentlemen. I'll have Julio see to your drinks right away."

As she left, Reno said, "We got good people working here, Rich. They don't deserve a guy like Mesmer coming in here fucking things up."

"Any other bombshells, Stan?"

"Oh, get this. He's going to recommend to Mr. Brolin that with the next big convention we get in here, COMDEX, that we charge our guests five dollars for parking in the parking garage *and* ten dollars if they use valet."

"Brolin will never go along with it," said Domingo. "The guy's got too much class."

"Well the way Mesmer tells it, the fourth quarter projections aren't good. He says this hotel has got to make money any and every way it can. He says these computer geeks are used to paying for parking and no matter what, the million dollar companies are footing the bill. It's a big fat write-off for them," said Reno.

"All right. There's a point," admitted Domingo.

In fact, here are some other revenue generating ideas he's going to run by Brolin: Start charging a dollar for toll free calls made from the guestrooms. Mesmer says the other hotels in town are doing it and when we don't, we leave hundreds of thousands of dollars on the table at the end of the year. He wants to start penalizing guests who say they're checking in for, let's say, a four-day stay, but they want to check out after only three days. He wants to charge them fifty bucks for the early departure. No more free rollaway beds. He's recommending a daily charge of twenty-five bucks."

"Anything else?"

"Not today, but I've got a feeling he's holding the better part of his list of recommendations close to the vest. It's my bet we'll hear about them later," said Reno.

Domingo cupped his hand over his ear like a radio announcer: "Ladies and gentlemen, that noise you just heard was the sound of shit hitting the fan." They both chuckled in helpless resignation.

"How's Missy?" Sharon murmured, her voice barely audible.

"Ornery as ever," said Sal smiling. "In fact she was released an hour ago. How are you feeling, sweetheart?"

"I've got a headache and I feel a little woozy," she said. "What time is it?"

"Three fifteen," said Sal.

"Aren't you supposed to be at work?"

"Called off," he said. "I had something more important to attend to." He lightly ran his fingers through the front of her hair, caressing her forehead.

"How long have you been here?" she asked.

"I got here around noon. You were totally out of it. You woke up once, saw me and smiled, then you were gone again."

"What did the doctor say?"

"Mild concussion, nothing serious. The swelling on your face has gone down a lot. You should be good as new in a couple of days."

"What about the money?"

"They had it at the nurses' station and turned it over to me when I got here." Sal patted his pants pocket. "Missy got hers, too. That was a stroke of genius, Sharon. Missy said it was your idea to hide the money in your bras. Brilliant!"

Sharon's attempt at a smile turned quickly to a wince as a shot of pain darted through her head. "When can I get out of here?"

"The doctor is supposed to be here around four. You'll probably be released then. Why don't you just rest for now."

"Hold my hand," Sharon said. "Talk to me. The sound of your voice makes me feel safe."

He took her hand. "Do you fully understand what happened to you today?" Sal asked.

"I think so," said Sharon. "What do you know?"

"From what I understand, you and Missy were attacked in Harrah's parking garage this morning while you were getting out of Missy's car. The guy struck you both in the face, grabbed your purses, and took off in his car. When you fell, your head struck something, maybe another vehicle. No one actually witnessed the attack, but Missy's screams brought people running right away."

"Do they know who did it?"

"Not yet. But Missy told me she scratched the hell out of the guy's arm before she went down."

Sharon giggled faintly. Suddenly her mood reversed. "What about our purses? All my cards, my keys ... "

"They haven't turned up yet, honey. And they probably won't. We'll need to contact the credit card companies and you'll have to take care of getting a new sheriff's card, drivers' license, and social security card. But don't sweat that stuff right now. Work on getting well first."

She thought for a moment, then was able to relax and smile. She closed her eyes, as he continued to caress her forehead. He ached to tell her about last night's meeting with Rolly and Nappa, but decided here and now was not the time and place.

Chapter Ten

*Do you think you two guys are the first Bozos
to think you can steal from the casinos?*

It was twenty minutes past eight. Monday evening prime time summer repeat television droned on in the Mooring home. Sal was sleeping soundly on the overstuffed recliner. He'd had barely two hours of sleep in two days. Sharon was only semi awake, lying on the sofa. The two had stopped off at Marie Elena's Mexican Restaurant for dinner after Sharon's discharge. The experience was unusually quiet for them. Sharon's aching head made chit chat an uncomfortable non-essential. Sal, on the other hand, wanted dearly to share with her what he and Rolly had discussed the previous night. Each time he thought he had built up the nerve to begin, he would look into Sharon's eyes, see discomfort and pain, and scoop up some refried beans instead.

The phone rang jolting Sal into awakened confusion. He reached beside him for the cordless. "Hello," he said, trying to sound awake.

"Hey, Slick." It was Rolly.

"Hey, what's up?"

"How's Sharon, man? Word is all over the pit."

"Who is it?" asked Sharon.

Sal covered the mouthpiece. "Rolly. He's asking about you. She's home now. She suffered a mild concussion, but she'll be all right."

"Did the guy get her money?"

"Actually, no. She and Missy hid their stashes in their bras. Can you believe it?"

"No shit?" Rolly cackled. "Hey, ah…have you, ah…talked to her about…you know?"

"No. I don't think now is the right time under the circumstances."

"Well, like I said before, I really do think you ought to leave her out of it."

Sal didn't respond. Sharon was watching him.

Rolly suspected as much. "Man, you should hear what Mesmer did today. He's got everybody fired up."

"The man needs to go," said Sal. "What'd he do now?"

"We'll talk when you get back. Don't worry about it now. By the way, I'm setting up a meeting in a few weeks to…"

Sal interrupted. "Hold it, Rolly. Let me get to a different phone." Sal carried the cordless into the kitchen, picked up the wall phone, and turned off the power to the cordless . "Okay, go ahead," he said.

"Like I was saying, I'm setting up a meeting for a couple of weeks from now to announce the details of the 'project.'"

Sharon entered the kitchen wearing a curious look. She pointed to the phone and mouthed "What's going on?"

Sal covered the mouthpiece and whispered "Oh – you know Rolly."

"Ah sounds, good, Rolly," he said, returning to the phone. "I haven't played poker for a long time."

Sal's tone told of Sharon's presence.

"Not alone, huh?" Rolly asked.

"That's right. You bet," said Sal.

"All right, kid. We'll see you when you get back to work. Give Sharon our best."

"Will do." Sal hung up.

Sharon cocked her head to one side. "What's that all about?"

"What's what all about?"

"Sal, please. There's something going on with you and Rolly. It's obvious. Why not tell me about it?"

"What makes you think that?"

"Come on," Sharon said. "You're out all night last night with him. You take the phone in the kitchen to get out of earshot. When I walk in, you change the subject and get off in a hurry. I don't know. Maybe it's me. But I get the feeling something's up."

Sal looked at her. Perhaps it was the right time. He knew he'd feel a lot better about everything if he had her support. But, he also knew that support wouldn't come easy.

"Let's go into the living room," he said. "I do have something to talk to you about. I'm not sure how you're going to take it. But, if my gut is right, this conversation could change the rest of our lives."

"Oh, Christ," she whispered to herself. "You're having an affair."

She followed him into the living room. He gestured for her to sit in the recliner while he continued walking across the room with his hand massaging the back of his head. He reached down and turned off the television. He knew it was critical to start this conversation exactly right and for the moment he felt at a loss for just the perfect words. He lingered, still facing away from her, and stared searchingly through the sheer curtains out into the summer dusk.

"This is scaring me, Sal," Sharon said through the tensing in her throat. "Please talk to me."

Sal turned and walked toward her, settling on one knee at her chair. "Honey, what do you think of our lives right now?"

"Our lives are fine, Sal. What kind of a question is that?"

"What I mean is, do you think ten or fifteen years from now we'll be living any differently? Any better?"

"I don't know. I suppose it'll be better. What..."

"Better how, Sharon? Every day we do the same things. We dress up in our black and whites, drive to the strip, wait for table assignments, and then start ripping off tourists of their hard-earned money pretending we're playing a game they have a chance of winning. And if that isn't enough, the money we win goes into the pockets of those corporate nobodies. They could give a shit less about us standing on our feet all day, numbers flying through our brains, smoke in our faces, taking the crap off the losers and acting like we're happy for the winners so they might throw us a bone. I don't know, I just..."

"Sal?"

"What?"

"Where the hell are you going with this? We knew what we were getting into when took these jobs. What do you want to do now, move back to Ohio and start a farm?"

"No, no, nothing like that. I like it here. In fact I love this town. But this town's like every other town. You've got the 'haves' and the 'have nots.' And, frankly, I have no desire to spend my life wishing and dreaming for something that just isn't going to happen. Look at those goons we work with. They've been pitching cards for twenty-five years, some of them. They walk to and from their breaks with their head bowed, their backs hurting and a scowl on their face that screams 'Man, I really fucked up a long time ago.' I just don't think I want to spend my life making other people – thankless people – people I don't even know – rich! I want something more – for you *and* me."

"You weren't kidding about this maybe changing the rest of our lives."

Sharon was beginning to wring her hands, a nervous gesture that tipped Sal, this was making her quite uncomfortable. Following a brief, awkward silence, Sharon asked, "What's happened, Sal? What's soured you on dealing all of a sudden?"

"Oh, dealing's fine," he said. "It gets us from payday to payday. But, I can't help wondering how it would be if we had a real stash, a huge bundle of money at our disposal so that we could really enjoy what life has to offer."

"No argument there," she said. "So let's start saving. I gave us a good start last night - six grand."

"Bigger than that," Sal said, "much bigger."

"Are you trying to tell me you're thinking of doing something wrong, something illegal?"

"Haven't you ever noticed that whoever the hell develops the list of rights and wrongs is always much better off than the rest of us. Look at politics, government, police, judges, company presidents. I tell you, honey, when you step back and take a look at the state this world is in today, you realize that you better do everything you can to take care of yourself because nobody else gives a shit about you."

"Are you thinking about cheating the casino?"

"You haven't heard a word I said."

"I heard you. Now tell me are you cheating?"

"Rolly has found a way to take financial care of him and Beatrice by simply stepping into a parade that's already in progress." Sal paused for a beat. "And he wants me to join him."

Sharon pressed her head into the soft recliner back. Her eyes closed while her mouth dropped to permit the escape of a resigned sigh. Sal's words ricocheted throughout her cluttered, confused mind. Her words were slow and pained. "And *are* you?"

This was the moment of truth. Sal knew there'd be no turning back now. "I'm seriously thinking about it, Sharon. But, I want your support."

"You are out of your ever loving mind! Do you think you two guys are the first Bozos to ever think you can steal from the casinos? What the hell's wrong with you? My God I can't believe what I'm hearing. I cannot believe it!"

"Listen," pleaded Sal, "I know exactly what you're thinking and I understand perfectly."

"No you don't! "If you did, you'd never even *consider* it! What am I supposed to do with a felon husband spending the rest of his life in prison? You can't get away with it, you know."

"I don't blame you for reacting like this. To tell you the truth, when Rolly first started telling me about this opportunity, I felt the same way."

"*Opportunity?* You're calling this an *opportunity?*"

"Sharon, all I want is a chance to discuss this with you and I promise that after you know all the details, if you still feel strongly that I shouldn't, you have my word that I won't."

"I can't believe I'm even in this conversation. And I'll tell you up front, the way I feel right now, there's nothing you could tell me that would make me support such a ridiculous stunt. In fact, I'm ashamed that you would even allow yourself to consider something so stupid."

"But you will let me try to explain?" His imploring face was irresistible.

"Explain away," she said. And she leaned her head back once again and closed her eyes as Sal's mind raced to grab the elusive brass ring.

Ralph Tamhagen took the final drag of his cigarette and squeezed it out in the dust coated ashtray. The nightly perch on his balcony would have to be cut short this night. Tomorrow morning, he'd have to attend that loathsome training program. The man known as the Colonel to his small cadre of friends and co-workers, absolutely dreaded the mere thought of going through this awkward experience the next day. But, as he rose for the walk to the bedroom, the thought that by tomorrow night at this time the class would be well behind him, provided the consolation he needed to face the pillow. Within moments, while the radio talk show droned on, Tamhagen ended yet another of his many days.

Missy Mangen and Officer Harve Dedman slowly untangled their moist, nude bodies following their third orgasm in the past two hours. Dedman had mustered up the grit to place a follow-up courtesy call late that afternoon. Missy, touched by the gesture, invited him to join her for some dinner at her apartment. Harve happily accepted, and their evening of whispers and giggles blossomed in the glow of scented candlelight. Exhausted now, they cuddled on the dampened sheets, nose to nose, lips to lips, breath to breath, and gave themselves to sleep.

Sharon Mooring lay in her bed, staring at the slowly whirring ceiling fan. Sal's sector of the mattress remained vacant. He had given up begging her to unlock the bedroom door more than an hour earlier. She struggled to make sense of his intruding bombshell of early evening. Her husband actually believed that it was not only possible to dupe the casinos out of a fortune in money, but that it was okay to even consider it. The strain of the very long day that had followed a very long night began taking its toll and she allowed her eyelids to slowly flutter to a close. She prayed that her tenacious resistance to his hair-brained scheme had chiseled an impact on his own perspective. But that, she thought, was a long shot. She had just learned earlier that evening that she didn't really know him very well after all. He was apparently capable of most anything. She would have to leave him. And that would be discussed tomorrow.

Chapter Eleven

Spying on workers on TV monitors don't take no special skill! You hear me?

The next morning at nine-forty AM., Ralph Tamhagen struggled to climb the dozen and a half steps up to the Desert Empire Training Room. The outside stairs rose from the fringe of the employee parking lot to what used to be the company's Purchasing Department. A faded, rusting sign riveted to the Quonset-like, prefabricated steel exterior implied the former occupant. Less than halfway up, the Colonel was forced to pause. The muscles in his legs were tightening and painful. Though no one else was on the stairs, he pretended to look out over the parking lot to mask his retarding fitness. During the drive from home, Tamhagen had rehearsed what would be his self-introduction. Rather than announce he was an agent in the Surveillance Department, he would simply say he was in Security. That would negate having to answer curious questions from other participants in the class about surveillance. He'd learned that ploy long ago and it has always served him well.

The mid-morning sun was promising a dog day. He patted the perspiration forming at his temples. He looked up at the remaining steps and, grasping the railing, resumed his slow climb. He was grateful that he had arrived early enough to avoid having to share this climbing misadventure with anyone else. His age was beginning to bother him more and more. He was quite aware that his character-worn face betrayed any attempt to hide his years. The Desert Empire, like her corporate neighbors, was quietly purging the workforce of the tired and weary, making way for the energetic, naïveté of the less expensive, more youthful models. He knew he stood out in a crowd of peers in a way that made him extremely uncomfortable. He longed for the quiet seclusion of his workstation.

The baritone voice startled him.

"Morning!"

"Morning to you," Tamhagen said, controlling his breathing so that it appeared effortless. "How are you?"

"Excellent, thanks. I'm Jeremy Reed, Training Manager." He extended his hand.

"Ralph Tamhagen. Pleasure," returned the Colonel. "You must be new here."

"About a year. Don't think our paths have crossed yet, have they?"

"Don't reckon. Course I work late swing. I guess you HR types don't get around here much that time of night."

"Not if I can help it," joked Reed. He was a plump, balding gentleman in his mid forties. His face wore that natural smile normally found on a used car salesman, etching telltale lines beside and beneath his deep, brown eyes. He dressed well, sporting a white shirt, navy suit and power red tie. The matching handkerchief puffing out of the jacket pocket may have been a bit much, Tamhagen thought. But the guy seemed nice enough.

"What do you do here?" asked Reed.

There it was. "Security," said Tamhagen, "I'm in security."

"Great," said Reed, his obvious response to any answer to that question. Tamhagen was hopeful that would be the end of that.

He edged up the final two steps, involuntarily wincing at the aching in his legs.

"Well, welcome to our training room," smiled Reed.

"Thanks. I have been here before, though," offered Tamhagen.

Reed pulled out a pack of cigarettes as Tamhagen ambled past him and entered the training room. He was the first to arrive. Several tables, providing a dozen seats awaited the eleven remaining participants.

Neatly arranged workbooks, name tents, and pencils adorned each of the seating positions. A sign-in sheet beckoned on a small round table just inside the entranceway. Tamhagen obligingly printed his name and scrawled *Security* in the department column. A scribbled signature completed the entry.

The aroma of freshly brewed coffee lured him to the back of the room, where two carafes of regular and one carafe of decaf sat warming, surrounded by stacks of white Styrofoam cups, containers of condiments, napkins and stirrers. A platter of assorted pastries summoned, and Tamhagen reached for one of the chocolate fingers, which he placed on a napkin. He poured a cup of high-test black coffee and carried his meal to a seat in the back of the room.

The large screen television in front of the room displayed a colorful graphic extending a welcome to *Diversity in the Work Force.* Two blank flip charts stood on either side of the television, while an immaculately clean white board stocked with a rainbow of markers occupied center stage. Tamhagen peered under his napkin at the professionally printed workbook, which was already open to the first page, a welcome letter from the company president, Thomas Brolin. While nibbling on a small bite of chocolate finger, he skimmed the perfunctory lines extolling the benefits of the training he was about to experience and encouraging him to participate fully.

A combination of footsteps and voices drifting through the open door distracted him. He looked up and could see through the doorway Jeremy Reed smiling and extending his right hand in another welcoming gesture.

"Jeremy Reed," he heard.

"Rolly Hutchins," came the distant response.

Tamhagen checked his watch. The session would begin in ten minutes and all in all, it looked like it might not be as bad as he'd initially feared.

Sharon Mooring slowly stirred the half and half into her third cup of coffee. She hadn't slept very well. Her head ached and she had no energy. She peered into the living room. Sal was still asleep on the sofa, covered by jackets from the hall closet. He looked innocent, like he always had when he slept. She wondered whether anything she'd said last night would make any lasting difference in his attitude.

The telephone rang. The caller ID showed that it was Missy.

"Good morning," Sharon whispered. She sauntered toward the patio doors that emptied onto the pool deck, carrying the wireless phone with her.

"How are you, feeling, Sweetie?" asked Missy.

"I've had better days. You?"

"Apparently a whole lot better than you are. What's up?"

"I don't know where to begin," said Sharon with a sigh.

"Same here. This past twenty-four hours has blown my mind."

"You go first," said Sharon. She sat down on one of the patio chairs and sipped her coffee.

Sal continued to lie on his back, his eyes focused on the ceiling, his ears straining to hear. When Sharon slid the patio door closed, he figured it must be Missy. That would not be good.

He rolled off of the sofa, a jacket tangling his legs, causing his head to bounce off of the coffee table. He unscrambled himself from the heap and shot through the dining area, past the kitchen, to the patio door. His eyes locked onto Sharon's lips, which at the moment were idling in the listening mode. He fumbled for the door handle and pulled the massive carriage of glass open. The noise surprised Sharon.

Instinctively, he raised the index finger of his right hand to his clenched lips. Sharon rolled her eyes as if to say 'do you think I'm an idiot?' Sal cocked his head in semi embarrassment, pulled the door closed and headed back to the sofa. His spilled secret would be safe with Sharon – for now. Within moments he was fast asleep.

"Mind if I join you?"

The Colonel looked up from the lunch table to catch the glimmer of Rolly Hutchins' smile. He'd gone out of his way to choose this corner booth to ensure some privacy at lunch, a particularly challenging feat since the dining room was especially crowded today. Now this guy wanted to join him. His gut told him he should not be sitting with a baccarat dealer. Policy was Surveillance and dealers just don't mix. He looked around the table as though searching for a reason to decline the invitation. Unable to find any, he looked up at Rolly.

"Course not," he said. "Please, sit down."

"Thank you, Ralph." Rolly slid into the empty seat on the other side of the booth and placed his tray opposite the Colonel's.

"That blueberry pie sure looks good," admired Rolly.

"Yeah. I don't normally eat like this, but what the hell. It's a school day, right?"

"So, what do you think of the class so far?" asked Rolly.

The Colonel chewed a hunk of buttered bread while contemplating his answer.

"Tell you the truth, it's not as bad as I thought it was going to be. Not bad at all."

"That Reed guy's pretty good at teaching. Don't you think?"

"Not bad," said the Colonel nodding.

"Sure beats walking the property all day, don't it?" asked Rolly.

"How's that?"

"You Security dudes. That's pretty much what you do all shift, ain't it? Kind of just walk around making sure everything's safe and secure and all?"

"Oh, yeah," said the Colonel squirming. "It sure does beat walking all day."

Rolly scooped up a helping of green peas. The Colonel tried to ignore Rolly's stare as he chewed the helping with a smirk.

"Yeah, sure beats walking around the property," repeated Rolly. "Especially when your wheels ain't rolling like they once were, huh?"

This conversation was making the Colonel very uncomfortable. All he could do was nod, while staring at his plate.

"I heard you say during the introductions that you've been here at the Empire over twenty-five years."

"That's right," came the Colonel's breathy reply.

"Funny I ain't never seen you around, ain't it?"

The Colonel had a strong feeling that Rolly was intentionally backing him into a corner, but why?

"I've seen *you*, before," said the Colonel. It was the truth. The Colonel had seen Rolly nearly every day, but mostly in black and white. "In fact, I remember seeing you the other day when there was all that confusion over at the baccarat pit...all those Chinese guys?"

"You saw that?" said Rolly with a grin. "Wasn't that a hummer?"

"There was quite a crowd outside that pit. A lot of folks had never seen that kind of action before," said the Colonel, trying to steer the conversation away from himself.

"So you were there? How about that? You need to stop over and say 'hey' next time you're in the area."

"I'll do that," said the Colonel.

The two sat eating in silence for the next several minutes. The Colonel dreaded further discussion. Now he began to question his own decision to lie about what line of work he was in.

"Hey, Ralph."

The Colonel looked up. "Yeah?"

"Why don't you come clean with me, Ralph? You ain't no more in Security than I am a kitchen worker. Am I right?"

The Colonel locked eyes with Rolly and involuntarily glanced to either side of Rolly's face. "Why do you say that?"

"I was in my car in the parking lot about five minutes before you got there. I was readin' the RJ, killing a few minutes before I went up. I saw you climbing the stairs, Ralph. I didn't think you were gonna make it, man."

This really annoyed the Colonel. His silence stoked the fire.

"A guy walking like you ain't in no Security, Ralph. And that's okay. Shit that's just fine by me. But you can't blame me for wondering why in hell a person would say he was a Security officer when he damn sure wasn't, now can you?"

All the Colonel could do was nod rhythmically while he chewed the final bite of his sandwich.

"I'm making you uncomfortable. Is that a fact?" asked Rolly. "I don't mean nothin' by it, Ralph. But damn, it sure is strange that a fellow employee wants to lie about where he works..." Rolly stopped short. It suddenly occurred to him there's only one department in the company whose employees notoriously want to keep a low profile and Rolly now knew just which department that was.

"Oh, shoot," said Rolly. "You know it just occurred to me why you would want to keep your department a secret."

Collusion on the Felt

The Colonel just glared at him.

"Ain't this a hoot?" said Rolly laughing. His laughter began to draw unwanted attention, further stiffening the Colonel.

Rolly leaned over and whispered directly into the Colonel's face, "You're in the fucking eye, ain't you?"

"You know the policy," said the Colonel through gritted teeth.

"Yeah…it's a fucking policy," returned Rolly. "What do you think, Ralph, that we don't think there are human beings up there?"

"We're not supposed to fraternize. You know that!" The Colonel's tone was heating up.

"Why is that, Ralph? You fuckers too good to be associating with us working stiffs?"

"Look, Hutchins, I didn't come looking for trouble with you. I was sitting here minding my own business. Why don't we just leave it right here?"

"Leave what right where?" Rolly was clearly agitated. "What makes you guys think you're so goddamned special up in that sky, Ralph? You act like you're part of the fucking CIA or something." The volume of his voice was bouncing echoes off the corner walls. The Colonel breathed deeply, his jaws pulsating.

"Hear me out, Ralph. I'm up to my ass with guys like you and your Desert Mounties. This is a fucking casino where people play cards – they *play* cards, Ralph! It ain't rocket science in this building and you and your buddies aren't landing 747s in the goddamned fog! You're no better than I am. Spying on workers on TV monitors don't take no special skill, you hear me? You wanna play Columbo, get a real job." Rolly slammed down his empty glass of milk, picked up his tray, and exited the booth.

The Colonel sat still, staring at the space where a second ago, Rolly's face had been scowling at him. Well, he thought, at least he never did admit he was with Surveillance. The policy was preserved. He picked up his dessert fork and pulled the blueberry pie to the center of the tray. The second half of the Diversity class was going to be uncomfortable as hell, he sighed.

It was all but a normal Tuesday at the Desert Empire. Word of Mesmer's 'meeting of doom' the previous day had spread through the entire property like a California wild fire. A coalition of dealers from the Dice Pit were waiting in the Human Resources Department, alternately standing and pacing outside the Labor Relations Manager's office. They had already garnered sixty-seven dice dealers' signatures on a hastily prepared petition protesting the elimination of odds bets for the craps dealers. They were livid. How dare Mesmer come in and rip away a significant portion of their income and seriously threaten their very livelihoods!

There had always been murmurs in the Vegas casinos among the dealers to unionize. Every few years the effort seemed to peak and then it would peter out. Recently, the United Transport Workers' Union had expressed interest in representing the thousands of Vegas dealers. At first thought, many were excited about the prospect of being represented, of getting paid a normal wage, having job security, and being treated with respect by the hard core casino management. Then there were the more senior dealers who had been there, done that many times over the years and were well aware of the likely outcome. When the chips were down following voluminous company held "information" and doom and gloom meetings with the dealers, union hopes for dealers had always been voted down.

The biggest and most powerful union in the city was the Culinary Union who claimed tens of thousands of kitchen workers, cooks, chefs, housekeepers, porters, change and slot attendants among their ranks. But they had no interest in absorbing the city's thousands of dealers. Now here comes the UTW who was already established in Las Vegas having organized the truck drivers and vehicle and bus operators at the city's airport. They were national and they were interested.

"But, they don't know squat about the casino business," a dealer of twenty-two years was heard to say. "All they'll do is take more money out of our pockets in the form of dues, settle on a half-assed contract, and forget about us. We'll be worse off than we are now!"

Several of the city's major casinos had already gone the first step with the National Labor Relations Board and secured the required two-thirds signatures of casino employees. That would lead to an election for each of the properties. Those elections were scheduled to begin in about six weeks.

A dozen of ornery twenty-one dealers and craps dealers had forged the unionizing effort at the Desert Empire. It surprised no one that the first to suggest unionizing was Natalie Waynor, the recipient of Mesmer's wrath on his first day at the property. Natalie had been a rather content, quiet employee up till then. But when she experienced the horror of humiliation she'd often heard about from fellow dealers, she decided to lead the union cause. Within a week, she had the coalition eating out of her hand. Of course, they were now known as the 'dirty dozen' by management. At first, the unionizing effort received only a luke warm response from the dealer population. Since the 'meeting of doom' yesterday, the effort suddenly took on monumental significance, especially among the craps dealers.

In order to understand the impact of Mesmer's rule that players would no longer be permitted to place odds bets for dealers, one needs to know a little about the game of craps. Players place their bets on the table. Although there are a lot of possibilities, the two most common initial bets are either the Pass Line or Don't Pass. Pass means you're betting that the number that comes up on the "come out" roll – the initial throw, will be repeated before a seven comes up. If the roller throws a nine (the point), he and the pass line bettors want him to throw another nine before he throws a seven. That would be considered "passing."

The Don't Pass bet is just the opposite. Bettors here believe that the roller will throw a seven before he repeats his point.

Players must place their wagers before the initial roll. A seven on the come-out roll is a winner for everyone on the pass line. The seven is never a "point." An eleven on the come-out roll is also a winner for everyone on the pass line. It, too, is never a point. Two, three and twelve are craps. On the come-out roll, a craps loses for the pass line. So, the only possible numbers that can be points are four, five, six, eight, nine, and ten. As soon as the point is established, players can place odds bets behind their initial bet. Each casino has different odds limits allowed. The tables will have a sign that says something like ten times odds. This means if a player has bet five dollars on the pass line, once the point is established, that player can add up to ten times his initial bet as an odds bet. In the case of a five dollar bet, the player could add another fifty dollars behind his bet. In effect, the player has fifty-five dollars riding on the bet. The payoffs vary somewhat depending on which number is the point. It's never less than even money, but could be more.

Many players have traditionally expressed their gratitude for the service and assistance rendered by the craps dealers by placing an additional chip or several chips behind their original bet as an odds bet for the dealers at the table. That way, if the point is thrown before a seven, the dealers benefit by winning the odds bet, which again is always at least even money, but could be more.

The loss of this extra income ability hit the craps dealers very hard, and when James Fraley, the Labor Relations Manager returns from lunch, the dealers are prepared to have their say in a big way. Unbeknownst to the dealers, however, Fraley's return would be considerably delayed. The traffic in the employee dining room was incredibly heavy.

Today was the first day in over twenty years, the management had to eat in the employee dining room. Of the 525 supervisors, managers and directors from all three shifts and from all departments, a solid 300 worked day shift. The most popular lunch breaks occur between eleven AM. and one PM. Neither the dining room's physical space, nor the chef's department food supply was capable of serving 300 more people for lunch than had been customary. It was absolute pandemonium.

Jaws were tight in the casino, as well. Business had been flourishing since around ten AM., and the floor supervisors and pit bosses, most of whom were long time smokers, had been unable to leave the pits for their usual twenty minute breaks. Nerves were on edge. Unable to light up, the jittery pit keepers huddled in pockets sharing their misery. Their shredded patience with giddy guests and grumbling dealers helped paint a painful picture of staff discontent in the Empire's house of cards.

Word of Mesmer's proposition to charge guests for valet and self-parking during major conventions seeped outside to the valet attendants at the porte cochere. Their having to run around in the steamy August heat wearing stiff, safari-type jackets had already taken its toll on their normally low morale. Derek LaSalle, the lead valet attendant, brought the bad news back with him from lunch. He knew just whom to tell first. He hurried over to Len Ostrosky, a thirty-seven year old valet runner whose sole existence is devoted to finding a tear in every silver lining. Ostrosky is known throughout the front services department as a chronic discontent. Derek knew this latest news would provoke him, and he relished giving him something big to whine about.

"Hey, Len!" Derek called.

"What's up?"

"You'll never guess what Mesmer told the management staff yesterday about us."

"You're right, I ain't gonna guess. Just tell me."

"Effective with the COMDEX convention, this hotel is going to charge guests ten dollars to park valet and five dollars for self-park."

"Get the fuck out of here." Ostrosky turned to walk away.

"It's true, Len. Mesmer wants to 'maximize income potential.' From now on when those big conventions come in, we're fucked."

"He's charging ten bucks for valet?"

"And five for self-parking," reminded Derek.

"Nobody's going to pay that! What the hell's he thinking? Christ almighty every time you turn around in this hell hole, they find another way to fuck you!"

"This really does suck," Derek said, egging him on. "There goes our holiday stash."

"We live for that shit every year," moaned Len. "Damn it, if we charge everybody ten bucks, they ain't gonna tip us! Son of a bitch!"

"Why do you think I'm so upset?" asked Derek. "We're going to have to bust our asses for these geeks at the busiest time of the year and make jack shit!"

"I'll be damned if I'm going to sit back and let them take food out of my family's mouths like this," screamed Len. "I'm going in and call the union!"

"Won't do any good … " Derek hollered after him. Then almost to himself he muttered, "The company has a right to manage." And therein lies one of the most regrettable contract lines the unions ever conceded.

Removing the opportunity for the valet attendants to get tips was only a scant ill-affect of Mesmer's decision. The valet crew stood to lose many hundreds of dollars during the major conventions, and it wasn't just in tips. A little known fact about the valet game in Las Vegas is the way the valet attendants prematurely close the valet when the valet lot is only two-thirds full. Legions of guests have driven up to one of Las Vegas's many hotel valets on a busy Saturday night only to be greeted by the "Sorry, Valet Full" sign. It's a scheme the valet forefathers learned years ago that works like a charm. By closing the valet when the lot still has plenty of room, the attendants make untold dollars from insistent guests who simply must get to a sold-out show or a standing-room only convention gathering. They eagerly wave a ten or twenty dollar bill asking the attendant if there is any way they could possibly squeeze in just one more vehicle. The attendant pretends to ponder the thought, looks to his right and left and whispers, "All right, I'll take care of you."

The guest impresses his lovely companion with his Vegas savvy, and the attendant brings in ten or twenty times what that car would have brought under normal circumstances. During the major conventions when the hotels are full and guests are exhausted from walking the seeming miles in the convention center, they're willing to pay big-time to have a valet squeeze in just one more vehicle. Now, thanks to Mesmer, those days would be just fading memories.

Attitudes were teeming, too, at the hotel's front desk just inside the main entrance. Mesmer's pronouncements concerning the one-dollar charge for all toll-free calls made from the hotel rooms hit the already vanquished front desk agents very hard. Every day a hassled public dangling from their wits' end trounces the agents both when checking-in and checking-out. They're fed up with standing in long, crawling lines of exhausted, hot and hungry visitors, forming a huddled mass inching its way toward the huge counter where only three windows are open to receive them.

The turnover at the front desk is unusually high at the Desert Empire. The working life span of the agents is about three years. It hadn't always been that way. In the early days before Howard Hughes dragged Las Vegas into corporate America, the city's visitors were truly welcomed and treated like royalty. The word of the casino owners was good as gold. Today's old timers revere the memories of early Vegas when "the mob knew how to take care of customers." Now, in the twenty-first century, there was no trust, no belief. For example the hotels have adopted the airlines' approach to booking rooms. You call the Room Reservations agents, tell them you want a king size bed in a non-smoking room. You give them a credit card number to hold the room for you. The agents input your preferences into the computer and process your payment. But, in reality, no room has been set aside for you. When it's finally your turn in that mass of waiting humanity to reach one of those three windows, it's a crap shoot as to whether ANY room is available for you.

The fact is the hotel overbooks rooms because over the years, they've realized a certain percentage of no-shows. When, in fact, they do run out of rooms, it's worth the goodwill to pick up the tab at another hotel. But, the fact remains the front desk agents have to wade through truckloads of customer grief day in and day out. Many simply can't take the pressure or the verbal abuse.

Now they have to contend with telling guests when they're checking out that every toll-free call they made from their rooms, including internet hook-ups weren't free after all. The one-dollar per call charge is going to ambush many guests when they're checking out. And the fallout will be on the front desk agents. To top it off, Mesmer was also suggesting to Brolin that the hotel penalize guests fifty dollars when they check out a day earlier than they had originally stated. One only has to imagine the holy hell that will come down off the mountain when a guest receives an emergency call to leave a day earlier than planned only to face the hotel's fifty dollar punitive fee. The agents were furious over this.

Casino bosses were swapping stories about what their wives had to say when they learned that their men had to buy new wardrobes. And they'd need to do it by this coming weekend to have them altered in time for the two-week deadline.

It seemed as if everyone at the Desert Empire had reached new lows in their disdain for management. And Mesmer was tucked up in his cool, quiet haven dreaming up more misery for next week's meeting.

Chapter Twelve

"If there's a breeze outside, I want to know from what direction it's blowing and how many miles per hour the breeze is. Got it?"

"I told you not to tell her." Rolly was genuinely upset. He turned away and began walking briskly toward the parking lot. "Once something like that is out of the bag, you can't put it back in, kid."

Sal picked up his own pace to keep up with Rolly.

"Look I don't need to be involved in whatever it is you're planning, Rolly. And you know goddam well I would never say anything."

"It ain't that, Slick. What bugs me is you don't even know your own wife. It makes me wonder about your judgment in other things. When I tell you you're better off not bringing her in to this, you got to trust me, man. I know what I'm talkin' about."

The two walked in silence over the hot asphalt employee parking lot. Sal had run into Rolly while on his way to work. Rolly had just left the training room and was headed home.

"Rolly, I've got to make my shift. I only have a few minutes."

"Well, tell me how it ended up, then. What did she do after she got off the phone with her friend?"

"She came in the house - didn't speak to me at all. Of course, I was half dozing on the couch. She put the radio on and started doing the laundry. Pretty normal stuff."

"Did she talk to you at all before you left?"

"When I got up, she was singing quietly along with the radio. I figured maybe she was over her anger, so I walked up to her and gave her a kiss on the back of the neck."

"That was good," said Rolly smiling. "She liked it, huh?"

"She pulled her head away and stormed into the laundry room. I showered, dressed and left without the two of us saying anything to each other."

"Well, kiddo, that's something you're going to have to deal with. I sure as hell don't want her talking about this deal to anybody. Either she's on board with it, or you got to get off. That's all I can say."

"There is one other alternative."

"What's that?"

"I tell her I'm out, but I stay on. Then when it happens and we're rich, she'll get over it in a hurry."

"And if you get caught – not by her, I mean, by the law? What about that?"

"It won't matter a whole lot, will it? Besides, you guaranteed me this deal will work."

"Ain't no guarantees in life, Slick. You make your own."

"Listen I need to get going. When is this big meeting you told me about last night?"

"Day after Labor Day. Here's the address." Rolly jotted the address on the back page of his training handout and tore it off for Sal. "You're off that day after that big weekend, and so am I. All the others will be there, too, and I'll lay out the plan."

Sal took the torn slip of paper and placed it in his wallet.

"What time that day, Rolly?"

"High noon," said Rolly, winking.

Sue Min Wong hurried up the mezzanine stairs and into Nathan Mesmer's outer office. Startled, Rhonda Bethtold looked up from her computer.

"Sue Min, may I help you?"

"I need to see Nate right away. He is in, isn't he?"

"Let me check."

"Never mind, I'll see for myself." She tore past Bethtold's desk and burst open Mesmer's door without knocking.

Mesmer quickly closed a folder from which he was reading and looked up angrily. "We have doors in this country and we knock on them!"

"Why won't you answer your phone, Nate? I've been trying to get ahold of you for twenty minutes."

"What's so urgent?"

"I got a call from Cyril Queck's people. Mr. Queck is in town and wants to play this afternoon."

"Who the fuck is Cyril Queck?"

"No one told you about him?"

"No, no one told me about him. Who is he?"

"Mr. Queck has not been in here for about ten months. That's probably why you don't know about him. Mr. Queck has been singularly responsible for thirty-three percent of this property's baccarat revenues every year since the early 1990's."

"Thirty-three percent! Jesus Christ, what the hell are we doing chatting in my office? Where the hell is he now?"

"His people have told me he has finished his business at the Bellagio and wishes to spend this afternoon and perhaps tomorrow here at the Desert Empire. My guess is his luck has not been favorable at the Bellagio."

"What's his line?"

"Five million."

"Have you contacted Credit?"

"I have. Everything is ready for his arrival."

"Of course, he gets the penthouse suite?"

"He is one of the few people, along with his family, to ever stay in that suite."

"Where does he play?"

"He always plays in the private salon."

"Any special requests?"

"Well, Mr. Queck is, shall we say, extremely superstitious."

"Tell me."

"He will fly only on an airplane with an even number of passengers including himself, excluding the crew. Either someone unsuspecting gets a free ride when he travels, or some poor soul is bumped off the plane."

"That's strange, but I've heard worse."

"I'm just beginning. The temperature outside must be within five degrees of the record high temperature for whatever day he is playing. If there is a breeze, it must be blowing south to north. The miles per hour of the wind must be an even number…"

"Or he doesn't play?"

"Or he doesn't leave his bedroom, Nate."

"This guy sounds a little nuts!" Mesmer opened a humidor on his credenza and gently lifted a cigar to his lips. As he lit it, he mumbled, "Go on."

"Any food served to him must have been alive no less than twelve hours before. He is always to be served over his left shoulder."

"Yeah, go ahead."

"Before he sits down to play, he must determine which table will be his lucky table. In order to uncover his lucky table, he walks the perimeter of the baccarat pit in a counter clockwise direction. During this walk, he experiences vibrations from the tables. When he feels the strongest vibrations, that is where he plays."

"Wait a minute. Wait a minute. You said he plays in the private salon."

"That is correct."

"Well, how the fuck is walking around the baccarat pit going to get his vibes going for a table up in the salon?"

"It does not. He gets the vibrations from the tables in the baccarat pit. We must move the table from the baccarat pit into the private salon when he has made his selection."

"You mean I've got to get a fucking crew to stand around in the pit until this guy gets his jollies, and then they have to uproot the fucking table and haul it up to the private salon?"

"Perhaps you can do without thirty-three percent of baccarat revenues?"

"What time is he due in?"

"Could be any time between now and late tonight."

"Anything else?"

"Oh, yes. He always has the dealer Hutchins deal to him. It's his good luck dealer."

"Hutchins, huh?"

"That's right."

"If this guy Queck is so fucking lucky with all his bullshit shenanigans, how is it he's responsible for a third of our baccarat revenues?"

"I can only answer your question with another question. If his shenanigans, as you say, are bullshit, how is it he can afford to play with a five-million dollar line of credit at ten of our city's biggest casinos?"

"Let me know when he gets in."

"You'll be the first." Sue Min turned and left his office as quickly as she had entered.

Mesmer pressed the intercom button. "Rhonda, get Kaiser up here immediately."

"Right away, Mr. Mesmer."

Mesmer swung around in his overstuffed leather executive chair to watch the baccarat monitor. He enjoyed watching the reaction of others when they're told he wanted to see them. He puffed his cigar in anticipation. He could see Kaiser being summoned by the pit clerk. Kaiser walked over to the clerk as she told him that Mr. Mesmer wanted to see him right away. Kaiser's reaction was to immediately check the knot on his tie and ensure the tie lay squarely under the buttoned suit jacket. He whispered something to one of the floor supervisors who laughed and made a cutting motion with his finger across his own neck. As Kaiser scurried up the stairs to the mezzanine, the floor supervisor whispered to another supervisor, pointed in Kaiser's direction, and they both laughed. Mesmer puffed on his cigar, and rotated his chair back to its desk position. He could hear Kaiser in the outer office mumbling something to Rhonda Bethtold. Kaiser cleared his throat and knocked on Mesmer's door.

"Come in and take a seat, Kaiser," growled Mesmer.

"Yes, sir," replied Kaiser. "What can I do for you?"

"Well for starters, you can tell me why a couple of minutes ago I made a complete ass of myself with the China doll."

Kaiser shot Mesmer a bewildered look. "I'm not sure I understand…"

"Does the name Queck mean anything to you, Kaiser?"

"Cyril Queck? Why yes it does. He's one of our biggest whales, possibly the biggest."

"Then you do know this Cyril Queck?"

"Absolutely, sir."

"Then perhaps you can explain to me why the name Cyril Queck wasn't mentioned to me in that meeting we had when I first got here and I wanted to know who our whales were."

"I didn't tell you about Mr. Queck?"

Mesmer glared at him. "Didn't I just say that!?"

"Mr. Mesmer…I…I can't explain why I didn't mention Queck to you…if I didn't…because…"

"What do you mean 'If I didn't'?" Mesmer shot out of his chair and circled around his desk toward Kaiser. "You think I'm not going to remember a player's name who provides thirty-three percent of your department's annual revenues?" Now Mesmer was standing over Kaiser.

"God, I'm sorry, Mr. Mesmer. Maybe I didn't mention him because he hadn't been here in a few months. Maybe I forgot about him. That's all I can think of."

"You know, Kaiser, I didn't like you the day I met you and I've liked you less every day since. Give me just one reason I should keep you on here."

Kaiser couldn't think of any reason that would be acceptable to Mesmer. But, the thought of being fired right now made him light headed. He could feel the pounding of his heart.

"One reason!" Mesmer repeated.

Kaiser's face reddened, a vein stood out on his neck. "Go ahead fire me, Nate! Christ, anything would be better than putting up with your shit for one more day!"

That retort caught even Mesmer off guard. He continued his glare at Kaiser for another few seconds, blew cigar smoke in his face, and turned back toward the desk. Facing away from Kaiser, he said, "You're lucky I'm in a good mood, Kaiser. But,

I'm putting you on notice. One more fuck-up and you're out. Is that clear?"

Kaiser's own outburst had brought him to the brink of fainting and he could barely control his own hyperventilating. He managed a weak, "Yes. It's clear."

"Anyway," continued Mesmer, "Queck's in town and he's headed our way. I want everything the way he likes it. Do you understand?"

"Perfectly, sir."

"Do you know about his eccentric superstitions, Kaiser?"

"It's lore around here, sir."

"Good."

"I want you to call the weather people and find out what the current temperature is relative to the record for today. Got it?"

"Yes."

"If there's a breeze outside, I want to know from what direction it's blowing and how many miles per hour the breeze is. Got it?"

"Got it, sir."

"Get a hold of food and beverage and make sure we have something to feed him, something that died less than twelve hours ago. Got it?"

"Yes, I've got it."

"Have a crew standing by to carry and install whatever the fuck table vibrates his balls up in the salon. Got it?"

"Yes."

And one more thing. Make sure that dealer Hutchins is standing by. I understand that's Queck's choice."

"Yes, that's right. But…"

"Did you say 'but'?"

"Well, yes…you see…"

"What the fuck is wrong with you? There can't be any 'buts!' We're talking about thirty-three percent of your annual revenue. HOW THE FUCK CAN YOU SAY 'BUT!'"

"Hutchins is off. He's home. He went to training today!"

"Does Hutchins have a phone, Kaiser?"

"Well, yes.…"

"Do you have any other questions or concerns, Kaiser?"

"No, sir, none at this time."

"That's good. That's very good. Now get the fuck out of here and make sure we're ready for Mr. Looney Toon when he gets here! I'm counting on you, Kaiser."

"Yes, sir. I'll take care of everything."

As Kaiser hurried out of the office, Mesmer sank into his leather chair. "He's going to fuck something up. There's no doubt about it," he sighed.

Chapter Thirteen

And no one could ever accuse him of keeping a low profile. He brought the casino to its knees.

Shortly after eight-thirty PM., little more than the soft background music could be heard in the Desert Empire casino. And it wasn't for lack of players. On the contrary, for a Tuesday night the casino was packed as this week's conventioneers settled in for a night of gambling. But, little by little, the action at the tables ground to a halt. The clicking of clay cheques resonating off the high ceilings was reduced to utter stillness. The players, table by table, had begun pulling back their bets and signaling to the dealers to "hold on a minute." Dice lay at the foot of the stick, awaiting the roller's resumption. The attention of the many players had been diverted to the unusual goings on just outside the baccarat pit. Many actually left their tables to get a closer look.

Cyril Queck, known and recognized only by the Desert Empire's casino staff had arrived with his entourage. He was a short man, barely five-feet tall. His head was totally shaved and masking his Asian eyes were large round, very dark sunglasses. His age, as with most Asians, was extremely difficult to judge. Even his hands were smooth, young looking – free of wrinkles or any other clue of seasoning. As was his custom, he was in white tails, carrying a matching top hat which no one had ever seen him wear. In his other hand, he toted a white baton. Even his shirt and bow tie were void of color. The crease in the pants could score a cake, and the cuffs rode perfectly on the pure white shoes.

Cyril Queck's wardrobe fashioned a spectacular contrast to the casual, colorful desert attire now a cultural element in twenty-first century Las Vegas. And no one could ever accuse him of keeping a low profile. He brought the casino to its knees.

"Is that some movie star?" asked a woman from Bowling Green, Kentucky.

Her friend just shrugged her shoulders. "I know Telly Savalas is dead...and Yul Brynner...."

"No, they were both much taller."

Dealers and other casino employees were less impressed. In fact, the room looked like a festival of eye-rolls, with heads lowered to conceal their smirks of impatience. Queck was a rather frequent and long time patron of the Desert Empire, and the employees had, over the years, grown rather bored with his antics. But, to the guests of the Empire and the casino management, Queck's return was an event of major proportions.

This little man with the huge credit lines was, in fact, sixty-two years old. He was rooted in Chinese tradition and consequently enveloped in superstition. His was a fairy tale life of poverty in youth, an insatiable desire for education, and unbelievable success in land development. He spoke several languages fluently, including English. He religiously pursued a philosophy of live now for the end is at hand. He believed his hard work over the years had earned him respect and admiration and he demanded the former and relished the latter. His outrageous demeanor spoke volumes about his expectations. To him, there was room at the center for only one centerpiece. And he lavishly assumed the position. His reported net worth of five point four billion dollars secured that position.

Nathan Mesmer pressed himself against the mezzanine railing, leaning over to get a better look. Although he'd never met Cyril Queck, there was no doubt whatsoever where among the crowd Queck was. Mesmer watched helplessly as Art Kaiser fumbled over himself to greet Queck with a combination handshake and half-assed bow.

"Look at that simple shit," Mesmer whispered to Sue Min Wong. "For the life of me, I don't understand how the hell he has lasted at this hotel for eighteen years."

"His heart is in the right place. I believe you intimidate him," she whispered back.

"People being intimidated by me is not my problem," snapped Mesmer. "It's theirs!" His voice began rising above whisper now.

"Shhhh," she cautioned. "Sound travels easily in here, and all is so quiet."

"Do I really need to go down there?" Mesmer asked.

"To ignore Mr. Queck would be a strategic and shall I say fatal error on your part, Nathan. He is aware we are under new management and is probably wondering already why he hasn't been greeted by you."

"I'm not real comfortable with this kind of shit," he admitted.

"I don't understand what you mean," she said.

"I don't know what to say, what to do…all I know is that oriental crap is dangerous. If you do one thing wrong it's all over. There's too many rules."

"Not at all," she said. "Tell you what, I'll go down there with you and you simply follow my lead. Okay?"

"Do I need to stay long?"

"If I know Mr. Queck, the sooner you are out of the picture, the better he will like it."

"What the fuck's that supposed to mean?"

She was already leading the way down the mezzanine stairs.

Sal Mooring stood parade rest at BJ 102 which was two rows away, but facing the baccarat pit. His players, like others, had ceased wagering, and had spun their seats around to see what all the excitement was about.

"Who is that guy, Sal?" one player asked.

"That's Mr. Queck," said Sal. "Interesting, isn't he?"

"Is he some big deal?" asked another.

"He's one of the wealthiest players who come here," said Sal. "He's probably our biggest whale."

"Whale?"

"That's the term for very high rollers," Sal said.

"Well, he's certainly a whale of an interesting character," chuckled a woman who had been standing behind her husband during his play.

"Who's the guy in the suit walking up to him...with the Chinese woman?"

"That's our casino vice-president," said Sal. "His name's Nathan Mesmer. I think this is the first time the two of them will meet."

Art Kaiser smiled at Mesmer and Wong as they approached.

"Mr. Queck," said Kaiser, "I would like you to meet our new vice-president of casino operations. This is Nathan Mesmer. Mr. Mesmer, this is Mr. Cyril Queck."

Queck's stoic expression put Mesmer off balance. Mesmer didn't know whether to extend a hand or bow. He smiled awkwardly to Queck who quickly turned his head in Sue Min's direction. Mesmer held the smile and also looked at Sue Min, not knowing what else to do. Sue Min's face lit up with a full-toothed smile as she extended her hand, palm down, in Queck's direction. Queck slowly reached for the hand and brought it slowly up to his lips for a light, respectful kiss.

Mesmer's smile withered and he shot a glance in Kaiser's direction. Kaiser made a slight motion with his head as if telling Mesmer 'do something, say something.'

Mesmer took a deep breath and extended his hand toward Queck.

"Mr. Queck, on behalf of all of us here at the Desert Empire, I want to welcome you and your party to our hotel and casino."

The hand was still extended, but had not been accepted. Mesmer didn't know whether to pull it back, leave it there or make a fist and knock this marshmallow-dressed pompous bastard on his ass.

Queck very slowly lowered Sue Min's hand and just as slowly turned in Mesmer's direction. He lowered his head, as if looking at Mesmer's outstretched, now quivering hand. Mesmer mistook the move as the beginning of a bow and withdrew his hand just as Queck's hand rose to meet it. Mesmer failed to see Queck's hand on the rise because he was in the midst of his own bow and smacked his forehead on Queck's thumb. Kaiser tried desperately to contain a rush of laughter, expelling nasal debris instead. Sue Min judiciously bit her lip.

Mesmer swallowed hard and shook his head slowly while still in the down position. Queck broke up the bumbling by speaking for the first time.

"Please take my hand, Mr. Mesmer. Let us shake hands in deference to the bow. I fear if I return your bow, one of us will sustain regrettable cranium injury."

Relieved, Mesmer grasped Queck's hand with both of his and let the man know through his vice-like grip how genuinely appreciative he was of his empathetic gesture. "Welcome, Mr. Queck. If there is anything I or my staff can do for you during your visit, please allow us the opportunity."

"Much thanks," smiled Queck. "You can begin by permitting me to win exorbitant amounts of money."

"Well, we'll certainly do all we can to ensure a fair game," chuckled Mesmer. "I hope conditions are favorable for you."

"The weather and the wind are ideal," reported Queck. "Now, if you will excuse me, I must select my lucky table."

With that, Queck began his counter-clockwise pacing around the perimeter of the baccarat pit. His entourage followed at a distance of some ten feet. Mesmer leaned over and whispered to Sue Min, "Stay with this guy and keep me posted. I've got a feeling we're going to kick his arrogant ass."

"He is overdue for a lucky session, Nathan. And he has the capital to see him through the rough spots. It could go either way."

Standing parade rest in the corner of the Baccarat Pit was Rolly Hutchins. He was somewhat annoyed at being called back to work, but more captivated by the flagrant audacity of this Asian hero of heroes. Queck was Rolly's kind of man. He looked forward to dealing to him.

Cyril Queck seemed to levitate as he glided through his deliberate stroll along the outskirts of the baccarat pit. Most surmised his eyes were closed, but the mystery would forever remain unsolved beneath those blackened shades. As he moved closer to the various baccarat tables, the dealers seated at those tables did their level best to stare straight ahead, avoiding any hint of their abounding curiosity. The entourage adopted Queck's identical pace, foot for foot, stride for stride, maintaining a holy silence throughout.

Outside the baccarat pit, in the heart of the casino, a player whispered to his dealer: "What's he looking for?"

The dealer whispered back, "He's not looking for anything. He gets vibrations from the tables. That's how he picks the one he wants to play at."

"How long does he do that?"

"It varies. Last time he was here, it took him two hours before he settled on one."

"Two hours? Did he end up winning?"

"Dropped four million," said the dealer with a grin.

"Hell, he could have hand-built his own table and installed a vibrator in it for a lot less than that," the player whispered.

At approximately ten-twenty PM., Cyril Queck's pace began to slow significantly. He and his entourage had been circling the baccarat pit for nearly two hours. Once or twice during the circumnavigation, Queck appeared to walk hesitantly, perhaps receiving spurious vibrations from one of the tables. But his pace would quickly hasten again, alerting onlookers his quest for the lucky table would continue. Long ago, the attention spans of casino customers who had been curiously watching had expired, enlivening the action at the tables again. Sporadically and during shuffles, they would glance in the direction of the baccarat pit. When they saw the bleak procession still in progress, they turned to chat with their fellow players and the dealers.

But this time, Queck actually came to a stop. Art Kaiser, who along with Sue Min Wong, had been sitting at the entrance to the pit, reflexively stood up.

Queck's head turned slowly toward the table to his immediate right. He stood still, tilting his head one way and then the other, not unlike a dog investigating a high pitched sound. He turned and walked slowly toward the table with his hands in front of him, palms out, as though being pulled there by a divine power. When he reached the table, he placed his palms on the felt and lowered his head. One of the men who had been following in the entourage motioned for Kaiser to come to him. Kaiser willingly obliged.

"I believe Mr. Queck has found his table."

"How will we know for sure?" asked Kaiser.

"When I say 'I believe Mr. Queck has found his table.'"

The verbal slap was not without its pain. Kaiser sheepishly pointed in Sue Min's direction. That was the cue for her to alert the moving crew.

"You may advise Mr. Queck that we will have his chosen table in the private salon and ready for his enjoyment within forty-five minutes," said Kaiser.

"Excellent," said the man. "Perhaps Mr. Queck and his party can enjoy some of your excellent cuisine in the meantime."

"Allow me to arrange that with our Maitre'd. Our exquisite Palace of Palms restaurant has been alerted concerning Mr. Queck's visit and I'm sure you'll find the food and service up to our usual standards."

"Excellent," said the man. "We shall go now."

The casino crew was already heading into the baccarat pit with a flatbed truck on which they would load the baccarat table for the journey upstairs to the private salon. Rolly Hutchins, who had been sitting in the pit waiting for such a moment, excused himself for a quick bite in the employee dining room. Sue Min cautioned him to ensure his return to the private salon within forty-five minutes.

"Wouldn't miss it for the world, Sue Min," Rolly said smiling and winking. "No, ma'am, wouldn't miss it for the world," he repeated.

Chapter Fourteen

"All right, let's get it back," he mumbled to himself, while gripping the cigar with his clenched teeth.

The final preparations were being concluded for Cyril Queck's rendezvous with the Desert Empire. The baccarat table, massive and ornately crafted, was now carefully placed and installed in the luxurious, private salon, one floor above the main pit, accessible only to a privileged few. A complement of support staff, meticulously selected for their level of skills and service, assumed their respective positions. Arlena Rosario would tend the satellite casino cage. Sam Peterson took his position behind the bar and was joined by Nanci Lee, Mr. Queck's preferred cocktail server. Jim Dennis was selected to provide armed security. Of course, Sue Min Wong was on hand to facilitate any public relations challenges that might arise. And handling the gaming duties were dealer Rolly Hutchins and floor supervisor Harry Fetters. Rounding out the contingent was Arthur Kaiser, ordered by Nathan Mesmer to personally oversee the entire operation "to its successful conclusion."

With the exception of Officer Dennis, tapped at the last minute for the security role, this group had banded before on several occasions during Mr. Queck's visits to the Desert Empire. They all knew going in, they may not see the outside of that room for up to thirty-six hours, maybe more, depending on Queck's play and more importantly, his luck. There were lavatory facilities adjacent to the salon and food would be provided around the clock, compliments of Room Service.

The silent partners in the group were the eyes beneath the black bubbles, set and focused by Charlie Palermo's graveyard surveillance man Isaac Nester.

At eleven-twenty PM., the stage was set. Arthur Kaiser telephoned the Palace of Palms restaurant.

"Please let Mr. Queck's party know that whenever they are ready, we are ready in the salon. Thank you." He turned to Harry Fetters. "Harry, go ahead and unwrap eight decks and purge them. Rolly, commence the shuffle as soon as you get the cards. I'm going down to escort the Queck group up here."

As Kaiser left the room via the private elevator, Harry Fetters began breaking the seal and unwrapping the first of eight decks of playing cards. Before turning them over to Rolly, he purged them of the four extraneous cards that if left in the decks would wreak havoc on the game. There were the two jokers. They had no value in the game of baccarat and needed to be purged. There's the courtesy calendar card provided by the deck's makers *The United States Playing Card Company* in Cincinnati, Ohio who proclaim themselves the standard for casino play since 1892. And finally, Fetters pulled the bar code card, inserted for security control purposes. He placed the remaining cards, presumably fifty-two of them, face down in one pile in front of Rolly. Rolly lifted the deck, turned it over, and spread the deck in one sweeping, semi-circular movement face-up on the table. Then in an intense inspection, he touched each card ensuring the sequence of all fifty-two cards divided evenly among the four suits. Then in another skilled movement, Rolly slid his hand under the far right card, twisted his wrist quickly, causing the complete line of cards to flip face down on the felt. Here, again, he quickly touched each card, ensuring the Desert Empire logo was on the reverse of each and every card. This process was repeated for each of the remaining seven decks. Once they were all checked, Rolly began the house shuffle, a predetermined series of stripping and fanning and stacking, designed to randomly integrate all 416 cards, thereby giving the house and the players an even playing field from which to start. Rolly would hold the stack, center table awaiting Mr. Queck's cutting.

Collusion on the Felt

The elevator door opened. Art Kaiser stepped out first and made a sweeping arm gesture to the Queck group. Cyril Queck was the last to exit. He nodded to Sam Peterson and Nanci Lee, at the bar. They smiled a return greeting. He handed his top hat and baton to Officer Jim Dennis. Awkwardly, Dennis thanked him, but it was evident he neither expected the articles, nor did he know what to do with them. For now, he simply held them.

Freed of his hand props, Queck rubbed his hands together, not unlike a new shooter in a high stakes craps game. He walked up to the baccarat table. Rolly stood for their customary bow. Queck sat down at the lucky eighth table position. In reality it was position number seven. There was no fourth position. The position numbers on the table ignored the luckless four, a gesture appreciated by the Asian players. Westerners can totally understand the depth of the superstition, as they rise in elevators from the twelfth directly to the fourteenth floor. Four is the Asian thirteen.

Queck raised his right hand in a call for one of his group to approach the table. The gentleman, dressed in a dark suit, responded quickly to the beckoning. Queck whispered in Chinese, after which the gentleman spoke to Harry Fetters.

"Mr. Queck requests a marker in the amount of one point five million dollars U.S., please."

The request was not unexpected. It was Queck's usual initial stake. Fetters turned toward Arlena Rosario at the satellite cage and nodded. Rosario knew what that meant. She touched a few keys on the computer keypad and within seconds the inkjet printer delivered the marker. She handed the marker to Arthur Kaiser who signed it and carried it to Cyril Queck. Queck signed it and slid it across the felt in Rolly's direction. Rolly picked it up, verified its contents, and laid it down face-up on the felt, in plain view of the ceiling camera. He then methodically counted out one-and-a-half million dollars in hundred-thousand dollar cheques. The three neat stacks of five hundred-thousand dollar cheques were placed next to the marker.

"Marker up one point five million," said Rolly.

"Okay," replied Kaiser.

Rolly slid the three stacks across the felt to Mr. Queck. He picked up the marker, folded it, lifted the paddle, and slid the marker into the locked cash box attached to the table's underside.

"Good luck, Mr. Queck," said Rolly smiling.

Mr. Queck motioned for the gentleman in the dark suit to sit next to him, on his left.

Kaiser leaned over to Sue Min Wong, "Who's the shadow?" he whispered.

"That's his brother-in-law," said Sue Min, softly. "His name is Prinya, Mr. Liu Prinya. This is his first trip with Mr. Queck."

"What about the other two guys?" asked Kaiser. "They've been with him before. Damned if I know who they are."

"Just bodyguards," said Sue Min. "They are low on the food chain and are not introduced."

"Been there," said Kaiser.

The bodyguards took seats against the wall, on the opposite side from Kaiser and Sue Min. Jim Dennis carried a straight-back chair and placed it in front of the elevator, where he settled in for what, by all accounts, could be a long watch.

When everyone was settled, Nanci Lee took the first round of drink orders.

While Sam Peterson scooped ice into the line of glasses, Cyril Queck pierced the horizontal stack of cards with the yellow, plastic cut card, dividing the stack by a third. Rolly separated the two stacks, slid the short stack to the rear, and inserted the yellow cut card approximately one-deck in from the rear. The cards behind the cut card would be out of play.

Queck slid his first one-hundred-thousand dollar wager into the Banker's circle. The bet made, play was underway. Rolly slid the first card, facedown, to the Player position; the second card, face down, to the Banker position. This order is required by the rules of the game. The third and fourth cards are also placed in the Player circle and Banker circle, respectively. The Player Position acts first. Rolly flipped over the first card: a seven of diamonds. He flipped over the second card: a nine of diamonds. Player Position totaled six. According to the rules, if the Player's two-card total is zero to five, Player must take another card. With a two-card total of six or seven, the Player must stand.

Collusion on the Felt

"Player shows six," Rolly announced.

Rolly nodded to Queck that he may turn over his own cards in the Banker's Position, if he chose – which he always has. Queck picked up the first card and flipped a ten of clubs, Banker had zero points. He flipped over the second card: an eight of diamonds.

"Banker shows eight," said Rolly, "Banker wins."

Rolly slid a one-hundred-thousand dollar cheque next to Queck's original bet. And since the house gets five-percent of all winnings in the Banker's position, Rolly also placed a five-thousand dollar cheque on Position Eight's Commission box. Commissions are due and payable to the house at one of several occurrences: end of the shoe, change of dealers, departure of the player, or at the player's whim. Some players, particularly Asian players don't like accumulating a lot of commission debt and habitually clear their commissions frequently during the round. Queck was an exception. From his perspective, the more he owed the casino in commissions, the better he must be doing. High commission debt was a symbol of success. And, so far, Queck was up ninety-five thousand dollars after a single hand.

Up in his darkened office, Nathan Mesmer, lighted only by the monitor screen, leaned back in his leather chair, propped up his feet, and lit a cigar. "All right, let's get it back," he mumbled to himself, while gripping the cigar with his clenched teeth.

Sal Mooring pulled into the driveway and pressed the garage door's remote control. The double-sized door lumbered up. All the way home, he wondered if Sharon would be there when he arrived. The garage was empty. It was nearly one AM. and the end of an especially long day. Sal didn't think he could muster the energy to worry about her, let alone search. He pulled in, staying close to the left side, as always, preserving her space on the right. He exited the car, hoping to find a note or perhaps a message on the answering machine. Maybe the sound of her voice would let him know that she's no longer mad and that she'd be back shortly.

The house was dark. No warming light in the dining area. His eyes found for the answering machine, but the message light stared back without a blink. He felt for the wall switch and the florescent hummed to life. A quick glance at the refrigerator found the magnetized notepad blank. He looked on the kitchen table, no note. He hurried through the living room into the bedroom, flicking on lights as he passed them. The bed was neatly made. Nothing seemed out of place. He went over to the caller I.D. on the nightstand and surveyed recent incoming calls. The latest was received just forty-five minutes earlier. And it was from Missy. Perhaps the two of them got together for a drink or something. Surely, she'll call once she realizes it's time for her husband to be home. Sal looked at the phone and contemplated calling Missy. It would probably be an important gesture to let Sharon know he's concerned. He sat on the bed and pressed Missy's speed dial number.

"Hi, this is Me," her machine said. "Talk at the beep."

"Missy, this is Sal. I'm concerned about Sharon. If she's with you, could one of you please call and let me know? Thanks."

He hung up the phone. Something made him glance in the direction of their walk-in closet. Dimly lighted by the nightstand lamp, he noticed the suitcases that normally occupy the overhead shelf were missing. Immediately, he crossed to the closet and switched on the light. Not only were the suitcases gone, so were most of Sharon's clothes. She appeared to have left behind only those "once in a lifetime" outfits, covered in plastic. He ran to the dresser and pulled open her drawers, one by one. Empty. Empty. Empty. Back in the closet, he checked for her shoes. All the newer ones were gone. He slammed the closet door shut and ran to the dining room hutch. He pulled open the glass door and picked up the fancy sugar bowl. He quickly lifted the lid. No money. She took the money, too!

"Son-of-a-bitch!" he shouted. "Fuck her then! I'm down for it, Rolly! Bring it on!"

Floor Supervisor Harry Fetters tried unsuccessfully to stifle a yawn. At two-twenty A.M., Wednesday morning, he, and the salon crew had not had a break in several hours. Their fatigue, however, was not a result of boredom. On the contrary. Over the past nearly three hours, Cyril Queck had amassed a king's ransom through meticulous, if not superstitious, baccarat play. With his brother-in-law, Liu Prinya, busily

Collusion on the Felt

engaged in tracking the outcome of winning hands and logging them on a notepad, and Queck, following a self-designed prognostication, the Desert Empire was down over eight-million dollars. And neither the trend nor the play showed any signs of cessation any time soon.

Rolly was having a great night. At the end of each shoe, Queck cleared his commissions and slid a thousand-dollar chip in Rolly's direction. They were now in their fifth shoe. This was the baccarat situation all baccarat dealers dream about. Here was one of the biggest whales in the world, with more money than he knew what to do with. He was a known "George," meaning he tipped very well when winning. And he was winning, and winning big. Rolly stood to make untold thousands in tips before the dust would settle on Queck's vacated chair.

Noticing all of this from the salon podium, Art Kaiser's lower jaw unconsciously jutted forward, his lower teeth encasing his upper teeth. It was a patented Kaiser manner when things were going very badly. Kaiser knew that Mesmer was watching all the action from his office, so he hadn't needed to contact him as these huge amounts of money changed hands. But, he also knew that Mesmer was surely about to blow as the millions trickled from the company coffers. And the shrapnel would invariably decapitate Kaiser. To make matters worse, Kaiser could look forward to making about four hundred dollars for this extended shift, while his dealer was collecting down payments for real estate. The lower jaw crept forward a little more.

About an hour earlier, ahead by three million dollars, Queck began doubling his wagers per hand from one-hundred-thousand to two-hundred thousand, the value of his current wager. The new shoe was now ready for cutting. Rolly pushed the horizontal stack of cards center table, holding the yellow, plastic cut card out for Queck's ceremonial cut. Queck leaned over and whispered something to Prinya, which obviously pleased his brother-in-law. Prinya raised his eyebrows and allowed a shallow smile. Queck took the cut card and swept it back and forth slowly over the top of the stack, as if searching for just the right cut point. When he found it, he carefully inserted it into the stack. As Rolly assembled the freshly shuffled and cut decks into the shoe, Queck pushed three-hundred-thousand dollars in cheques onto the Player's circle. Prinya nodded his approval.

"Good luck, Mr. Queck," said Rolly. And he really meant it.

Rolly slid the first card to the Player's circle; the second to Banker. The third followed to Player and the fourth to Banker. Since Queck was betting on Player, Rolly nodded to Queck that he may now turn the cards. Queck turned over a two of hearts and a three of clubs.

"Player shows five," said Rolly. Queck nodded. According to the rules, if Player's first two cards total zero to five, Player may draw another card, depending on the Banker's two-card hand.

Rolly turned over Banker's cards: an Ace of Clubs and a Seven of Diamonds. "Banker shows eight," said Rolly. Kaiser mentally began raking in the three-hundred-thousand. The score was eight to five. Banker had to stay with the eight, but player was allowed another card.

"Player takes another card." Rolly slid out the third card. Queck motioned for Rolly to turn it face up. It was a four of spades.

"Player shows nine," said Rolly. "Player wins."

Kaiser was nauseous. Burning nervous energy, he walked over to join Sue Min Wong. "He's killing us," Kaiser whispered.

"As long as we can keep him here, we have a chance to recoup," she whispered.

Such was the mantra of Las Vegas. Keep them playing. Over the long run, the house will win. If they leave with the house money, there is no chance of getting even. Keep them playing.

Sue Min could see the perspiration soaking Kaiser's shirt collar. He was clearly out of place in high stakes baccarat, she thought. The man was a shuffle shy of turning into one big ulcer.

"Art, this is baccarat," she reminded him. "You cannot take our losses personally."

"Mesmer does," he said. "You've seen him with me whenever we deal a big losing game. The man blames me personally."

"Art?" The call came from Harry Fetters.

Kaiser walked back toward the table. "What is it?"

"I just wanted you to be aware that Mr. Queck has just bet on the tie."

"Oh, Jesus," said Kaiser swallowing hard. He looked down at the table and verified that three-hundred-thousand dollars sat on the tie circle. Normally, a bet on the tie is good news for the house. The bettor has a 14 percent disadvantage when betting on the tie. On average, a tie occurs in about one of every ten hands. However, a bet on the tie brings eight to one odds if a tie indeed occurs. And Queck was red hot right now. If he were to win this hand, the house would be down another two point four million.

Queck's brother-in-law was obviously excited about this bet. According to his tracking pad, a tie had not occurred in the last twenty-two hands. It was very, very ripe statistically.

Kaiser squeezed out a forced, tight-lipped smile and simulated a bow as he made eye contact with Mr. Queck's sunglasses. "Good luck," he said.

Rolly slid two cards to each of the betting circles. He turned over the Player's two cards first: a ten of diamonds and an eight of hearts.

"Player shows eight," said Rolly.

He reached for the Banker's cards. Every eye in the room followed his hand. Kaiser fought the lump in his throat. He reflexively glanced over at the phone, his umbilical to Mesmer. But it remained silent. Not that there was anything a hundred Mesmers could do now to thwart destiny.

Prinya reached over and anxiously clasped Queck's wrist.

Rolly turned over the first of the two cards: an eight of spades.

Queck remained constant, cool, and confident. Prinya's legs were bouncing rhythmically on his springing toes. All of his teeth were visible.

"No ten...no picture card...," Kaiser's concealed tongue silently formed the words.

Sam Peterson, Nanci Lee, Jim Dennis, Sue Min Wong, and the two bodyguards all were on their feet anticipating the revelation that was now in progress.

It was a Jack of Diamonds.

"Banker shows eight," said Rolly. "Tie wins."

Prinya jumped from his seat and began slapping Queck on the top of his head. Not only were all his teeth visible, so were his gums and molar fillings. He jumped up and down screaming something in Chinese.

"What's he saying?" Jim Dennis asked Sue Min, gesturing toward Prinya.

"It's the Chinese equivalent to 'no fucking shit!'" she said.

Kaiser, hyperventilating, was massaging his chest.

Harry Fetters stood motionless, his eyes locked on the twin "eight" hands still sitting on the table. Rolly was counting out two point four million dollars in cheques. Queck was up over ten-million.

"I wish the fuck Mesmer would come here," breathed Kaiser. "I can't take not seeing his face, not knowing what the hell he's thinking! This is killing me!"

"Please, Art, sit down for a minute. You're embarrassing us," said Sue Min somewhat harshly.

Kaiser collapsed into an overstuffed chair, still rubbing his chest.

"I need to talk to you a second," said Harry Fetters.

"Can't it wait, Harry?" pleaded Kaiser in between breaths. "I'm having a situation over here."

Fetters looked at his watch. "You need to get somebody to relieve me, Art. I need a break badly."

"Can you call someone from downstairs?" Kaiser asked Sue Min.

"Who?"

"I don't know...Dale Bouviet. Just tell him to hurry."

"Appreciate it, Art," said Fetters.

Cyril Queck obviously decided it was time to stretch his legs. He rose up from his chair and allowed Prinya to continue dancing around him. When Kaiser saw Queck get up from the table, he instantly thought he was leaving the property with the ten-million dollars. It was as though a blood clot the size of a V-8 engine shot through his heart. His eyes bulged and all he could manage was an involuntary wheeze.

Fortunately, neither Queck nor Prinya were paying any attention to him. The bodyguards had joined in the celebration now. They were all chanting around Mr. Queck.

Amidst the jubilation, Kaiser wasn't certain, but he thought he heard the phone ring. Sam Peterson picked it up.

Kaiser knew it had to be Mesmer. No one else would ever call the salon.

"It's Mr. Mesmer for you, Art," said Sam handing the phone to Kaiser.

"Yes, sir."

"Art, I seemed to have dozed off. How are we doing?"

Kaiser's face froze. He tried imagining swear words of sufficient magnitude to secretly say to himself, but found his brain impotent. Mesmer dozed! Mesmer doesn't know we're down ten-million? Kaiser's pulse was racing out of control.

"I asked you a question, Kaiser! How are we doing?"

"Oh, God!"

"Oh, God? What the fuck is that?"

"Oh, God! Oh, God!

"How the fuck much down are we, you spineless hairball!?"

"Oh … Oh, God!"

"I'm coming over there, cockroach! You hear me!?" Mesmer slammed the phone down.

"Oh … Oh, my God," moaned Kaiser. "Oh, my God."

Kaiser was still frozen, holding the phone up to his ear when the EMT arrived. They pronounced him dead of a massive coronary occlusion at three-twelve AM.

Mesmer apologized to Cyril Queck and his party for the unfortunate interruption. There had been no further play since the tie hand some thirty minutes earlier. In the meantime, Dale Bouviet had relieved Harry Fetters as floor supervisor. With Kaiser's passing, Mesmer, himself, would oversee the operation. The remaining staff had been put on break while the emergency medical technicians performed their duties. It was nearly four AM., when the game was about to resume. Mesmer took his post at the salon podium. Bouviet stood parade rest just behind Rolly. Peterson and Lee manned the bar. Davis sat by the elevator. The bodyguards seated themselves as before. Sue Min walked over to join Mesmer.

"We are very fortunate Mr. Queck did not leave," she whispered to Mesmer.

"The condition we're in, the word 'fortunate' does not belong," mumbled Mesmer. "When we get that ten mil back, talk to me about fortunate."

Sue Min merely shook her head and retreated to her seat.

Queck pushed five-hundred thousand dollars in cheques onto the player's circle. Mesmer swallowed hard. The old man was up to half-a-million per wager now. Would there be no end to this nightmare?

Rolly slid the cards from the shoe, placing them facedown in their respective circles. Just then, the elevator doors opened and Harry Fetters, fresh from his break, re-entered the salon.

Queck hesitated in turning over the pair of cards on the Player's circle, as Prinya was whispering something to him. Queck listened and then nodded. At that, Prinya slid a one-thousand dollar cheque into the Player's circle. He was betting with Queck. Queck reached for the cards, only to be interrupted by Dale Bouviet.

"No bet," said Bouviet sharply, holding out his hand as if stopping traffic.

Rolly remained motionless. He knew why Bouviet made the call. House rules prohibit wagering once the cards are out of the shoe, even if they haven't yet been turned over. It was legally the right call.

Queck, who hadn't said a word aloud since coming into the salon, finally broke his silence.

"What is the meaning, this 'no bet?'" he asked Bouviet.

"Mr. Queck, I cannot accept Mr. Prinya's wager because the cards were already out of the shoe," explained Bouviet, obviously somewhat nervous.

"But, we cannot see the card values," countered Queck.

"That's it for me, folks, my relief is back," announced Bouviet. He clapped his hands for the cameras and headed for the elevator.

Sue Min squeezed her eyes closed and lowered her head. Mesmer walked to the elevator to intercept Bouviet.

"What's going on?" Mesmer asked.

"I think you heard me, Nate. Cards were out of the shoe. It's no bet. I didn't make the rules."

Mesmer knew Bouviet was correct, but this situation did not feel right. All at once, Mesmer noticed Queck pulling back his three-hundred-thousand dollar wager. Prinya pulled back his one-thousand dollar bet. Queck rose.

To Rolly, Queck said, "You may color me out now."

Those words threw a chokehold on Mesmer. "Oh, hold on here, Mr. Queck, there's no need to ... "

"I said you may color me out," repeated Queck to Rolly.

"Mr. Queck, please reconsider. I would be happy to...."

Queck turned directly toward Mesmer. "There will be no further discussion on this matter."

"You must understand, Mr. Queck, our house rules prohibit...."

"Nate," interrupted Sue Min, "please walk with me a moment." Her look gave him few options.

"You don't understand, Nathan. There will be no further negotiations with Mr. Queck. Bouviet made him lose face. There is no recovery."

"What do you mean 'made him lose face'?"

"He turned away from Mr. Queck without addressing his question and said he was leaving. He may as well have slapped Mr. Queck square across the face. Mr. Queck is not only leaving, he most assuredly will never return."

"No, no. I'll talk to him," said Mesmer.

"As you wish," said Wong. "Don't say I didn't warn you."

Arlena Rosario was accepting Queck's cheques at the cage window from Prinya. She was preparing a check in the amount of ten-million, four-hundred thousand dollars. Prinya instructed her to wire the money to Mr. Queck's bank.

Queck tipped Rolly another five-thousand dollars, bowed and thanked him. Rolly reciprocated. Queck and Prinya began walking to the elevator with Mesmer in tow. Mesmer continued talking, but he alone was doing the listening. Queck was going; Prinya was going; and the ten-million dollars was gone. In about thirty minutes, when Mesmer tires of being ignored by Queck, Dale Bouviet will receive an expensive lesson in finance and diversity. As to the finance, he will learn that to protect the house from possibly losing one-thousand dollars to Prinya, he cost the house the ten-million dollars to Queck, plus all of the untold millions Mr. Queck's future business would have brought to the Desert Empire. As to diversity, it would never again be an issue. Bouviet would never work in any casino, in any town, in any country again.

Chapter Fifteen
He wanted something naughty and she ached to give it to him.

With Labor Day just two weeks away, Sal could focus on little else. During the past two weeks since Sharon moved out, he'd adjusted well to living alone. He hardly saw her before, anyway, so the adjustment wasn't difficult. Two days after she moved out, Sal received a long letter from her. In it, she apologized for the way she left, but felt if she'd waited for him to come home that night, they would have had a nasty fight. She was staying with Missy. She admitted taking the money, but promised she would handle it wisely. She said she missed him and she loved him, but was very disappointed in his bazaar thinking. She had always imagined him way above that sort of thing. His willingness to risk everything they had worked for on a hair-brained scheme that was sure to fail was more than she could handle. She said he could call her if he wanted and she was anxious to talk to him.

Sal hadn't called - not that he hadn't felt like it many times. It was just the circumstances of how she attacked him when he opened up to her and how she just packed up and left without any warning. He knew anything he'd try to say to her would turn into a heated argument and make things worse. With the meeting set in only two weeks, it was better if Sharon wasn't around.

As for Rolly, Mesmer offered him a promotion to floor supervisor in baccarat, now that he was short both Kaiser and Bouviet. Rolly turned it down as he had so many times before. But Mesmer was relentless. After hours of insistence, Rolly reluctantly acquiesced. So now the big guy was wearing a suit, and there was no shortage of razzing from his former colleagues. Even before Rolly had told Beatrice about the promotion, he invited Sal to the Neon Lantern for another late night chat. When Sal learned of Rolly's promotion, his first inclination was to feel betrayed. It just didn't seem right planning a major casino heist with a floor supervisor. Rolly assured him nothing had changed. In fact, his new position could prove to be a major asset.

While they were at the Lantern, Debbie the waitress took advantage of the opportunity to do a little flirting with Sal. Rolly had egged her on, saying Sal had begged him to bring him back to that "cute girl's" place. She'd remembered that Sal had ordered the Spanish omelet last time and asked him if he'd like to have one "tomorrow morning." Sal stuttered his way out of the invitation, but Rolly could see it was a real struggle. He wasted no time reminding Sal, in Debbie's absence, that Sharon was long gone and that Sal must be horny as hell. To Rolly's surprise, Sal didn't argue. When they left the Lantern, Debbie told them to "hurry on back now."

In the past two weeks, Rolly and Sal hadn't seen much of each other. The meeting was locked in for day after Labor Day, at noon. Rolly had scribbled the address on a scrap of paper and given it to Sal a couple of weeks ago. They would be meeting in an abandoned Montgomery Ward building off of Fremont Street. Rolly knew the real estate agent and had arranged a satisfactory rental agreement for the few hours of occupancy. The quick two-thousand dollars, under the table, would keep the agent otherwise engaged that day.

Harve Dedman was still calling on Missy, and the two were going out nearly every evening. With Sharon as a houseguest, Missy and Harve were spending most of their time at Harve's apartment. On this Monday night, the two were just finishing a wonderful Italian dinner at Mama Olivo's Restaurante on Spring Mountain Road. The cuisine was masterful. Basking in the corner booth's candlelight and anesthetized by the chilled, red Chianti, Harve gently pulled Missy closer to him. She willingly obliged.

"You're breathtaking," he whispered.

"You're drunk," she giggled. "But, I won't hold that against you."

"You know the more I see you, the more I want to be with you. I don't ever remember feeling that way about any woman."

She looked into his eyes. "You make me feel special, Harve. I've always wanted to feel special in a man's life. I'm almost afraid of our relationship maturing past this level. It's so good now. I don't want to lose it."

He squeezed his arm around her, pulling her lips to his. He loved the way her scent captivated his senses. She felt so perfect pressed against his body; so soft, yet so independently capable. Her exploring tongue sought his and their tongues swam madly, wetly, back and forth. It was a moment, among many, they wished frozen in time. And they remained locked in this bonding, yet fleeting tenderness for more than a minute.

Missy slowly allowed their lips to separate. She was panting in short, quick breaths. As her eyelids fluttered open, she focused on his. They were peering deep into each other's eyes.

"There is nothing on this earth I wouldn't do for you right now," she sighed furtively. "Nothing, Harve. I'm totally yours. Test me," she said with an impish smile.

Harve stared back at her. "I believe you mean that," he whispered.

"I do."

His gaze took on a musing air.

"What?" she smiled. "What are you thinking?"

"Nothing," he lied. "Why?"

"There's something going on in there. Let me in," she mouthed seductively.

He laughed somewhat nervously.

"Oh, you devil," she said. "This must be good. What?"

Harve reached for the bottle of wine and refreshed their glasses.

"Uh oh, more wine, huh? I can't wait to hear this," Missy said.

He handed her glass to her and touched it with his own.

"To us," he said.

"To us, indeed."

They both sipped their glasses dry. The velvety smooth, sensuous feeling grew more deeply in both of them. With tingling faces, they pressed their numbing lips together, and delighted in their feeling of virtual solitude.

But there was something on Harve's mind. As intoxicated as Missy was, there was no mistaking his mental preoccupation. He wanted something naughty and she ached to give it to him.

When they stopped for air, she placed her finger on his lips, removed it, kissed him, and replaced it.

"Say nothing more," she said, "until you share with me what you're thinking. Believe me that I want to know…and more… I will do it for you…whatever it is. As long as it will make you happy."

"When you said there was nothing on earth you wouldn't do for me," began Harve, "something did pop into my mind. But, to be honest, I'm afraid to say it because I'm afraid you'd take it the wrong way and…"

"Would it make you happy?" she interrupted.

"Well, yes…"

"That's the only measurement that counts. What is it, darling?"

"It's something I've thought about for a long time. Curious, you know?"

"No, I don't know…because you're not telling me."

"All right. It involves sex."

"Not surprised." She winked.

"A somewhat unconventional sex," he said.

"The best kind," she said, licking her lips.

Harve had his entire foot in the water, and so far so good. The next step, however, would be a point of no return.

"I'm waiting," she said.

He closed his eyes. "Three people."

Her eyes twinkled. "Oh, you nasty little boy," she giggled. "Am I one of the three?"

"Of course," he said, a huge weight lifted from him.

"Are you one of the three," she played?

"Uh huh." He smiled.

"That leaves room for one more, huh?"

"Yep," he breathed heavily.

"Girl or boy?" she asked, as if playing a game.

"Oh, a girl for sure," he said.

"Me, you and another girl? And I thought this was something that was supposed to make *you* happy," she laughed.

Harve was in a drunken glory. If he could get past the final piece of the puzzle, he was in.

He swallowed hard. Missy knew he was having difficulty with this.

"I won't make you say it, honey?" she said.

"Say what?"

"Sharon's name," she said smiling.

"Yeah?" He blushed. What makes you think I was going to say Sharon?"

"This," she said. And her hand floated down between his legs in time to feel the burgeoning. "You can run, but you can't hide, mister."

"Guilty," he pleaded. "You're not upset?"

"Why would I be? Listen, stud, there's a very attractive female staying in my apartment right now. No husband for a couple of weeks. You don't think she's horny? I see her watching me parade around in the buff. I do the same with her. This little fantasy of yours could make several people happy."

Harve took pause to reflect on the imagery.

"Pour me some more wine. I have an idea," she said.

His hand trembled as he poured the last of the Chianti into her glass. She was up for it! He couldn't believe it. Could she really pull this off with Sharon, he wondered? A married woman yet. Harve was experiencing a very strong sensation bordering on burst. Missy sipped her wine, giggling. She shot him an eyes-only glance and let her tongue crawl around the rim of the glass. Her anticipation was as immense as his.

"So what's your idea?" he asked.

"Just follow my lead," she said in her soft, sultry voice.

Missy reached for her purse and retrieved her cell phone.

"You're not calling her, are you?"

"Hush, Stud. Save your energy," she said, as she touched the buttons. Her speech was beginning to slur. On her, it sounded so cute, Harve thought.

"Hey, what's doing?" she asked on the phone. "Sounds boring. I need a favor," she said. "Harve and I are a little boozed and, you know, him being a cop and all, it wouldn't be a terrific idea for either of us to drive, so I was…oh, you would?" Missy glanced at Harve with an incredibly devilish wink.

"We're at Mama Olivo's over on Spring Mountain. Meet you outside in ten. Thanks, sweetie." She flipped the phone closed. "Viola," she beamed a toothy grin.

Sharon reached down and switched back to line one.

"That was Missy," she said. "She needs me to pick up her and Harve. They're apparently in no shape to drive."

"Sounds like they're really hitting it off, huh," said Sal.

"Looks that way. They're together almost every night," said Sharon.

"That's how we used to be, remember?" asked Sal.

"Oh, I remember," said Sharon. "I remember it well."

"We could have that again," said Sal, after a short silence.

"It's hard to be together when one of us is in prison," said Sharon dripping with sarcasm.

"Look," said Sal. "Would you rather I had never confided in you about this?"

"Is that my only choice? You tell me, then you do it; or you don't tell me and then you do it? Either way, I spend the rest of my life without you. Not much of a choice if you ask me."

"Sharon, I know you feel strongly about this. God, do you think I want something to happen so that I end up in prison? I don't! I would never get involved unless I was a hundred percent sure."

"Are you?"

"Truthfully, no. Not yet. I'll know a lot more after that meeting we're having. I want to listen and ask a lot of questions. If it doesn't sound absolutely fool proof, I'm out. It's that simple."

"That's my point," said Sharon. "There can't be any fool proof way to knock off a casino. Only fools try it. And you know they always get caught."

"All right. We're still at the impasse. I'm not willing to back out just yet. All I want to do is be able to size up the situation, give it a lot of thought, and then make a decision – hopefully with your input."

"I can tell you right now, I don't care what kind of plan Rolly and the rest of those clowns dream up, if you decide to risk everything, including me, I'm not so sure I married the right man. I'll never support you in a scheme like this."

"I promise, if after I explain the plan to you, if you still feel that way, I'll respect your wishes and back out. Will you go that route with me?"

"Sal, I need to get going. Those two are waiting for me."

"Just say you agree, Sharon."

"Fine. I agree."

"Thanks. I love you."

"I love you, too."

"Any chance you'll be coming home soon?"

"We'll see, okay?"

"All right. I want you here with me."

"Good night," said Sharon.

"Good night, Sweetie," said Sal.

That had been the first time the two of them had spoken since Sharon left. Sal had called her. She'd been napping and sounded so warm and cuddly when she answered the phone. The call got off to a rocky start with Sharon questioning why he hadn't bothered to call her up till now. In the middle of Sal's list of excuses, the call was interrupted by Missy's call waiting beep. Both Sal and Sharon remained seated for a moment in their respective living residences, staring into space, contemplating each other and their future. As if on cue, the two of them rose – Sal to head over to the Neon Lantern where Debbie's smile was sure to comfort him; Sharon to pick up Missy and Harve and face the most difficult decision she'd ever have to make.

At nine-forty PM., Sal slid into a corner booth at the Lantern and pulled a menu from the clip on the napkin holder. He pretended to study the fare while a lump grew in his throat. There were only two other tables with two customers each. He was glad he'd made contact with Sharon, but felt unsettled about the ease with which she could seemingly cast him aside. All he wanted was to make their lives better. He wasn't a fool. He fancied himself a realist. It was simple, he thought. If the plan had all the bases covered and if, after thorough analysis, he felt there was no chance of getting caught, what the hell else could she want? It irritated him to think that if he did get away with it, she'd waste no time basking in the fruits of the triumph. Not so fast, sweetheart, he thought. Where were you when I needed some tolerance, maybe even a little encouragement? Maybe I don't want *you* around, kiddo. How about that?

"Who are you talking to?"

"Huh?" Sal was startled.

"Your lips were moving," said Debbie with a smile.

"Oh, they were? I, uh, I was just thinking about something. How are you?"

"I'm good," she said. "Where's your friend?"

"Oh, Rolly? Not sure. I just decided to come by for a bite. Kind of a last minute thing."

"I'm glad you did," she said. "We almost missed each other, though. Harold - she gestured toward the kitchen – just told me to take off at ten tonight. We're kind of slow."

Sal just gazed at her. She was even cuter than the mental version he carried around with him. Her shoulder-length, sandy hair was made up in two ponytails that sprouted out the rear of her short-billed waitress cap. Her lips were dressed in rich pink lipstick that matched the vertical stripes in her uniform. The spread between the top two buttons of her blouse allowed a hint of ample cleavage to peek over the top of her frilly apron.

"So, what can I get for you? Are you ready?"

"Huh, uh, yeah." Sal quickly shifted his attention to the menu.

"I think I'm in the mood for chicken fingers and…can I see you tonight?" He turned and looked up at her again, raising his eyebrows. "I'm sorry, but I can't seem to get you out of my mind. I'd really like to spend some time with you."

Debbie nodded slowly and knowingly. Sal couldn't help but notice the shroud of blushing that was taking form. She reached down and put her hand on his.

"Like I said, I'm out of here at ten. I wouldn't mind spending some time with you, too." Her smile was most inviting.

Sal returned the smile. "Excellent," he said. "Fabulous."

"Now what would you like with those chicken fingers?"

"Chicken fingers…oh…yeah…just some coleslaw," said Sal.

"How do you like your fingers?" asked Debbie.

"How do I like them?" asked Sal.

"You know, mild, medium, hot?"

"Which one is better for the breath?" he asked.

"Probably the mild," she said.

"Let's do the mild," said Sal.

"Mild is good," she said. "Something to drink?"

Sal thought about it for a moment and announced, "How about some Southern Comfort on the rocks?"

"Deal," she said. "I'll bring the southern comfort – you bring the rocks."

She laughed and started toward the kitchen, while the lump in his throat was heading due south.

Missy and Harve were huddled outside Mama Olivo's when it occurred to them that the horn tapping had been for their benefit. Sharon had arrived. Giggling, they hurried toward the car holding hands. Missy was in the lead. She opened the rear door and slid across the seat. Harve followed.

"Hi, sweetie," said Missy. "You're the best! No way could we have driven home."

"We appreciate it, Sharon," Harve chimed in.

Sharon smiled and glanced up at the rearview mirror. They were snuggled in the center of the back seat.

"Hey, glad to do it. So where are we headed, you two?"

"You know what? Let's stop by Royal Video on the way. We want to pick up a movie," said Missy, knowingly nudging Harve with her elbow.

"Why Royal?" asked Sharon, "Blockbuster's right around the corner."

"Blockbuster doesn't have what we're looking for," giggled Missy.

"Oh, I get it. You guys are in a special mood tonight, eh?"

"Real special, kid. Matter of fact, if it's okay with you, we'd like to pick up some wine, too."

"Wine it is," said Sharon smiling. "Anything else?"

Missy looked at Harve; he looked at her. "Oh, we'll let you know," said Missy. They chuckled and kissed. Sharon caught the action in the mirror.

The remainder of the ride to Royal Video was accompanied by breathy sounds of passion as Missy and Harve brewed the anticipation of the evening. Sharon frequently sneaked reflected glances and tried flimsily to deny her own secret yearnings. Harve's big, brawny hands were caressing Missy's face and fondling the crests of her bosom while his mouth pressed firmly against hers in an obvious open and penetrating fashion. Sharon caught herself breathing deeply, massaging the rawhide steering wheel cover with her thumbs. Some wine, she thought, sounded like an excellent idea right now.

She pulled into the parking lot at Royal Video and stationed her LaSabre perpendicular to the building's front entrance. Royal Video was a much smaller, independent video rental store who found its market differentiator where family-oriented stores like Blockbuster designedly passed – adult videos. Missy whispered something in Harve's ear and opened the car door.

"Be right back," she said to Harve. Then knocking on the driver's side window, Missy invited Sharon to join her. "Come on in with me," she said, "but leave the motor running so Harve can cool off." Everyone laughed at that.

Harve watched Sharon exit the car. Her long legs were sleek in her thigh-high cut-off denim shorts. The high-cut, amply tight belly shirt, and her long, shiny auburn hair flowing down her back to just below her shoulders helped too. He knew that by the time the two women returned to the car, Missy would have discussed their proposal with Sharon. Harve had his fingers crossed.

"It'd be kind of silly to get something to eat right now, wouldn't it?" remarked Sal. Debbie looked over at him. Peripherally, he noticed her gaze, but kept his look straight ahead on the road.

"I don't know," Debbie said. "I don't think anything we would do right now could be silly. I mean, I've been thinking about a moment like this for quite a while now. I'm just enjoying being with you."

Surely she'd seen his wedding ring, Sal thought. Just in case, he wanted to clear the air.

"You do know I'm married, right?"

"I know you wear a wedding band," she said. "Beyond that, I don't know much about you at all."

"Well, I just want to be up front with you. I am sort of married."

"Sort of?"

"Things aren't going very well right now, but that's what I am. I'm also damn intrigued by you."

"Do tell," she whispered as she rested her hand on the back of his seat, and began lightly fingering his hair at the nape of the neck.

"First of all, you need to know I don't screw around on my wife," said Sal. "Because I don't…I mean…haven't."

"I believe you," she said. "In fact, only one of us seems concerned about you being married. That's got nothing to do with me."

"Well, okay," he said smiling. "At least it's out in the open. That's the last of it. Your turn."

"My turn for what?"

"I don't know much about you, either, except that you're drop dead gorgeous and I can't stop thinking about you. I want to hear your story?"

She slid closer to him and nibbled on his ear. He could feel her soft, warm breath ushered by a low, throaty groan as she outlined his ear with her moist, flittering tongue. It was an overwhelming moment - as erotic as it was wrong. Sal struggled to order the emotional chaos in his mind, but the pleasured turmoil in his body was triumphing. After a long, sensual moment, Debbie slowly eased away and resumed her finger stroking at the base of his neck.

"That's some story," panted Sal.

"That's only the introduction," breathed Debbie.

"Where are you from – originally, I mean?" asked Sal.

"Heart of Texas," she said, proudly. "You?"

"Boring Ohio." Sal smiled.

"Is that the name of the city or an editorial comment?" she said with a giggle.

He laughed. "Actually the mid-west is okay. You don't really know how ho-hum it is until you move someplace like here. I could never go back," said Sal.

"The jury's still out on that for me," said Debbie.

"Why is that?"

"I don't know," she sighed.

A moment of silence followed, during which Sal surmised Debbie was gathering her thoughts. When she didn't speak, he decided to probe.

"Is it your job?" he asked.

"Waitressing? I don't remember growing up saying I want to wear a frilly apron and wait on people, if that's what you mean. I could waitress anywhere. I left home in search of more. I...I just haven't found it yet."

"What do you want to do?" asked Sal.

"You'll laugh."

"Why would I laugh? I'm not going to laugh."

"I came out here to be a dealer. Thought there'd be big bucks in it for me," she said.

"And I'm supposed to laugh at that? What the hell do you think I do?"

"Oh, I know you're a dealer," she said.

"How? I never said anything about that."

"I just figured, you're always with your friend...and I know he's a dealer."

"Rolly? He told you he was a dealer? When?"

"Long time ago. He's been coming to the Lantern forever – with all kinds of people. One time he was wearing his black and whites. I asked him if he dealt and he said yeah."

"So have you tried becoming a dealer?"

"Looked into it. Can't seem to put anything together."

"What do you mean?"

"Dealing school takes about six to eight weeks. You don't make any money in dealing school. I'd have to go to school during the day, and still wait tables at night."

"So?"

"I wouldn't have any time with my daughter."

"Oh. You've got a daughter." There was some news Sal wasn't expecting. "I never figured you for having a kid," said Sal.

"What's that supposed to mean?"

"You seem...so single...and all."

"I didn't say I wasn't single, silly. I'm single with a daughter."

"Who watches her while you're at work?"

"My neighbor. She lives in the apartment across from mine."

"How old's your little girl?"

"Tarin's seven."

"Tarin? That's an unusual but beautiful name. What's it mean?"

"Does it have to mean something? I just liked the way it sounded. Right before I had her, I read one of those romance novels, and the woman's name was Tarin. No mystery."

"How about Tarin's father?"

"That *is* a mystery. I suppose he's somewhere in Texas. We never hear from him."

"Did you two divorce?"

"Oh yeah, about eighteen months after the wedding. It was one of those stupid things that never should have happened. But Tarin's worth every miserable month I spent with him."

"Is that when you moved to Vegas?"

"No, we didn't move right away. My parents took us in for a while. My mother watched Tarin while I tried to go to college, but not surprisingly, that didn't work out. My mother was never one to put herself out."

"She kept throwing it up to you?"

"Oh that, yeah. But worse, she'd scream at me when I wanted to go out on the weekend. I mean, I can't blame her. She was tied down all week. But I needed some chill time from school, too."

"Did you finish?"

"No way. That plan lasted about a year. That was all I could take. So about four years ago, at the age of twenty-three, I packed up Tarin and we took a bus ride to 'lost vagish.'"

Sal laughed. "That's what Tarin calls it?"

"Darling, isn't it? Been here ever since. Harold hired me at the Neon Lantern – that was the first place I applied – and the rest is history."

"Except that you're not happy," said Sal.

Debbie leaned over and kissed him softly on the cheek.

"Wrong," she said. "Right now I'm very, very happy."

Harve had been sitting in the back of the Buick nearly 35 minutes, waiting for the girls to return. His disposition passed "panic" ten minutes ago. Now, he was even afraid to go inside after them. There was no telling what was going on inside Royal Video. Just as he was about to call Missy on her cell phone, the two women pushed open the glass door and exited. And to Harve's astonishment they were giggling! They obviously found a video they agreed on. Missy was toting a Royal Video plastic bag. The girls looked over at the car and Sharon made an obvious attempt to fluff the back of her hair. Missy laughed and mimicked the move. From all accounts, it looked as though Missy had pulled it off!

The two got in the car, only this time Missy sat shotgun. She tossed the bag over her head to Harve.

"Got you a good one, stud."

"I thought maybe you were making your own in there," Harve retorted.

They both snickered. As Sharon put the car in reverse, Missy turned around and winked at Harve.

"Check out the video," she said with a smirk.

Harve reached into the bag and pulled out the tape case and read the title – *A Knight to Remember.* He looked back up at Missy. She winked again.

"Time to pick up that wine," said Sharon. "Better get two bottles."

With his heart pounding against his rib cage, Sal turned off the ignition and initiated the closing of the automatic garage door. Debbie slid out the driver's side, ensuring that her uniform dress rode high up her thighs. After standing up, she feigned modesty and pulled down the tight fitting hem. When she looked up, her eyes locked with Sal's. At that instant, the garage door landed closed and they were enveloped in total silence. She stepped toward him relishing his admiring stare. Sal pulled her to him. Their bodies pressed against each other and they kissed with forceful passion. It was a long, tender fervent embrace. Her feel was excitingly unfamiliar; her scent potently alluring. When they finally broke for air, they stayed pressed and they joined themselves at their foreheads.

"Let's go in," breathed Sal. "I'll fix us a drink and we can go for a swim. How does that sound?"

"Au natural?" she smiled.

"I wouldn't have it any other way," he murmured.

Sal took her hand and guided her into his house.

"I've got some catching up to do," said Sharon. "So when you get that cork popped, Harve, just put a straw in the bottle and hand it to me."

"Everything okay, Sharon?" Harve felt compelled to ask.

"How do you mean?" she teased.

"What I mean…did Missy talk to you at the video store…?"

"Yeah, we talked. Why?"

The cork burst out of the bottle. He poured into Sharon's glass.

"Look," he said, "The only reason I'm trying to talk to you about this is because I don't want something to go wrong and…"

"You two want to fuck me, right?" She raised the glass to her lips and the luscious liquid began the journey through her veins. She drained the glass and held it out for more. Harve poured. "At first I was upset," said Sharon. "I've never done anything like that in my life. But then I thought, 'what the fuck?' Since when is that the measuring tape?" She downed the second drink. Harve poured some more.

"I'm not so sure I wouldn't like to have two beautiful people, one who's my best friend; the other my best friend's lover, make me feel like a beautiful woman again, for a change." She downed the third glass. Harve poured.

"You *are* a beautiful woman, Sharon," Harve said.

"And you, you prick, you're a beautiful man." She emptied the fourth glass. Harve poured another for her, and one for himself.

Missy came into the kitchen wearing a sheer, white, waist cut negligee and an equally sheer white thong. "Don't you two start without me," she said.

"You are ravishing," said Harve. He poured a glass for Missy.

"Have you got something like that for me?" managed Sharon, happily experiencing the numbing effects of the wine. "I want to look…what was that…ravishing, too."

"You bet I do, girlfriend. I've got it laid out on my bed for you."

Sharon started for the bedroom.

"Take your glass, honey," called Missy, handing her a refreshed drink. "Keep sipping."

Sharon took the glass from Missy and purposely eyed her slowly up and down. She blew a sensuous Marilyn Monroe kiss to both of them as she turned and left for the bedroom. She turned on the stereo, as she passed it, and soft MOR music filled the apartment. Harve took Missy into his arms and they slow danced. After a few minutes, he whispered in her ear. "I don't know how you did it, babe, But my pants are about to bust. How did you do you it?"

"Easy," Missy said smiling. "I told her you bet me a thousand dollars I couldn't talk her into it. And that I'd give her half, if she would. At first she pretended to be insulted that we were even thinking about her that way. Then, with a little coaxing, she realized what a compliment it is to have both men and women hot for your body. After we looked at a few pictures on the video boxes, she admitted the thought of a threesome sounded exciting. Being horny didn't hurt, either. So she agreed to do it.

"When you two were walking out of the store, you were both giggling. What was that all about."

"Oh, yeah. After we paid for the tape, Sharon pulled me aside and said there was one little change in the deal. I said what's that? She said she wanted the whole thousand."

Harve looked concerned. "And you said what to that?"

"What could I say? You were out there in the car over half an hour and I knew you wanted it…so I said yes. After all, I didn't need my five-hundred anyway."

"So this little fantasy is going to cost me a thousand dollars?"

"Look at the bright side. I'm not taking my half."

"What are you talking about? You don't have a half...she doesn't have a half! There are no halves! I never bet you anything on this."

At that moment, Sharon glided slowly into the kitchen. She had donned the outfit. And she looked like a dream. It was a burgundy sheer top that hung open in the front daintily veiling very little of her ample mounds. Along the inside edges, the bottom, and around the neck was a matching burgundy fur trim. Underneath, she wore a very tiny burgundy bikini bottom. Her long hair was brushed so that it all wrapped around her left side. She wore long, golden earrings, freshly applied, glossy red lipstick and emanated the fragrance of a very expensive French perfume.

She held out her empty glass.

Missy's mouth had fallen open. Harve gulped down his wine, poured another, and began some creative financial thinking.

"Aren't you going to say anything?" asked Sharon. "Harve, you told Missy she looked ravishing. How about me?"

"Ravishing is the most powerful word I know," said Harve. "I have to use it for you, too." He gulped down another drink.

"How about you, Missy?" Sharon asked.

"I'll tell you what," said Missy, "I'd like to have about thirty minutes with you alone...without Harve...that's how I feel."

"What do you say we take a look at that video?" said Sharon, who then turned and headed for the living room where she turned off the lights and slipped the tape into the VCR.

"Okay...a thousand dollars," whispered Harve to Missy. "It'll be worth every nickel."

Missy laughed. "Guess what," she said. "I was only kidding about the thousand, you lucky buck." She switched off the kitchen light. "Now get down to your skivvies and bring in the other bottle. It's time for '*A Knight to Remember.*'"

Her pink striped uniform and white frilly apron lay neatly over the back of a lounge chair. Her bra, panties, nylons, shoes, and waitress cap collected on the seat. On the neighboring lounge chair, his clothes lay strewn. With the singing of desert crickets providing the only sounds, and the pale blue moon glow the only light, the dealer, and the waitress, virtual strangers, clung to each other, moist flesh against moist flesh, amidst the tepid pool water. She locked her hands around the back of his head and pulled his willing mouth to her breast. Her nipple was wet and eagerly protruding as it found his stroking tongue. His hands enveloped her buttocks and supported her legs as they wrapped around his waist. He had entered her long ago, she, so willing a recipient. No words were uttered; no words were needed. The two beings who had quietly lusted for each other were now speaking in the only language that mattered. And it felt so unbelievably good. For neither of them could there be a logical explanation why this physical euphoria was other than so right.

Sal's overwhelming need for biological release had swallowed up his moral commitment to Sharon, but could not push her completely from his thoughts. This was Sharon's house, too, after all. They were in Sharon's pool. Debbie was enjoying Sharon's man. But, in the heightened chaos of physical craving and emotional drain, no man could be persuaded that this bodily elation could somehow be against the will of any being, spiritual or otherwise. It was indeed possible, concluded Sal, that human beings had not escaped the basic polygamous desires craved by other living creatures during human evolution. Love was love and…this was this. Both could exist in tandem.

The pounding rhythm of his penetration had incrementally intensified as his mind cried out for moral reconciliation and he was unconsciously bringing Debbie to delicious heights of ecstasy. Her fingernails dug frantically into his scalp; her breathing escalated to frenzied whimpers of delight. Her agile body fought back, reciprocating each and every one of his animal thrusts. He squeezed her buttocks as she dug into his head. Both were unaware of the giant ripples developing waves around them that slapped against the sides of the pool. His masculine growls of rhapsody punctuated each of her fevered whimpers until the inevitable, mutual climax – so shattering it left them breathless.

The video had spent only twenty minutes before its presence earned only a secondary prominence. The three of them had been sitting on the sofa directly across from the television. Harve, dressed only in his skimpy blue briefs sat sandwiched in the middle of the two sweet smelling, semi-nude women. Both bottles of wine were long ago emptied, and all three were basking in the glow of intoxicating severance from reality. The scenes on the video had delivered the desired steaminess and the heat had transcended to the sofa. One needed only look at Harve and his feelings of urge were hugely evident. One at a time; sometimes two a time, the girls had lightly run their fingertips over the length of his blossoming staff. One would begin at the tip; the other at the bottom and they would caress in opposite directions until, for his benefit or theirs – it wasn't clear to Harve – their fingers would meet and caress each other. While that was going on down below, up top the two of them would be leaving traces of lipstick on his neck, ears, cheeks, eyes and shoulders. Harve had had considerable experience, but nothing had ever come close to this. He started out feeling like he would burst and the feelings had only since multiplied. Several times while watching the threesome on video, Missy or Sharon would whisper into Harve's ear that she'd like to experience what they were watching. Harve could also tell that occasionally the girls arms, which were on the back of the sofa behind his neck would begin exploring each other. This drove him absolutely wild…and they knew it.

Missy removed her arm from around the back of the sofa and, with considerable difficulty, rose. She staggered toward the television.

"I'm going to fire up a candle," she said.

Both Harve and Sharon, whose arm was still around Harve's neck, watched as the illumination from the television shown through Missy's sheerness outlining her shapely body.

"Nice, huh?" whispered Sharon into Harve's ear. "You lucky boy," she said.

Missy lighted the candle and turned off the television and the VCR. She walked over and turned on the stereo.

"I don't know about you two, but this baby's ready," she said.

Only the flickering of the candle flame provided any light at all in the suddenly dark apartment.

"To the bedroom," Missy slurred.

Harve rose and assisted Sharon who felt like she was in a slow motion movie.

"Here hold this, sweetie," said Missy, handing Harve the candle. He took it and watched as she removed her negligee.

"Sharon, your turn. Let me help you." Missy reached out for Sharon who crept up to her and allowed Missy to remove her fur trimmed top. Missy dropped the garment on the floor on top of her own and extended her arms to Sharon. Sharon willingly complied and the two shared a warm, full embrace, kissing each other's lips while their hands explored each other's bodies.

Harve watched this in the flickering light, nearly extinguishing the flame with his panting.

"Harve's turn," Missy said, "Sharon, maybe you should help him with his shorts."

Harve carefully placed the candle on the coffee table and dutifully raised his arms in submission as Sharon knelt and slid her fingers inside the elastic of his briefs and drew them down over his knees and feet. As he stepped out of them, she gasped at the sight of his swollen manhood.

"I need some help now," Missy said to Sharon. Still on her knees, Sharon rotated toward Missy and let her fingers creep leisurely up Missy's thighs. She inserted her thumbs into the silky thong and as her breath warmed Missy's front, she slowly freed her girlfriend of her remaining clothing. Before Missy would step out of them, she reached down and placed her hands on the crown of Sharon's head and slowly massaged her. Sharon melted at the feeling and allowed her friend to slowly pull her inward until her face was lost in the forbidden junction of Missy's thighs.

Still massaging Sharon's head, Missy said to Harve, "She's the only one with clothes, Harve. Help her with her panties."

The anticipation of Harve's hands on her body dispatched chills and tingling all over Sharon. With his touch, she moaned. Harve removed her scanty covering to below her perfectly round, protruding buttocks and paused to lick her all over. She ached for him to take her from behind and conveyed as much through a high pitched groan and by ever so slightly spreading for him. She raised her quivering hands and placed them over Missy's nipples, rubbing and kneading her girlfriend's breasts, losing herself in the most exalted level of erotic sensuality.

Harve stared at Missy. The candle glow twinkled off her intense face as she squeezed her eyes closed and breathed deeply. Her stroking of Sharon's hair was in synchronous rhythm with the sway of her hips and the beat of the stereo's music. Beads of perspiration dribbled from her neck and traced the outlines of her tremulous breasts, disappearing between Sharon's groping fingers. Missy was unmistakably lost in paradise. Sharon groaned again, this time with added insistence. Harve reached around her and tenderly cupped her fleshy breasts in his massive hands, taking care to sample her hardening nipples with his thumbs and forefingers. He felt her push back toward him with a pleading groan, spreading even more.

"Fuck her, you animal," whimpered Missy. "Fuck my girl!"

Sharon emitted a muffled, pleading scream and Harve immediately plunged into her wet, hot, starving entrance. The fervor among the three of them built steadily. Harve pummeled; Sharon bucked. Missy squeezed handfuls of Sharon's flowing hair, pulling her face deep inside and pulsating repeatedly in response to her frenzied tongue action.

The naked trio were lost in ecstasy. This man and two women were for this single fantastic moment united as a couple of three – a threesome of one. And they never did make it to the bedroom.

Chapter Sixteen

Sharon's heart raced. Her chest rose and fell in rapid step with her breathing. Her eyes darted repeatedly as if searching for a life preserver. There were no words.

For all intents and purposes, Labor Day weekend was over for Las Vegas by late morning on the holiday, itself. More than 135,000 physically and financially spent summer-ending revelers descended upon McCarran Airport by taxi, bus, rental car, shuttle, and relatives as they began their journeys back to rules and responsibilities. Interstate Fifteen, southbound, was already bumper to bumper for more than twenty miles, as a hundred-thousand Californians crawled along the desert highway back to power black-outs, no smoking signs, and second mortgages.

Jerry Lewis, a Las Vegas resident for years, still had five hours to go during his annual telethon to raise money for "his kids." Too bad "his kids" don't own the casinos. Early estimates were that the visitors had left behind sixty million dollars in "non-gaming" revenue, alone. That's the way the media liked to report it. One had only to imagine the untold additional millions they lost to Lady Luck.

In the Mooring household, things had changed again during the past couple of weeks. Two days after her tryst with Missy and Harve, Sharon called Sal and guided the conversation toward a conditional reconciliation. They agreed Sharon would move back during her next days off. That had been a week ago.

Harve, still reeling from his night to remember, got the terrific news that he'd earned his sergeant stripes. He and Missy, closer than ever, were now discussing marriage. Sharon and Missy remained close, but at Sharon's insistence, remained mum, even to each other, about the threesome.

Sal hadn't returned to the Neon Lantern, nor had he tried to call Debbie. When he'd taken her back to get her car that night, they both agreed that it would be best to let things settle back to normal. It was obvious to Debbie that Sal had been only on temporary loan from his marital commitment. She would not make things uncomfortable for him.

Rolly had stayed continually busy learning his new role as floor supervisor and he hadn't talked much to Sal recently. The last time they'd spoken, Rolly shared how busy he'd been preparing for the big meeting and went through yet another of Sal's teeter-totters regarding his intended involvement. As always, though, Rolly's optimism and charisma brought Sal around.

At just before noon, the telephone rang and Sharon picked it up. "Hello," she said.

"Hey, Sharon, how's it goin'? This is Rolly."

"Hello, Rolly," she said, with a chilling lack of enthusiasm.

"Ouch," said Rolly. "I just felt a cold stabbing in my ego."

"I'm sure you'll bounce back," said Sharon. "I'll get Sal for you..."

"No, wait," interrupted Rolly. "I'd like to talk to you first...that is if it's okay."

"Me? What for?"

"Look, Sharon," said Rolly, "I know you blame me for a lot of the problems you and Sal are having recently. But, I...."

"How dare you think for me!" Sharon blurted out.

"Whoa take it easy," said Rolly. "I'm trying to apologize here..."

"Apologize? Why should you apologize? All you've done is *ruin* our marriage!"

"That might be a little strong, don't ya think?" asked Rolly.

"Well, let's see," said Sharon sarcastically. "You've lured my husband into a scheme that's bound to send him to prison and turn me into a virtual widow. Hmm...maybe you're right! Perhaps I am overreacting!"

"You know I did warn Sal about telling you."

"Somehow I believe that," said Sharon. "You're a deceitful slime bucket, Rolly Hutchins! I don't know what the hell he sees in you!"

"I'll tell you what he sees. He sees a way out, Sharon."

"Out of what?"

"That hole we're all in. The one we keep trying to climb out of, but the dirt keeps crumbling off the sides and burying us deeper and deeper."

"Is this the same speech you give all your future cell mates?"

"You're not being the least bit fair to me," said Rolly with an exasperated sigh.

"Fair? Why the hell should I be fair with you?"

"Because I'm about to do you a huge favor."

"Oh, this ought to be good," said Sharon. "And just what favor is that?"

"I'm about to cut the Mooring family in for a *double* share."

"What? What the hell are you talking about?"

"I've got a role for *you* in our project, Sharon. It's worth over a million."

"Jesus Christ, I don't believe what I'm hearing!"

"Now, wait..."

"No! *You* wait!" screamed Sharon. "I don't even want to hear this garbage! The gall! You know full well how I feel about this ridiculous scheme and you have the audacity to even *pretend* that I would be a part of it?"

"You two would be set for life," said Rolly.

"Yeah – life in prison!"

"You keep saying that, Sharon, and yet you know absolutely nothing about this project."

"And that's exactly the way it's going to stay," said Sharon.

"Well, I hold a differing opinion," said Rolly.

"Rolly, I don't give a *fuck* about your differing opinion."

"Well I do have something that *just might change* your mind," Rolly said, his tone bordering on the devious.

"If a million dollars won't change my mind…"

"A night to remember?" interrupted Rolly.

Sharon froze.

Rolly broke the short silence. "Ah, apparently I have the lady's attention."

Sharon's heart raced. Her chest rose and fell in rapid step with her breathing. Her eyes darted repeatedly as if searching for a life preserver. There were no words.

"As I was saying," continued Rolly, "I'm doing you two a huge favor here. You spend a couple of hours on the project. Sal spends a couple of hours on the project. Each of you is a millionaire in your own right. And the night to remember is totally forgotten."

Sharon forced a gritted whisper through tightened jaws, "You motherfucker."

Rolly chuckled. "I kind of thought you'd see things my way."

"You motherfucker," Sharon repeated.

"Yes, yes. You'll thank me someday," said Rolly.

"How do you know?" asked Sharon, her voice quivering.

"You can probably figure that out," said Rolly. "There were only three of you there."

"That son-of-a-bitch," she muttered.

"Now that's no way to talk about one of Metro's finest," said Rolly mockingly. "And just so you know, he's in on the project, too. We go way back."

"So *you* put him up to that?"

"It wasn't like it took a lot of coaxing," Rolly said, chuckling. "You're an incredible woman."

"Fuck you."

"Let's just leave it at everybody had a good time and nobody got hurt. If you cooperate, it'll stay that way. You have my word."

"But…why?"

"To tell the truth, I figured the only way Sal could be assured a place on the team was with you on the team, too. And I knew *that* was not going to be easy to pull off."

"I hate you."

"I'd rather you didn't. *Esprit de Corps* and all that."

"I'm warning you, if Sal ever finds out I will personally kill you."

"You do what I ask, and you'll never have to worry about it."

"What do I have to do?"

"Okay, get Sal on the extension and I'll tell him we have a new recruit. That'll blow his mind! Then I'll give you guys the lowdown on tomorrow's meeting."

"Hold on."

Sharon placed the phone on the kitchen counter. Feeling apprehension, she rubbed her face with the palms of both hands, then headed for the master bath where Sal was just finishing shaving.

"Sal?"

"Yeah, honey?"

"Rolly's on the phone. He wants to talk to both of us."

"Both of us? What's going on?"

"He wanted to surprise you," she said, "but I'm not going to let him." She smiled broadly. "Guess what?"

"What?"

"I'm on the team, too! We're getting a double share!"

"What the fuck?"

"It's okay," she said, smiling. "He offered me a role and I figured what the hell? Now we're both in!"

"Holy shit!" Sal exclaimed, beaming. "And we get *two* shares?"

Sharon nodded with a toothy grin, her hands clasped in front of her.

"Damn, baby! Hand me the phone. This is great!"

The Desert Empire had undergone quite a few changes over the past couple of weeks. Thomas Brolin, the property president was reassigned to one of the corporation's smaller properties in Reno. To mask the apparent demotion, the corporate big wigs at Monarch Resorts also put him in charge of an additional property on the California-Nevada border up in Lake Tahoe, a small, slots-only neighborhood joint. The reassignment had come rather suddenly, and coincidentally, within 48 hours of the Queck episode. Nathan Mesmer, a corporate favorite, was given additional duties as acting president at the Desert Empire, along with his casino responsibilities, pending a final decision on the top job's appointment.

As Acting President, Mesmer wasted no time performing the impossible. Single-handedly, he managed to take an already dispirited, forlorn employee morale, and squeeze the vestiges of life out of it. All of Mesmer's prior announced changes had taken full affect, managing to alienate a great majority of the employee and management population. Now, as top dog, he answered to no one about the day-to-day operation. Among his first dictums was to institute a mandate that trimmed the number of employees permitted to work any given day, based on hotel occupancy. For example, if the hotel was only eighty percent occupied, twenty percent of the service staff would not be permitted to work. As occupancy fluctuates greatly, particularly during the slower summer months, employees would not be able to count on a steady paycheck, causing many of them to face serious financial crises at home. This daily staffing adjustment also played havoc on the department managers who had to juggle schedules, reassign duties to already overworked staff, notify those who were to remain at home, and field complaints from angry guests who didn't appreciate the long waits and surly attitudes of the employees.

Mesmer ordered the managers to swiftly discipline employees whose poor performance or attitudes generated customer complaints, resulting in stacks of paperwork and serious deterioration of management and employee relations. With no internal avenue of redress, those disciplined employees who were represented by a collective bargaining agreement marched directly to their union shop stewards to file grievances. Non-union staff had nowhere to go but to each other. Pockets of them could be seen hiding in the back halls of the property, out of sight from the surveillance cameras, their criticisms and complaints echoing throughout the corridors.

Especially vulnerable were the suits. As a group, they were a costly expenditure and in periods of economic decline, were among the first to dust off their resumes. Middle managers were continually reminded by Mesmer how dispensable they were. And they were downright scared these days. They shuttered at the mere sound of Mesmer's name. He was vicious, insensitive, and egotistical. Many of the managers would pass each other in the halls or on the floor and simply raise their eyebrows in greeting as if to say 'we're still here, how about that?'

The Labor Day weekend had been expectedly busy. Like most of the hotels in town, the Desert Empire had enjoyed a hundred percent occupancy since Friday. Now, as the Monday swing shift began reporting for work, the restaurants and casino were quiet, their tables virtually empty, but for the few locals taking advantage of their day off to visit a strip casino.

Sal parked his car in the employee parking lot and began the walk in the hot sun toward the building. There was a definite bounce in his step. He and Sharon had punctuated their conversation with Rolly by having outrageous sex on the bedroom floor. She was unusually aggressive and delivered him to uncharted heights in physical pleasure. Sal was certain the excitement of the project, along with the prospect of millions, stirred feelings in her neither of them knew she had. Now that they were both on board, they could openly share their innermost feelings. And they were both looking forward to tomorrow's big meeting.

Rolly assigned Sharon the role of ATM which he defined as Administrative Team Member. She would check in the participants, compare IDs to Rolly's list, provide the team members with their pre-assigned numbers, and assist Rolly during the meeting. For that and for a few tasks following the actual project, she'd earn a full share of the take, a sum exceeding a million dollars. The prospect made Sal smile as he crossed the hot asphalt heading for the employee entrance.

He noticed other employees making the walk from their cars, too. But, many of them had their heads down and barely acknowledged each other. They walked with a tentative stride, their faces full of concentration. Then it occurred to Sal. He knew he was going to tomorrow's meeting, but he had no idea who else was going. And if Rolly's approach to the others was consistent with his approach to Sal and now Sharon, none of them knows who's going either. He would be surrounded today by people at work who would be thinking about tomorrow's meeting, saying nothing to anyone, yet suspecting everyone.

When he walked into the cool, air-conditioned building, he shot glances at the various employees he passed along his way to the casino. The first leg took him through the Retail area where some of the employees at the shops acknowledged him with a nod or a smile. Others let their eyes meet his for an instant, before they shifted their attention elsewhere. This is ridiculous, thought Sal, why would Rolly have recruited Retail people for this operation? He quickly dismissed his hypothesis. There would be no sure way of identifying project participants by their behavior today, and nothing to be gained by trying. He vowed to abandon the notion completely and let tomorrow take care of itself.

Chapter Seventeen

He sat down, and like the rest of his comrades, faced forward and listened to his own breathing.

On Tuesday morning, the alarm sounded at ten AM. Sal reached over and turned it off. Sharon had awakened on her own two hours earlier. The aroma of freshly brewed coffee filled the house. He laid in bed contemplating the next several hours. This day had been something he'd been looking forward to for weeks. Sharon was already asleep when he returned from his late shift last night, but when she heard him crawl into bed, gave him the sweetest kiss and snuggled up against him.

He rolled out of bed and sent his feet feeling for his slippers. Finding them, he slid them on and walked out to the kitchen.

He read her handwritten note reminding him she had to go in early to help Rolly set-upfor the meeting. He pressed his lips against her red lip imprint on the note.

He poured some coffee and dropped a couple of slices of wheat bread into the toaster. Walking over to the patio doors, he looked out at the late summer morning. Birds were sneaking sips of chlorinated water from the Jacuzzi, pausing every second or so to quickly scout the areas to their right and left. Spider webs were beginning to appear wherever two solid objects were separated by six or eight inches of open space. The sky was cloudless and blue. It was, by all accounts, a beautiful September morning in the desert.

Sal turned and headed for the refrigerator where he pulled out a stick of butter. He lopped off a quarter of it with a kitchen knife, placed it on a saucer and into the microwave. He hated tearing up bread with solid butter, but Sharon had recently sworn off the chemically challenged margarine. So now Sal had to nuke butter to get it to spread smoothly on his toast. He spread the hot, soft butter over the toasted wheat and ate both slices standing over the sink. That's something Sharon would appreciate, he thought. He made sure the crumbs fell into the side with the garbage disposal. He sipped his black coffee, swashing a mouthful around his teeth.

"Okay, the chairs are set-up the way you wanted," said Sharon.

Rolly looked up from his notes and removed his glasses. "Twenty four?"

"Twenty four," she said. "Four rows of six, each spaced a chair apart. Mine's up here near you."

"Excellent," said Rolly. "Now go ahead and set-up the check-in table out by the door. Match up the names on the list with their corresponding number card. Then put up the signs on the wall behind the check-in table."

"Anything else," asked Sharon.

"Yeah. You can start smiling," said Rolly.

"That would cost you another million," said Sharon. "Not a nickel less."

"Have you figured out who you're maddest at?" he asked.

"What do you mean?"

"You're walking around here hating me. What you did was all about *you*. Those choices and decisions were *all* you."

"Maybe I am mad at myself," said Sharon. "Maybe I did make those choices. But you're the one who's turned them into blackmail. And I resent you with every fiber of my being."

"You resent me, huh? Tell me that a year from now."

"I won't know you a year from now. I won't know you the moment this thing is over."

"So say you."

"Is there anything else?"

"Not at the moment," said Rolly.

"Then I've got work to do," said Sharon. "They'll be arriving in less than an hour."

Rolly shook his head, repositioned his glasses, and resumed the review of his notes.

At eleven-fifty A.M., the checkered cab turned right off of Fremont Street at the intersection of Boulder Highway into the sprawling vacant parking lot of the former Montgomery Ward's. It continued on a route farthest from the building, hugging a path along the white guard-railed perimeter until it turned left and entered the lot behind the building.

"Up ahead there," said Sal, rather nervously. "Pull up near that smog inspection station."

"Ain't no one there," offered the cabbie. "Been closed all year."

"Yeah, I know. A couple of us are looking over a business opportunity," said Sal. "This is fine."

"Fifteen-fifty," said the driver.

Sal counted out eighteen dollars. "Here you go, pal. Thanks."

"Good luck with the business," said the driver.

Sal stood and waited as the cab made a u-turn and drove off. Then, he headed directly for the Ward's building. Across the lot, he could see the industrial blue door at the receiving dock just as Rolly had described.

When he reached the door, he knocked once, paused, and followed with three quick ones. He heard a clicking noise from the other side and the steel door opened an inch or so, inviting his entrance. Sharon instantly recognized her husband and threw her arms around him, planting a warm kiss on his lips.

Inside, the area was very dimly lighted and only by candlelight. That was Rolly's way of controlling the noise level, thought Sal. Low light, low volume.

"Hi, baby," said Sal.

"Hi," said Sharon. "Nearly everybody's already here."

"Did you recognize anyone?" asked Sal.

"I recognized some names of people I hear you talk about," she said.

"Like who?" Sal whispered.

"You'll see when you go in," she giggled.

"Rolly in there?" asked Sal, gesturing down the darkened hallway.

"Yeah, he's here. He's in kind of a strange mood," said Sharon.

"I can hardly blame him," said Sal. "This is huge."

"Here's your number," she said, handing him an index card. "Rolly will be referring to people by their number. Don't ask me why."

Sal read a small sign taped to the wall. It said PLEASE NO TALKING. As he turned to leave, someone knocked once on the door, paused, and knocked three more times. Sharon signaled a goodbye by daintily waving her fingers at him and blowing a kiss. Then she opened the door.

Sal looked down at the number on his card. It was difficult to read in the poor lighting. He moved to a candlelit area a little farther down the hallway where he could read 505. That was easy enough to remember, he thought.

He proceeded slowly down the darkened hallway. Up ahead, just at the end of the hallway, he could see that it opened to a very large, equally dimly lighted room.

As he entered, he saw the room was actually a small, corner area of the entire single story building.

Rolly sat at a small table at the head of the rows of chairs, facing the group. He appeared to be going over some reading material. Behind him was a large white board on wheels, stocked with a variety of dry-erase markers. It would no doubt to be a major visual aid player in today's meeting.

The people sitting in the chairs were absolutely silent and for the most part motionless. They sat staring straight ahead in Rolly's direction. It seemed so surreal. He slowly scanned the group and gulped as he recognized some of the participants. There was Stan Reno! My God, he thought, my own boss! Sue Min Wong – a fucking vice president! He recognized Nappa who looked over at him and winked.

Collusion on the Felt

There were others he didn't recognize at all. Some he swore he'd seen in the employee dining room, but didn't know their names.

Outside the seating area, Sal could see the huge warehousing layout that was once Ward's. Some broken shelving stood scattered among countless cardboard boxes strewn all over the area. The only sunlight was what sneaked in through the tears in the paper window coverings clear at the far end of the building. The meeting area, itself, was surrounded by candles, which added to the aura of it all.

Sal moved toward the third row of chairs where he noticed an empty seat, one of only two remaining. He sat down, and like the rest of his comrades, faced forward and listened to his own breathing.

The short-lived silence was suddenly interrupted by the slapping sound of flesh on flesh echoing from the hallway. Instinctively everyone turned to see Harve Dedman entering, sporting a blush of embarrassment, and massaging his cheek. Sal's curiosity was interrupted by the sound of Rolly clearing his throat. With everyone now on board, the meeting was about to begin.

Rolly, rose from the chair as Sharon entered the room from the hallway and walked directly toward him. She handed him a sheet of paper and whispered something directly in his ear. He half-smiled as she took a seat at the table, opposite his.

"We all know why we're here," he began. "I have spoken to each of you, some several times, and I'm proud to see that you've all lived up to your commitments by being here today, and by being on time. Now that you've all stepped up to the plate, it's time to play ball."

The group murmured its approval.

"Many of you likely do not know each other. Some of you work the swing with me; some work days; some are on grave. Some of you don't even work at the Empire. I've assigned each of you a three-digit number, partly for simplicity during this meeting and partly so that we can avoid the use of names as much as possible."

Rolly ran his hands through his thick hair. "One word before we get to the details." He walked a few paces to his left. "What is said here today must absolutely stay here today. The success of this project depends totally on unqualified secrecy. There may be no discussions about anything with anyone at any time." He paused, raised his arm level with the group, and scanned a pointed finger at everyone in the room. "If you are not willing or not able to commit to total silence, we will wait now as you do us the courtesy of leaving the building." Rolly walked over to his chair and sat down.

After a symbolic brief wait, Rolly rose and stepped to the rear of the staging area accompanied by Sharon. Each grasped an end of the mobile white board and guided it downstage closer to the seated group. Rolly again took center stage, this time, carrying a note tablet. "Well," he said, "from this point forward we sink or swim together. Let's begin." He flipped open the cover of the notebook. "This operation has a name." He picked-up a black marker and printed in large letters at the top of the white board: '*COF*,' and underlined it. "We'll refer to it as COF– that's the acronym for collusion on the felt. Make no mistake!" he cautioned. "If you live to be a thousand, you will never be part of a more serious effort. COF will either *make* us or *break* us and there ain't *no* in between."

Next to COF, Rolly printed a colon and the words '*One Week From Today.*'

"COF launches in one week," he said. The strategy will be cacophony." He wrote out the word: *cacophony* and placed a dash after it. "By that I mean," and he wrote, "*chaos* - we're going to come at that company from every which way, all at once. They'll never know what hit them – and, more importantly, they'll never be able to prove a thing."

That last point acutely piqued the interest of the group and induced a low wave of muffled muttering offered up as a chance prayer of praise. After all, the contemplation of failure and capture was the single most powerful deterrent erected by the casino Goliaths. Rolly had just ripped down that wall and summoned a room full of Davids. Sal's eyes met Sharon's, clear across the room. They exchanged smiles. Rolly told them that they would have one more contact prior to COF. That would take place on Sunday. More about that later.

Next, he printed the word *Tactics*. "Now let's get specific," he said. "This is how we're going to pull this off."

Everyone leaned forward in grand anticipation.

Rolly turned and nodded to Sharon, who rose from her chair and left the room, entering the hallway from which they all had come. She would return momentarily with trays of cold, bottled water for the group, who heartily welcomed the needed refreshment.

For the next hour and forty-five minutes, Rolly detailed the specifics of COF, referring often to his notebook, drawing diagrams on the portable wall board, providing pinpoint times and durations when explicit assignments would be carried out, and by whom, by assigned number.

For example, he assigned #521 the task of producing six hours of digital music recordings, to be hooked into the casino's playback system. Rolly asked 521 to self-identify by raising a hand. He motioned to Sharon who retrieved an envelope from a box on the chair next to her. She studiously delivered it to 521. Rolly said the envelope contained a specific list of songs and a specific order in which those songs were to be recorded. The songs, indeed certain lyrics, even beats would provide casino-wide precision synchronization cues for many critical strategic moves.

He then asked for three others to self identify: 511, 523 and 505. Sal immediately recognized that last number as his. He hesitated momentarily until two others raised their hands. Then, he followed suit. Rolly told them they would each be preparing four eight-deck shoes, two filled with red decks, two filled with black. The cards in each shoe would be prepared in an order specifically prescribed in the envelopes now being delivered by Sharon. Each of them, as they left today, would pick up a box of materials, gestured by Rolly to be on the floor, against the wall behind him.

Rolly told the group that at precisely four-ten P.M., Monday afternoon, the casino host's office will receive a telephone call. The call will advise that Mr. Archie Yen and his group plan to visit the casino's Baccarat Pit at around seven-thirty PM. It will be a good-natured call predicting the group would, this time, "even the score."

"Most of you may recall," said Rolly, "several weeks ago, on a Sunday afternoon, we had a tremendously high stakes game going in Baccarat. That was the day Mesmer showed up in his 'goof off' clothes and made everybody nuts."

Many nodded, making audible sounds of recollection.

"Well, that entire afternoon was merely a set-up," announced Rolly. "It was a set-up for what will play out beginning next Monday evening. If you thought those stakes were high a few weeks ago, you just ain't seen high. And, in case you're wondering – yes – that's where several of those pre-made shoes some of you are working on will end up. While Mesmer and his henchmen scramble to prepare for the invasion of Mr. Yen and his group," Rolly continued, "another call will be made to the host's office, about forty-five minutes after the Yen call. This call will advise that none other than Cyril Queck has had a change of heart and has decided to give the Desert Empire another crack at his credit line. He and his entourage will be arriving at the Empire at around eight PM. that same evening. Mr. Queck's return, too, is nothing more than a planned sequel to his earlier set-up visit a few weeks ago."

Sal's face crinkled in pure adulation. He stared in absolute wonderment at his friend Rolly who was positively captivating. He had no doubt that this room full of cronies shared his deep admiration for this brilliant, heretofore untapped leader.

"Both Mr. Queck and his entourage, and Mr. Yen and his group will be requesting dinner service on site. Numbers 509, 512, 518, and 520, you will ensure that you are the ones who deliver the room service orders. It is by way of your covered trays that we will slip the pre-made shoes into their respective games."

Rolly paused as he referred to his notebook. He flipped a couple of pages. Finding what he was looking for, he tapped the tablet repeatedly and walked a few steps to his right with his head raised facing the ceiling. The group could sense an announcement of significant magnitude was forthcoming.

"The eye," began Rolly. "From talking with each of you over the past few months, it's clear that the "eye" is one of your major concerns. Let me talk about that now in some detail. Obviously, I've given an awful lot of thought to surveillance, and I've concluded that we have one very favorable thing going for us – management's frugality. They're so fuckin' cheap when it comes to manpower – they may have helped lay the groundwork for COF. I started thinking about what the eye actually is. It's a perch where management can watch everything and anything that's going on in the hotel, the casino, and all public areas. They can visually verify that everything goes on according to their plan. And for their evidence, they roll the tapes in the VCRs. Well, I thought, that sounds like the very set-up *we* could use to make sure *our* plan is proceeding as scheduled. So rather than trying to work *around* the eye, for which I had an initial plan, I've decided on an approach to *take it over*."

A group murmuring, mixed with audible gasps punctuated Rolly's statement.

"Now," he continued, "they have two people on the swing shift – Palermo, the director, and some old geezer they call the Colonel. They used to have Palermo plus three. But when Mesmer took over as acting president a couple of weeks ago, he cut out two surveillance positions during Monday's swing because Monday's normally such a slow day. That really frosted Palermo. But, he decided to keep the Colonel because of his seniority – and the guy *is* pretty good. The good news is he's a tired old fuck who can barely walk – an easy take-over, the way I see it. Now for Palermo…he's got a fourteen-year-old daughter, Alicia. She's a sophomore at Holy Rosary Catholic High School. Number 502 – self identify."

In the front row, the right arm of a male, small in stature and youthfully thin went up. Sal didn't recognize him. Sharon rose from her seat and carried an envelope to 502.

"This is Alicia's photograph, 502, along with Holy Rosary's address and time of dismissal. Your job is to see to it that she doesn't get on the school bus after school on Monday, but that she is otherwise safely entertained. In other words, she must not know she's being detained, nor do I want her harmed. To assist you with this challenge, see me after this meeting. I've got a priest's outfit for you to wear. Number 515, self-identify."   An arm in the third row shot up. Sharon responded with another envelope.

"This is Palermo's home phone, office phone, and cell phone, along with the time the school lets out. Fifteen minutes after dismissal time, you call Palermo from a pay phone. Start with his cell phone. You'll say exactly what is written for you to say in that envelope, nothing more; nothing less. Guaranteed, no way Palermo will be at work."

"This will leave the Colonel alone in the eye. It so happens these morons get special privileges. Instead of eating their dinner in the employee dining room like the rest of us, they get *room service* to deliver their meals!" Rolly had raised his voice for the first time, and his words echoed in the huge warehouse.

"Number 517, self-identify." From the middle row, an arm went up.

"You will ensure that you deliver the Colonel's meal on Monday evening. He normally eats around seven-thirty PM. No matter when the Colonel calls to make the order, you wait until you hear Neil Sedaka on the house sound system singing *Calendar Girl*. That should occur within moments of seven-forty-five PM. At precisely the first time in the song when the lyric goes: *April – you're the Easter Bunny when you smile,* on smile–knock on the door to the eye, and knock hard! It's during the refrain: *Yeah, Yeah, my heart's in a whirl, I love – I love – I love my little Calendar Girl –* on 'girl' is when I make the switch to the first pre-arranged shoe for the Yen group."

Number 517 nodded.

Rolly gestured toward Sharon. She reached for a small, wrapped package, and carried it to 517.

"In that package are two items. One's a stun gun, 517. I want the Colonel out of commission–no pun intended–and then blindfolded, gagged and tied. Drag him inside the storage closet in the corner of the eye. The other item in that package–I'll get to later."

Number 517 nodded.

"Numbers 506, 507, and 508, self-identify," said Rolly.

Three arms went up, one from each row. One of them was Nappa's.

"You are the command control center crew. Once 517 puts the Colonel on ice, he will open the surveillance door for you. Be in the hallway, outside that door by seven-oh-five PM. Number 506?"

Nappa raised his arm again.

"You are the commander." Nappa gave a thumbs up.

"507, 508, and 517 are your crew. You three, give me a thumbs up." They did.

"The three of you must do exactly as you're told by 506. One of your immediate assignments, 506, will be to have the crew eject the videotapes from every one of the video recorders."

A black thumbs up followed from Nappa.

"So, where are we so far," said Rolly. "We've got our music playing, the Yen group is in the pit, Queck's got the salon, and we own the eye in the sky. Not a bad start, don't you think?"

The group exploded into applause.

"Just the beginning," said Rolly, raising a hand to subdue the applause. "There's lots more. At this point in COF, no one on the floor, including Security, has any reason to believe anything is wrong. Frankly, I don't like that. Security needs to feel that they're on top of things —so we're going to give them something to get on top of. Numbers 500, 504, 510 and 513 self-identify." Four arms went up from various areas of the group.

Sharon began delivering one envelope to each of the four.

"These envelopes contain the following information," said Rolly. "There's a specific twenty-one table indicated where the four of you will begin to play at exactly seven PM. Number 519?" Stan Reno raised his hand. "You will ensure that the table indicated in your envelope is closed until seven."

Sharon carried an envelope to Stan Reno.

"You will also ensure that 501…501 where are you?"

A hand shot up from the second row.

"You will ensure that 501 is the dealer who is assigned to that table. 501 will approach you at exactly six-fifty-nine PM. Thumbs up, you two."

Thumbs went up from 501 and 519.

"All right, back to 500, 504, 510 and 513. You'll like your assignment. I want you to arrive at the table wearing cowboy hats and at least sixty percent drunk. All of you drink about five beers before you arrive. Play and drink for the next ninety minutes. Play multiple hands so all seven table positions are taken. Let no one else in the game. Be boisterous. Drink a lot. Draw attention to yourselves. Celebrate the wins; cuss out the losses. At approximately eight-thirty PM., the sound system will begin playing *Monday Monday*, by The Mamas and the Papas. By that time I want you guys to at least appear to be three sheets to the wind. I mean dead drunk! When you hear that song start, I want you all to sing along with it, as loud as you can. Change the words, if you want. I don't care. But, I want you to cause a commotion. I want people looking over at you. The bigger the crowd of onlookers, the better. Then, at the point in the song when they begin the second verse, I want you to break into a huge fight at the table – with each other and with anyone else who gets involved. You will have accomplished your task if you can draw seven to nine security officers into the fray. Of course, they'll all be unarmed, thanks to Nathan Mesmer and another brilliant piece of leadership. So it'll be brute force against brute force. And, if you've seen the builds on these over-rated night watchmen, you know you've got nothing to worry about. During the fight, 519, you volunteer to call Metro. Of course, you won't. You'll call the cellular number that's in your envelope for number 525. Self-identify 525."

Harve Dedman raised his hand. Sharon delivered the envelope to him and lightly smacked it against his chest.

"525, you will be dressed in a metro uniform. Pick it up from me after this meeting. You'll arrive within eight minutes of the cell call from 519. Your envelope contains your detailed instructions. Among those instructions is your need to load down the security officers with statements, paperwork, and reports. I want them to spend the next two to three hours in an administrative office filling out forms. You'll tell the officers you're removing the four fighting cowboys for booking downtown and you'll be back for security's statements. Then get our guys out of there."

Dedman gave a thumbs up.

"Then, 525, I want you to return to the Empire by nine-thirty PM. Go straight to the Surveillance Room. Knock twice, pause, and knock five more times. Did you hear that, 506?"

Nappa gave a thumbs up.

"506 will let you in to the eye – of course you'll still be in your police uniform. Now, 517 –for the second item in your package. Along with the stun gun is a portable voice recorder. When 525 shows up in his uniform, give him the voice recorder and the stun gun."

Thumbs up from 517.

"Then, 525, take that voice recorder and stun gun to the closet where the Colonel will be. Identify yourself as being from Metro – the uniform will help…" Rolly smiled broadly.

The group laughed.

"Pull the tape off the Colonel's mouth. Ask him his name. Record it. Ask him if he's okay. Record his response. Keep recording until you get him to say 'okay.' Got it?"

Thumbs up from Dedman.

"You'll use that recording if Palermo should happen to call to check on things."

Another thumbs up from Dedman.

"We're just about through this," announced Rolly, "but, I do have a couple of more details to discuss with you."

He walked over to the table and downed a bottle of water, then returned to face the group.

"Last time Archie Yen's group demanded that I remain their dealer. In fact Cyril Queck *always* has. They'll both be in the building at the same time and will both request that I deal to them. One: that's impossible. I can't be in two places at once. Two: I'm not a dealer anymore. I'm a suit. Yen and Queck will still insist that I deal to them. Mesmer will, no doubt, arbitrate. I am going to suggest that all of them play at one table up in the salon, and that I do the dealing, providing Mr. Queck doesn't mind. I have it on good authority he won't." Rolly smiled as the group laughed.

"Yen and Queck will know the sequencing of the cards – in other words they will know whether to bet player, banker or tie. At first, Yen will purposely lose a few big hands, while Queck will win. Yen and his group will then decide to bet with Queck – and that's when the money will begin to roll. The split of the Yen/Queck take will be 25% for the Yen group, 25% for Queck, and 50% for us. We estimate that by the time that game breaks up – and that should happen at just before shift change at eleven P.M., our share should be around one point one million dollars *per person* in this room."

The group gasped in unison. Some grabbed the top of their heads and simply shook them. Rolly stood proudly and smiled at them. Then, following the lead of several, the group erupted in a melding of screaming and applause.

Sal glanced across the room and his eyes met Sharon's. Instantly the hint of her smile vanished and her eyes shot to the floor in front of her. Why wouldn't she want him to see her smiling, he wondered. As if catching herself, Sharon looked back up at Sal and forced a closed-lip smile. Strange, he thought.

When the jubilation died down, Rolly continued.

"All right. That's it until Sunday," he said. "You all have a major role to play in COF. Between now and Sunday, you must devote your time to accomplishing and thinking about your assignments exactly as I have laid them out for you. On Sunday, I will telephone each and every one of you in the order in which we made our assignments today. I will start making the calls at eight AM., so I can make sure I'm available for work at three. I do *not* want to hear any busy signals or answering machines when I call. During the call, I will give you any last minute instructions and answer any questions you have at that time. Speaking of questions, I will answer any you may have at this point. Just raise your hand."

There had to be tons of questions, yet no one seemed to want to be the first. Many looked around to see who might be the first speak. It was Nappa

"I got one," said Nappa, breaking the silence. "How, ah, how do we go about taking personal possession of our individual booty?"

Several participants chuckled. Most nodded in agreement.

"If I understand your question," said Rolly, smiling, "you want to know how you get your share?"

"Yeah, that's it," confirmed Nappa.

"I don't have that totally worked out yet," said Rolly. "But that will be something I will let you all know during our Sunday call. Okay?"

The group nodded and murmured.

"Anything else?" asked Rolly. No one stirred.

"Okay, that's a wrap. Talk to you Sunday!" said Rolly.

Chapter Eighteen

Nappa and Rolly made eye contact and suddenly cracked each other up. It was obvious to Harve the two were experiencing a drunken giddiness.

Beginning at three-twelve PM., the COF team began pouring out of the abandoned building. Several of them carried boxes of various materials, given to them by Rolly as part of their COF assignments.. They blinked and squinted into the bright September sunlight. The air hitting their perspiring faces was very invigorating, however, and a refreshing climatic change from the stuffiness of the room.

Sal, among the last to leave, carried a box containing an envelope, thirty two decks of Desert Empire playing cards, and four empty dealing shoes. Half the cards were in red tinted boxes; half in black. He wondered how in the world Rolly was able to get his hands on 128 decks of brand new, cellophane-wrapped playing cards. The card room, where such controlled materials are stored is accessible by only a very few, highly placed casino executives. Getting one's hands on 128 decks alone boggles the mind, but actually removing them from the building – that had to take major collusive involvement, Sal thought.

During his solo ride home – Sharon had to stay and help Rolly clean up - it was clear to Sal that he and Sharon were a mere week away from financial security for the first time in their lives. All he had to do was put together four shoes of dealing cards. He'd have that finished before bedtime tonight. A million and change - no evidence – no video. And he didn't have to worry about explaining it all to Sharon. She was now part of it. He wondered how Rolly did it, how he got her not only to accept the idea, but to be part of it.

Exhausted, he laid his head back on the taxi seat and closed his eyes. The meeting with Rolly replayed over and over. Rolly certainly had lived up to his promise of defeating the casino's security. The plan was magnificently thorough. The stakes were definitely worth the risk – minimal as it was. The fog in his mind had completely lifted. He was now totally commitment to COF.

Inside the Ward's building, all was quiet. Only Rolly and the Sharon remained, folding the chairs, and otherwise gathering their things. They worked in silence for a few minutes. Then Rolly spoke.

"How do you think it went?" he asked.

She looked up at him. "I guess I have to hand it to you. That was impressive."

"Oh, yeah?" said Rolly. "You mean that?"

"Don't let it go to your head," she warned. "I won't easily forget the underhanded way you got me involved with this. You may be brilliant, but you're still a snake."

"You know, I've always believed this was gonna work," he said, apparently ignoring her remark, "but now, more than ever, I'm convinced beyond a doubt."

"So am I done now?" she asked. "I'm gonna be a millionaire just for doing what I did today – playing hostess?"

"That was the deal," Rolly said. "Deal's a deal."

"If you don't mind, I'll believe it when I see it," said Sharon. "But now that I've done this, don't you ever breathe a word to Sal about why I got involved." Her look was threatening.

"Lips are sealed," Rolly said.

The taxi was snagged in the afternoon shift change traffic. In the back seat, Harve Dedman stared at the vehicle's interior ceiling. He laughed to himself as he remembered Rolly saying he could pick up his Metro uniform after the meeting. That was a nice touch, he thought. So he was going to be a millionaire, huh? This was too cool. Even on a sergeant's pay, it would take several lifetimes and he was sure he'd still never be wealthy. And all he had to do was play a cop, while he's in uniform and on duty.

It had been such a chance meeting that night last April when Harve had pulled Nappa over for speeding on Boulder Highway. He and Rolly had had a few beers and weren't feeling much pain.

"Evening, sir," Harve had said. "I'll need to see your license and registration."

Nappa and Rolly made eye contact and suddenly cracked each other up. It was obvious to Harve the two were experiencing a drunken giddiness.

"License and registration, please," Harve repeated.

"Oh, certainly, officer," Nappa managed, visibly trying to subdue his ache to laugh. "I know I got that here somewhere." Nappa patted his shirt and windbreaker pockets, repeatedly.

Rolly, watching his friend's futile search, lost it and belted out a hearty laugh.

Patiently, Harve waited for Nappa to produce the documents, knowing full well this would end up as a DUI.

"Sumbitch," slurred Nappa. "Somebody ripped me off of my shit."

Rolly was nearly convulsing, sliding off the front seat.

"You might want to check in your wallet and your glove box, sir," Harve offered.

"Oh yeah? How much you want, man?" asked a confused Nappa.

"Sir, please look in your wallet for your license – and your glove box probably has your vehicle registration." Harve's patience was beginning to wane.

Rolly volunteered to search the glove box, while Nappa pulled out his wallet. Between his blurred vision and numbed fingertips, the wallet search was a complete failure.

"Sumbitch, I know it's in here," Nappa managed.

"Got the registration," said Rolly. And he handed it across the front seat to Harve.

"Way to go, man," said Nappa. "See if you can find my license in here." He handed his wallet to Rolly.

Harve shined his flashlight on the registration. "You're Napoleon Jackson?" he asked.

"Friends call me Nappa," said Nappa smiling. "That Napoleon shit makes my skin boil. Know what I'm sayin'?"

Harve leaked the beginnings of a smile at Nappa's malaprop. "Mr. Jackson, I'll need you to step out of the car," said Harve. Shining his light on Rolly, he said "You sir, please remain seated with your hands on the dashboard."

"I'm looking for the license," said Rolly, holding up the wallet.

"Please return the wallet to Mr. Jackson. And I'll need your identification, as well."

Nappa took the wallet and fumbled with the driver side door trying to get out without falling. A horn blare from a passing car startled him.

"This is embarrassing, man," Nappa mumbled. "My homies be drivin' by watchin' this, laughin' their motherfuckin' asses off at me. Know what I'm sayin?"

"Please step to the rear and place your hands on the hood of my cruiser," Harve said.

"There I go steppin' to the rear again," said Nappa, barely to himself. "What about this wallet?" Nappa said, holding it up.

"Place it on the hood."

"You know I counted that money, man. I know how much I got in there."

Harve smiled. "Don't worry," he said. "Your money's safe."

"Two-thousand dollars," said Nappa. "That's how much I counted."

"That would be a lot of cash to be carrying around with you," said Harve. He picked up the wallet to look at it. To his surprise, there *were* at least twenty hundred-dollar bills inside. "Where did you get all this cash?"

"Oh, no you don't, man. Here we go! A black man with a stash – must be a drug kingpin or somethin'. No, you don't, man. I earned that. That's *my* money."

"Where do you work?" asked Harve.

"Gold Mine Casino downtown," Nappa said. "My ID's in there, too."

"What do you do there?"

"I'm like you, man. I'm in surveillance. You dig?"

"Oh, the eye, huh?"

"The eye, the ears, the nose and the throat, man. We're wassupp. Know what I'm sayin?'

"Mr. Jackson, have you been drinking tonight?"

"You mean booze?"

"That's right."

"Yeah, man. We had a couple of beers. Wassupp?"

"I have reason to believe you were operating a motor vehicle while under the influence of alcohol. I'll need to administer a sobriety test."

"You mean DDU?"

"DUI," corrected Harve.

"Man, I'll lose my fuckin' job, I get a DIU. We got to work something out here. Know what I'm sayin'?"

"I'll pretend I didn't hear that," said Harve. "Now…"

"Wait a minute, man. You don't understand. It ain't only me I'm worried about. My buddy in there – he's a big shot baccarat dealer at the Empire. He…"

"I understand completely, Mr. Jackson. All of us have jobs. Right now mine is to check you for intoxication and issue a citation for speeding. Don't complicate things by trying to bribe me. It won't work."

"Bribe?! Ain't nobody said nothin' about no bribe, man. Don't be tryin' to hang somethin' like that on me!" As loudly as Nappa shouted those words, he quickly lowered his voice and spoke through frozen lips, almost at a whisper: "Take a grand, man. It's yours."

Harve heard it, but pretended he didn't. Instead, his eyes shot to the red light barely visible through the cruiser's windshield, just above the rearview mirror, then back to Nappa. "Don't say any more," he said under his breath. "It's all being recorded."

"What do you want to do, man?" Nappa asked softly. "It's yours."

"We need to get off the highway," said Harve. "Get back in your car and I'll follow you to the Denny's right down the road. Pull in the back."

"You're okay, man," smiled Nappa.

When they met at Denny's, Harve parked beside them and lowered the window.

"Pass it over," he said, while his eyes darted in all directions.

Rolly handed him a thousand in cash. As Harve took it and began rolling up the window, Rolly held up his hand to tell him to wait.

"I need to talk to you – when are you off duty?" Rolly asked.

"What about?" asked Harve, nervously.

"Look – you obviously need the money. You just risked a hell of a lot. And we appreciate it. Now, I want to talk to you about real fuckin' money. And all you gotta do is be a cop. We're talkin' millions."

Harve swallowed hard. He looked around the quiet, dark parking lot. His mind was going a mile a minute. He wasn't exactly sure why he just took a thousand-dollar bribe – he'd never even considered it before. But the cash looked so good to him. And all of a sudden the word 'millions' is being tossed in his direction. As long as nothing out of the ordinary happened for the rest of the night, the videotape would be recycled on the next shift. There would be no evidence of his stopping and talking with these guys.

"I'm off at midnight," he said. "Say where."

So on that cool April night at the Neon Lantern, Nappa, Rolly, and Harve Dedman connected. Rolly instantly knew the value of having a cop on the crew. They exchanged names and phone numbers and didn't speak again until a few weeks ago. Rolly had called him to let him know about the meeting day after Labor Day. During their chat, Harve talked about the Balastrieri mugging at Harrah's garage that particular morning, and said he had done some work on it. Rolly told him how he knew the husband of one of the women – that he and the husband had just been together that night. Rolly suggested that

Harve do what he could to get close to the single woman – that the two women were best friends – and it might be a good idea for Harve to be in the loop. Agreeing, Harve called Missy later that afternoon, and had been in the loop ever since. In the past few weeks he'd banged Mooring's wife, made sergeant, and started making marriage plans with Missy.

Now, here they were a week away from COF. That thousand dollars seemed so miniscule now. To Harve it was merely a down payment on a life of luxury. He ran his hand through his hair and rested his head against the seat back. Traffic was beginning to move again.

Chapter Nineteen

He found it both at once exhilarating and terribly perplexing to accept that absolutely everything he'd designed was now in irreversible motion.

The Dominos Pizza driver retrieved the large warming bag from the passenger seat, shoved the door closed with her hip, and approached the front door. Finding the doorbell, she pressed the button, and waited. Momentarily, the door opened a mere two-feet. Sal Mooring handed the young lady a twenty-dollar bill and accepted his piping hot pepperoni, sausage and extra-cheese feast.

"Keep the change," he said with a smile.

Her eyes lit up as she quickly calculated the more than six-dollar tip. "Thanks," she said, "thanks a lot."

"You bet," he said warmly, and closed the door quietly so as not to wake Sharon from her nap.

He carried the large pizza box to the kitchen and placed it on the far corner of the table, prudently away from the piles of pristine playing cards, shoes and, above all, Rolly's methodically prepared spreadsheets. Sal had marveled at the surgical-like precision with which Rolly had laid out the predetermined order of each of the four shoes, prescribing everything down to the suit for each of the cards.

It had taken Sal more than two hours to prepare the first shoe, taking critical care to be absolutely sure he followed the instructions perfectly, and he triple-checked his work. One card out of place would be disastrous. It was now six-thirty-five P.M. He hadn't eaten anything since his morning toast and was now ready for a pizza devouring. He sprinkled on a layer of crushed red pepper, grabbed a few napkins and a cold diet soda, and sentenced the first slice to oblivion.

At a pay phone on Valley View Road, outside one of Vegas's many Seven-Elevens, Rolly deposited a quarter and a dime. He looked around nervously and listened for the connection to complete.

"Yeah," said the voice, following the first ring.

"It's done," said Rolly.

"How'd it go?"

"Like a well greased machine."

"No bugs?"

"Not a flea."

"Good. Good," said the voice, just before the click.

Nathan Mesmer loosened his red tie. He reached down to his desk's bottom drawer and found the pint of Kentucky Bourbon. He poured two-fingers into his empty coffee cup and rotated his executive chair around toward the window. The administrative staff was gone for the day and he relished these peaceful moments alone. The ever-present television monitor off to his right, flashed picture after picture of the casino's goings-on downstairs. But his mind was elsewhere right now.

Rolly's call sent his adrenaline rushing. He found it both at once exhilarating and terribly perplexing to accept that absolutely everything he'd designed was now in irreversible motion. The massive locomotive was barreling swiftly on a one-way track through a long, dark tunnel and wouldn't see the light of day until its engineer was rich beyond his wildest dreams. He sipped the bourbon.

One of his greatest feats, he reflected, was having the insight and gut smarts to choose Rolly Hutchins as the patsy. Hutchins was ripe. Here's a guy who's got the respect and trust of virtually everybody who knows him; who's approaching the end of his working career and still lives paycheck to paycheck. The *piece de resistance* is his immense disdain for corporate frigidity. *And* he's smart. What a catch, thought Mesmer.

His eyes drifted to the framed photograph of him and his family displayed on the credenza. He hoped they were well. It had been two weeks since he had sent Helen and young Bradley off to Lansing, Michigan to set up housekeeping and get the boy enrolled in the third grade. He'd told her he'd be joining them shortly, once corporate finalized a partnership agreement with one of the Indian tribes in that area to jointly operate a new casino there. It was all bullshit. There was no Indian casino deal. And as for corporate, a week from now no one would know where in the world he was.

He leaned forward in his chair and lifted a briefcase onto the credenza. He spun the dials for his personal locking code and lifted the lid. He inserted his hand into the elastic compartment and retrieved the airline ticket folder. Following another sip of bourbon, he reread the flight information:

Southwest Airlines, Flight 34
Departs Las Vegas: 8:05 am, Tuesday, September 11
Arrives Los Angeles: 8:55 am
TWA, Flight 300
Departs Los Angeles: 11:50 am
Arrives London   9:40am, Wednesday, September 12
British Airways, Flight 9
Departs London 9:20pm, Wednesday, September 12
Arrives Sydney, Australia 6:10am, Thursday, September 13

The ticket folder wore three months of handling. He sipped some more. He felt he must have pulled it out and salivated over it at least thirty times. He always ended his review with another scan of the passenger information: *Roland Hutchins, Las Vegas, NV.*

Part of him felt sorry for Hutchins. So far, he'd carried out the plan to virtual perfection —did a lot of leg work rounding up the chumps, connecting with the whales, putting together the meeting, and so on. He's got everyone involved believing they're pulling one over on me. Mesmer smiled to himself. He reached into his humidor and selected a fat cigar. As he lit it, he leaned back in his chair and propped his feet up on the credenza. One more time, he wanted to mentally play out the scenario:

I take a taxi to work on Monday, bitching to the office staff that the Viper's on the fritz and in the shop. That night, the whales break up the game at around eleven. They cash in their chips and demand cash. The cashier calls me for approval in my office where I always wait while whales are playing. I behave irascibly, as expected, but finally give my approval. The whole time the whales think they're doing business with Hutchins and his chumps. Hutchins thinks he's double-crossing the chumps and doing business with me. After the game, Hutchins leaves to meet up with the whales to split the take, having promised the chumps he'd be meeting them behind Sam's Club in an hour with their shares. Instead, he meets me in the parking lot and we drive over in his car to the rendezvous point way out on Blue Diamond Road, at the foot of the mountain. Exactly three miles before the meeting point, I tell Hutchins to pull over so I can get out of the car. After all, we don't want the whales to know I'm involved. Hutchins goes on alone, meets with them, and brings back fifty percent of the total take – upwards of thirty million dollars. We divvy it fifty-fifty. Hutchins takes a bullet in the back of the head. Oops, now it all belongs to me. I fill two footlockers that I had hidden in a pre-dug hole with the money. I bury Hutchins in the pre-dug desert grave, some three hundred yards from where I had him pull over. I drive his car to the airport long-term parking lot and leave a copy of his itinerary to Australia in the sun visor. Then I take a taxi home with my footlockers. When Hutchins doesn't show behind Sam's Club with their take, the chumps will know they've been suckered, but won't be able to do or say a damn thing about it. If any heat comes down, my perspective is the whales won their money fair and square. All the whales know is they gave half the money to Hutchins. If there's any sniff of foul play, the police will be looking for Hutchins. Ashamed and humiliated about the huge loss, I resign my position – that's if I'm not fired first. I go off into the sunset a very wealthy man.

Mesmer re-deposited the airline ticket folder in his briefcase, closed and locked it. He leaned back and drew on his fat cigar.

"Sal? Sal? Are you awake?"

Sal opened his eyes and quickly inventoried his surroundings. He'd dozed off at the dining room table.

"What time is it?" he asked.

"Nine-thirty," Sharon said. "You were really snoring."

"Yeah," he said yawning. "One hell of a day."

"Did you get finished?" Sharon asked.

Sal surveyed the materials in front of him.

"No, not yet," he said. "I'm in the middle of the fourth shoe."

"Come on, Mr. Millionaire!" she said with a smile. "Let's get moving here."

"Tell me," said Sal. "What turned you around?"

"How do you mean," Sharon asked, knowing exactly what he meant.

"One minute you were on the verge of divorcing me if I participated. A minute later you're not only in favor of it, but participating yourself."

"I told you," Sharon stalled. "I couldn't turn down that extra million."

"What about the risks you were worried about?"

"I'm sure there are still risks," she said. "But you heard Rolly today. This thing is extremely well planned. Besides one risk that is gone – I won't be left here without you."

Sal smiled and shook his head.

"What?" Sharon asked. "What are you smiling about?"

"There's just something magical about your logic," Sal said. "Always has been."

Sharon playfully blew on her fingernails and then buffed them on her T-shirt. "Well, now my logic is telling me you're going to kiss me," she said seductively.

"Right again," said Sal. And they kissed passionately.

<hr>

At eight-fifty-three AM., Sunday morning, the phone rang. Sal quickly checked the caller I.D. It read "not available." Disappointed it wasn't Rolly, and against his customary judgment, he picked up the receiver.

"Hello," he said stoically.

"Hey, Slick." It *was* Rolly.

"Hey, you're not at home," said Sal, rather surprised.

"Listen, Slick, don't say my name or anything, okay?"

Sal realized what was going on. Rolly didn't want any phone records–cell or otherwise–documenting his calls.

"Gotcha. We'll talk in code," said Sal.

"We're set for the party tomorrow," said Rolly.

"Good," said Sal. "Everybody coming?"

"So far, so good. You got your present taken care of?"

"Yeah," said Sal. "Not sure how to get it in without spoiling the surprise, though."

"I hear that," said Rolly. "A van will be making the rounds later today to pick up all the presents. Copy?"

"Copy that," said Sal. "What time?"

"Around noon. Make sure it's wrapped nice and pretty."

"Think the box ought to be taped closed?"

"Absolutely," said Rolly. "I'll see you at work. Might be best if we don't talk, though – know what I mean?"

"Yeah, I do."

"Later, Slick."

"Whoa!" said Sal. "Aren't you forgetting something?"

"Like?"

"Like *after* the party? Aren't we supposed to *meet* somewhere?"

Rolly laughed. "Damn, I keep forgetting about that. Funny how everyone wastes no time in reminding me." Rolly cleared his throat. "We'll get together in the parking lot behind Sam's Club off of Pecos, near Trop."

"Got it," said Sal.

"Okay," said Rolly. "Got some more calls to make. Later."

Sal immediately went to the hall closet and retrieved the box of pre-set shoes. He stuffed it with rolled up sections of newspaper and taped the flaps securely with wrapping tape. He placed the box on the table by the front door to await arrival of the "party" van. With Sharon already at work, he decided to shower now, so he'd be ready for the van when it arrived.

Shortly after twelve noon, Sal heard a horn honking in the driveway. He carried the box out the front door to the passenger side of the vehicle. The windows were very darkly tinted. The driver was a shadowy form and appeared to be wearing a ball cap. When Sal approached the passenger door, he heard the whir of an electric window opening from the rear of the van. As he placed the box through the window, he tried to steal a peek at the driver from behind, but couldn't make an ID. However, he did snatch a glimpse of other boxes in the rear compartment. The instant his hands let go of the box, the window began its upward climb, causing Sal to retract them quickly. Just as quickly, the van shifted into reverse. Sal spun to his left, nearly falling, as the blue Windstar departed. Not a word was exchanged between them. As he watched it disappear around the corner, he couldn't help mentally celebrating the de facto beginning of COF.

Rolly deposited thirty-five cents into the pay phone and dialed the final number on his list.

"Yeah."

"In the can," said Rolly.

"Any lumps?"

"Not really. Maybe a couple of jitters. Otherwise good."

There followed a silence as Mesmer lit a cigar. Rolly could hear him sucking and puffing – a rude, but Mesmer-like mannerism.

"Those jitters – calmed down?" mumbled Mesmer.

"Like always," said Rolly.

"You are good. I'll say that for you. You should have sold cars."

"Yeah – missed my calling. Speaking of cars, how long do you have the minivan rented for?"

"Goes back Wednesday."

"Good."

"Anyway, nothing until rendezvous now," cautioned Mesmer, referring to their late night ride to Blue Diamond Mountain tomorrow night.

"That's a ten-four," said Rolly.

"Out," said Mesmer, just before the click. He turned to the video monitor to, once more, take in the action. He leaned back in his chair, blowing smoke circles into the air. He clicked through the switching mechanism on his desk, browsing the many camera shots and angles at his disposal, many focused on hands, cards, chips and cash; still others provided wider shots, where he could scrutinize the chumps' behaviors. Several of COF's covert operatives were already on duty. Mesmer detected their mental distractions through their obvious insulated mannerisms. People weren't talking to each other. There were no smiles. Minds were noticeably preoccupied.

Those who weren't involved in COF merely mirrored the apathetic demeanors of those who were. The malaise was feeding off itself.

Mesmer basked in the warm glow of his powerful control. Although he hadn't used drugs since his late twenties, he was ever mindful of the intense physical high brought on by the combination of his genius and this overwhelming anticipation of COF. Like any junkie, he wanted more.

He crushed the cigar in the ashtray, and double-timed it to his outer office.

"Going down on the floor," he barked to Rhonda Bethtold, as he breezed past her desk.

"I'll warn the carpet," she muttered to herself.

Aside from the continual clatter of clinking chips, dice calls from the stick men, and the occasional smoker's cough, the casino was relatively quiet. These personal visits to the floor by Mesmer were intentionally infrequent so as to generate hyperventilating among the hired help. He walked with the gait of an inspector general stepping between open ranks, replete with the locked, protruding lower jaw and dagger eyes.

He savored the emotional rush as dealers and the pussies in suits glanced in his direction and immediately shifted their attention to non-existent matters. Occasionally, he'd lock eyes with one of the floor supervisors and stop dead in his tracks. He could actually watch their faces turn from rose to gray as the blood headed south. To Mesmer, that spectacular feeling gave ejaculation a run for its money.

But his pompous, abusive behavior was much more than a mirror of his persona, it was *intentional* and *strategically purposeful*. He knew immediately upon his arrival at the Desert Empire that this would be his final assignment. He had long tired of the frequent intra-corporate moves, the policy changes, and the demands from those above him to continually break and set profit records. The stress of the greed had taken its toll on this once bright and tenacious ladder climber. And after years of ulcers, it had become crystal clear that the top of that ladder would likely remain out of reach.

As he began his architectural design of COF, he incorporated the over-the-top behavior that would become the Mesmer way. He was well aware that the more of a *son-of-a-bitch* he was, the more those who worked for him would be eager to rip him and his casino off. His strategy had worked. The COF team was now crammed with Mesmer haters. And now, on the eve of the great heist, it was time for one more behavior reinforcement.

As he strutted past pit two, he noticed floor supervisor Rich Domingo appearing to be doodling on a piece of paper at the pit stand. Mesmer stopped, folded his arms, and glared. He was standing behind players at BJ twelve, but the dealer, Josh Keaton, was well aware of Mesmer's presence. Knowing better than to address Mesmer, Keaton lowered his head and tended to his game. Keaton knew Mesmer was eyeballing Domingo, who should have been eyeballing Keaton's game. He ached to get Domingo's attention, but that would be suicide.

To make matters worse, the player seated at Keaton's table directly in front of Mesmer pounded his fist on the felt.

"What are you doing?" he yelled.

Caught totally off guard, Keaton instinctively met Mesmer's eyes, as he addressed the player.

"Sir?"

"You took my money! I didn't bust. I had twenty!"

Domingo looked up from the pit stand and immediately recognized Mesmer standing behind the player. He discreetly laid down his pencil and approached the table.

He whispered to Keaton, "What happened."

"I thought this gentleman busted, so I took his money and cards. He says he had twenty."

Mesmer purposefully inched closer to the table, ensuring Domingo noticed.

"All right, check the cards," said Domingo.

Keaton placed his hand on the discard pile, but was stopped short.

"Hold it," ordered Mesmer. "Why are you checking the cards?"

"Mr. Mesmer," Domingo began, "I need to verify this gentleman's claim."

"What's his claim?" asked Mesmer, as if he didn't know.

"He says he had twenty, but we..."

"Well, did he?" asked Mesmer.

Domingo knew immediately a career change loomed in his immediate future.

"I...I don't know, sir."

"You don't know?" asked Mesmer.

"No, sir. I don't."

"I don't understand," said Mesmer. "Correct me if I'm wrong, but isn't that why I have you here–to know what the fuck is going on?" Mesmer laughed mockingly, as he put his arms around the three players in front of him. "What do you guys think?" he asked them, "isn't that why we have these overpaid monkeys here? I mean, if I'm wrong–tell me."

The players, shocked, looked at each other, shaking their heads.

Mesmer looked up at Domingo. "I'm waiting for my answer," he growled.

"You are right, Mr. Mesmer. It is my job to watch the games. I know I am wrong, sir."

"I am wrong, sir," Mesmer mimicked with a forced Hispanic accent.

"Yes, sir," said Domingo.

"Don't you mean 'si, senor'?"

Domingo's nostrils flared. His jaws tightened. His breathing quickened. But, he fought successfully to control his rage. Not only was his job on the line, so was his freedom to search for another.

"Well, let's see, shall we?" Mesmer said, "What would you do, hot shot, if you were me?" He glared directly at Domingo.

Domingo lowered his head. "You need to do what you need to do."

"Excuse me," interrupted the player, turning around to face Mesmer. "What the fuck's wrong with you?"

"Keep out of this, asshole," ordered Mesmer.

"That's it!" the player screamed, slamming his fist on the felt covered table.

At once, all three players jumped off their chairs and pounced on Mesmer, throwing him to the floor, pounding him with their fists. Domingo nudged Keaton, and both fought desperately to stifle their smiles knowing, full well, Mesmer would later be reviewing the surveillance tape.

Three security officers abandoned their casino posts and rushed to pit two.

"Call 911," shouted one to a pit clerk, who placed her hand on her cheek and imitating Scarlett O'Hara said, "Now wherever did I put that silly telephone?"

"Charlie! Melee in pit two! They're beating the fuck out of Mesmer!"

Palermo immediately looked up from his desk through the glass window at the twenty-seven inch color monitor above the console. He hit the intercom button to his agent at the console. "If they don't knock it off in fifteen minutes, let me know," he said snickering. The agent responded with a thumbs-up.

When the security officers piled on, some of the cowboys from the craps table yelled at others: "Watch my chips!" and four of them dove onto the fray.

The slugfest continued. Crowds of casino players mixed with cocktail servers, casino porters, and slot attendants converged around the heap of bedlam. Screams of "Kick his fucking ass! Kill the bastard! Don't stop, he's still breathing!" could be heard above the laughter each remark generated.

Action ceased at the table games. Dealers, floor supervisors, and pit bosses all assumed the required positions of game and bank protection. That's what Mesmer would want, they mused.

Chapter Twenty

The phone had yet to ring. The few who would have truly cared, didn't know. Those who did know, truly didn't care.

Word of Mesmer's beating and subsequent transport to University Medical Center's trauma unit, bloody and unconscious, spread like melted butter on a hot cinnamon bun throughout the Desert Empire and from shift to shift. Verification calls from the hotel to the hospital by various staffers inquiring about his critical condition fueled the rumor mill with loads of timber.

Among all, Rhonda Bethtold, Mesmer's Administrative Assistant, was in most frequent contact with hospital officials who were trying desperately to contact Mesmer's next of kin. Rhonda, totally unaware that the Mesmer family had left town, kept insisting the hospital continue calling the number she had first given them. Her phone was constantly ringing as various department heads called to ensure the rumors they heard were not rumors. Everyone delighted in this man's condition.

Rich Domingo was enjoying celebrity status among his peers. In addition to stumbling into the center of attention by way of his doodling, it was his idea to stanchion off the bloodstained carpet area in the casino under the guise of crime scene protection. In whispers, he announced it was a " … shrine to Our Lady of Retaliation."

With the entire property buzzing about the incident, it's no surprise that Rolly was aware something was up even before he swiped his ID card at the time office. Having heard scatterings of conversations from off-duty passersby while walking in from the parking lot, Rolly inquired with the security officer at the employee clock-in area.

"Hey, what's everybody talking about? Something happen here today?"

"I guess you ain't heard," said the security officer, "Mesmer's in the hospital. Damn near dead, from what I hear."

Rolly was stunned. "What?"

"Yeah, got into a clobber-fest with some pissed-off guys in the casino. He didn't stand a chance."

"Where is he?" asked Rolly, careful to mask the depths of his interest.

"UMC," said the officer. "He ain't come to, yet."

"What's the prognosis, have you heard?"

"They ain't made one that I know of. I know one thing, he's out for a ton. If he ever comes back, I don't expect it to be less than a couple weeks. 'Tween you, me and the fence post," he leaned forward and covered his mouth with his hand, "I hope the fucker dies in there. He deserves to go straight to hell, far as I'm concerned."

"I hear that," said Rolly. He swiped his ID through the time clock. "See you later – need to get goin'."

"Yeah, later."

Rolly's mind shifted into overdrive during his walk to the casino. That stupid fucker getting into a fight! Now what? Should COF continue? Should it be postponed? How could he possibly notify everyone in time? This really screws things up. What if he dies? If he dies, Rolly would have the entire take to himself. But, if he doesn't die by tomorrow night, he'd be sure to start talking when he remembers what's supposed to go down. In that case, Rolly could have Mesmer's share stashed away for him. But, Rolly would have to somehow tell him that before he left town. This really does screw things up. He cringed.

"Rolly! Hey, Rolly! Wait up!"

Rolly turned around to see Sal jogging to catch up. He was out of breath.

"Did you hear?" Sal managed.

"Yeah, I heard," said Rolly grimacing.

"What's it mean?" asked Sal.

"Shhhh, it don't mean nothin'," whispered Rolly. "Watch what you say."

"Okay, cool. Just checking."

"Everything's still a 'go'," said Rolly. "Pass the word."

"Got it," said Sal. "I need to get some water."

"Later," said Rolly, and he pressed forward at a quickened pace.

Inside room 621 at University Medical Center, Nathan Mesmer lay flat on his back with intravenous tubes funneling liquid nourishment and antibiotics into his veins. By eight-forty-five PM., it had been over seven hours since the incident, and he'd yet to regain consciousness. The room was filled with the hum of air conditioning and the rattle-like snoring from its only resident. There had been no visitors – not because of doctors' orders, but because no one cared to visit. There were no flowers or cards in the sparsely furnished room. The phone had yet to ring. The few who would have truly cared, didn't know. Those who did know, truly didn't care.

Back at the Empire, the three injured security officers were all treated for bruises and lacerations and released back to work from Desert Springs Hospital. The three players and the four cowboys were merely eighty-sixed from the property immediately by Security Director Chester Pulski and warned never to return. They all threatened to sue, but Pulski laughed at them. "You all attacked our man," he said. "You're lucky we're not pressing charges. Now get out before I change my mind!"

Many at the Empire knew of the tremendous animosity between Pulski and Mesmer and viewed Pulski's lenient treatment of the fighters as a token of his gratitude for pulverizing the bastard. Even Palermo made sure the videotapes that captured the incident were "accidentally" recycled back into the operation immediately.

After work, Rolly caught up with Sal in the employee parking lot and told him to meet him at the Neon Lantern for an emergency meeting.

They arrived at the Lantern's parking lot at the same time and parked next to each other. On the way there, Sal speculated that Rolly should actually be elated that Mesmer wouldn't be on property during COF. It seemed a huge break to Sal. Mesmer's absence would only make the operation easier. All of this added to his mounting curiosity.

"Inside," said Rolly, as he noticed Sal about to speak. The look on Rolly's face was tense. His eyes squinted like a scientist pondering complex theorems. His bushy eyebrows were heavy and furrowed. He was more tight-jawed than Sal had ever remembered seeing him. And his breathing was audibly rapid. They took a booth at the rear of the Lantern, far from the late night few. Sal looked around for Debbie, but so far she hadn't appeared.

Rolly began as soon as they were seated. He leaned forward and spoke in forced whispers.

"Look," he said, "all through this operation I haven't been able to talk to anyone. I may have wined and dined, but that was all salesmanship. When it comes to the details, I've had to keep everything absolutely hushed, couldn't bounce anything off anyone. This thing with Mesmer now has got me in a fuckin' quandary. I need to talk it out. I need you to listen and maybe give me some advice."

Sal's face took on the pain he saw in Rolly. "Yeah…sure. You got it. Anything. You know that." His voice was equally hushed and his speech choppy. His heart pounded contemplating what would follow.

"All right. Good. Glad to hear that," said Rolly. "Let's get a beer. I need to calm down."

As though on cue, the kitchen doors swung open and a middle-aged, overweight woman with very thinning hair scooped up a couple of menus and headed toward Rolly and Sal.

"Here comes the waitress," said Rolly. Sal turned around in anticipation. "It's not her, though."

"Evenin' gents," she said in a cold monotone, dropping a menu in front of each one. "My name's Lucille. Somethin' to drink?"

Rolly collected the two menus and handed them back to her. "Just a couple of beers," he said. "Bud Lights."

"Excuse me," said Sal. "Is the other waitress – Debbie – working tonight?"

"Sorry, sweetheart. She up and quit the other day. So you're stuck with me. Now that's two Bud Lights. Be right back."

"Wonder why she quit," said Sal.

"Ah, waitresses – they come and they go," said Rolly.

"I would have thought she'd say something to me," said Sal. "We did spend some time together."

"Maybe that's why she's gone, Slick. I mean you did pull the plug on that, didn't you?"

"What was I going to do? I mean she was terrific, but I didn't want it getting out of hand, you know?"

"You did what you had to do. It's probably best she's gone. At least you were able to keep all that from Sharon."

"Shit, that would have killed her," said Sal. "I'd never be able to bounce back from something like that."

"That begs the question – why did you do it?"

Sal thought for a moment. "I really don't know. I suppose it was the animal instinct, the challenge, the attraction. Know what I mean?"

"Do you think that justifies it?"

"Thank God I won't have to justify it. That's all I've got to say. I enjoyed it and it's over."

Lucille arrived with their drinks. "Two Bud Lights. Anything else, gents?"

"No, this is good, thanks," said Rolly. Lucille dropped the check and departed.

Rolly lifted his beer. "To animal instincts," he said, toasting.

They clinked their mugs and heartily sipped.

"Now," said Sal, "What's up with you?"

"Everything." said Rolly. "Everything seems like it's collapsing in on me."

"What are you talking about? What's collapsing in on you?"

"Mesmer's in the hospital. He could be dying...."

Sal looked incredulously at him. "And your point? Sounds to me like that would make things even easier."

"It might have, but we found out during the shift tonight that corporate is sending in one of their VPs to oversee the place while Mesmer's out. He arrives tomorrow."

"Rolly – you're losing me. What the fuck difference does it make whether Mesmer's up in that office or this new guy?"

"With Mesmer, we know what we've got," said Rolly. "You can set your watch by his predictable behavior. I felt comfortable with COF because I was comfortable with Mesmer. This new guy – I don't know."

"All right," said Sal. "You call this off now, there will be no second chance, mostly because those involved have worked so hard to muster the courage to even consider this. The trust factor goes down the toilet forever – and so does the brass ring."

Rolly listened. He admired the level-headedness Sal was bringing to the discussion. He found himself nodding his assent. "Is that how *you*, feel?" Rolly asked.

"Yeah, I guess it is," said Sal. "Right now I'm committed. That didn't come easy. Damn near ruined my marriage – and if it doesn't work – my life – and now Sharon's life!"

Rolly chugged down the remainder of his beer. The alcohol was beginning to kick in. He propped his elbows on the table and rested his face in his hands. Through the cracks in his fingers, he watched Sal. Here was a guy, like so many others, who was risking all that was dear to him, and he unknowingly stood to walk away with nothing at best, with a felony at worst. Then there was Mesmer. Rolly now deeply regretted getting involved with him. The miserable bastard couldn't keep his fat mouth shut just one more day. Things would be so much easier If Mesmer *would* die. If he died, Rolly could actually go through with the share-splitting with all the COF team as announced and none would be any the wiser. They certainly deserve it, he thought. In the midst of his current mental turmoil, he couldn't understand how he could possibly *ever* have intended to defraud them, while partnering with that no good son-of-a-bitch.

"What are you thinking," asked Sal.

Rolly motioned to Lucille for two more beers.

"I've got to let you in on something, Slick. But you're gonna have to hear me out, okay?"

Sal leaned in closer and nodded eagerly.

Rolly instinctively looked both ways and leaned in closer to Sal. His voice lowered to a mere whisper. "Everything about COF is not exactly as it seems."

"What does that mean?" asked Sal, a flush filling the pores on his face.

Rolly hesitated, knowing he was at the point of no return. He stared at Sal and breathed in through his nose. "COF was Mesmer's idea, not mine." There. It was out.

Sal's eyes widened as his lower jaw dropped. Rolly immediately held up his hand, cocked his head, and raised his eyebrows indicating there was more.

Lucille delivered the second round of beers and swept up the check for updating – all in one motion.

"You mean he *knows* about this?" asked Sal, shock dripping on every syllable.

"Oh, he knows," said Rolly, nodding. "Like I said, it was *his* idea."

"Jesus Christ!" whispered Sal, his torso slamming against the back of the booth bench. "How the fuck…?"

Rolly shushed him. "Remember – you gotta hear me out."

Sal's eyes shifted toward the ceiling. Both hands covered his mouth as the impact of this news reverberated through his consciousness. Not only did the acting president know about the collusion – it was *his* fucking idea!

"Rolly, this scares the absolute fuck out of me!"

"Keep it down, Slick," warned Rolly, pressing his finger against his lips.

Sal took a deep breath and chased it with a healthy gulp of beer. Rolly nervously sipped his own beer. The direction of this conversation was now anybody's guess.

When Sal leaned in again, Rolly knew he could continue. "All right, it gets worse now, so try to relax and control yourself, huh?"

Sal closed his eyes and slowly nodded, bracing for the next wave.

"As far as Mesmer thinks," Rolly continued, "he and I are splitting the take and you guys get nothing." The words tumbled onto the table like iron dice. "But," Rolly interjected hurriedly, "that's not the way it's gonna be, I promise you."

"We get nothing?" Sal was horrified. "What the fuck kind of a plan is that?"

"Listen," said Rolly, "that's how it started out, but believe me, that was never gonna happen."

"How do I know that?"

"What do you mean?"

"How do I know that was never going to happen? If Mesmer hadn't gotten his ass beat, we wouldn't be having this fucking conversation, would we?"

"You don't believe I would have actually fucked you all, do you?"

"What the hell else *is* there to believe?"

"Slick," said Rolly, exasperated, "I had to play the game with him the way I did to make this work. I had to pretend it was me and him all along. There's no way I could have told you guys this was Mesmer's plan. Don't you see?"

"Hold it! Sal ordered. "Let's say Mesmer's beating never took place. It's tomorrow night. We pull this thing off. How do you and Mesmer split the loot and still give the rest of us our shares? How were you going to pull that off?"

Rolly stared at Sal. Their eyes locked. Rolly took a deep breath. "The only way I *could*, Slick," he said. "Mesmer would have to be eliminated."

"Kill him? You expect me to believe that?"

"Why not? What else could I do?"

"You're no killer, Rolly!"

"What choice would I have? I know goddam well Mesmer would never let *me* live through this? Get a grip, man! That motherfucker would *never* split that money with me and let me live to tell about it."

Sal's look told Rolly that last thought got through.

"And another thing," said Rolly. "There's a chance Mesmer will die in that hospital. Why the fuck do you think I'd tell you all this now? I could have kept quiet hoping he would die. Then no one would ever have known."

"Good question. Why are you telling me now?"

"Cause It's been bothering me, man. Even before Mesmer's fight, I've been struggling with the inevitable that someone has to die over COF. There's just no way around it. And I wanted someone I trust to know the whole story…just in case."

Sal sat there shaking his head. "So what do we do now?"

"Well, the show goes on. We'll keep close tabs on Mesmer's condition. If it looks like he might survive, I'll find a way to take him out. I may need your help. Can I count on you?"

Sal swallowed hard. "I never figured this thing could get so far out of hand, Rolly. I mean murder? I don't know."

"Do I need to remind you that both you and Sharon are up to your asses in this thing already? If this thing blows up because of Mesmer, and you two get fingered, your worst nightmare will become reality, my friend. Twenty to life. Think about that."

It was all too true. It wasn't as though Sal and Sharon could back out gracefully. Their deeds were already done.

"Rolly?" asked Sal. "Can we keep all this from Sharon?"

"Absolutely. In fact, I'd rather *none* of the others ever know about all this."

"Okay," said Sal. "I'm with you for long haul. Whatever you need."

Rolly nodded. "Damn that makes me feel a whole lot better." The two men clasped their hands in a high five.

Chapter Twenty-one

It was obvious, at once, who he was. The tall, handsome, sandy haired stranger in the pinstripe suit was a standout in any crowd.

At nine-twenty AM., Monday morning, a Desert Empire fire engine-red stretch limousine with license plate "Mpire 1" pulled to a stop at the hotel's front entrance. The driver quickly walked in front of the parked limo and opened the passenger's side back door. A tall, sandy haired gentleman in his mid forties, exited. He wore a gray pinstripe suit, white shirt and gray and red striped necktie. The driver opened the trunk and retrieved a suitcase, clothing bag, and a briefcase. The sandy haired man walked directly into the hotel followed by the luggage toting driver.

As soon as they entered the lobby, the on-duty bell captain hurried over to the driver and signaled for him to stop. The sandy haired man kept walking toward the casino. "You need to turn that baggage over to a bell person," the bell captain said.

"You don't understand," said the driver. "That's Mr. Frederick from Monarch Gaming. He just flew in to watch over the place while Mr. Mesmer is out."

"What's there to understand?" asked the bell captain. "This is a union hotel. We carry the bags. Period. Now if you'll…"

"Don't even think about touching these bags, man. Mr. Frederick gave me explicit orders to carry these bags for him all the way to his office. Now if you've got a problem with that, I suggest you file a grievance. Now, I need to get going so I don't lose him."

The driver moved through the hotel foyer, down the marble steps into the casino. He saw Frederick way up ahead, walking at a brisk pace toward the casino host office. With some difficulty, the driver hurried after him.

"H.R. Frederick," he said, extending his right hand. His voice was loud and very deep, with seemingly very little effort.

"Sue Min Wong," she said, accepting and shaking his hand. "I'm Vice President of Casino Marketing. Welcome."

"Thank you, Ms. Wong. I don't know how long I'll be here–depends on Nathan's recovery–but I look forward to working with you. How is he, by the way?"

"Uh, we haven't heard any updates this morning. I'll give a call…"

"Not important. I'll have his secretary call. Now where do I go from here to get to his office?"

"Allow me to escort you," she said.

As they exited the host's office, the baggage laden driver had just arrived, completely out of breath. Frederick motioned for him to follow them. One look at Sue Min and the driver got his second wind. Sue Min led the two up the stairs to the casino management office. As they entered Rhonda Bethtold was filing her nails.

Sue Min cleared her throat as soon as she entered the office. Rhonda quickly dropped the file into her open drawer.

"Rhonda Bethtold, I'd like you to meet Mr. H.R. Frederick from Monarch. He'll be sitting in for Mr. Mesmer for a few days – or more," she said smiling. The two shook hands.

"Rhonda, get me an update on Mesmer's condition, please," he said. Rhonda was taken back by the powerful bass in his voice. "And do your nails on your own time."

"Yes, sir," she said, and quickly began dialing the medical center.

"I suppose that's the office I'll be using," said Frederick gesturing toward Mesmer's office.

"Yes, sir," said Sue Min. "Do you drink coffee?"

Frederick moved quickly past Sue Min, signaling the driver to follow him.

"Had plenty on the plane," he said. "Caffeined out."

Sue Min hoped that it was the caffeine that made this man move and talk at such warp speed. Maybe, he'd slow down a little once he settled in.

"I'll be getting back to the office," said Sue Min. "Again, good meeting you."

"Hold on," called Frederick. "I'm going to need a briefing. Can you help me by organizing a combination hotel and casino department head meeting? Let's have it at ten o'clock. You folks have a conference room or something?"

"Yes, we…"

"All right, have them in the conference room at ten. Tell them to be prepared to give me the lowdown on what's going on."

"I'll be happy…."

"And tell them I like short, succinct, powerful sentences, Ms. Wong. I'm not impressed with that 'dazzle them with bullshit' stuff. Are we clear?"

"Yes. Very…"

"And Rhonda!" he called out.

"She's on the phone with the hospital, Mr. Frederick."

"Still?"

"Tell her to see me when she's through. Now you'd better get going."

"Where would you like your luggage, sir?" asked the driver, who had been waiting in the outer office.

"Oh, yes. There's a closet. Put them in there. I'll take the briefcase."

Sue Min returned quickly to her office. She fetched her cellular from her purse and dialed Rolly's number. The phone rang four times and went to his voice mail. When she heard his announcement finish, she spoke. "Rolly, this is Sue Min. I know I'm not supposed to call you, but I just met Mr. Mesmer's replacement from corporate. We need to talk. Call me on my cell."

"Yes, Mr. Frederick?"

"Rhonda, I'm going to need...oh, by the way, how's Nathan?"

"I'm afraid it's not good news, sir. Mr. Mesmer still has not regained consciousness. They're watching him very closely."

"What exactly happened here?" he asked.

"Well it all started when...."

"Rhonda, I want one sentence. What happened?"

"Three players attacked Mr. Mesmer in the casino while he was reprimanding a floor supervisor."

"That was very good, Rhonda. Now, one more sentence. Why did the players attack him?"

"Because he supposedly called one of the players an 'asshole,' sir."

"I see. Is Nathan in the habit of calling our customers 'assholes?'"

This flustered Rhonda. "I...I...well...ah...I've never heard...I mean..."

"That's fine, Rhonda. I want you to keep hourly tabs on Nathan's condition and no matter what I'm doing, interrupt, and give me the update. Okay?"

"Certainly, sir."

"No need to call me 'sir.' H.R. will do just fine."

"I appreciate that, sir, however, I'd be more comfortable addressing you as Mr. Frederick...if that's okay."

"Have it your way, Rhonda. Now we don't have a lot of time. I've called a meeting in the conference room for ten o'clock. Ms. Wong is working on that for me. What I need from you is a list of all the department heads and a two-week out calendar of scheduled events, groups, players, etc. I'll need it by nine-forty-five to give me time to review it." Frederick checked his watch. "That gives you ten minutes."

Word spread throughout the casino that the corporate guy was on board and appeared to be a no-nonsense type, personal, but highly professional and he talked and moved quickly. Department heads were receiving very short calls from Sue Min telling them about the ten o'clock meeting. Many asked why she was notifying them. Her response: "He told me to."

Of all the people involved in COF, the only one who was currently on duty was Sue Min, herself. The other employees wouldn't be reporting until their swing shift, which for some began at one PM.; for others, as late as three PM. The staggered hours were developed years ago to help regulate traffic on the busy strip, and, as the resorts continued to grow, it helped spread out the demand for employee parking.

Sue Min checked her watch and determined she had just enough time to make one more call. She dialed the number.

"Yes."

"Archie, it's me."

"Is there a problem?"

"Don't know yet. I met Mesmer's replacement – a hot shot from corporate."

"Are we still on?"

"So far."

"When will you know?"

"I'm waiting for a call."

"From him?"

"Yes."

"I need to know as soon as possible. There are others I must contact. What's your gut?"

"Hard to say. This guy's no pushover."

"All right. Notify me at once."

"I will."

The instant she terminated the call with Archie, her cellular rang.

"Yes?"

"Sue Min?" It was Rolly.

"I met him. He's tough."

"Met who?"

"You know, the guy from corporate."

"Oh! You met him? Tough, huh?"

"No pushover."

"What are the chances he'll even be on property tonight?"

"Well, once we report the players are coming in, he should stay, shouldn't he?"

"Most others do, but this guy's from corporate. I doubt he has any heavy casino background. Try to find out what he does at corporate.

That's going to be important. That's it – get me a little resume. Call me back."

"How will I…" Rolly was gone.

Sue Min looked at her watch. She had three minutes to get to the meeting. She grabbed a binder and headed upstairs to the conference room. When she got there, the conference room was buzzing with curiosity. There were more managers than there were chairs around the huge mahogany table. Normally the attendees for these meetings were just from the casino side of the resort. But you add in the hotel side, along with food and beverage and accounting, there were at least twice as many attendees as there were chairs. Once Hal Howard, the Keno Manager offered his seat to Sue Min, other men did the same for some of the women who were standing. The chair shuffling was still going on when H.R. Frederick entered the room.

It was obvious, at once, who he was. The tall, handsome, sandy haired stranger in the pinstripe suit was a standout in any crowd. And when he opened his mouth and that deep voice vibrated: "Good morning," all noises ceased and everyone immediately settled themselves wherever they were.

"I'm H.R. Frederick from the corporate office," he said. "Of course I'm here only temporarily until your acting president, Nate Mesmer, is back on his feet. But, since we don't know how long that will take, I thought it important to get a briefing from all of you – and I promise to stay out of your hair and let you run your departments." He smiled and they smiled back.

"First," he continued, "a little about me. At corporate, my title is Vice President of Development. It's a fancy way of saying I'm involved in designing or contracting all of the management and leadership training and development programs for all of our properties. I'm sure many of you have attended some of those courses here."

They all looked at each other without the foggiest notion of what he was talking about, but they smiled and nodded in his direction.

"To be honest," he continued, "I haven't worked at the property level in fifteen years, and back then I was in Human Resources. So I don't have a lot of casino or hotel background per se. That's why I said I'd leave you all alone to run your departments. All right, enough about me. Let's go around the table and let me hear your very succinct reports about what's going on here at the Desert Empire."

"He doesn't know a thing about casinos."

"You're certain?" asked Rolly.

"He said so himself," said Sue Min.

"Super. Okay. We go just like we planned. I've got a feeling he won't know any better to stay around for the whales. But, even if he does, I don't think he'll give us any trouble about converting the chips to cash."

"I don't follow you," said Sue Min.

"I was…talking out loud," Rolly said catching himself. "You see when the whales cash out tonight and they ask for cash instead of checks or direct deposits, I had every faith that Mesmer would honor their request. My concern was that the new guy wouldn't, but since he has no background. It's worth the shot."

"Okay, then. We go," said Sue Min.

"It starts with you when you get the call. Good luck."

"Good luck to you," she said.

Rhonda Bethtold ran into Frederick's office. "Mr. Frederick! Excuse me, but I just got word from the hospital that Mr. Mesmer has regained consciousness." She smiled for Frederick's benefit.

"Terrific, Rhonda. Get me a limo. I want to go visit him."

"Certainly, sir."

Rhonda dialed Sue Min's number. The host's office normally arranged limousine transportation.

"Sue Min?"

"Yes?"

"Sue Min, you need to arrange for a limo to take Mr. Frederick to the hospital. Mr. Mesmer has come to."

"When does he want to go?"

"He wants to go now."

"Okay. I'll call you back with the details."

Sue Min quickly called Rolly on her cellular.

"Yeah," said Rolly.

"Mesmer's come to. I just got a call from Rhonda. Frederick wants a limo to take him to the hospital to see Nate. Just thought you ought to know."

"Yeah, thanks." Rolly clicked off his cell. Jesus Christ! he thought, and he ran for the front door. His BMW was parked in the driveway. He jumped into it and reached for his cellular. He punched in Sue Min's number.

"Yes," she said.

"Stall on the limo!" yelled Rolly, as he started his car. "I'll explain later. Give me an hour, okay?"

"Okay, one hour," said Sue Min, as confused as ever. She picked up the desk phone and called Rhonda. "Rhonda, Sue Min. The limo will be here in one hour. We have one in the shop today and the other is on an airport run. Okay?"

"I'll tell him," said Rhonda.

Sue Min called the limo service. "I need a limo here one hour from now to take our acting president to see Mr. Mesmer in the hospital. Okay? Thank you."

The BMW sped through the neighborhoods of southwest Las Vegas and out onto busy Tropicana Avenue. Rolly was breathing heavily, and sweating profusely. He absolutely had to get to Mesmer before the hotshot corporate guy did. What he really wanted was Mesmer out of the way. But in the light of day, that was out of the question. It pained him to try to mentally sort all the details and have them make sense. He had to be dressed and at work by three PM. It was eleven forty-five AM. now. The corporate guy would be arriving at the hospital at about one PM. Rolly knew whatever he did in the next hour would affect the rest of his life.

Chapter Twenty-two

*I'm the only one I trust. This isn't about trust.
It's about greed, and you know it.*

The cellular phone rang incessantly. Sue Min hurried into her office and rummaged hastily through her purse.

"Hello," she said, nearly out of breath.

"You didn't call," scolded Archie Yen.

"Damn! I forgot. Sorry. So much has been happening…"

"Are we on?"

"Yes. Absolutely. Yes."

"There, that didn't take so long, did it?"

"Look…" she heard the click on the other end. She sat down to collect her thoughts. What else might she have forgotten? She checked her watch. It was just past noon. Now, she remembered. Lunch.

The traffic on Charleston Boulevard was heavy, rife with eighteen-wheelers and trucks, as well as cars. The perennial construction on the parallel east-west thoroughfare, Sahara Avenue, sent commuters and delivery trucks scurrying for Charleston, which already had its own daily share of traffic challenges. Rolly glanced at the car radio's clock. It was twelve-oh-five PM. University Medical Center was just up ahead. All he had to do was negotiate this latest maze of orange traffic cones and find a place to park. With luck he'd be with Mesmer in ten minutes.

The nurse, carrying medications on a tray, pushed open the door of room 621. Unlike during previous visits, this time, the patient's eyes turned toward her.

"Good afternoon, Mr. Mesmer," she said quietly, but cheerfully. "Time for your medication. How are we feeling?"

Mesmer stared at her. She could see the pain in his eyes. He looked as though he wanted to speak, wetting his lips with his tongue.

"Still feeling some pain, are we?"

He nodded with his eyelids.

"Here," she said, "this will help." She placed two tablets on his tongue and held a cup of water to his lips. As he swallowed, he grimaced at the smarting from the pain.

"What day is it?" he mouthed, barely audible.

"What day?" she verified. "It's nasty old Monday. Don't you just hate Mondays, Mr. Mesmer?"

He nodded with his eyelids, again, this time accompanied by a smirk.

"Oh," she said. "I almost forgot. You know we tried to contact your family yesterday, but we're getting no answer at the number they gave us at the Desert Empire. Is your wife at home?"

Mesmer closed his eyes and barely shook his head.

"Well, we need to know how to get in touch with her then."

"No need," squeaked Mesmer, "I'll contact her myself – later."

"Well, it's good to hear you beginning to talk," she said. "I'll be by a little later to check on you."

His eyes widened. "Wait," he mouthed, then he motioned with his head and eyes for her to come closer. "I need to get out of here today."

"I'm sure you do," Mr. Mesmer. "However, the doctor has something to say about that. Why don't we leave that decision to him. You're more seriously hurt than you might know," she said.

Painful as it was, he thrust out his lower jaw to indicate his dissatisfaction with that reply. "When will I see the doctor?"

"He usually makes rounds around four or five."

She delicately fluffed his pillow, careful not to disturb his head, and left the room. Mesmer lay there staring at the ceiling. It by no means escaped him that today was COF. This was the last place he needed to be. He wondered what was going on at the Empire. Would Hutchins and the group be going through with COF? What would Hutchins do with Mesmer's share of the money? His chest tightened to think that the little bastard would actually be getting away with the entire take. His thoughts were interrupted by a knock on the door.

Rolly had stopped off at the hospital gift shop and picked up a newspaper and a box of candy. He didn't want to go up empty handed – it wouldn't look good to the floor staff. After receiving no response to his knock, he pushed the heavy door open and peeked in. His eyes met Mesmer's. The man looked pitiful to Rolly, severely bruised and linked to a web of tubes. The only expression on Mesmer's face was the familiar look of someone at odds with life.

"Hey," said Rolly, quietly, as though he were in a library.

Mesmer nodded ever so slightly.

"Brought you a paper and some candy. I'll put them over here," said Rolly. The starkness of the room, void of any personal warmth struck Rolly immediately. The absence of love was conspicuous. He placed the meager offerings on the end table, next to the telephone.

"No TV?" asked Rolly, noticing the television was facing away from Mesmer.

Mesmer responded with a faint wave of his hand. "Forget TV," he grumbled hoarsely, "start talking."

"We're on," Rolly whispered.

"You've got to get me out of here," Mesmer ordered. "I'll make it worth your while."

"What can *I* do?" asked Rolly. "Don't talk nonsense."

"I don't care–I've got to be there."

"Don't worry, nothing's changed. You're still in for half. But, you're gonna have to trust me," said Rolly.

"Trust?" Mesmer tried to laugh, but winced at the facial pain. "Listen to what you're saying–trust. I'm the only one I trust. This isn't about trust. It's about greed, and you know it. I need to be there. Period."

"What do you suggest?"

"Whatever we do, we need to do it before you go to work. I won't see the doctor till late this afternoon. I can't count on being discharged."

"So what are you gonna do, rip out the tubes and crawl out of here? That'll draw the kind of attention we don't need. Besides, there's a guy in from Monarch to watch over the place."

"Son-of-a-bitch!" Mesmer clutched his chest. "Whose goddamned idea was that?"

"Corporate's, of course."

"Bastards! Who is it?"

"Don't know his name. I can find out. Is it important?"

"Damn right."

Rolly picked up the phone and dialed Sue Min's cellular. Fortunately, she had her purse with her at lunch.

"Yes?"

"What's the guy's name from Monarch?"

"Frederick, H.R. Frederick. Why?"

"Never mind. Thanks." Rolly hung up. "H.R. Frederick. Do you know him?"

"Yeah, I know him. He doesn't know shit about a casino. I suppose that could be good."

"By the time this goes down tonight, he'll be fast asleep in his room," said Rolly. "Only thing is, we'll need to wake him up when the whales cash in."

"What for? I'm not dead. You have them call me here for permission. I'll take the heat."

Rolly smiled. "Works for me," he said.

"Now–the matter of my share."

"You tell me."

"Damn, it hurts to think," groaned Mesmer. In his mind he was re-writing the scenario. If he couldn't be there at Blue Diamond to dispose of Rolly, that meant Rolly was going to have full possession of the all money. He could take off for anywhere in the world. But, there was little choice if Mesmer weren't discharged. He would have to trust Rolly. "Look," he said. "I've got two footlockers buried in a shallow hole out there by Blue Diamond. It's about three hundred yards due north from where you were going to drop me off. It's marked with a plastic water bottle, half filled with dirt. Bring a shovel. Stuff my money in one of the footlockers and re-bury it. Leave the water bottle there to mark it. That's how we'll handle it."

Rolly nodded. "You got it."

"Hutchins."

"Yeah?"

"You fuck me and I will hunt you down. I will have every law enforcement agency in the world looking for you. Don't even think about fucking me. Are we clear?"

"Hey, how much money does a person need? There's plenty for both of us. I'm not gonna fuck you, don't worry."

"Now, if I get lucky and get out of here this evening, we're back to plan A, got it?"

"Got it."

"All right. Get going," said Mesmer. "Wait. Before you go – how bad is my face?"

"You definitely took a lickin'," said Rolly. "It hurts to look at you."

"Spare me your pain," said Mesmer. "Don't forget–don't fuck me."

"All right, you take care," said Rolly, shaking his head and smiling. "Pleasure doin' business with you."

Rolly closed the door behind him and walked directly to the nurses' station.

"The gentleman in 621 – any idea what the chances are of his being released later today?"

The nurse flipped through pages on her clipboard. Finding the subject of her search, she stopped to scan the document. "This morning the doctor wrote Mr. Mesmer could be released, once he regained consciousness and showed no vital ill effects. He's going to be extremely sore, though and will require an anti-inflammatory and anti-biotic. No release is permitted without a final review." She looked up at Rolly. "The doctor normally makes rounds late afternoon, between four and five."

"Thank you, ma'am," said Rolly, and he turned to leave.

"One moment, sir. Are you a relative of Mr. Mesmer?"

"An employee, ma'am."

"I see."

Rolly summoned the elevator. So there's a shot he may be out today, he thought. Sounds like Plan A. My plan A; not his. Rolly smiled as the elevator door opened. He moved aside as H.R. Frederick stepped off and approached the nurses' station. Since neither knew the other, Rolly selected the first floor and began his descent. It was one o'clock – three hours before COF.

"I'm looking for one of your patients – a Nathan Mesmer," Frederick said to the nurse.

"Well, Mr. Mesmer's popularity has certainly risen dramatically today. He's in room 621."

"Thank you." Frederick walked the short distance to Mesmer's room wondering just how popular Mesmer has become since yesterday. He knocked at the door. Unable to hear a response, he pushed the door open and walked in.

Mesmer recognized him immediately. The two had attended many corporate management and leadership functions, policy reviews, and the like together over the years. They were corporate friendly and polite, but neither liked the other socially.

"Nathan. Nathan. Nathan. You look terrible," said Frederick with a smirk. "I hope you don't feel as badly as you look."

"Hello, Harry. What brings you into town?" sighed Mesmer.

"Well, it's not a pleasure trip, if that's what you mean. Surely, you heard the company sent me in to keep an eye on things for you."

"I didn't get the memo," Mesmer said sarcastically.

Frederick walked around the room, noting the blank walls and tables. "Where's all the flowers and cards, Nathan?"

"Here, have some candy," said Mesmer, pointing to the end table with his thumb.

"Thanks, I'll pass. Just had lunch. Have you eaten?"

"No, I'm hoping they come around pretty soon. I haven't eaten since yesterday."

"Oh, you want to laugh?" asked Frederick.

"Frankly, no," said Mesmer. "Have you seen my face?"

"Remember when you and I went on that week long retreat up in Lake Tahoe a few years ago?"

"Yeah, I remember," said Mesmer. "The company wanted to create synergy or some shit like that."

"Yeah, that's it. Remember how they gave us all matching brief cases with the company logo?"

"Yeah, why?"

"Funny thing," said Frederick. "This morning I reached down to pick up what I thought was my brief case. I dialed in my code–which incidentally is the same default code all those brief cases come with–0 0 0. Well, the lid pops open and I'm digging around inside looking for my day timer, see–and next thing I realize is the damn thing's not my brief case at all. It's yours! You never changed your default code either, did you?"

"I don't suppose I did. That was a long time ago." Mesmer didn't like the fact that Frederick was rifling through his personal belongings, and he was sure he was leading up to something.

"Well, I just thought you'd enjoy that little story, Nathan. I was so embarrassed, even though I was alone in the room. Know what I mean?"

"Yeah. Anyway, you may as well head back to New Jersey, Harry. I'm expecting to be discharged later today. No need for you to hang around."

"Mind if I pull up a chair, Nathan?"

"Make yourself at home."

Frederick dragged one of the padded chairs from against the wall over closer to Mesmer's bed and sat down. There was an awkward moment, during which neither man spoke. Mesmer sensed there was something on Frederick's mind. He didn't have long to wait to find out.

"Nathan, I need to speak to you about what happened yesterday," said Frederick.

"There's nothing to say. A few guys jumped me in the casino. I'll recover."

"You realize I've had to launch an investigation into your conduct yesterday? Not only are you accused of publicly humiliating one of your floor supervisors, you are accused of telling one of our customers to quote 'keep out of this–asshole.' I need to hear your side of this, Nathan. It's not sitting well with corporate."

"Are you telling me you guys are going to take the word of a candy-ass floor supervisor and a drunken two-bit gambler over mine?"

"I haven't heard your word yet, Nathan. Tell me what happened."

"Fuck you!" yelled Mesmer, reflexively grabbing his face which throbbed with pain. "You're not putting Nathan Mesmer on trial here. Get the fuck out of my room!"

Frederick stood. "I will leave, Nathan, but it's my duty to inform you that you are suspended pending investigation. You are prohibited from returning to the Desert Empire until such time as this investigation is completed. Between you and me, my friend, if this investigation confirms the allegations, you will be terminated for cause.

"Fuck you, you sneaky son-of-a-bitch! Nurse! Nurse! Get this son-of-a-bitch out of here! Nurse!!!

Chapter Twenty-three

Frankie Valli and the Four Seasons' "Big Girls Don't Cry" came tumbling out of the speakers. Rolly checked his watch and smiled.

At two-fifty P.M., Rolly was on his way to the baccarat room when pit clerk Melinda Fields motioned for him to come to the pit stand.

"Hey, Melinda. How's it going?"

"Hi, Rolly. Got a message here for you." She handed him a phone message from Rhonda Bethtold asking Melinda to send Rolly up to Frederick's office as soon as he comes in.

"Any idea what this is about?" asked Rolly.

"Sorry, Rolly. I just took the message."

"I suppose this Frederick guy is up in Mesmer's office?"

"Yeah, that's what Rhonda told me."

Rolly crinkled up the note and tossed it into a trash can. He looked at his watch. It was an hour too early for the whales to have announced they're coming. What the hell could Frederick want? How does Frederick even know his name? Nervous, he climbed the stairs to the mezzanine. He walked into Rhonda's office and waited until she looked up from her computer keypad.

"Hello, Rolly," she said. "Let me tell him you're here."

Collusion on the Felt

Rolly nodded. She rose and walked into Frederick's office. Rolly swished his tongue around the inside of his mouth trying to repair the extreme dryness that was setting in.

"Rolly, Mr. Frederick will see you now. Please come in."

Rolly entered. Frederick looked up and smiled. What concerned Rolly was that Rhonda pulled the door closed on her way out.

"Hello there, Hutchins," said Frederick.

"How do you do?" said Rolly.

"I do fine. Here have a seat." Frederick gestured to one of two overstuffed chairs directly in front of his desk. Rolly moved to the one nearest him.

"What can I do for you?" asked Rolly.

"Oh, I don't think there's anything you can do for me – at least not at the moment, but there is something I can do for you," said Frederick.

"Oh?" asked Rolly.

Frederick reached inside his suit jacket and pulled out what was clearly an airline ticket folder. "Won't you be needing this tomorrow?" he asked.

"That looks like an airplane ticket," said Rolly. "Why would I be needing that?"

"It's got your name on it – Roland Hutchins. That's you, isn't it?"

"That's me. But I don't have any travel plans for tomorrow."

"To Australia? By way of London?" asked Frederick.

"Australia?" Rolly broke into a nervous laugh. He had no idea what was going on, but this attention was making him feel extremely uncomfortable. "There must be some mistake," he said.

"So that I perfectly understand now, this is not your ticket? Is that right?"

"That's right. I don't know anything about it. I swear."

Frederick nodded. "If I were to tell you that—on accident, mind you—I found this ticket in Nathan Mesmer's brief case, what would be your reaction?"

"Same as it is now. I'm dumbfounded." That motherfucker, thought Rolly.

"I did take the liberty of checking with human resources and they have no record of your having requested any vacation. So that, pretty much, supports your claim. One thing does trouble me, though."

"What's that?"

"This is one-way passage."

"One way? That's ridiculous. Why would I go one-way to Australia. And why would Mesmer have my ticket? Can you tell when that was purchased?"

Frederick put on a pair of glasses and examined the ticket. "Looks like it was purchased in June of this year. June 18th. Paid for in cash." Frederick took off his glasses. "So, it's not yours, right?"

"Not mine," said Rolly.

"Well, it's certainly a mystery, that's for sure."

"Will that be all, Mr. Frederick?"

"There is one more thing, Hutchins. I'm putting out a memo in the next few minutes explaining that Nathan Mesmer has been relieved of his duties here—more or less permanently. We've placed him on suspension pending investigation of yesterday's events."

"He won't be coming back?"

"Doesn't look like it. Let the others know, please. Any rules Mesmer had concerning casino operations are still in effect. Any decisions he would have to make will now be deferred to me."

Rolly was stunned. By the time he realized it, his mouth was hanging open, and his eyes were locked in a far off gaze.

"I'm sorry to have to hit you with all this just as you come on duty, but that's what makes horse racing, as they say. Okay, that's it." Frederick rose.

Rolly rose slowly. His mind was on overload, processing data, sorting through decisions that would have to be made or confirmed quickly.

"Are you all right, Hutchins?" asked Frederick.

"Yeah. Yeah, I'm okay. Just totally lost on that Australia ticket. I hope there's a good explanation for that," said Rolly. "Imagine how you'd feel if someone showed you a ticket to someplace like Australia—one way—with your name on it. It blows your mind."

"I can certainly understand that," said Frederick. "Well, have a good shift."

"Yeah. Thanks." Rolly opened the door and walked zombie-like to the baccarat pit. The first phone call from Archie Yen and company was due in forty-five minutes. As the magnitude of what just occurred settled in, Rolly began to fume. What did that one-way ticket to Australia mean? Why was it in Mesmer's brief case? Was it supposed to be a gift tomorrow? Would he actually present him with a ticket to Australia as a gift for COF? Why just Rolly? What about Beatrice? The ticket was bought in June. Why didn't he buy one for Beatrice, too? Even today, at the hospital, if he had the slightest suspicion he would not be discharged today, wouldn't he say something like "Oh, by the way, pack your bags, you're going to Australia tomorrow morning – one way, no less."

Something was terribly wrong. How could Mesmer use that ticket to his advantage? There's the key. How could Mesmer benefit by Rolly flying off to Australia? Rolly arrived at the baccarat pit. He told Harry Fetters to pass the word that Mesmer no longer had authority at the Desert Empire. He couldn't help wondering how Mesmer felt about that on this, of all days.

In many corners of the Desert Empire, and indeed, in many corners of the city of Las Vegas, anticipation, the likes of which had never before been experienced, was churning in the hearts and minds of the COF team. In just a matter of minutes, the sequence of events outlined a week ago would be triggered by a seeming routine incoming telephone call. Within the Empire, lone, anonymous COF partners tried desperately to focus on the tasks at hand, only to find themselves driven to incessant clock watching. Like thespians drilling lines before an entrance, they mentally rehearsed their assignments, replayed Rolly's expectations, and attempted to project their lives twenty-four hours into the future. Those outside the Empire, still in their homes, their cars, or other places of employment, paced, stared, and tracked the time. It was now four PM.

The cellular phone emitted its programmed melody. Charlie Palermo saved the document he was typing in his word processor and reached into the pocket of his suit jacket, draped over the back of his chair.

"Palermo," he said.

"Listen carefully," began the nervous sounding voice of a man. "I will only say this once. Alicia is safe…"

"Who is this?" demanded Palermo, fear quickly evident in his voice.

"… but whether or not you see her again depends totally on you," the voice continued.

"Listen here, you bastard, if you so much as touch one … "

"All right, asshole, have it your way." Click.

"Hello! Hello! Jesus Christ! Hello!" Palermo jumped up from his seat. His screaming bled through the glass walls isolating his office from the surveillance agents' area. The Colonel rotated his chair around to investigate. He observed his boss standing and yelling into his cellular. The look on Palermo's face was horrific. The Colonel slapped his hand on the intercom and yelled, "CP, what's wrong?"

Nearly out of breath, Palermo hit the intercom button in his office. "I just got a call…" His cellular rang again. "Palermo!" he shouted in desperation.

"Last chance," threatened the same quivering voice.

"Go on," pleaded Palermo, nearly hyperventilating. "Go on."

"First, you are being monitored. Second, if you even think of getting law enforcement involved, pretty Alicia will need extensive reconstructive surgery in order to look even hideous. Do you understand?"

"What is it you want?" panted Palermo.

"*Do you understand?*" shouted the voice.

"*Yes! Yes*, I understand! Now, what is it you want?" gasped Palermo, clutching the back of his head.

By this time, the Colonel had climbed the three steps to Palermo's elevated office and opened the door. He stood at the entrance, watching and listening.

"Our demands are meager," the voice said, "Bring five-thousand dollars in small bills to the Las Vegas Speedway. Make certain you're alone."

Palermo began scribbling on a notepad.

"At the speedway entrance, off of I-15, there is a phone booth. Look in the phone book on the same page as your name for further instructions." Click.

"Hello! Son-of-a-bitch!"

"What can I do?" asked the Colonel, somberly.

"They've got my daughter," choked Palermo. "I've got to get to the bank before they close."

"Are you sure someone's got her?" asked the Colonel.

The possibility of a lie had evaded Palermo. He immediately dialed his home number. The phone rang until the answering machine picked up. He hung up. "No one's home," he said. "She's usually home by this time. I can't take any chances."

"Do you want me to call your wife at work or the police?"

"No! Don't call anyone, please," ordered Palermo. "I've got to handle this."

"Whatever you say, CP."

As Palermo started for the door, he stopped and turned to the Colonel. "Colonel, call Mesmer's office and tell Rhonda to let the corporate guy know I had to leave on a personal emergency. Under no conditions do you tell them what has happened. Okay?"

"Sure. Sure."

"And, Colonel. Call me on my cell if you need anything."

"Don't worry about here, CP. Take care of your kid."

With that Palermo was gone. It was now four-ten PM.

Down in the casino, the COF-involved employees who had been scrupulously monitoring the time, looked up in virtual unison toward the hosts' office. Those who were able, glimpsed through the open door in time to see Sue Min answer the telephone. The reality of COF in motion sent tingling sensations up, down and through their central nervous systems.

Sal could barely concentrate. Following his look toward the hosts' office, his fingers became like thick stumps, unable to grasp or hold on to each successive top card. The blood was rushing through his body so fast that perspiration was escaping at his temples and above his upper lip. The realization that nothing could or would stop COF was overwhelming to him and to his anonymous fellow confidants.

In the Baccarat Room, only one table was active with two Middle Easterners betting a thousand dollars a hand. Paul Hawkins tended to the dealing chores with Rolly standing behind him, unwrapping fresh decks of cards in preparation for the next shoe. After checking his watch, Rolly looked up and across the casino in time to see Sue Min leave the hosts' office, make the turn, and climb the carpeted stairs to the mezzanine. He smiled confidently to himself. H.R. Frederick was about to learn that the Desert Empire was expecting company.

On the sixth floor of the University Medical Center, Doctor Syd Jacoby checked in at the nurses' station to begin his late afternoon rounds. He requested the charts of the patients in the east wing and began perusing them.

"How's patient Mesmer been responding to the medication?"

"It's apparently working well. He had a visitor earlier today and it ended up in a screaming tirade. We had to ask the visitor to leave."

"Well, maybe we'll be able to send him home tomorrow ... "

"He won't like that, doctor."

"Why is that?"

"I believe he's counting on you releasing him this evening. For some reason, he's insistent on being home tonight."

"All right, I'll check on him now, and we'll see what we can do."

Doctor Jacoby picked up the chart and headed for room 621. He opened the door and found the bed empty. The bathroom door was closed and its light was on, so the doctor sat on the edge of the bed to await his patient.

The late model black Lexus swerved into the Wells Fargo parking lot on Maryland Parkway and screeched to a stop. Charlie Palermo slammed the door, chirped the lock, and ran into the bank. He hurried to the customer service stand and scribbled his needs on a savings withdrawal slip. With only a few minutes before the bank was to close, he took his place in a line with three other people. He looked at his watch. It was four-twenty PM.

Sue Min made her way across the casino. She placed her hand on the gold railing and climbed the plush steps to the baccarat room. She walked directly over to Harry Fetters, who had, since the untimely death of Art Kaiser, assumed the role of Baccarat Shift Manager.

"Hello, Sue Min," Harry said smiling. "Welcome to our humble abode."

"The new guy sent me down, Harry. A few minutes ago I got a call from Archie Yen who told me he and his group are coming in tonight for some high stakes action. He said they wanted to 'even the score' from last time, if you know what I mean."

"Oh, here we go," said Fetters. "It was starting out to be a nice quiet little shift, too. What time we are expecting them?"

"Yen said they'd be in around seven-thirty PM. They only have a few hours in town and they want food service in the Baccarat Room."

"I'll put the order in right away. Do they want to eat as soon as they get here?"

"It'll be seven-thirty, Harry. It's a good bet they'll be hungry."

"Just asking," he smiled.

"By the way," Sue Min said, "Mr. Frederick said to take very good care of them and that he leaves them in your capable hands. He's starting to come down with jet lag and is looking forward to retiring early tonight."

"They're in the best of hands," said Fetters. "Between Rolly and me–we'll see to it they go home broke, too. Tell that to Mr. Frederick."

Rolly, overhearing the conversation, looked up and smiled. He gave Sue Min a thumbs up, which she happily returned.

Palermo filed the thick envelope of bills in his inside pocket and fired up the Lexus. He fastened his safety belt and pointed the hood ornament north to the Las Vegas Speedway. With drive-time traffic flooding the interstate, it would take him over an hour to get there.

Doctor Jacoby looked at his watch. He'd been sitting on Mesmer's bed for some eight minutes and hadn't heard a sound from the bathroom. He rose and knocked on the bathroom door. There was no response. Fearing his patient was hurt or otherwise incapacitated, he opened the door. The bathroom was empty. There was no sign of Mesmer. He opened the patient's clothing cabinet and sure enough, his clothes were gone. Mesmer had disappeared.

Sal had watched as Sue Min walked down the stairs of the mezzanine and made the trek across the casino to the baccarat room. He found it terribly difficult to keep his mind on his game. His players were becoming increasingly wary of his continual looking away. While he was watching Sue Min talk with Harry Fetters, he missed a player's signal for an additional card.

"Hey, Sal," the player said. "Got a minute?"

"What's that?" asked Sal.

"I want another card," said the player. "What's distracting you?"

Stan Reno overheard the exchange and walked over to the table. He stood to Sal's left and observed.

"I'm sorry," Sal said. "I've got something on my mind. It won't happen again."

"Something bugging you, kid?" asked Reno with a hint of a wink.

"Nothing really, Stan. I'll be fine."

"Try to stay in the game, okay?"

"Sure, Stan," said Sal. As he scooped up the cards, he glanced at his watch. It was four-fifty-five PM. Sal remembered that Queck's call was due in now.

At that instant, the secretary from the hosts' office picked up the phone. After a few seconds, she hurried outside the office and visually scanned the casino for Sue Min. Seeing her in the Baccarat Room, she walked briskly toward that location. Sue Min saw her coming and excused herself from Harry Fetters.

The two met mid-way. "Sue Min, there's a call for you. It's Cyril Queck's people."

Sue Min hurried back to her office and picked up the phone.

During his shuffle, Sal eyeballed Rolly across the room. The big guy had that familiar smirk. They were now knee-deep in COF.

Rhonda Bethtold was turning off her computer and collecting her things when the phone rang.

"Desert Empire, Mr. Frederick's office. Certainly. Please hold." She pressed the phone intercom to H.R.'s office. "Mr. Frederick, it's UMC. They need to speak with you."

"H.R. Frederick."

"Mr. Frederick, this is Pauline Sheedy at UMC. Doctor Jacoby asked me to notify you that Nathan Mesmer has disappeared from the hospital."

"What do you mean disappeared?"

"Before the doctor could evaluate him, Mr. Mesmer removed his IV's, dressed himself and, somehow, sneaked out of the hospital without any of us seeing him."

"Well, Ms. Sheedy, I appreciate your call, but Nathan Mesmer's a big boy. I can't explain why he would have done that, but then again, all of us do things that are inexplicable. If I should hear from him, which I doubt, I'll ask that he contact you at the hospital."

"We can't be responsible for his well being, Mr. Frederick."

"Nor can I, Ms. Sheedy. Thank you." Frederick terminated the call. He took a deep breath. What the hell is this guy up to? he wondered.

At precisely five PM., Curtis Lately, a sound technician from the production department, hit the play button on the house digital audio system, and ratcheted up the volume three notches. Frankie Valli and the Four Seasons' *"Big Girls Don't Cry"* came tumbling out of the speakers. Rolly checked his watch and smiled.

The driver of the white Dodge Intrepid, traveling south on state route ninety-five, pressed on the brake, slowing the car from sixty miles per hour to twenty-five as the vehicle approached the tiny community of Searchlight, Nevada.

"Ever ride down through here before?" he asked.

"No, I don't think so," said his female passenger. "Why, Father?"

"They love to get speeders coming through here," he said. "The town's so small and it pops up out of nowhere, a lot of times people sail through here at highway speeds."

Alicia looked at her watch. It was a little after five PM.

"We're almost there," he said. "Are you getting hungry?"

"A little," she said. "You're sure my folks know where I am, Father?"

He looked at her and laughed. "Are you insinuating I would lie to you, Alicia?"

"No, but…"

"No buts about it. I told you, I asked your principal to recommend one of her brightest students and she didn't hesitate to mention your name. I called your father at work and ran it by him. He said it was okay with him if it was okay with you. I'll have you back before eleven. So quit worrying. What do you say we stop for a quick sandwich at that truck stop up ahead?"

"Okay," she said. "So tell me about this guy I'll be reading to. What's his story?"

"We can discuss that while we eat. There's really not a whole lot to say about him. I do know that you'll like him—and he'll like you."

What's not to like, he thought? Alicia was a very attractive young lady with an incredible build, particularly for a fourteen-year old. She seemed very mature for her age. They didn't make fourteen-year olds like this when I was growing up, he thought.

They pulled into what appeared to be the only major business in the town of Searchlight, a dinky little gas station with a short order counter. He got a kick out of the reaction he was getting from people who actually believed he was a Catholic priest. Their deference to him almost made him feel deferential. On the way into the store, he looked at his watch, wondering how Alicia's old man was doing. Most likely he was beside himself with worry and fear. God bless him, he thought.

"So how do you propose we handle this Mr. Queck along with the other group that's coming in? Sounds like an immense volume of action between the two."

"Well, Mr. Frederick," said Sue Min. "We do have room in the high roller salon to accommodate both groups, actually. So as long as each group doesn't mind being accompanied by the other, perhaps they can play at the same table. That way, Rolly Hutchins can deal to all of them."

"Who?" asked Frederick.

"Rolly Hutchins," she repeated. "Of course, we'll need your permission to allow him to deal. He was promoted to floor supervisor since these groups were last here."

"Why Hutchins?" asked Frederick. His interest seemed more than passing.

"He happens to be their lucky dealer," said Sue Min, smiling. "Chinese people are very superstitious, as I mentioned about Mr. Queck. Once they have a good luck charm, they must always have it."

"Hutchins, huh?" reflected Frederick. "That's interesting."

"Why is that interesting," asked Sue Min.

"Just something that happened earlier. It's not important," said Frederick, waving his hand.

"I hope I'm not prying," said Sue Min, "but what happened earlier?"

"It doesn't concern you or the hosts' office, Ms. Wong," said Frederick.

Sue Min didn't feel comfortable with this "unknown" still floating in the air. She hoped perhaps Rolly could fill her in. She also felt it important to let Rolly know that Frederick appears a bit suspicious.

"All right then, Ms. Wong, I trust you'll handle all the details and coordinate with Fetters on this?"

"Absolutely, sir. With pleasure."

"What is the policy here with regard to notifying the president when certain amounts of money are at stake?"

"Well, you are the policy maker, Mr. Frederick. It is whatever you wish it to be."

"Please don't patronize me, Ms. Wong. What was Mesmer's policy?"

"Baccarat shift managers may accept cumulative table wagers up to one-million dollars. Cumulative wagering above one-million must be approved, each round, by the property president. Also, whenever the baccarat bank wins or loses two million dollars or more on one hand, the president must be notified and kept abreast of the situation."

"Pretty hands-on stuff, huh?"

"Mr. Mesmer did prefer to remain in control. Delegation from him did not come easily," said Sue Min.

"Well," Frederick said as he massaged his chin, "based on what you've told me about our guests, we can expect extremely high wagers tonight – from both groups. I know I'll never be able to stay awake. So for tonight, I will modify the policy as follows – perhaps you should jot this down."

Sue Min gave him a look. It wasn't the first time today he inferred by his actions that he viewed her as administrative help. It rubbed her the wrong way. Reluctantly, she picked up a pen and tablet from his desk. "I'm ready for your *dictation*," she said, smugly.

"Effective this date," Frederick said, "and continuing until further notice, the Baccarat Shift Manager has unconditional authority to accept cumulative table wagers up to three million dollars per baccarat hand. Wagers beyond this amount must be pre-approved by the property president or person acting as property president. There, how does that sound?"

"It sounds good, Mr. Frederick."

"You sound tentative, Ms. Wong."

"Well, I know these players. They like to let winnings ride. They will be at the limit in two or three hands."

"I see," said Frederick. "In that case, add the following: The Baccarat Shift Manager may, without fear of rebuke, accept 'let it ride' bets up to a limit of, what do you think – fifteen million?"

"Can we go with twenty?"

"Twenty it is," said Frederick. "Excellent, now type that up and...."

"Mister Frederick!"

"Excuse me?"

"Must I remind you that I am a vice-president here. Your demeaning treatment of me, apparently because I'm a woman, is insulting–with all due respect."

Frederick just glared at her. His expression slowly turned from one of surprise to one of admiration. "I'll sign the pen and ink copy, Ms. Wong. And I apologize for my obvious indiscretion. It won't happen again."

He signed the paper and watched her leave. He stretched and yawned. It had been a very long day. He looked at his watch. It was five-forty-five P.M., or eight-forty-five P.M., *his* time. He'd been awake since ten o'clock last night, preparing for his red-eye from New Jersey. Exhausted, he turned off the light in his office and locked the door. Out on the mezzanine, he took the elevator to his suite on the twenty-seventh floor. He wasn't in the room five minutes before he was snoring.

Palermo saw the motor speedway up ahead on the horizon. He sneaked a look at the scrap of paper. The phone booth would be at the entrance of the speedway, off Interstate Fifteen. As the entrance came into view, he could see for acres and acres the absence of any vehicles. He signaled his right turn, pulled onto the exit ramp, and left the highway. At the stop sign, he looked to his right. In the distance he saw the booth. In a burst of acceleration, he headed straight for it. When he reached the booth, he hurried inside, lifted the tattered phone book onto the shelf, and immediately tore it open more than halfway. He found the P's. As he turned to the second page of P's, a folded typewritten note slid out of the book onto the floor. He bent down and snatched it. It read: *We're still watching you. So far, so good. One more stop. Continue driving north to St. George, Utah. Cross the border. Tourist Information Center. Phone booth. Phone book. P's.*

"Goddamn it!" Palermo muttered through his teeth. *"Bastards!"*

The hot water felt wonderful as long as it pounded against his back. The face was still too tender, sensitive, and bruised to withstand the beating of the exhilarating shower. Nathan Mesmer stood, with a white-knuckle grip on the metal bar, yielding to the therapeutic soaking. This was the feeling he'd craved the entire taxi ride from the hospital. It also gave him cessation during which he could sort through the collection of possible tactics that had amassed in his head, since his apparent terminal suspension from the Desert Empire.

One thing was certain, he needed to act, and he needed to act now. He'd already confirmed that COF was underway, having anonymously called the surveillance room and been told by Tamhagen that Palermo would be unavailable the rest of the evening. Poor sap was undoubtedly worried stiff right about now, Mesmer thought. If his calculations were correct, he supposed Palermo was on his way to St. George at this moment with a rapid heartbeat and five G's in small bills. Fuck him.

So Hutchins is going through with COF? Surely word is out about my suspension, Mesmer speculated. What's Hutchins really going to do with all that money? Mesmer snarled at the obvious response. He didn't believe for an instant that Hutchins would bury Mesmer's share in the footlocker. The piece of shit underestimates his foe, Mesmer muttered to himself. That's a costly error.

He finished showering, dried himself off, and slipped into his favorite silk smoking jacket and slippers. He felt like pouring himself a drink, but decided against dulling his wits while he laid out his plans to intercept the money and settle a score with a certain traitorous baccarat floor supervisor.

The Intrepid made the left turn off of state route ninety-five, onto the four-lane highway leading to Laughlin, Nevada. The imposter padre, alias Father Coquet, and his clueless hostage were hitting it off, in a priest-student sort of way. Alicia was full of questions and Father Fraud was having to do some fancy brain footwork to keep the charade credible. The premise under which he successfully lured her from the front of her school was that he was new to the Holy Rosary parish. He had asked another student to point her out to him, after showing the student Alicia's photograph. He told Alicia he came from Laughlin where a former parishioner, up in years and blind from diabetes, enjoyed having someone read to him. And since it was this man's birthday, the priest asked the school principal to recommend a bright student who may be willing. He told Alicia the principal recommended her. It sounded legit and he *was* wearing the priestly collar. Alicia fell for it easily.

"You're kind of young to be a priest, aren't you, Father Coquet?" Alicia asked.

"Well, I'm older than I look, Alicia. I've always looked younger than my years."

"With me, it's the other way around," she said. "People always think I'm older than I really am."

He laughed. "That's fine when you're young," he said, "but later, that's not such an asset."

"How long ago were you ordained?" she asked.

"It's only been a couple of years," he said.

"Was it tough?"

"Was what tough?"

"Giving up everything and going through what you went through to be a priest."

Fortunately, he had been raised Catholic, himself, so he was able to comfortably field these questions. "It's never tough to do God's work," he said. "It's a work of love."

"You're a nice priest," said Alicia. "I'm glad we got you at the parish."

"Thank you," he said smiling.

They drove in silence for a few minutes, then Alicia hit him with it.

"Father, do you have to be in a confessional to do confession?" she asked.

"No … not really," he said. "There's nothing magical about the confessional. It's just a convenient way to have both privacy and a sense of sacrament." He didn't know where those words came from, but he was proud of his response.

"Could I go to confession to you now?" she asked.

"What–here?"

"Sure."

There was a situation he had not anticipated. This was getting way too serious now, he thought. Though his religious nature had diminished in recent years, the upbringing was still indelibly etched in his being. No telling what a fourteen year old girl is going to confess in this day and age, he thought. But, then again, how could he refuse?

"Is that something you want to do?" he asked.

"Yeah, it's been a while for me and this would be a good opportunity to clear the slate."

"Is there a lot on that slate?" he asked.

"Are we already into the confession?" asked Alicia.

"Not yet," he said quickly. "We're still in conversation."

"I don't have a lot—but what I do have is pretty heavy," she said.

"I'll tell you what," he said, stalling. "Right now, I'm driving outside my parish district. To hear your confession here may not be altogether sanctioned. Why don't we wait until we're on the way back and we re-enter the district?"

"Okay," she said.

The pretend priest let out a silent sigh of relief. But his masculine curiosity was peaking and he anticipated the return trip with mixed emotions.

Chapter Twenty-four

Tamhagen responded to a seasoned premonition.
He dialed the security booth in the casino.

As Charlie Palermo continued his heart-pounding journey north on Interstate Fifteen to St. George, Utah, his daughter and her priest impersonator were just descending the long, steep hill leading to the southern Nevada border town of Laughlin, situated on the Colorado River, on the Nevada side of Bullhead City, Arizona.

Back in Las Vegas, the exhausted H.R. Frederick, wrapped in sheets and blankets to neutralize the effects of the intentionally low thermostat setting, was lost in deep, satisfying sleep.

Downstairs of the Desert Empire, in the basement's heart of the house, Francisco Mercado checked his watch. It was six-forty-three PM. The room service captain sauntered over to the dispatch desk to check the incoming orders. None had yet been received from the surveillance department. He would check back in about ten minutes.

Upstairs, in the thick of anticipation, Rolly talked with Harry Fetters regarding their procedures for dealing with the heavy action that would, very soon, befall the Empire. Fetters was not part of COF, one of Rolly's few unforeseeable regrets. When Rolly had been recruiting for COF, Arthur Kaiser, then Baccarat Shift Manager, was his logical target and an easy mark. Fetters had only been a supervisor but of long standing with the company. It was Kaiser's death and Mesmer's subsequent appointment of Fetters, a seniority-dictated move to avoid undue attention, that forced a rethinking of the disabling of surveillance. It wasn't as though Rolly had never considered Fetters for involvement. He had. But during his customary initial talks with extended feelers, Rolly concluded Fetters didn't have the bravado needed to challenge any system. Further attempts with him could have been COF's death knell.

Now sneaking those pre-arranged shoes into the game tonight without Fetters' knowledge was likely the most significant challenge facing COF. One sloppy move; a single slip would be catastrophic. Fetters, after all, was still operating in the world of normality.

Upstairs in the surveillance room, the Colonel's mind played pingpong with casino observation and the crisis terrorizing his boss. He and Palermo had a very close relationship. In fact, the Colonel idolized him. He prayed all would be resolved with the safe return of Alicia. He was also concerned about being alone for the remainder of swing shift. Palermo's absence could be tolerated, provided the action remained at its current level.

But, the Colonel couldn't help wondering why Sue Min Wong had made so many trips across the casino floor to baccarat, including two trips to the corporate guy's office, all within a very short time span. That level of host-casino-management interaction usually preceded the arrival of heavy action. And it's always followed up with a call to Palermo, alerting surveillance of the impending need for higher alert. No such call had been placed.

Trusting his polished judgment, the Colonel decided to initiate an inquiry. He picked up the phone and called the hosts' office.

"This is Sue Min," she said.

"Sue Min, this is Tamhagen, upstairs."

"Yes, Ralph."

"Just curious. We got anything cooking for tonight? I noticed you made quite a few trips on the floor a little while ago."

"In fact, we do," she said. "I'm glad you called. We've got very heavy baccarat action due in within the hour or so. Two groups. Archie Yen and the Queck group."

"Why weren't we notified?"

"Didn't Mr. Frederick call Charlie?" she asked, knowing full well Palermo was long gone from the building.

"We got no call," said the Colonel. "And that irritates me."

"I'm sorry, why is that?" she asked.

"Frederick knows Palermo's off property with a personal emergency. That leaves me up here alone. As soon as he knew we had action coming in, the man should have called me. Now, I've got to bring in one of the other agents to assist, and I've got damn little time to do it."

Immediately Wong realized a serious problem. COF hadn't counted on overtaking *two* surveillance agents. This would make things much more difficult. She quickly decided to pull rank.

"Just a moment Ralph," she said, her tone cooling. "You're talking overtime. All overtime has to be pre-approved by department heads or executive management…"

"With all due respect, Sue Min…."

"Please don't argue with me, Ralph. As a member of the executive management team and in the absence of our acting president who will not be disturbed, I must deny your request for overtime authorization."

"You've got to be joking," said the Colonel, exasperated. "I can't handle everything alone up here with that kind of action going on."

"Well, you'll have to," she said. "Make do. Cover the heavy action and concentrate less on the small stuff. That's how we'll handle it."

"What if I call Charlie on his cell and…"

"You do and you'll be in violation of a direct order."

Tamhagen was savvy enough to know he was wobbling on thin ice. The last thing he wanted was to give them a reason to reevaluate his employment. "As you wish," he said bowing. "I'll handle it your way."

"Thank you, Ralph. Is there anything else I can help you with?"

"Nope."

"Again, I'm sorry we failed to notify you. It was obviously a breakdown in communication with Mr. Frederick."

"Yeah. Okay," the Colonel said, hearing himself sound beaten. "Thanks."

He looked at the clock. It told him what his stomach already knew–six-fifty-nine–time to order dinner. He picked up the phone and dialed the four-digit extension for room service. He knew it by heart.

"Room Service," said the dispatcher, Ellie O'Donnell. "May I help you?"

As he placed his usual order: Cheeseburger, onion rings, small salad with ranch dressing and an orange juice, he observed four men who appeared to be in their mid to late twenties, dressed in cowboy hats, shirts and jeans, enter the pit. They looked to the Colonel to be feeling little pain as they approached a closed blackjack table with their arms around one another's necks.

They signaled for Stan Reno and asked if he could open up the game for them; they wanted to play all seven spots. At that moment Chris Mooney approached Reno for a table assignment.

"Go ahead and open this game," said Reno. "These guys are covering all seven spaces."

"Evening, gentlemen," said Mooney. "While I prepare the shoe, would you like a cocktail server?"

"We'd like four of 'em," joked the tallest, "about yo big," he held his hands out in front of his chest. The others laughed and voiced their liquored agreement.

"Cocktails," Mooney called out over his shoulder.

"We have first class availability tomorrow morning on flight three departing Las Vegas McCarran at nine-fifteen AM.," the Hawaiian Airlines reservationist said, "arriving Honolulu at three-forty PM.

"Book it," said Mesmer.

"And your return date?"

"One way," he said.

"All right, Mr. Mesmer, "I'll need your credit card to secure this seat for you."

"Right," he said, reaching for his wallet. "What time do I need to be at the airport?"

"For a nine-fifteen AM. departure, we would recommend arriving around eight o'clock," she said.

"Fine," said Mesmer. "Here's my American Express number … "

The Desert Empire's north tower parking garage elevator door opened on the first floor. Nappa Jackson, dressed in a black dress shirt and black slacks exited. He looked at his watch. Seven PM. He cocked his head and smiled. His energized step reflected the anticipation within. He had five minutes to join his command control center crew outside Surveillance. He would just make it.

Meanwhile, Francisco Mercado, wearing his black, duty-worn waist jacket and black bow tie paced nervously outside the room service kitchen. He had seen Ralph Tamhagen's dinner order posted on the order board moments after it was received. Shortly, he'd be heading upstairs to deliver his contribution to COF.

Upstairs, Tamhagen, still simmering from his bout with Sue Min, sat glued to monitor nine. The four cowboys who had commandeered BJ three hadn't stopped laughing and carrying on since they sat down. And they were putting away the liquor. Sandy Mills, the cocktail server, had made several lucrative trips to the group already and appeared to delight in the amorous attention the boys lavished on her. The dealer, Mooney, wasn't doing badly either. Tokes were streaming his way. Tamhagen responded to a seasoned premonition. He dialed the security booth in the casino.

"Security."

"Tamhagen, upstairs."

"Yeah."

"Keep an eye on BJ three. Alcohol's flowing freely. Not sure those boys can handle it."

"Got it."

Sporting plate number Mpire 3, the stretch limo pulled up in front. Doorman, Justo Gustav approached and opened the two rear doors. Archie Yen was the first to emerge, followed by his four fellow countrymen. The last and eldest, Mr. Nim, required assistance which Gustav provided. Gustav then reached inside his jacket to retrieve his walkie-talkie. He called for Sue Min to meet the gentlemen just inside the front doors.

Immediately after they stepped foot onto the glorious marble foyer, Sue Min, her make-up refreshed and her smile blazing, glided up to them and extended her hand in a warm welcome. It made for a great show.

She escorted them to the Baccarat Room, moving slowly to accommodate the aged Mr. Nim's lack of agility. Harry Fetters was most gracious, greeting them at the podium. Rolly remained conspicuously inconspicuous, choosing instead to remain standing at the rear of the well-appointed room.

Sue Min asked Fetters to join her out of earshot of the group.

"Has their dinner been ordered?"

"I did that as soon as you told me," said Harry.

"Excellent. I know they are hungry. Let's have room service deliver immediately," she said.

"Will do," he began to leave.

"Another thing," she stopped him. "Mr. Yen wants Hutchins to deal, as always."

"What about Queck?" asked Fetters. "He always wants Rolly, too."

"I'm going to ask both groups if they will play at the same table – up in the salon – once Mr. Queck arrives."

"What if they don't want to?" asked Harry.

She smiled her bright smile. "Leave that to me," she said, seductively.

Fetters shrugged. He knew if it can be done, Sue Min can do it.

"Mr. Frederick said it's okay for Rolly to deal." she confirmed.

"Fine by me," he said.

"Incidentally," she said as she reached into her jacket pocket and retrieved the signed policy amendments, "Frederick signed these revised policies giving you authority to accept much larger wagers tonight. He really doesn't want to be disturbed," she said.

"You don't have to tell me twice," he said with a grin, placing the folded paper in his jacket pocket.

"Okay, let's eat then," she said.

Francisco Mercado felt his right chest. The stun gun was in place. He set Tamhagen's freshly prepared meal onto an equally freshly prepared room service table. The starched white cloth extended to just above the table's wheels. On the second shelf, hidden beneath a food warming cover were a coil of rope, a box cutter, a roll of silver-gray duct tape, and several large, folded napkins. He placed another food warming cover over Tamhagen's meal. He'd be heading upstairs momentarily.

On the other side of the room service hallway, several servers busily prepared the Archie Yen dinner service for five. It was important that all of them, including Francisco, leave at exactly the same time. Francisco checked the time, it was seven-thirty-eight PM.

Upstairs, in the back hallway around the corner from surveillance, Nappa waited with his pair of assistants. None of the three had seen each other before last week's meeting. And this was the first time they had actually met. Nappa, the other two knew from Rolly's meeting, was the boss. Nappa learned they wanted to be called Jesse and Marv, acquaintances of Rolly's, but neither worked at the Empire. They preferred their actual identities remain confidential. Nappa, taking their cue, told them to call him chief. He always liked the sound of that.

The hallway outside Surveillance received little employee traffic. But when someone did walk by, the three huddled and spoke quiet babble. No one ever questioned anyone in back of the house as long as they looked like they knew what they were doing. Nappa checked the time. "We roll in about five," he whispered. The two nodded.

Bill Haley and the Comets' *"Rock Around the Clock"* exploded from the sound system. The cowboys wasted no time keeping rhythm with their hands on the padded rim of the blackjack table, singing along: *"One, two, three o'clock, four o'clock rock! ... "*

Players at nearby tables looked at them and laughed. They'd been having a terrific time since they'd arrived. Others throughout the casino began mouthing the rock 'n roll classic.

Downstairs, the Yen dinner crew began pushing their tables toward the exclusive baccarat elevator. Francisco Mercado began pushing the Tamhagen meal toward the regular service elevator.

Upstairs, Rolly had removed his suit jacket and necktie and donned a dealer's string tie. He'd been shuffling the eight fresh decks of cards given him by Harry Fetters and was now offering the horizontal stack to Mr. Nim, the group's good luck charm for a cut. Mr. Nim accepted the red plastic cut card, dragged it back and forth quickly across the felt, and inserted it about three inches from the rear of the stack.

Rolly thanked him and moved the rear selection of cards at the point of the cut, to the front of the stack. He tapped the stack against the side of the empty shoe to tightly pack the cards, then lifted the stack with both hands, and fitted them into the shoe.

As if to punctuate the action, the saxophone riff from Neil Sedaka's *"Calendar Girl"* sounded the COF trigger.

At that instant the elevator door opened at the rear of the baccarat room, and the food servers wheeled the three tables toward the baccarat table.

The service elevator opened on the second floor, just a short distance from the surveillance room. Francisco pushed the table out into the hallway.

In Baccarat, the lead server gave the room service bill to Harry Fetters. Fetters took it to the podium and placed it under the light. He reached into his inside pocket for his glasses.

"March – I'm gonna march you down the aisle; April you're the Easter Bunny when you smile! Yeah, Yeah…!"

Francisco pounded on the surveillance room door. The Colonel rose to answer.

Rolly reached under the tablecloth of the room service table nearest him and grabbed one of the pre-made shoes. He made certain it was one with the red cards, like the one he'd just prepared. At the same time, he placed the freshly shuffled shoe in its place and let the tablecloth fall.

At the podium, Fetters pulled out his pen and signed off on the meal comp. He carried it over to the lead waiter and handed it to him.

The Colonel opened the door.

"Room service," said Francisco, standing in front of the table. And immediately, he jabbed the stun gun into the Colonel's waist area. The big man gasped with pain, inhaled a vocal scream, and toppled like a sack of flour.

Hearing the noise, Nappa and his team rounded the corner and infiltrated the room. Francisco dragged the Colonel behind the open door, hurried into the hall and quickly pushed the dinner table inside. He slammed the door closed and locked it.

He reached under the tablecloth to the second shelf and retrieved his stored materials.

Behind him Jesse and Marv were ejecting videotapes from the VCRs and punching out the record safety tabs. For good measure, they were yanking the video- tape out of the cassettes and tossing them all in a conveniently placed trash barrel.

The Archie Yen group was positioned around the huge baccarat table. The cigarettes were lit and dangling. Rolly slid the first three cards, face down, from the bogus shoe and placed them in the discard pile. Mr. Nim opened the game with a wager of a thousand dollars on Player. To Nim's left, sat Archie Yen, holding a pencil against a baccarat score pad. Very lightly printed on the score pad in lead pencil, virtually invisible at any distance to the naked eye, was the sequence of winning spots each shoe was designed to serve. The sequence for each shoe was identical, so it didn't matter which shoe they were playing with. The strategy to avoid suspicion was for the Yen group to lose their first four wagers, win one, and lose two more to each one they won, until they began playing with Cyril Queck.

"Here's the first pitch," announced Nappa from his perch at the surveillance console. "The ball game is underway!"

Behind him, on the aisle floor, Francisco was pulling a stretch of duct tape off the roll and affixing it to the Colonel's mouth. Marv, at the Colonel's feet, was banding them together with rope. Jessie tied a square knot, securing a large linen napkin as a blindfold. They tied his hands behind him with rope, trimming it with the box cutter. And as Rolly raked in the first win for the house, they dragged the Colonel across the floor and stowed him in the rear of the walk-in storage closet.

At seven-fifty-seven PM., Harry Fetters, alive and well in his world of normality, smiled to himself. The Desert Empire was a thousand dollars richer.

Chapter Twenty-five

The siren was a nice touch. It masked the sounds of five men laughing themselves silly behind those dark, tinted windows.

Alicia, mostly over her initial discomfort when she and Father Coquet first arrived, had settled in to her task of reading to the elderly blind man introduced to her as Mr. Bogovitch. The old man inexplicably resided in a tiny, musty guestroom at the aging Riverside Hotel and Casino at the foot of Laughlin's single street gambling oasis. His story of choice – Edgar Allen Poe's short story: *"The Tell Tale Heart."*

According to Father Coquet, Bogovitch was allegedly in his mid-seventies and sightless for the past fifteen years. He lay on the bed on top of the bedspread, his head propped up on two pillows, wearing large, dark sunglasses. Alicia, herself a Poe aficionado, welcomed this particular selection, both because she liked the story and because the story was relatively short. Across the room, Father Coquet sat close to the television with the volume low, watching the season opener of *Monday Night Football*.

Several hundred miles to the north, an exhausted Charlie Palermo exited off Interstate Fifteen and entered the city of St. George, Utah. As darkness began to settle in the Pacific West, Palermo ventured northeast in search of the tourist information center and its phone booth. He was certain his frightful journey was nearing its end. As long as Alicia is all right, the return trip to Vegas would be a breeze. He passed a green highway information sign promising the tourist information center in five miles. He pressed down on the accelerator and the Lexus lunged forward with determination.

His reservation made for a one-way escape to Honolulu, Nathan Mesmer set about packing his belongings, at least those he wished to take with him. There would be plenty of money for a new wardrobe, so he could afford to be very selective. A single suitcase for personal items was his self-imposed allocation.

He checked his watch. Eight-oh-five PM. Cyril Queck would have arrived just moments ago at the Empire. Mesmer had about three hours before he needed to leave for his intervention. He started to smile, but his face hurt too much.

The players in the casino had stopped their wagering ten minutes ago. None wanted to miss the spectacle of the baton toting little man, dressed head to toe in white formal. He was both preceded and followed by members of his entourage as he made his way from the casino entrance to the Baccarat Room. Members of COF who were on duty couldn't help snickering at Rolly's little private tribute. As if by magic, as Queck entered the casino, the house PA system began playing Sammy Davis, Jr.'s *"Candy Man."*

Even the Archie Yen group pulled back their wager and stood by the room's railing to catch an elevated view of the Queck parade. As Queck approached the Baccarat Room, he stopped, bowed, and saluted the Yen group with an extension of his top hat. The Yen group laughed and applauded, their cigarettes dangling. Rolly took advantage of the break in the action to stand and stretch his legs. So far, the group had been playing about fifteen minutes and were conveniently down about ten-thousand dollars. Harry Fetters, elated over the house's early luck, stepped from the podium to the top of the Baccarat stairs to greet Mr. Queck and his group.

As Queck completed his salute to the Yen group, his brother-in-law, Liu Prinya broke ranks from the parade's rear and hastened up the stairs to speak to Fetters.

"Good evening, Mr. Prinya," Fetters said, extending his hand.

"Good evening, Mr. ... ," Prinya strained at Fetters' name tag, " ... Fetters," Prinya returned. "Mr. Queck feels exceptionally lucky today. He wishes to bypass his usual table selection process and move expeditiously to the salon to begin his play."

"Very well," said Fetters, just as Sue Min arrived. She offered her hand to Queck who raised it gently to his lips and planted a sensuous kiss on the back of it. She said something to him in Chinese, then hurried up the steps to join Prinya and Fetters.

"Welcome, Mr. Prinya," she said with a smile.

"Thank you," said Prinya.

"Mr. Queck wants to go directly to the salon," said Fetters. "Would you like to offer him our proposal concerning Hutchins and the Yen group?"

"Absolutely," Sue Min said, and she returned to Queck, placing her mouth very near his ear, whispering in, what Fetters believed to be, Chinese.

It was all for show, however. Queck knew perfectly well what the plan was. But for added suspense, he pretended to ponder Sue Min's suggestion. Fetters fell for it immediately, believing the Queck action could be at risk.

"If that's unsatisfactory ... " he began, "we could ... "

Sue Min held up her hand and brought her finger to her mouth. "Allow Mr. Queck to consider," she said to Fetters.

While Gene Chandler's *"Duke of Earl"* played, Queck lightly tapped his baton against the side of his bald head. Fetters held his breath. Rolly hoped Queck wouldn't over do it. At length, Queck summoned Sue Min to his side and simply nodded his approval. The Yen group cheered and applauded. Fetters asked them to gather up their chips and other belongings. They were all headed for the private salon upstairs.

Charlie Palermo arrived at the Tourist Information Center at eight-ten PM. The building was closed and shrouded in darkness. Just outside the entrance, he found the phone booth. Repeating his search through the phone book, he discovered another typewritten note: "Good job," the note said. "Your efforts shall be rewarded with the return of Alicia, unharmed, as promised. Leave the money in the phone book, same page. Go home. If it's all there, she will be home by eleven tonight. Do something stupid–she'll never forgive you."

Palermo looked around. Except for the occasional speeding car traveling the highway, all was quiet and vacant. He hated the thought of leaving the cash and not knowing his daughter's fate for nearly three hours. But, he also knew he didn't dare risk her life. He slipped the cash-filled envelope into the phone book, which he left sitting on the small shelf near the phone. As he exited the booth, he looked around and listened one more time. He felt very much alone. He folded this recent note and stored it in his jacket pocket next to the first. These were the only tangible pieces of evidence he'd have if things went awry. With another long trip ahead of him, he headed southwest to Las Vegas. Every ounce of his original fear went with him.

In the dealers' break room, Sal sat quietly and uncharacteristically alone. He avoided holding anything in his hands for fear others would see how uncontrollably they were trembling. He barely made it from the cafeteria with his cup of hot coffee without burning himself. Try as he might to appear nonchalant, his nerves were getting the best of him. He took deep breaths, exhaling slowly, keeping his eyes closed to avoid visual contact with those sitting nearby.

His mind involuntarily generated suppositions laced with failure and discovery. He felt like he was in the middle of a long fall from a tall building with absolutely no physical control over his incontestable fate. He knew there was no turning back; that the fuse was lit. Most of all, he was absolutely stunned at his own impotence to cope serenely with the pressures associated with COF. It was one of those moments when he wanted to bury himself, face down, between the sheets with a soft pillow over his head, blocking out the world. It disturbed Sal to realize, deep down, he was a coward.

"Mooring, you all right?" asked Corine Pollard, as she walked past him to pick up a newspaper.

Sal opened his eyes. "Yeah, I'm good," he said, hurriedly. "Thanks."

"Your wife's upstairs asking for you," said Corine.

"My wife?"

"I *guess* she's your wife. A cutie. She asked Reno if you were here."

"Thanks," he said. Sal took a hurried swig of his coffee and tossed the cup into the trashcan. Finding new energy, he sprinted up the stairs to the casino.

As soon as Stan Reno saw him, he pointed to BJ two. Sitting at third base was Sharon, looking like she stepped off the cover of Glamour Magazine. Reno made a hand-shaking motion at his belt line as if to say "Mama Mia!" Sal, mindful of casino rules to stay inside the pit while in uniform, hurried into the pit and went directly to Reno.

"Let me have BJ two," Sal said.

"Hell, I was thinking of dealing that, myself," Reno said. "Sharon looks like a vision tonight!"

"I'll say," said Sal with a smile.

"Keep your mind on your game," warned Reno. Then he said to himself "fat chance."

Sal tapped out Josh Keaton. "What are you doing?" whispered Josh under his breath. "I don't want a break." He motioned toward third base with his eyes.

Sal smiled, apologetically. "Reno's orders," he said. "Besides she's my wife."

The instant Sharon saw Sal, she lit up like Rockefeller Center at Christmas. Sal had never seen her look so beautiful. Her hair was done up in a French twist with sweeping tendrils cascading down both sides of her picture-perfect, richly made-up face.

Her deep blue eyes were exquisitely outlined in ember black mascara; her lips, immaculately coated in mystical pink with a hint of gloss. She wore long, shimmering gold and zirconium earrings with matching necklace that rested daintily at the cleft of her imposing cleavage. Her pleated, crimson cocktail dress hugged at the waist and hung loosely a daring eight inches above the knees–more now as she sat cross-legged on the BJ stool.

Collusion on the Felt

"Ooh, a new dealer," she said lighting up and slowly sliding a five-dollar chip into the betting circle.

"Good evening, everyone," Sal said smiling in her direction. "Let's see if we can't win you folks some money. Looking directly at Sharon, he mouthed: "You look fantastic!" The two other players, a husband and wife, each bet five-dollars. Sal slid the first card out of the shoe and into the discard pile. "A king," he announced as the first card landed in front of the woman. "Another king," he called for the gentleman. "And an ace," he said triumphantly, placing the card in front of Sharon.

"All right," said Sharon, wiggling in her seat. "Picture card, picture card, picture card," she repeated, crossing her fingers.

Sal dealt himself a card face down; then a nine to the first king, a six to the second, and a queen to the ace.

"Yes!" Sharon squealed excitedly.

Sal dealt his second card face down and flipped over the first to show a nine.

The woman stood with her nineteen. The man hit the sixteen and busted with a seven.

"I win," said Sharon. "Pay me, sir," she said playfully. Sal paid her seven-fifty for the blackjack. He turned over a ten, gave the push sign by touching his clenched fist against the felt in front of the woman's nineteen, and collected the cards. As he placed them in the discard pile, the house system began playing The Mama's and the Papas' *"Monday Monday."*

At the first sound of the chorus, up in the surveillance room, Nappa, alias Chief, rubbed his hands together in delightful anticipation.

"Stand by," he yelled to no one in particular. "We are about to ratchet things up a notch or two. Everybody, take a look at monitor seven!" As though he were directing a television show, Nappa lifted his pointed finger and cued the monitor. "Action!"

At the table next to Sal's, the cowboys burst into accompaniment with the sixties group. Sharon knew it was coming, but turned and smiled at them, believing it a natural guest reaction. One of the cowboys, the one singing loudest and most off-key, noticed this beautiful woman smiling at them. He nudged his buddies and motioned in her direction. Both Sal and Chris, the dealer at the cowboys' table, knew the fight was about to erupt, but Sal didn't want Sharon to have any involvement in it. It was apparently too late.

Sharon was enjoying the guys' singing and began joining in. The cowboys ate that up. Each one wanted to put his arm around her and harmonize, but there were obviously too many arms. Sal could sense she was beginning to feel uncomfortable. The cowboys grew louder and more physical in their struggle for Sharon's attention.

"Guys!" Sal called out. "Guys, you'll need to leave the lady alone, please!"

Sharon was now attempting to politely push them away from her. The tall one looked up in Sal's direction and slurred, "Ain't no one talkin' to you, monkey. Stay out of this!"

"She's with me," called out another cowboy.

"Fuck she is – she's mine, motherfucker!" hollered the third.

"Gentlemen, you need to leave the lady alone!" warned Sal sternly.

The commotion drew everyone's attention, including Stan Reno's, who hurried over between the two tables.

"You'll need to break this up now!" he yelled.

"Fuck you, old man!" yelled one of the cowboys. "She's with me!" And he slugged the tall cowboy who fell against the man playing at Sal's table. The man toppled over backwards, knocking his wife off her stool.

Sharon instinctively screamed. Glasses and bottles were knocked off the tables, crashing to the floor. Fists were flying. Security officers hurried to the pit from all corners of the casino.

"I'm calling Metro," yelled Reno, and he picked up the pit phone and dialed Harve Dedman's cellular.

Dedman was cruising in the vicinity of the Empire, anxiously awaiting this call from Reno.

"We've got a drunken brawl here at the Desert Empire casino," Reno hollered into the phone. "Send help immediately!"

Upstairs in the private baccarat salon, one of Queck's bodyguards had been observing the main casino through the glass window. Broadcasting the fight was his COF contribution. "Huge fight in the casino – people everywhere!" he yelled.

The timing couldn't have been more perfect. Rolly knew the fight would be starting and had precisely timed the shuffle and cut of the second shoe.

Nappa's eyes ricocheted from monitor seven to monitor two, whose camera was set on the baccarat table in the private salon.

"Okay, Rollo," he whispered to himself, "Now's your chance."

As Harry Fetters hurried over to the window to check out the fight, Rolly switched the shoe of black cards with the pre-made shoe on the covered shelf of the room service cart.

Nappa broke into a wide, toothy grin. "Yes!" he shouted.

Rolly waited for Fetters' to return, before burning the first three cards.

It had been about halfway through that first shoe when the Archie Yen group huddled and decided to place their bets with Cyril Queck. Fetters acknowledged the move, but had no veto power. From that point forward it was the table versus the house. At the moment the house was down thirty thousand dollars.

Prinya, sitting next to Queck, pretended to make an entry into his baccarat score pad. Instead, of course, he was noting the winning hand on the initial deal. He, betting for Mr. Queck, slid five thousand dollars into the Banker's circle. As agreed, Mr. Nim slid five thousand dollars from the Yen group's stash into the Banker's circle. As Rolly was about to pull the cards from the shoe, Queck managed a vocal groan and held up his hand to stop the action. Everyone at the table looked toward him. Queck glanced down at his ample stash, looked out onto the table at the wagering circle, and back down at his stash. Then he reached down into his stash and located a pink check worth twenty thousand dollars and added it to his current five thousand dollar wager. Prinya was relegated to properly place the highest value chip on the bottom of the stack. Members of the Yen group looked at each other and mumbled amidst their streaming cigarette smoke.

"We will match," announced Mr. Nim, as he slowly placed a twenty thousand dollar chip on the bottom of his group's wager.

"Total wager is fifty-thousand," said Rolly. Fetters nodded.

Rolly slid the first and third cards onto the Player position and the second and fourth cards onto the Banker position. As a courtesy, he looked up at the two bettors, Prinya and Nim. They bowed to him.

The interaction was ceremonial. Player's cards are always acted on first. Since the table was betting Banker, Rolly turned over the Player's cards, a three of clubs and a four of clubs.

"Player totals seven," said Rolly.

Nim and Prinya looked at each other. Nim bowed to Prinya as if to say: you may have the honor of turning over Banker's cards. Prinya leaned in and flipped over a two of spades and a six of clubs.

"Banker shows eight," said Rolly. "Banker wins."

"What a fucking shock!" said Nappa laughing sarcastically. "Who'da guessed it?"

The table erupted into their usual victory jubilance. The house was now down eighty thousand dollars. Forty thousand of that belongs to COF, thought Rolly. And he scooped up the cards.

Downstairs, Harve Dedman left his unit with flashers blazing, and ran into the main entrance of the casino. The huge crowd that had gathered around the lower end of Pit One, alerted Dedman where he needed to go. By this time the four cowboys were slugging it out with each other and with seven or eight security officers. Sal had pulled Sharon from the fray just before security arrived. At the moment she was out of breath and being comforted by Sal.

Blackjack stools were strewn over a thirty-foot area and the fracas participants were rolling all over the floor as the house system played Barry Sadler's *"Ballad of the Green Berets."* Dedman pushed his way through the crowd. "Police Department! Out of the way, please!" he shouted, repeatedly.

Once he made his way through the crowd, he pulled a police whistle from his belt and let loose a trilling blare, causing bystanders to cringe, and cup their ears. "Police Department!" he yelled. "On your faces, now!" The security officers instinctively responded, pushing themselves away from the cowboys and rolling over on their faces. The cowboys were slower to respond, continuing to whack each other until Harve drew his weapon and blew the whistle one more time.

"On your faces, now!" he screamed. The cowboys, drunk, exhausted, and sore, rolled over on their bloody faces. "Security, please cuff and search them," he commanded. "You guys, put your hands behind your back, now!" he ordered the cowboys.

"Are you okay?" Sal asked Sharon.

She looked up from her sanctuary, buried against his chest, and nodded. "As long as I can stay right here, nothing can hurt me," she said with a big grin.

"Let's march these guys out to my unit," ordered Harve to the security officers. "And I've got to get some forms filled out and statements from you guys. It'll probably tie you up for a little while."

"No problem," they mumbled, barely able to move themselves. "No problem."

The cowboys actually were severely inebriated. Getting them to rise to their feet was no easy chore. But deep below their drunken surfaces, they hung on to the fact that their contribution to COF had been a big hit. Their shares would go a long way to soothing their aches and pains. Limping and involuntarily side-stepping, the four paraded through the casino followed by officer Harve Dedman, equally proud of the money he'd just earned.

Outside, in full view of gawkers in and around the valet area, the four were loaded into Dedman's police car. Harve gave instructions to the seven security officers along with an armload of paperwork.

"I'll be back in a little while to pick this stuff up from you," he told them.

They nodded.

Then with all the fanfare he could muster, Harve turned on the siren and removed his charges from the Desert Empire. The siren was a nice touch. It masked the sounds of five men laughing themselves silly behind those dark, tinted windows.

Nappa turned his attention back to the baccarat salon. He liked what he saw. The piles of chips in front of Mr. Nim and Mr. Prinya had more than tripled since the last time he checked. Harry Fetters stood at the podium, nervously massaging his chin. Nappa panned, zoomed, and focused the camera above and behind Fetters down to a close-up of Fetters' notepad. If he was reading the numbers correctly, the house was down seven point five million already.

"Motherfucker! We are doin' it!" yelled Nappa. Marv and Jesse were busy munching on the remaining morsels of Tamhagen's confiscated meal.

Stan Reno had contacted the porter department to send over someone to sweep up the broken glasses and bottles around Pit One. While they were cleaning up, Sal re-assumed his position behind the table; Sharon climbed the stool at third base, not without attracting a lot of male attention.

"Forgive me for staring," said Sal. "I mean, I've always found you attractive, but you are an absolute vision tonight."

"I wanted to look special for you," she whispered. "After all this is a special day – for both of us. I clean up nice, huh?"

"You clean up terrific," he said. He leaned closer to her. "How do you think it's going?" he whispered.

"Like a well greased machine, I'd say," she said. "How about you?"

"Inside, I'm a nervous wreck," he said. "It seems to be going smoothly. Maybe that's what scares me. I'm not used to things going exactly my way."

"I'd like to be able to do some celebrating later," she said. "Got any plans?"

He just looked at her. "I'm sort of formulating them right now," he said with a devious grin.

A couple of men took seats at Sal's table. They each tossed a hundred-dollar bill onto the felt. "All green," said one.

"Green here, too," said the other.

Sal spread the bills face up on the felt, placing two stacks of four twenty-five dollar chips beside them. "Change two hundred," he called to Stan Reno.

"Got it," said Reno.

"Good luck, gentlemen," Sal said to the men, and he slid a stack of chips in front of each of them.

"I'm sticking with red," said Sharon. "Green's too rich for my blood." And she slid a five-dollar chip into the betting circle.

Sal's hands went through the motion of pitching the cards, but his mind was a million dollars away.

At precisely nine-thirty P.M., a panting Harve Dedman, after winding his way through the back of the house maze, arrived at the surveillance room door. He'd had to ask directions, but the uniform proved only an asset in his obtaining quick assistance. He knocked twice, paused, and knocked five more times.

Inside the room, Nappa instinctively checked the time. "Open the door," he commanded. "It's our cop friend."

The man known as Jesse opened the door.

Harve nodded a greeting and made his way inside. Jesse locked the door. As soon as he saw Nappa, Harve let go a loud whoop, and the two embraced like long, lost relatives.

"Man, you were incredible," said Nappa. "I seen the whole thing right there," he said, pointing to the monitor. "You da man!"

"Where's our guy?" asked Harve. "And I'll need the voice recorder."

Nappa pulled the recorder out of his pants pocket. "Here you go, man. Dick head's in the closet," he said, pointing.

Harve moved to the closet and opened the door. The Colonel was lying on his side, blindfold, duct tape and rope all in tact. The old man was sweating profusely. His clothes were wringing wet. It was incredibly hot in the closet, thought Harve. He had already begun to sweat, himself. He knelt down in front of the Colonel and pulled the blindfold up over his eyes. Even the dimly lighted closet proved too bright for the Colonel's aging irises. He squinted and groaned weekly. Harve made sure the Colonel got a glimpse of the uniform, then he replaced the blindfold immediately.

"Too harsh on your eyes," he said. He held the recorder near the Colonel's mouth. "I'm Officer Parker with Metro," he said. "What's your name?" He immediately pressed record.

"Tamhagen," said the Colonel. Harve stopped the recorder.

"How are you?" asked Harve, pressing record.

"Okay, I guess," said the Colonel, in slow bursts of breath. "I'm starving, though." Harve pressed stop. "Officer?" said the Colonel.

"Yes."

"I'm a diabetic," he gasped. "I know my blood sugar is dangerously low. If I don't eat…"

"Hey, I need some food in here now!" ordered Harve.

Jesse repeated the order to Nappa who didn't quite make out what Harve was saying.

"You shit-faced motherfuckers ate that food, too," Nappa said, shaking his head. "Ask him why he needs the food."

Harve was standing at the doorway to the closet, facing the room. "I think we've got a diabetic coma coming on," he said. "We've got to get some glucose in him immediately."

"What am I gonna do?" asked Nappa, "call room service…hey send up about a pound of glucose, man."

Harve walked over to Nappa. He looked as serious as his next sentence. "If this man dies, we're all accessories to murder."

"Get me some motherfuckin' glucose up here now, motherfuckers!" screamed Nappa.

The two ran out of the room. Once in the hall, Jesse turned to Marv. "What the hell is glucose?"

"They'll know in the kitchen. That guy who first let us in – he'll help us out," said Marv. The two headed for the service stairs, hoping to run into Francisco Mercado and still stay relatively invisible.

Meanwhile, Harve hurried back into the closet. He knelt down in front of the Colonel and whispered, "Do you have anything up here in the office I could get for you?" he asked.

"Charlie always has some candy in his desk," said the Colonel, weakly. "Middle drawer."

Harve hurried outside the closet. "Where's Charlie's desk," he asked Nappa.

"Charlie who?"

"What the fuck do I know 'Charlie who'?" He began looking around. Noticing Palermo's office up and behind the surveillance area, he leaped up the three steps, opened the door, and saw Palermo's desk plate with his name on it.

"Charlie!" he yelled. He pulled open the center drawer and found the little hard candies wrapped in yellow cellophane. He scooped up a handful and hurried back to the closet. He unwrapped one and put it in the Colonel's mouth.

"Here," he said. "Suck on this. I'll unwrap another."

Like fish out of water, Jesse and Marv, standouts in their street clothes among a sea of kitchen uniforms, tried in vain to stroll unnoticed through the room service kitchen. It didn't help that they had no idea what they were looking for.

"Excuse me," called out Clarence Buckman, a black room service captain. "This area is not open to guests. Let me show you the way back to the casino..."

"Just a minute," said Jesse. "My dad has an emergency and needs some...what was that?" he asked Marv.

"Glucose," said Marv. "He's sick and needs some glucose."

"Glucose? Isn't that something you get at a drug store?" asked Buckman.

"I don't know," said Jesse. "All I know is he's heading for a coma."

"Is he diabetic?" asked Buckman.

"Yeah."

"Wait here, I'll get you some orange juice."

Buckman disappeared through an open doorway and returned with a large glass of orange juice. "Here," he said. "Take this to him right away, and then get him something substantial to eat."

"Thanks," said Jesse.

"No problem."

On their way up the stairwell to the second floor, Jesse and Marv confronted a security officer on hotel patrol. They tried to nonchalantly pass by the officer with a nod and smile, but their attire and the large glass of orange juice screamed investigation.

"Hold it right there," said the officer.

"Who, us?" asked Marv, looking around.

"What are you two doing here?"

"Just getting some juice for my father," said Jesse. "He's a diabetic and needed some glucose."

"Where did you get that juice?"

"One of the guys in the room service kitchen gave it to us. And, frankly, I think he should be commended. He probably saved my dad's life."

"That's for sure," chimed in Marv.

"In fact, I'm certain my father will be writing a glowing letter to your president about how this hotel's staff takes care of their guests," added Jesse.

"Are you folks staying with us?"

Not sure what the better response would be, Jesse nodded and Marv shook his head.

"Which is it – yes or no?"

"Me and my dad are staying here," said Jesse. "He's just visiting."

"What's your room number?" asked the officer, removing a small notebook from his rear pocket.

"Ah, I believe it's 1415," said Jesse.

"Let me see your key," said the officer.

"I don't have it with me. I left in such a hurry when my dad needed glucose, I forgot it. Now, I really need to get going." He held up the orange juice. "My dad?"

"I'll need your name for my report," said the officer.

"Jesse," he said. "Jesse Stevens. The room's in my father's name… Marshall Stevens."

The officer made a few notes in his tablet. "All right, let me ask you, Mr. Stevens, why are you climbing fourteen flights of stairs instead of taking the elevator?"

The men looked at each other. Jesse said, nervously, "We…ah…we didn't know how to get to the elevator from down there and didn't want to waste precious time…"

"Follow me," said the officer. "I'll take you to the guest elevator."

Reluctantly, the men traipsed after him. As they walked, the officer reached up to his left collar and pressed the talk button on his radio. "Dispatch. Check guest registration name, room 1-4-1-5."

They exchanged a troubled glance.

"Where the fuck are those boys at?" screamed Nappa.

"Well, this candy is helping a little," said Harve. "But he's going to need some liquid. He hasn't got enough strength to chew this stuff. And the sucking takes forever. See if you can find them on camera."

Nappa swung around in his chair and began switching through the hotel and casino cameras. During his random switching, he punched up a camera just as Marv and Jesse, following a security officer, emerged from a stairwell into the hotel lobby. "There they are," said Nappa. "Shit, they're with Security."

Harve hurried from the closet entrance to the video console. "He's talking on his radio," said Harve. "I think we've got problems. The one fellow is carrying a glass of something." On the black and white monitor, the liquid in the glass was indiscernible.

"Punch it up in color," said Harve.

Nappa did.

"It's juice," said Harve. "That's exactly what this guy needs."

They watched as the officer's head leaned toward his shoulder radio, followed by the officer's quick turn toward the two men. All of a sudden, Jesse threw the juice in the officer's face. The two pushed the officer out of their way, causing him to fall over backwards, and they began running through the hotel lobby to the exit doors.

"Get out, you motherfuckers!" Nappa yelled to the screen. "And keep goin'!"

"Look," said Harve, "those hotel suits from the front desk are chasing them."

"We're in trouble now," blurted Nappa.

"Why is that?"

"We're gonna get a call from somebody – either Security or Hotel – or both – wanting to know if we got the video of those two. Shit. Now what?"

"Take it easy," said Harve. "I'll deal with them. I've got the guy's voice on tape."

Chapter Twenty-Six

He intentionally kept his eyes riveted on the road.
He knew if he looked over at her, the texture of
this confession could change drastically.

It was ten-twenty PM. Alicia and the man she believed to be Father Coquet were traveling a long, dark stretch of two-lane highway back to Las Vegas. Thus far, the charade had proven extremely successful. Alicia felt gratified that she was able to bring some enjoyment to the elderly, blind man she knew only as Mr. Bogovitch. The young counterfeit priest enjoyed the satisfaction of knowing he pulled off his contribution to COF without a hitch. And in a few short hours, he'd be worth more than a million dollars. All that remained was delivering his captive safe and sound to her home and avoiding detection by her father. With luck, she'd be home before he arrived.

The ride, since Laughlin, had been mostly in silence, with only intermittent attempts at tuning FM radio between bouts with static. As the Intrepid whizzed by the sign promising Vegas in fifteen miles, Alicia resurrected her earlier request.

"Are we back in the district?" she asked.

"Beg your pardon?"

"Are we back in the district, so you can hear my confession?"

He'd forgotten completely about their earlier conversation. Everything had gone so well, so far, he wanted to do nothing to jeopardize it. "You still want to have confession?" he asked.

"Sure," she said.

"All right." He made the sign of the cross on himself and her. "You may begin," he said, trying to sound reverent.

"Bless me, Father because I have sinned," she said. "It's been about eight months since my last confession."

He nodded, looking straight ahead.

"I missed Sunday Mass twice last March when I had a bad cold," she began.

"It's not a sin if you're truly sick," he said, still braced for the main events.

"I've not been as respectful to my parents as I know I should," she continued, "but I'm trying to do better."

"Good," he nodded.

"Then there's the sex issues," she said.

"Issues?" he asked, clearly curious and equally apprehensive.

"I met this guy at a dance. I think it was at the end of the school year. He was a sophomore in college, you know?"

"Whoa," he said, "a sophomore in college?"

"Well, he's a junior now," she said. I told him I was nineteen–which was a lie, of course, so I need to confess that...."

"Okay."

"I felt good when he like believed me, you know?"

"Sure."

"And I really liked him. I still do. But we've sort of...like been together...you know what I mean?"

"Go on," he said.

"Do I need to tell more?" she asked.

"Only if you care to," he said, his heart thumping. "For instance, did you go all the way?"

"Is that *more* of a sin?" she asked.

"More than what?"

"More than like laying together with our clothes off and touching each other."

"Just touching?"

"Basically, but sometimes the touching was like with our mouths and stuff, you know?"

"Did you ah…go down on him?"

"You mean BJ?"

"I believe that's one way to characterize it," he said, finding it increasingly difficult to breathe.

"Uh huh. Just a few times, though," she said.

"A few times," his voice cracked. He cleared his throat. "I see. Did ah…did you enjoy that?"

She hesitated a few seconds. "I really did," she said, meekly. "He did, too."

"I see." He intentionally kept his eyes riveted on the road. He knew if he looked over at her, the texture of this confession could change drastically. "Did he…ah…did you let him, you know…go down on you?"

"I'm ashamed to say that that was the best of all, Father. I can't seem to get enough of that."

Christ, she's a nymph, he thought. I'm sitting here with a little nymph and I'm wearing a priest collar. He was rock hard now and tormented as to how to continue.

"Have you ever done that, Father?"

"Done what?"

"You know…gone down on a girl. I mean before you were a priest, of course."

He cleared his throat. "Well … in all candor … yes I have. And, of course, it was before I … ah … heard my calling."

"Is it normal … I mean … in God's eyes … is it normal for us to enjoy that?"

His mental control was fast slipping away and the subject matter was blanketing his entire being. For the first time, he turned to her, looked at her lovely face, and spoke. "It's perfectly normal," he told her. "It's called being human. Now, do you have anything else you'd like to confess?"

"No, that's about it, Father."

"Excellent," he said. "Now for your penance, say five Hail Mary's and make a good Act of Contrition." He waved the sign of the cross in her direction and breathed a sigh of relief as she began mouthing her prayers.

Nathan Mesmer pulled his Viper between two pick-up trucks in the self-parking lot, a considerable distance from both the building and the employee parking area. He wore tan Dockers and a brown tweed sports jacket over a button-down, open-collar, white shirt. As he walked slowly toward the side entrance of the casino, nearest the stairs to the mezzanine, his muscles and bones still ached and his face downright hurt. His decision to return to the Empire had not been reached hastily. But, in the end, he determined he had no choice. There remained that huge loose-end up in his old office that he unquestionably had to resolve. No matter how COF ended up, Mesmer knew he'd never escape suspicion as long as the Hutchins' airline ticket was still tucked away in his briefcase.

Obviously Frederick hadn't found it. If he had, Mesmer guessed he would have grilled him about it. Furthermore, it certainly wasn't too late to use the ticket as it was originally intended.

He reached the glass door, pulled it open, and with his head down avoiding eye contact, limped the twenty-five yards to the mezzanine stairs, just around the corner from the hosts' office. Peripherally, things appeared to be moderately busy. He reached the stairs, and though wanting to leap them three at a time, carefully placed both feet on each step, ascending them like an arthritic old man.

The telephone rang its fourth ring. Harve Dedman, sweating billiard balls, was trying frantically to cue the pocket-sized tape recorder.

"Will you please hurry up," begged Nappa, staring at the caller I.D. "It's an outside call!"

"I'm ready," panted Harve. 'Let's do it."

Nappa picked up the phone and placed the mouthpiece directly against the tape recorder and nodded. Harve let go of the pause button.

"Tamhagen," sounded the tape. Harve quickly brought the receiver up to his ear.

"Colonel, its Charlie," came Palermo's voice. "How's everything going?"

Harve played the tape. "Okay, I guess," came the Colonel's voice. "I'm starving though." Harve grimaced. He didn't mean for that to continue.

"Well, get something to eat," said Palermo. "I was going to stop by, but if everything's okay, I'll go on home. Talk to you tomorrow."

Harve mumbled into the mouthpiece, "All right, bye." He gave the receiver to Nappa who quickly hung up.

"What do you think?" asked Nappa.

"I think it worked," said Harve.

"What about him?" asked Nappa, pointing toward the closet.

"He's still sucking on candy. Hell, his sugar may get too high now."

Nappa checked the time. "Phase one is almost over, man. We need to get ready for that graveyard dude. He'll be coming in that door in a few minutes."

"Not a problem," said Harve. "Let me have the stun gun."

Nappa began patting his pockets. His face took on serious concern.

"You have it, don't you?" asked Harve.

"No, man. I never did have it. That fool from room service – he's the one that's got it."

"Shit. All right, I'll use my pepper spray. That'll keep him distracted while we tie him up."

"Cool," said Nappa. "Let's see how much our boys raked in up in the salon." He sat down at the console and zoomed the salon camera over the podium to the pad where Fetters had been continually making entries. The most recent scribbled entry was sixty-nine million.

"I don't believe what I'm seein'," gasped Nappa. "What's that look like to you, man?"

Harve squinted at the monitor. "Sixty nine million. Holy shit! Sixty nine fuckin' million!"

"Do the math, man. How much we get?"

"Harve picked up a pad and started calculating. "...divide by 2...thirty four and a half... Hang on," he said, "How does one-point-three million apiece sound?"

"Oh, my God! Oh, my God!" said Nappa, slapping his hand on his forehead. "I'm a rich motherfucker! You, too!" he said.

"Shhhh," said Harve, pointing to the main door, where he heard a key insertion. Harve ran toward the door feeling for his pepper spray. As the door opened, Nester's eyes widened at the sight of a uniformed policeman running frantically toward him, apparently reaching for a weapon. Nester froze, instinctively raising his hands, as Harve pointed the pepper spray directly at his partially obscured face. He sprayed, much of it landing on Nester's outstretched palms, but some made it onto his face. The burning sensation caused Nester to squeeze his eyes shut and scream. Harve sprayed again, soaking his target. Nester rolled onto the floor, still screaming.

"Get the stuff," Harve yelled to Nappa.

Nappa looked around for the rope and the duct tape. He saw them across the room, near the closet. He retrieved them and brought them to Harve.

"Tie his hands," ordered Harve, and give me that duct tape."

Nester screamed, "What the fuck is...!"

Mesmer still had his office key, a major blunder by Frederick. He opened the door to his former office, flicked on the light, and headed straight for the desk. He sat down, out of breath from the painful stair climb, and spun the chair around facing the credenza. Sure enough, there were two identical briefcases under the table. He lifted one to the desk, dialed in 0-0-0, and lifted the cover. This one wasn't his. Obviously, it was Frederick's. Curious regarding its contents, but pressed for time, he re-locked it, and placed it on the floor. He lifted the other briefcase, repeated the coding, and lifted its cover. He inserted his hand into the elastic compartment and felt around for the ticket. Finding it, he pulled it out, quickly opened it, and made sure it was all intact. Quickly, he deposited it in his inside jacket pocket. He scanned the other contents of the briefcase to see if there was anything else he needed to take. He'd have to leave the briefcase here. No way he could remove it. Deducing nothing else essential, he closed the lid, locked it, and positioned it next to Frederick's.

"Find everything, okay, Nathan?"

Terrified, Mesmer looked up.. Frederick, wearing a robe and slippers, stood in the office doorway.

"What's the matter, Nathan? You look like you've just seen a ghost."

"Shit, you scared the hell out of me," muttered Mesmer. "I just came back for my things."

"Is that why you placed your briefcase back under the table?"

"I decided I didn't want it anymore. What's it to you?"

"Oh, nothing, really. Is there anything else you wanted to take with you?"

"Like what?"

"Well, that picture of your family, for instance."

"Oh, yeah. Of course." Mesmer lifted the framed picture.

Frederick walked into the office. "I had a feeling you'd be back."

"Must be that executive intuition. Now, if you'll excuse me…"

"Don't run off just yet, my friend. Let's have a drink for old time's sake. You know, the bottle in the bottom drawer?"

"Look, Frederick, you've already fired me. Have the decency to let me take my few things and just go."

"Heard you 'escaped' from the hospital," Frederick said, laughing.

"I left, if that's what you mean. I hate hospitals."

"Had to be someplace in a hurry, huh?"

"What are you getting at?"

"Level with me, Mesmer. You've got something underhanded going on – I know it; you know it. Why don't you just level with me?"

"If you're so smart, you tell me," said Mesmer.

"All right." One syllable at a time, he said: "Australia."

Mesmer tried to sit motionless, but his right cheek flinched.

"The cards are on the table, Nathan. Just come clean and tell me what game we're playing."

Mesmer continued to stare at Frederick.

"Perhaps you need more," teased Frederick. "Australia by way of London." He paused. "Tomorrow morning." He paused. "Roland Hutch.…"

"You had no goddam business rummaging through my personal belongings, you son-of-a-bitch!" Mesmer was livid.

"Purely by accident, Nathan. After all our briefcases are identical, your honor."

"What do you want?" growled Mesmer.

"Maybe I want a piece, Nathan. Got enough to go around?"

"You're setting me up, you fuck! You've got that cold, corporate blood running through your veins. Don't snow the snowman!"

"I want only what you want, my friend, a little security, a chance at some of life's finer things. We both know we don't have that with our jobs. What would it take to show my sincerity?"

Mesmer felt like a trapped rat. His options were minimal, but he did have options. One, one of his two Smith and Wesson's was tucked inside his belt, under his jacket. He doubted if Frederick was armed, but you could never be sure about the sneaky bastard. If he blew him away, he'd eliminate the problem. Of course, that would set a whole other ration of grief in motion. Two, he could trust the fucker and buy him off with some of the take. That appeared to be the better of the two. Of course, if number two failed, he could always fall back on number one.

"If you're serious, Frederick. I'll cut you in. There's plenty to go around. You'll be rich beyond your dreams for the rest of your life."

"Like I said, how can I show my sincerity?"

Mesmer reached for the phone. He dialed operator. "Get me the baccarat salon," he barked.

"My pleasure, Mr. Mesmer," the operator said. She obviously hadn't gotten the word of Mesmer's firing.

Mesmer put the phone on speaker. "All right," he said to Frederick, "Ask Fetters how it's going with the whales."

From the speaker, Fetters could be heard. "This is Fetters."

"Fetters, this is H.R. Frederick." He called out to the speakerphone.

"Yes, Mr. Frederick?"

"How's it going with the whales?"

"Horrible, sir. Absolutely horrible," Fetters whispered.

"Give me numbers, Fetters."

"Sir, we're down seventy million and I think they're getting ready to cash out."

Mesmer struck a very facially painful smile.

"Fetters, we're on speaker phone. Did you say seven zero million?"

"Yes, sir." Fetters sounded like he was having a nervous breakdown.

"And no one has contacted me all fucking night?"

"We had orders you weren't to be disturbed, sir."

"Whose orders?" he shouted.

"Why yours, sir. Sue Min told me that. She gave me your new empowerment rules, as well. And, sir, their bets stayed within my authority all night. They were just so...so...well, they were very lucky, sir."

"Fetters...."

"Sir, please hold on a second." Fetters could be heard talking to Rolly in the background.

Mesmer maintained his painful smile. "Here's where you show your sincerity," he said. "Give your permission for the whales to take cash."

"What?"

"You heard me. If you're in, okay the cash."

"Mr. Frederick?" Fetters was back.

"Go ahead, Fetters."

"Sir, there's one more thing. Mr. Queck and Mr. Yen and his group want their chips exchanged for cash. Seventy million in cash, sir. I'll need your permission for that."

Mesmer stared at Frederick. Frederick stared at Mesmer.

"Give me a minute," said Frederick.

"Certainly, sir."

Frederick mouthed "Mute that," to Mesmer. Mesmer pressed mute.

"Well, I certainly underestimated you, Nathan. How did you pull this off?"

"Never mind that right now," said Mesmer. "There's time for that discussion later. Right now, simply for giving your permission for them to take cash–there's ten million in cash in it for you."

"Tonight?"

"Tonight."

"Go ahead, take it off mute."

Mesmer did.

"Fetters?"

"Yes, sir. I'm still here."

"Go ahead and approve cash."

"Affirmative, sir. Per your instructions, I will approve cash."

"Thank you, Fetters."

"Thank you, sir."

Mesmer hung up the phone.

"How did they do it, Nathan? How did they get so lucky?"

"Luck had nothing to do with it. You know as well as I do the harder you work, the luckier you get. I've worked very hard on this–for a long time. And it's all come down to now. What you just did, I would have done if you hadn't fired me. So, that firing cost me ten million dollars. I'll live."

"I say we have a drink to celebrate," said Frederick.

"You go ahead," said Mesmer. "I've still got things to do. I don't have time to celebrate."

"Don't mind if I do," said Frederick, and he walked from in front of the desk to the other side of Mesmer behind the desk, and reached for the bottom drawer. As he pulled the drawer open, he was bent down with the top of his head facing Mesmer. With split-second timing and one fluid action, Mesmer pulled the gun from his belt and called out Frederick's name. As Frederick looked up, Mesmer forced the gun's barrel against Frederick's chin and, grimacing with that jutting lower jaw, pulled the trigger.

Frederick's head exploded, splashing red and gray matter on the ceiling, chairs, and carpet. Shreds of human shrapnel sprayed all over Mesmer's hand and arm. He felt wet globules on his face. Disgusted, he pushed the gun's barrel against Frederick's collapsing carcass, helping it drop on its back.

"Oops, a suicide," growled Mesmer. "Poor fucker couldn't handle the big loss. And he used poor old Nathan Mesmer's gun, for which Mesmer had a license and kept in his desk drawer. But then again, it wasn't Mesmer's desk anymore. Mr. Corporate Frederick fired his motherfucking ass while he was in the fucking hospital today and took his key."

Chapter Twenty-seven

He walked into the outer office. He noticed that Frederick's door was slightly ajar and his office light was on.

Mesmer rinsed himself of Frederick's bloody residuum in the executive washroom, adjacent to the office. He placed the gun in Frederick's right hand, and positioned it at his side. He wasn't worried about fingerprints, after all this used to be his office. His fingerprints were everywhere.

He looked at his watch. It was now eleven-thirty PM. He eked a vestige of a smile. The graveyard shift was now on duty. Few, if any of them, knew what Mesmer looked like, since their paths very rarely crossed. His exit would be less stressful than was his entrance.

He switched off the office light and almost pulled the door closed, when he remembered two very important items. He switched the light back on and reached into his pocket. He removed his office key from his key chain, touched it against Frederick's thumb and fingers, and lifting it with his handkerchief, placed it in the clean ashtray atop the desk. The second item he remembered was to leave the office door nearly closed without switching off the light.

He made his way through the outer office, out into the mezzanine hallway where he descended the stairs slowly. With no apparent attention paid to him, he turned and slipped unnoticed out of the building and headed directly for his car.

Up in the Surveillance Room, Nappa received his first communication from Rolly by way of a special frequency radio.

"Hello, eye?"

Nappa pulled the radio from its holster around his waist and responded. "Eye, go ahead."

"How'd it look from there?"

"Looked, good, man. A few glitches along the way, but nothin' we couldn't handle."

"Excellent," said Rolly.

"So, how'd we do upstairs?"

"A little better than expected," said Rolly.

"Bitchin'," said Nappa.

"Your whole team still up there with you?"

"Not exactly. That's one of the glitches I mentioned. The two dudes got chased out of the building. I'll explain later."

"What do you mean they got 'chased out of the building'?"

"I sent them to the kitchen to get some shit, I forget what it's called, for the old dude in the closet cause he was having some sort of coma, according to the cop."

"Is the old guy all right?"

"He's still breathin'. Him and his replacement are still locked in the closet."

"Where's Harve?"

"He took off to gather up the statements from the security dudes for that fight."

"If you see him, tell him to take off. And leave those guys in the closet. They'll find them in the morning. I'll see you a little later at you know where."

"That's a ten-four," said Nappa. He clicked off the walkie-talkie and mumbled under his breath through a wide toothy grin, "I know *where* and I know *how much*." He laughed as he slid the walkie-talkie into its holster, dangling from his belt.

Meanwhile Cyril Queck and Archie Yen were standing just outside the main casino cashier's cage. They were patiently waiting for the cage's night supervisor, Diane Nieman and her staff to count out their seventy million dollars in cash. Harry Fetters, having been summoned by Nieman to certify authority for the unusual cash transaction, stood inside the cage, but out of the staff's way. The group methodically stacked blocks of ten thousand dollars comprised of one hundred dollar bills on a huge table in a room accessible from the cage, but out of sight from casino guests. Nieman disappeared into the cage's vault. When she returned, tapping a pencil point to her lip, she looked very concerned.

"Harry, I'm afraid we have a little problem," she whispered to Fetters.

"In fact, we have seventy million problems," lamented Fetters.

"I can't provide all seventy million in cash."

"Why not?"

"I'm required to maintain a balance of twenty-five million. We only have sixty million in cash in the vault. The best I can do is fund half of it in cash. That'll leave me with a ten million cash cushion overnight. Will they take half of it in cash and a cashier's check or electronic transfer for the balance?"

"I'll find out." Fetters excused himself and exited the cage. He approached the gentlemen. "Mr. Queck, Mr. Yen, I'm afraid we are unable to provide the entire sum in cash. We..."

"Excuse me. Did you not get the approval you needed?" asked Queck.

"I did, Mr. Queck. However, our vault – which is substantially stocked, mind you – does not have sufficient funds to permit total funding in cash of such a large amount. Now we have some options. One, if you wish, we can provide all of it in cash as soon as the banks open in the morning, say by ten AM. Or, we are prepared to provide thirty-five million in cash right now and either a cashier's check or an electronic transfer for the balance."

"I find this highly irregular, Mr. Fetters," said Queck. Archie Yen, nodded in agreement. "Word of a casino the stature of the Desert Empire unable to pay its gambling debts on demand would be an unfortunate piece of news on the streets, don't you agree?" asked Queck.

Collusion on the Felt

"Yes, it certainly would," said Fetters, visibly shaken. "It's my hope we have treated your parties fairly and with respect and that you would not find that necessary."

"All right," said Yen. "If that's the best you can do. Give us half in cash and wire the rest to our accounts."

"I will agree, with much disappointment," said Queck.

"Thank you. Thank you both very much," groveled Fetters. "I will also arrange for security to accompany you and your cash to our limousine which is already waiting for you out front."

"We will need two limousines," said Queck. "I may have agreed to allow these gentlemen to play at my table, but I have not adopted them. We arrived separately; we shall leave the same way."

"Of course," said Fetters. "I will arrange for a second limo immediately."

Fetters hurried to the cage counter and asked for Dianne.

"Half cash is fine. The other half will need to be wired," he said.

"Do each of the gentlemen get fifty percent of the half in cash?"

"Yes. Then half of the balance needs to be wired to each of their accounts."

"One more thing," said Dianne.

"What's that?"

"Containers. It's not as though we have Desert Empire shopping bags back here. What do we put the money in?"

"Shit. Let me ask them." Fetters turned and approached the men. "One more thing, gentlemen." Fetters cleared his throat. "We will need some containers for the cash."

In a gesture intended to insult, Cyril Queck frisked himself. He patted down his chest, coat, and pants. He even lifted his top hat from the cage counter and looked inside it. Archie Yen watched, smiling, and shaking his head.

"Nothing here," said Queck, sarcastically. "How about you, Yen?"

"I'm afraid I can't help, either," said Yen.

They both turned toward Fetters and stared at him.

"Ah, perhaps I can have the hotel assistant manager open the gift shop," said Fetters. "Would that be acceptable?"

"Is it your intention that we purchase containers?" asked Queck.

"Well, you are walking out with seventy million…" Fetters reversed direction in mid-sentence. "…and that's a lot to carry. The least we can do is comp the suitcases for you," he said, with beads of moisture creeping along his upper lip.

"It is much appreciated," said Yen.

"That gesture secures my future visits to your property," said Queck.

"Nothing pleases me more," said Fetters. 'If you'll excuse me, I'll tend to the suitcases while they're preparing your money."

Meanwhile the employee parking lot was fast becoming a temporary hangout for the exiting COF team. There were hushed giggles and stifled laughter amid streams of high-fives and back slaps. Acutely aware that they must draw no attention to themselves, yet bursting with pent up celebratory energy, the group passed whispers to each other, sharing what tidbits of information they did know.

"Okay, what's the next move?" someone asked.

"Sam's Club," another answered. "Don't you remember?"

There were scattered snickers.

"All I remember is I'm rich," said another.

"Hell, we're *all* rich," said Stan Reno. "Plenty to go around."

Sal and Sharon stood leaning against Sal's Voyager, locked in a loving embrace.

"Can you believe it?" whispered Sal.

"Mmm hmmm" moaned Sharon, smiling.

"Right now," he said, "we've got over two million dollars. Do you realize that? Sharon, we are richer than we ever dreamed we'd be."

"Darling, I don't mean to cloud the picnic," said Sharon, "but there is the small matter of possession, you know. So far, your wallet and my purse are still as under-nourished as ever." She noticed the emerging of Sal's frustrated look and hurried to continue. "Believe me, I want it as badly as you. I can't wait to have our hands on our shares. Kiss me."

Just as they started to kiss they heard a smattering of applause from among the group as Rolly made his exit from the building.

Collusion on the Felt

"Hey, here comes Rolly," whispered a voice. The hushed applause grew by several careful decibels. As the muffled sound reached Rolly, he signaled for quiet with his hands. But his face showed his pleasure. Several of the team walked briskly toward him, Nappa in the lead.

"It was brilliant, my man," said Nappa, slapping Rolly on the shoulder. "That was so well greased, it purred like a kitty raised on warm milk. You done really good, man."

Rolly looked at Nappa and smiled. "Couldn't have done it without you – all of you," he said, gesturing to the several gathered around him. "The hard part may be over, but the scary part still awaits us," he said. "There's still some distance between us and our payoff. And that's where I'll be heading in just a little while. They're still paying off the whales inside."

The cage cashiers deposited the last of the thirty-five hundred ten thousand dollar stacks of one-hundred dollar bills into the final suitcase. As each of the twelve suitcases was filled and accepted by Cyril Queck at the cage, a porter with a two-wheeled dolly accompanied by a security officer took over. They toted the loot through the casino, up the handicap ramp near the front entrance, and across the marble lobby, outside to the waiting limousines. Under the watchful eyes of Archie Yen and his group, and Liu Prinya, on behalf of the Queck entourage, six suitcases were neatly stored in each limo, using both the trunks and rear seats.

On the second floor of the parking garage, leaning over the concrete abutment, Nathan Mesmer squinted through hunting binoculars as Cyril Queck exited the hotel, stiffed the doorman, and climbed into the mid-section of the red stretch limo. Careful to avoid pressing his still bruised, sore eyes against the binocular's eyepieces, Mesmer had counted the suitcases as they were loaded one by one. With only twelve suitcases, he smelled a rat. No way seventy million in cash could be stowed in only a dozen suitcases, he reasoned. Something must have gone wrong. He surmised the cage was probably short on cash. He was comfortable that *half* would fit in twelve suitcases. That was the half he was concerned about, anyway. He collapsed the binoculars, tossed them through the window onto the passenger seat of the Viper, and buckled himself in for what was sure to be the bumpiest ride of his life.

Inside, Harry Fetters reaching the end of a long, haggard shift felt exhausted and terribly beaten. The dejected Fetters climbed the mezzanine stairs to the casino office where he would file a brief, final report of the night's salon action for review by Frederick and the comptroller tomorrow morning. At least, he thought, Frederick already knows about the huge loss. That was a tremendous relief.

He walked into the outer office. He noticed that Frederick's door was slightly ajar and his office light was on. Fetters wondered why he'd still be here at this time, particularly since he was so tired earlier. He opted not to disturb him, but instead flopped down at the shared casino managers' desk. He picked up a pen and a blank copy of a shift report. He scribbled in the sketchy details of the evening's action, ending with the additional expense of twelve Samsonite suitcases from the gift shop. He chuckled to himself. The suitcases will probably put them over the top, he thought. Seventy million, they can deal with–but a dozen suitcases? He shook his head, picked up the form, and placed it in Rhonda Bethtold's in-box. Yawning, he loosened his tie, unbuttoned his shirt at the neck, and headed for the door. Over his shoulder he called out, "Goodnight, Mr. Frederick!" No response. Typical, he thought, and he let his numb legs carry him down the stairs.

Chapter Twenty-eight

The unmitigated dormancy reflected in the LED displays tore his heart out.

Rolly looked at his watch. "Okay," he said, "looks like it's time for me to take off. I will see you folks at you know where. Let's plan on meeting there in an hour, hour and a half."

Sue Min motioned for Rolly to join her just outside hearing distance from the group.

"Yes, Sue Min?"

"Rolly, I'm just a little concerned about all the cars congregating late at night in that parking lot. Isn't that going to draw a lot of attention if someone notices?"

"I know what you mean. It's not that I hadn't been thinking the same thing. It's just that I don't have any better ideas."

"One or two vehicles – maybe," said Sue Min. "But we could end up with a couple of dozen."

"Couple dozen what?" asked Nappa, joining the twosome.

"Sue Min's concerned about the number of cars we'll have behind Sam's Club," explained Rolly.

"Yeah, nothin' like a late night spectacle," said Nappa. "But what choice do we have?"

Rolly looked around, thinking. He spotted a large step-van parked outside the showroom loading dock. It was the Empires' lights and sound van. "Hey, where's Curtis?" he asked.

"Who?" asked Nappa.

"Oh, our sound man," said Sue Min. "Curtis Lately."

"Yeah, have you seen him?" asked Rolly.

"I think he's over there with the group," said Sue Min.

Rolly walked briskly toward the group. "Curtis!" he called out.

"Yeah, Rolly?"

"You got the keys to that lights and sound van?" He pointed to the loading dock.

Instinctively, Curtis slapped his pants pocket. The jingling sound was pleasantly affirming. "Sure do," he said.

"Excellent," said Rolly. "All right. Everyone gather around here, huh?"

Curious, the group moved in among the parked cars to join Rolly at the edge of the lot.

"Listen up," he said. "Minor change of plans."

"Uh oh," Sharon whispered to Sal. Sal gave her a look. She crinkled her nose at him and smiled.

"For the time being, I want all of you to stay put here in the lot. But, for heaven's sake, don't congregate and draw attention to yourselves. When I pick up our shares, I'll radio Nappa. Then I want you guys to load up in that lights and sound truck over there and meet me at the original location. That way, we'll only have the two vehicles. We'll distribute the shares there and then take you to your homes with your money. You'll be able to afford a cab later to pick up your cars." Rolly laughed. "How does that sound?"

"Works for me," said Stan Reno. The others concurred.

"Excellent," said Rolly. "Okay, I'm on my way." Rolly headed for the rented blue minivan.

"So we're stuck here for a while, huh?" Sharon asked Sal.

Sal didn't answer. Instead his eyes were riveted on Rolly as he approached his car.

"Sal?" said Sharon. "Sal?"

"Just a second, honey," Sal said. "I think we need to follow Rolly."

"Follow him?"

"Yeah. It's about something he said to me the other day. I think it's best if we follow him."

"Well, that beats sitting here," said Sharon. "My car or yours?"

"Mine's closer," said Sal. "We'll take mine."

They hurried toward Sal's Voyager. Sue Min called out after them, "Where are you two going?"

"We'll be back in a little while," Sal said. "Got something we have to take care of."

"You think Rolly's not coming back?" asked Sharon, as Sal started the engine.

"Has that thought ever crossed your mind? Sal asked.

"I haven't really thought about it...."

"Think about it now," Sal said. "What's to stop him from taking off with all our money? What are we going to do call the police? Officer, some guy just stole the money we stole."

"Now's a fine time to...."

"Shhhhhh," Sal said. "Not now."

Clemente Duarte pushed his rolling trash barrel off the elevator at the mezzanine level. Carrying his broom and extended-handle dust shovel, he pushed the large, plastic barrel into the casino managers' outer office and began emptying the trash cans at the four desks, and sweeping up. He noticed the office light was still on in the vice-president's office, and felt uneasy about interrupting to empty trash. The few occasions Nathan Mesmer had been working when Duarte entered, the jerk waved him away. He knew, through the hotel grapevine, that Mesmer had been hospitalized and then suspended and replaced by a guy from corporate. He decided to go ahead and attempt to empty the corporate guy's trash.

He knocked on the nearly closed door. When he heard no response, he knocked again and called out, "EVS Department, trash pickup." Again, he heard no response. Slowly, he pushed the door open and rolled his trash barrel into the large, executive office.

It was twelve-forty-two AM. when Charlie Palermo, drained and extremely upset, finally arrived home. His wife Monica and daughter Alicia were both already in bed. He walked down the hall to Alicia's bedroom, pressed his ear to the door, and then opened it. She was fast asleep. Sweet, innocent girl, he thought. The sight of her safe and at home was a glorious contrast to the vivid imaginings that haunted him all the way to Utah. He was out five thousand dollars in the scam, but the loss was miniscule relative to the sight he beheld right now. He pulled the door closed and walked back into the kitchen. A cold beer would hit the spot, he thought.

While he sat alone in the family room with the TV on very low, his thoughts wandered to whom may have singled him out for this emotional trouncing. Clear possibilities were not forthcoming. He felt personally violated, and it angered him. And why only five thousand dollars? That was a ridiculously low ransom! It was almost as though they simply wanted him out of the hotel this evening. Why? He wouldn't be able to sleep unless this dilemma was resolved. He picked up the phone and dialed the Desert Empire's Surveillance Department. Perhaps Isaac Nester could shed some light on this.

The night was particularly dark with the quarter moon providing the highway's only semblance of light. Mesmer looked down at his odometer. He was seven miles from the point on Blue Diamond Road where Hutchins was originally going to drop him, on the way to rendezvous with the whales. Up ahead, perhaps three-quarters of a mile, Mesmer could still, but barely, track the dwindling taillights of the two limousines. He was pleasantly surprised the whales appeared to be keeping their part of the agreement. He'd half expected them to take off with all the cash. Perhaps they *were* men of their word, he thought.

He used to be. Alas, there was a time when the word of Nathan Mesmer was as binding as a contract with the devil. Laser straight. Integrity at all costs. Upward and onward. *Most* people enter the tunnel of life bursting with energy, drenched in optimism, focused on abiding by the side of righteousness.

Then through that tunnel, pointed straight at you, comes earned wisdom like a colossal locomotive on a collision course with idealism; at first gradual and deliberate, then gaining momentum during the formative wage-earning years. And just as you allow yourself to be lulled into feelings of security and confidence – wham! It's a runaway behemoth fueled with the brutal truth of human dominance, egos dripping with deceit, souls coated in envy, and engineered by schizophrenic haves bent on derailing the have-nots. And the track? A rigid bed, lined with all the voracity a lifetime of greed and glutton can marshal. Survival! That's what it's all about, concluded Mesmer. Survival of the fittest.

And he was feeling fit tonight. Despite the constant pain and discomfort slicing through his body like a surgeon's scalpel, he was at the top of his game. Nothing or no one could stop him now. Not Hutchins; certainly not Frederick. Fuck Frederick. May he rest in misery. Those fat cat suck-ups. They were all the same. As long as they had their cushy thrones and stock options, the hell with everyone else. It's all bullshit! This time Mesmer beat them at their own game. All that remained was to collect the winnings.

That reminded him. He unbuckled his seatbelt and leaned across the passenger seat to the glove compartment. He pressed the button, causing the door to fall open, revealing his second Smith and Wesson, a loaded copper-coated 357 Magnum. Behind it sat a nearly full box of ammunition. Alternating glances between the gun and the road, he reached inside and lifted the only partner he could trust. His lower jaw reflexively protruded as the coolness of the weapon encountered the moist warmth of his hand. It felt good – solid, heavy, obedient. He laid it on the seat beside him and flipped up the glove compartment door. In the distance, the two red chariots continued on toward the meeting point. All of the whales would have to live through this tonight, in order for any one of them to live, he vowed. It mattered not to him how that would play out.

He looked up into his rearview mirror. There were no car lights behind him. He knew Hutchins would be along shortly. He wanted to position himself *behind* Hutchins and make his surprise on everyone at once. He pulled left off the road onto a graveled parking lot of a roadside tavern and jockeyed the Viper alongside a parked eighteen wheeler, facing the road. He killed the lights and shut off the ignition. With his hand on the Magnum, he awaited the blue minivan.

Charlie Palermo ran past the Time Office security booth, flashing his ID card. After receiving no response to four telephonic attempts to contact Surveillance from home, he was convinced something horrible must have happened.

Nappa, standing just outside the lights and sound Truck, gasped as four Las Vegas Police cars, lights flashing and sirens blaring, escorted an EMT ambulance along the distant perimeter of the rear loading dock area, heading toward the front of the Desert Empire. Others quickly scrambled out of their cars as the sirens' intensity drew nearer.

"Into the truck, everyone!" ordered Sue Min as she ran toward the loading dock. Nappa took on the proverbial deer in the headlights posture, debating whether to run outside in the opposite direction of the police, or jump into the back of the truck. "Everyone in the truck!" Sue Min shouted.

Curtis Lately, out of breath and shaking nervously, fiddled with the keys to the truck.

"Curtis, give me the keys!" demanded Sue Min. She caught the toss and quickly unlocked the back door of the truck. "Everybody in!"

At the last second, Nappa joined his comrades and leaped into the back of the truck. Sue Min tossed him the keys. "Can you drive this thing?" she asked.

"I can drive anything," said Nappa.

"Go," ordered Sue Min. "I've got shotgun!"

"Where we goin'?" asked Nappa.

"Just drive," she said, pulling the rear doors closed, "We've got to get the hell out of here!"

Palermo slid his key into the lock and pushed open the surveillance room door. His worst fears were confirmed at the immediate absence of staffing at the console. He quickly eyeballed the bank of monitors. In the casino, it appeared to be business as usual. But monitor forty-two told a much different story. A bevy of policemen were cordoning off the area around the hosts' office with yellow crime scene tape. EMT technicians, carrying a stretcher and other medical equipment were just now entering the side door, rushing up the stairs to the mezzanine. Palermo instinctively looked behind him at the floor-to ceiling racks of video recorders, the bread and butter of his career. The unmitigated dormancy reflected in the LED displays tore his heart out.

In a gesture of religious proportions, he frantically shoved his flattened hand into several of the machines' tape slots, praying for the familiar touch of hard plastic cassette. The disappointment was crushing. He was breathing heavily now and soaking with perspiration. Next his eyes flashed the huge, round trash barrel, loaded to the brim with black videocassettes, loops of crinkled tape yanked from under the horizontal flaps.

The magnitude of this catastrophe was already incomprehensible. Palermo knew there would barrages of questions, incessant investigations, allegations of his own incompetence and possible involvement. Something disastrous had obviously adulterated the Desert Empire – on his watch – and he was not only unable to deliver on his responsibilities, the chief eye, himself, had been blinded.

He was hyperventilating and on the verge of dizziness. He hunkered down on the top step outside his office and deposited his head in his quivering hands, panicking as he anticipated the first of what would be countless phone calls.

While waiting for the minivan to pass by on the dark, quiet Blue Diamond Road, the exhausted Mesmer had inadvertently dozed off. Startled suddenly by the ignition sound of a nearby diesel truck, he awakened in a panic and immediately checked his watch. He'd been out fifteen minutes. In a frenzy, he accelerated, spinning the Viper back onto the highway. He was eight miles from the rendezvous point and, he feared, many minutes late.

"There, up ahead," said Sal. "See the limos?"

"I see them," said Sharon.

"See, Rolly's pulling over," said Sal. "When we get there, go on past them. We'll turn around and double back from the other side."

The Voyager cruised by the rendezvous point where the two red limos were now joined by Rolly in his minivan. Rolly got out of the car and hurried over to the driver's side of the Queck limo. Craig Stetson opened the door and embraced Rolly.

"I can't believe it, Rolly. We've actually pulled this son-of-a-bitch off!"

"What I can't believe is how fast my heart is beating," said Rolly. "This whole thing is a hell of a rush. How are you guys doin' back there?" Rolly asked the Queck group.

"We are happy for you," said Queck. "We are happy for ourselves, as well."

"You should be." said Rolly. "You picked up a quick—what—fifteen mil?"

"Actually seventeen point five," corrected Queck.

"Not bad for three hours work, huh?"

"What will you do, now?" asked Queck.

"What do you mean?"

"Do you intend remaining with the Desert Empire? Or are you leaving town?"

"It's open," said Rolly. "Might go join my wife, or I might bring her back here. I'll see how it goes for a while. I'll definitely be back to work on Thursday, though. I told everybody they needed to report as scheduled."

"Well, we wish you good luck," said Queck.

"Thank you, Mr. Queck. Always a pleasure."

Paul Toomey, driver of the other limo walked over and threw his arms around Rolly. "You need to run for President, man. You really pulled something off here."

"*We* did," said Rolly. "This was a damn fine team effort."

"You got room for twelve suitcases in your van?" asked Stetson.

"Hey, if I have to drive sittin' on the roof, we'll make room," said Rolly laughing. "Let's go ahead and make the transfer. I want to say 'hey' to Archie and his boys."

Stetson and Toomey began transferring the suitcases from the limos to Rolly's minivan, while Rolly went over to the second limo.

He opened the door to the center section and extended his hand to Archie Yen.

"See I told you," said Yen, "You are my lucky charm."

Rolly laughed. "You didn't do too bad by me, either, my old friend. Thank you."

About seventy-five yards from the rendezvous point, Sal slowed the Voyager and came to a full stop, just off the road, killing the lights and the engine. Sal and Sharon could barely make out the three vehicles, illuminated only by the interior dome lights from the open doors.

Sal opened his window, straining to see if he could hear anything. This remote part of Las Vegas was stone silent, but for the occasional cricket. He could make out very distant voices, like on an early morning golf course, but words and meaning were unintelligible.

"Let's just cool it here," whispered Sal. "I suppose he's getting the money now."

"Maybe you had nothing to worry about," whispered Sharon, smiling.

"Hey, I wasn't sweating him getting the money," said Sal. "It's what he does next that concerns me."

Sharon looked around at the blackness. "This is kind of romantic, don't you think?"

He looked over at her. "I'm really glad you're in this with me," he said grinning.

"Why is that?"

"If I were involved in this by myself, not only would we only have half the money, but the sheer rush of this thing would only be half as high. But with you – the sky's the limit."

"And that's a good thing?" she asked.

He leaned over to her, peering into her eyes, slowly nodding his head.

She leaned toward him with her lips parted, and pressed them against his mouth. "I've never kissed a millionaire before," she whispered. "Mmmm, it tastes good."

"Don't forget, you're a millionaire, too," he said.

"That makes me wet," she said. "You make me wet."

At that instant, the lights from a distant, but fast approaching car, bounced off their faces. Their eyes reflexively shifted toward it.

"Here comes somebody," said Sal.

"I hope it's not a cop," said Sharon.

They watched as the car made a skidding left turn into the rendezvous point.

"Looks like a Viper!" exclaimed Sal. "Mesmer has a Viper!"

"Mesmer? Your VP?"

"Never mind," he said. "Shit's happening!"

The bright lights from the speeding car stunned everyone, and they began scrambling out of the limos as the yellow Viper skewed to a dust-billowing stop. Rolly instantly recognized it was Mesmer. "Keep cool," he said to everyone. "I'll handle this."

Mesmer remained seated in the car, turning off the lights, but keeping the engine running. Stetson and Toomey, each carrying a heavy suitcase, froze in their tracks.

"Christ, is that Mesmer?" asked Toomey. "What the fuck…?"

"Oh, shit," said Stetson.

Rolly walked toward the Viper, calming everyone in the first limo. "Stay cool," he repeated.

Mesmer's power window lowered. In a low, slow grumble, he said "You want to talk?" He sat looking straight ahead through the windshield.

Rolly, placing his hands on the widow seal, lowered his head into the car and in the same low grumble, said, "What the fuck are you doing here? This isn't what we agreed!"

"Looking after my interest," snarled Mesmer. Then he looked directly at Rolly and barked, "No one else is!"

"What are you talkin' about? I'm here pickin' up our money just like we agreed. We're supposed to hook up back there," Rolly said pointing east.

"Been a slight change in plans," said Mesmer. "Get over it."

"Nathan, these people weren't supposed to know you were involved," he whispered. "This fucks everything up."

"No, *this* fucks everything up!" Mesmer growled, quickly pushing the muzzle of his 357 against Rolly's chest. "Get the fuck away from the car!"

"What's going on?" asked Sharon. "Can you tell?"

"Can't make anything out," said Sal.

The door opened and Mesmer emerged, with considerable physical difficulty. He grabbed Rolly from behind by the left arm and pushed the gun against the right side of his head.

"Tell your buffoons to continue loading up the van," he ordered.

"Guys, go ahead and load up, please," said Rolly.

Stetson and Toomey continued the transfer.

"Tell the Chinks to get out of the limos," Mesmer ordered.

Rolly made a hated, twisted face at Mesmer, and called out," Mr. Queck. Mr. Yen. Please have everyone exit the limos."

"Now you all listen up," shouted Mesmer.

"Shhhh, I think I hear something," said Sal.

Careful not to bump or touch Mesmer, Rolly very slowly inched his right hand to his right hip where his radio was holstered. Feeling with his fingertips, he found the VOX button, and slipped it ever so carefully to the "on" position.

Simultaneously, in the lights and sound truck traveling southwest of the strip, a similar holster attached to Nappa's hip emitted a belch of static.

"What was that?" asked Sue Min, nervously.

"What was what?" asked Nappa.

"Listen," she yelled.

"You people do as I say and you may get out of here alive," began Mesmer.

"That's Mesmer," she said.

"Who?"

"Shhhh!" Sue Min lifted the radio from Nappa's hip and held it to her ear.

"Most likely, you Chinamen already have your money, so don't be idiots," said Mesmer. "Just do as I say and you'll get to spend it. Now, we're going to finish loading the van with the suitcases. Then you folks get back in the limos and drive yourselves out of here. You two drivers, you're coming with me. Now hurry up!"

"We've got big trouble," said Sal. "Sounds like Mesmer has a gun and is taking the money."

"Oh, no!" said Sharon. "Do something!"

"Start the engine, keep the lights off, and slowly creep forward. I want to get a little closer," said Sal.

"There goes our money," said Sue Min.

"What are you talkin' about," replied Nappa, nearly losing control of the truck.

"Be careful" she ordered. "We've got to find Rolly and help him."

"Where is he?" asked Nappa.

"Don't know," she said. "I'll keep listening, maybe get some clues."

Chapter Twenty-nine

He gouged the writhing weasel's forehead with the gun barrel, while his own face contorted into horrific revulsion, exposing his lower teeth and gums.

Charlie Palermo looked up as the phone again rang. He knew if he didn't start answering it, security would be dispatched in short order. He crossed to the video console. "Surveillance, Palermo."

"Mr. Palermo, I've been calling this number for ten minutes. What's going on there?"

"And whom am I speaking to, please?" asked Palermo, grasping for a sound of authority.

"Messersmith. Detective Arnie Messersmith, Metro. I'm going to need to speak with you. Can you spare a couple of minutes?"

"Yeah. I'm alone here, so..."

"All right. I'll get Security to escort me."

The two limousines were gone. As directed, the Queck and Yen groups had each departed with their own people doing the driving. The twelve suitcases were loaded in the Ford minivan. Stetson and Toomey were forced to sit in the van's back seat to await their fate according to Mesmer.

In the Voyager, Sal and Sharon had stealthily rolled to within fifty yards of the rendezvous area. They had seen the two limos leave a few minutes earlier. And they presumed that Rolly and Mesmer were now alone with their vehicles – and the money.

The lights and sound truck had pulled into McGivens' Auto Wrecking on West Russell Road, and mingled with the vehicular rubble. Sue Min Wong and Nappa Jackson were audibly glued to the wireless radio, their lifeline link to Rolly.

Mesmer and Rolly, who was still held at gunpoint, wandered away from the minivan, out of earshot of the two other captives.

"So what are you waiting for?" asked Rolly. "You've got the gun. You've got the money. Why don't you just drive out onto Blue Diamond Road and make your getaway? Why are you hangin' on to me?"

"Quiet!" barked Mesmer. "I'm trying to think."

"There it is!" shouted Sue Min, her ear against the radio's speaker. "Blue Diamond Road! Everybody down in back! We're taking off!"

Nappa fired up the truck and backed it out onto the dirt path. "Blue Diamond Road, here we come!"

"While you're thinking, think about this," Rolly continued. "There's enough money in that van for everybody. Split with us and you won't have to sleep with one eye open the rest of your life." Anticipating a potentially incriminating response, Rolly nonchalantly reached down and slid the VOX switch off.

"Shit! What was that?" asked Nappa.

Sue Min shook the radio and began slapping it. "I think it cut out," she said.

"Months ago, it started out to be a two-way split, Hutchins, me and you. Do you remember that?"

Rolly forced a nod.

"And now you want to water it down to a one-twenty-seventh cut. What the fuck do you take me for?"

"There was never going to be a two-way split, Mesmer, and you know it. You were going to fuck me from the beginning."

"Never!" Mesmer lied.

"No? What about the plane ticket Frederick found in your brief case? Australia? Tomorrow morning? With *my* name on it! What about that, huh?"

Mesmer was aghast.

"Got anything yet?" asked Nappa.

Frustrated, Sue Min continued to hit the radio. "No. Maybe he shut it off."

"Well, when he wants to communicate, he will. I know the Rollo!"

Sitting in the back of the minivan, Craig Stetson noticed the keys were still dangling from the ignition. "Paul," he said nudging his friend, "the keys...."

Toomey peered over the front seat. "No shit," he said. "Then why the fuck are we still sitting here like ducks in a carnival game?" He made a move toward the front.

"Wait! We can't just leave Rolly here like that," said Stetson. "Let me think a second."

"All right, let's level," said Mesmer.

"Level?" asked Rolly. "How are we supposed to level with that gun pointed at me?"

"All right then, *I'll* level with *you*. I bought you that ticket the day after we first talked about this..."

"Save it, Mesmer. We spoke in March. You bought the fucker in June."

"Doesn't matter. Once I plant that ticket in your home, it's going to look mighty suspicious you flying one-way to the other side of the world...perhaps to get away after you killed your new boss at the Empire."

Instinctively, but without being seen, Rolly switched on the radio.

"Got him back," said Sue Min. "Shhhh."

"What new boss…you mean Frederick? You *killed* him? You son-of-a-bitch!"

"No, *you* killed him," said Mesmer laughing. "I was home recuperating from that beating I took. Besides no one saw me go in or out of the hotel. And we both know there's no videotape. Must be that guy who flew to Australia," Mesmer mimicked.

"So you killed Frederick. You rotten piece of shit! And now you're going to kill me."

"Life's a bitch, ain't it?"

"Mesmer killed Frederick! That certainly explains the police," said Sue Min.

"Who's Frederick?" asked Nappa.

"Shhhh," she said. "Now he's going to kill Rolly. We've got to get there!" The truck lunged forward.

"This plan of yours leaks like a sieve," said Rolly, desperately.

"Do tell," said Mesmer.

"First of all, they'll never be able to connect me to Frederick; no fingerprints, no witnesses, no motive, no nothin'. Second, I'm not going to be on that flight tomorrow, so I won't be on the manifest. Third, *you're* the disgruntled employee who Frederick fired. *You* had the motive. It's *you're* ass they're going to be after, not mine."

"You're forgetting that you and Frederick spoke today when he told you about the plane ticket. My guess is other people know of that meeting – Rhonda for one. Another guess is, that meeting was held behind closed doors. I think we can summon up at least a modicum of suspicion there, don't you?"

"Look," said Toomey. "If I jump up front and start the engine, Mesmer will instinctively turn toward us. Right?"

"Most likely," said Stetson.

"Well, as soon as he turns, Rolly will make his move. He'll disarm him. We drive over and jump in. It's our only hope. We can't just sit here waiting to die for Christ's sake."

Stetson pondered the plan. "Man, it better work."

"It's worth a shot, Craig. What do you say?"

"Do it!"

Toomey quickly squeezed between the two front captain's seats, twisting into the driver's seat. He turned the key and revved the engine.

As anticipated, Mesmer turned quickly, "What the...!"

Rolly leaped onto Mesmer's back, forcing him to the ground. The gun went off.

"He shot him!" screamed Sue Min. "My God!"

"Gunfire!" screamed Sal. "Get going! Now!"

Sharon fired up the Voyager and powered the skidding vehicle, zigzagging onto Blue Diamond Road, speeding toward the sound of the gunshot.

With the lights from the minivan piercing the rising clouds of flying dirt and sand, Rolly and Mesmer rolled over onto each other repeatedly, each clutching parts of the gun, Mesmer white-knuckling the handle; Rolly vice-gripping the barrel. Stetson and Toomey, leaped from the van and shuffled tentatively only feet from the two brawlers, fearing another stray discharge from Mesmer's weapon.

"Grab the gun!" grunted Rolly.

"I'll kill you all!" panted Mesmer. "Stay... the fuck...away!"

Just then, the sound of pebbles and dirt fiercely ricocheting off a car's undercarriage accompanied the hurried arrival of the Voyager.

"Hit the horn!" yelled Sal. And Sharon leaned on it, as the car skidded to a stop just inches from the two prone combatants. She and Sal hurried out of the car and joined Stetson and Toomey.

The audible distraction worked. Mesmer, pained by the deafening blast, screamed and lost his grip on the gun. Rolly, equally affected, but boiling over with loathing, swiftly yanked it from his weakened grasp. His chest rising with every wheeze, and blood streaming from the corner of his mouth, Rolly mounted Mesmer's chest, jamming his shoulders into the dirt with his knees. He gouged the writhing weasel's forehead with the gun barrel, while his own face contorted into horrific revulsion, exposing his lower teeth and gums.

"Give me one fuckin' reason – anybody!" he yelled, "why this bucket of dog shit should live! One fuckin' reason! That's all!" he screamed.

"No," pleaded Mesmer, panting. "No, please...."

"Shut your fuckin' trap!" ordered Rolly. "Ain't no one here talkin' to you!"

Suddenly, Rolly's radio erupted with a crack of static followed by Sue Min's voice. "Rolly Hutchins, you don't have a hair on your ass if you don't jam that gun in that cocksucker's mouth right now and blow him to Kingdom Come."

"Oooooeeeeee," said Nappa. "Mamma, I love when you talk dirty!"

Hearing his friends' voices delivered a calming to Rolly. He managed a trace of his trademark smirk. "You hear that, Mesmer? A lot of people want you dead. Ain't that a shame, man? Your life ain't worth filler's fuck. How does it feel?"

"It's not too late," whispered Mesmer, his lips quivering. "Take the money, let me live. You're not a killer, Hutchins. Don't do this to yourself. You're right. I'm not worth it."

"There you go again, Nathan, tryin' to bullshit me. Tell you what, I'll make a deal with you…"

"Anything. Anything," Mesmer pleaded.

"You're right, you ain't worth me bein' a killer. So, here's the deal. How about I give you this gun and you do the world a favor and blow your own head off. That way I'm off the hook and you get a chance to make things right."

"Hold on, there, Rolly," interrupted Sal. "You're not serious about turning that gun over to him are you?"

Rolly didn't take his eyes off Mesmer, but recognized Sal's voice. "Hey, Slick. How you doin? Now just hold on a minute, okay? Well, Mesmer, either you do it or I do it. What's it gonna be?"

No way Mesmer believed Rolly would be stupid enough to give him the gun, but this was definitely the end of the line. He'd have to play his final hand. "I'll do it," he said. "If that's my only choice, at least I can try to make amends. I'll do it myself."

"You heard him, guys," said Rolly. "Man says if I give him the gun, he'll do us all a favor and kill himself. How about that?"

"Rolly?" said Sal.

"Yeah, hey Rolly," said Stetson.

"I take it you guys don't believe Mr. Mesmer. Is that it? You don't believe this fine upstanding casino executive–excuse me–*former* casino executive, is that it?"

"Rolly," said Sharon. "We are begging you, don't give him the gun."

"Damn, Mesmer. Ain't nobody wants me to turn this baby over to you."

"I'm serious," Mesmer managed. "Trust me on this."

"Hear that?" asked Rolly. "He says we need to trust him on this."

"Rolly!" It was Sue Min. "Why are you playing games with this man?"

"Because this motherfucker has been playing games with us!" yelled Rolly. "His whole life has been one big game – one big game where he makes and changes all the rules just to suit him. That's why, Sue Min. Now it's our turn to play games!"

Rolly, much of his original anger returned, lowered his head so he was nose-to-nose with Mesmer. The gun was still digging into Mesmer's forehead, and the pushing pressure of both hands was now increasing. "I'm gonna let you play one last game, hog shit. You win – you live. You don't – you die."

Mesmer was trembling. "What is it?"

"We're going to play a little game of roulette – Russian Roulette. Now get up."

Rolly stood up with the gun trained on Mesmer. "I want you in the driver's seat of your car. Get moving."

Mesmer slowly and painfully rolled onto his stomach and with considerable difficulty, raised up from his knees to his feet. He stumbled his way to the Viper, with Rolly gripping his sport jacket and aiming the gun at the back of his head. The other four followed.

"I don't know if I can stand to watch this," said Sharon.

"You don't have to. You can wait in the car," said Sal.

"What about you?" she asked.

"Sorry, but I wouldn't miss this for the world."

"Are you sure this is what you want," asked Mesmer.

"Shut up," commanded Rolly. "And give me the keys."

Mesmer reached into his pocket and surrendered the keys to Rolly.

"Don't want you getting tempted," said Rolly.

"Rolly, this is Sue Min. You need to wait until we get there. I got a truck full of anxious puppies who want to see this."

"How far away are you?"

"Can't tell. We're on Blue Diamond now, headed west. Just passed some old tavern on the left."

"You're almost here. Less than ten minutes," said Rolly. "We'll wait."

"You fucking people are making a show out of this," said Mesmer.

"Yeah, and just imagine how much popcorn we can afford to buy now," said Rolly smugly. "Now get in."

Mesmer opened the door to the Viper and slid into the driver's seat.

"Don't worry about the seatbelt," said Rolly. "With luck, you won't be needing it."

Sal, Craig, and Paul snickered. Sharon just shook her head. Rolly emptied the gun of its seven bullets. He placed all but one in his pocket, reserving it in Mesmer's name.

"Well, we're all set," said Rolly. "Soon as the rest of the audience gets here."

"How many times do I need to do this," asked Mesmer, "before I might win?"

Rolly scratched his chin in thought. "I don't know. Guys, how many times do we want Mesmer to pull the trigger?"

"Three?" offered Sal.

"Three? No, we need more than that, don't you think?"

"No more than five," said Sharon. "If he gets by five, that should be enough."

"I think about twenty," said Sue Min.

"We'll go with five," laughed Rolly. "And let me tell you something, Mesmer. If you even think about pointing this gun at us, we will pull you out of that car and take you apart cell by cell, no questions asked. You understand?"

"But if I get by five attempts, you're going to let me go free?"

"We'll let you go, but you'll never be free, Mesmer. You'll never be able to outrun what you did to Frederick. So I'm not worried. Besides, if there is a God, you'll never make it past five, anyway," chuckled Rolly.

"You realize this doesn't look very good," said Arnie Messersmith.

"I know, I know," lamented Palermo.

"Have you tried calling any of your agents?"

"Yeah, I called the Colonel, nobody answered. I also called Isaac's home, same response. I'm worried about both of them."

"Have you searched this place?"

"What's to search? You don't see anybody, do you?"

"What about that door over there?"

"Storage closet," said Palermo.

"Have you looked in there?"

"No …."

Arnie moved quickly to the storage closet and pulled open the door. "Quick, get over here," he called to Palermo. "Two men down!"

"Oh, my God," said Palermo, as he hurried to the closet. "Are they still alive?"

Arnie was down on one knee. Isaac Nester squirmed and groaned, a stark contrast to the immobile Colonel. Arnie carefully pulled the duct tape from Nester's mouth. "Untie him," he said to Palermo. "This other fellow's hurting."

He removed the tape from the Colonel's mouth and immediately felt his neck for a pulse.

"He's diabetic," said Palermo. "He needs a doctor now!"

"He's barely got a pulse," said Arnie. "Untie him. I'm calling for help."

He ran out to the video console, picked up a phone, and called the hotel operator.

"Get me Security immediately."

"My pleasure, sir," said the operator.

"Security. Roscoe."

"Yes, this is Detective Messersmith. I need you to get the EMT people from the casino manager's office and bring them to Surveillance at once. We've got a man down – possible diabetic coma."

"I'm on it," said Roscoe.

Isaac Nester, freed from his confinement, wobbled from the storage closet.

"I need water," he said. "I'm dying of thirst!" Arnie obliged.

"Do you feel like talking?" asked Arnie.

"Sure," Nester said, gulping the liquid treasure.

"What happened?"

"I come walking in for my shift. First person I see is a cop. That blew my mind. Next thing I know, the cop lunges at me with pepper spray! Burned the hell out of my eyes and face. Pretty much knocked me out. When I came to, I was just like you found me. I didn't know where I was or what the hell happened."

"You say a cop lunged at you?"

"Yeah."

"Not a security officer?"

"A cop!"

"Ever see him before?"

"Nope."

"Did you see a name tag or a badge or anything?"

"I saw stars, man. That's it."

"Do you think you could ID the cop?"

"Hard to say. It happened so fast."

"Was anybody else in the room when you came in?"

"I have no idea. You come from the bright hallway lights into the darkness of this room, you can barely see anything for a few minutes."

"What time was that when you got here?"

"A few minutes before eleven – my usual time."

"Okay. That's it for now. Thanks."

"Is the Colonel going to be all right?"

"Help's on the way," said Arnie. "I think it's serious."

"Son-of-a-bitch!," cursed Nester. "This sucks!"

"Detective!" called Palermo. "Is a doctor coming?"

"On the way," answered Arnie. "Is he conscious?"

"I can't detect any breathing!"

The lights and sound truck could now be heard out on Blue Diamond Road. It was two-fifty AM. "We see some light on the left of the road, Rolly. Can you hear our truck?"

"Loud and clear. Make a left at the opening."

"Man, we get to become millionaires and watch a Russian roulette all in the same day," said Nappa smiling. "It's all good."

The truck pulled in to the rendezvous area and up to where they saw the group standing outside the Viper. Immediately, everyone began jumping from the truck, mixing with and greeting their comrades. There were hugs and high fives.

"It's show time, everybody!" Rolly clapped his hands.

The group immediately quieted down and moved toward the Viper, forming a semi-circle gallery.

Rolly spun the chamber several times, as Mesmer sneered his disdain.

"Here ya go," he said. "I already spun it for you, but you might want to spin, too."

Mesmer took the gun with his left hand and defiantly raised the pistol and pressed it to his left temple.

"Yeah, that's it," said Rolly, "aim thataway. Keep the mess away from us."

Mesmer's lower lip quivered as his eyes squeezed tightly shut. His lungs filled with air he drew in forcefully through visible, clenched teeth. His hand, rife with tension, began trembling. Not a decibel of sound was evident, as everyone held their breath. Some even looked away. Mesmer involuntarily emitted a high-pitched, muffled whine as his forefinger applied just a trace of pressure on the trigger. But that was all it needed.

The force of the springing hammer pounding against the carbon steel chamber created a safe clicking sound that was followed immediately by Mesmer's shrieking gasp.

The crowd exhaled.

"Son-of-a-bitch," panted Rolly to no one in particular. "That's *one*."

"Fuck you," muttered the still quaking Mesmer, sweat streaming down his face.

"All right, give it a good spin," ordered Rolly.

Mesmer grimaced. He grabbed the chamber with his right hand and spun it twice.

"Sal, this is horrible," Sharon whispered. "What are we going to do if that man actually blows his head off? Has anybody thought about that?"

"There's at least a hundred places I'd rather be right now," Sal whispered back.

The barrel of the gun was again pressed against Mesmer's left temple. His bruised and battered face was scrunched up in blatant dread. Shuddering and soaked from fear, he allowed his finger to exert on the trigger.

"Bang!" shouted Rolly.

Mesmer screamed. The group screamed. Rolly laughed, as Mesmer collapsed onto the seat into a pitiful blubbering pile. When it registered that the gun had indeed *not* fired, the gathering began babbling incoherently.

Nappa screamed "Damn!" for no apparent reason, but to let off steam.

"Don't make me do more," whimpered Mesmer. "I can't take it. Please"

"Three more," ordered Rolly. "A deal's a deal."

Rolly turned toward his COF mates, "Am I right? A deal's a deal, right? Come on, let me hear you. A deal's a deal. A deal's a deal."

The crowd, less than enthusiastic, was slow to answer, offering barely audible responses arising from perhaps a meager handful. Determined to raise their vivacity, Rolly shot stares at each of them, pointing to them individually, forcefully repeating his chant. His face broadcast his growing delight as the group's reluctant participation slowly grew in both number and volume. The chant "A deal's a deal! A deal's a deal!" now pierced the silence of Southwest Las Vegas, albeit in a vacuum of alien ears. While Rolly's attention focused on energizing the group, the crouching Mesmer quickly opened the glove box and snatched the stored box of bullets. With lightning speed, he flipped open the box, pouring the potent shells into a heap on the passenger seat. He scooped up a handful, flipped open the chamber, and with his back as cover, filled the revolving chamber counting seven insertions. If accurate, that meant there had been no bullets in the gun after all!

Satisfied that ample enthusiasm reigned, Rolly raised his arms and quieted his group. He turned toward Mesmer who still maintained his crouched position.

"Okay, Mesmer! Three more! A deal's a deal!"

Like a tightly wound spring, Mesmer lunged to the window, leading with the pointed gun raised to the heavens and pulled the trigger. The resounding detonation married to the blazing discharge first stunned, then staggered the incognizant crowd as they screamed and dove to the ground in a pile of hyper palpitation. First among them was Rolly, most traumatized of all.

"Game over!" screamed Mesmer, pushing open the car door and firing a second shot airborne for good measure. With full knowledge the five remaining rounds could not stave off everyone, should will overpower sense, Mesmer's eyes riveted the mass for the perfect hostage. His eyes met Sharon's.

"You!" he shouted, waving the magnum. "I want you here! Now!"

Sharon turned toward Sal, her face pleading. "No, Sal! Please!"

"Take *me*, Mesmer!" Sal blurted out. "Leave her alone!"

"No!" screamed Sharon. "No!"

"All right, hero – fine! Get your ass over here!"

Rolly spoke up. "No, Mesmer. This is between me and you. Nobody else move!" he ordered. "You want a hostage. Grow balls! Take me!"

"Nothing would give me more pleasure," Mesmer growled. "Up here, now!"

Rolly lifted himself from the ground, dusting the dirt from his clothes. He turned toward the sniveling crowd. "I'm sorry, guys," he began. "I should have taken him down when I had the chance. Whatever happens to me – I deserve it."

"Everybody stay put!" Mesmer shouted. "Flex one muscle and your guru is a dead man!" Pointing the gun at Rolly, he ordered, "In the van, now! You drive."

Chapter Thirty

Both men were doggedly focused on singular personal fulfillment, a reverie that could occur only at the other's ruin.

"You realize we let thirty-five million dollars just ride on out of here, don't you?" asked Nappa. "How many times in your life can you say that?"

"What were we supposed to do – jump him? He had that thing pointed right at Rolly," said Sal. "There was nothing we could do."

"Well maybe someone can tell me what we're going to do now?" asked Sharon. "What are we waiting for? What's next?"

"I think we should just wait here for a while. You never know what tricks Rolly may have up his sleeve," said Craig Stetson."

"I agree," chimed in Paul Toomey. "Rolly's gotten us this far. I wouldn't throw in the towel just yet."

"Frankly, I don't hold out a lot of hope for Rolly," said Stan Reno. "Mesmer's a snake *without* a gun. Mix in a gun and money, the man's a king cobra."

"All our dreams, man – out the fucking window!" moaned Francisco Mercado. "This is bullshit!"

"Well, we can't all just sit here," said Sal. "They can't be that far ahead," he said to Sharon. "Let's see if we can move in behind them. Keep an eye on things."

"You two go ahead," said Sue Min. "We've got the truck and Nappa's radio. If Rolly calls, we're out of here."

Sal and Sharon hurried to the Voyager and took off, headed east on Blue Diamond Road. Sal gunned the engine. They had considerable ground to cover quickly.

Craig Stetson and Paul Toomey jumped off the rear of the truck and wandered about 40 yards away from the group, disappearing into the late night shadows, ostensibly to smoke a cigarette. As they created distance from their comrades, they appeared to be whispering to each other.

"What are those two up to?" asked Curtis Lately.

"They're the limo guys," said Sue Min. "They live in their own little world."

"Think we should try Rolly on the radio?" asked Nappa.

"I wouldn't just yet," said Sue Min. "A blast of static could trigger a reaction from Mesmer. We'll let Rolly initiate any calls."

Rolly and Mesmer were heading east in the Ford Windstar, hauling the unparalleled mother load. No destination had been announced. Indeed, since Mesmer's initial "turn right" out of the rendezvous area, neither had spoken a word. The barrel of the 357 magnum bore into Rolly's ribs. The wheels of their minds vigorously spat out a plethora of images, grinding out frames of earlier events and flashes of hitherto options. Both men were doggedly focused on singular personal fulfillment, a reverie that could occur only at the other's ruin. At this instant, Mesmer owned the upper hand. But that edge had volleyed repeatedly during the past four hours. Rolly desperately clung to the hopeful prospect that somehow, someway, the tables would inexplicably turn just once more.

"Why did you kill him?" Rolly asked, breaking the silence.

"Kill who?"

"Frederick. Who do you think?"

"Had no choice. He stuck his nose where it didn't belong."

"I guess once you've killed somebody, the next one's easy, huh?"

"I'll let you know."

"It didn't have to be this way, you know."

"What way?"

"Me and you like this – bitter enemies. I mean, if you think about it, this is what we planned all along – me and you and thirty-five million in cash."

"No, It's all fucked up now," said Mesmer.

"How do you mean?"

"Frederick for one. And everybody in COF knows I'm involved, now. It's just all fucked up."

"You know killing me won't change any of that."

"But *not* killing you will make it worse. I don't need worse."

Silence returned for about a mile. Rolly, somewhat gratified that Mesmer was at least having a dialogue with him, decided to play his ace.

"You realize back there your gun was empty, don't you? There *was* no single bullet in the chamber. You could've spun that thing all night. Nothing was going to happen."

"See – you fucked up, too."

"Yeah," Rolly said with a sigh. "Apparently I did."

"Why?"

"What?"

"Why did you do that – no bullets?"

"I don't know," said Rolly. "Even though I despise the way you are right now, I'm stuck with the fact you and me had an agreement. I don't know, call me a pussy, but there's still a grain of integrity left in me."

"Don't bullshit me," said Mesmer. "You were going to fuck over your team all along – or at least that's what you said. In any case, you were either going to fuck them or me. No way you could keep your word to all of us."

"I said there was a 'grain' of integrity, Mesmer, not a shit load. What difference does it make anyway? I'll be dead in an hour."

"That's pretty optimistic, don't you think? An hour?" Mesmer laughed. "You'll be stone cold in an hour."

"Oh, is that right? Well, that bein' the case, there's no reason for me *not* to swerve in front of that eighteen-wheeler coming toward us, right?"

Mesmer looked quickly. Rolly wasn't kidding. There actually was a huge eighteen wheeler heading in their direction about a mile away.

"What about that, Mesmer? If I time it just right, I can die knowing your nasty face wore a Mack Truck logo just long enough for the grill to divvy up your head like a loaf of sliced bread."

Mesmer, even though armed and presumably in control, was developing pangs of anxiety. Rolly sounded serious. The barreling truck was now about a half-mile away.

"In fact, I have a better chance of surviving a broadside with that rig with you as a buffer, than I do a direct hit from that gun," grinned Rolly. "Yeah, the more I think about it, the more I like my odds."

"Don't be an idiot!" yelled Mesmer. "We'll both be crushed and millions of dollars burned!"

"What the fuck do I care?" Rolly faked a turn of the wheel into the truck's path.

"Pull back! We can deal!" screamed Mesmer.

"Deal, huh? Rolly straightened the wheel. " Better deal fast!"

"All right," bellowed Mesmer, biting his lip. "We can…split!"

The truck was getting closer. Mesmer could make out it was a tanker.

"Split? What kind of split?"

"We'll split even!" Mesmer pleaded.

"Fifty-fifty?"

"Yes! Yes!" Mesmer yelled.

The tractor was dark blue; the tank a drab gray.

"Toss the gun – now! Out my window!" ordered Rolly.

The truck was 75 yards away and fast approaching. Mesmer increased his grip on the gun and swallowed hard.

"All right," warned Rolly. "Have it your fuckin' way!" He quickly jerked the wheel to the left sending Mesmer slamming up against the passenger door, as the heavily loaded van tilted 40 degrees to the right on two wheels .

"No!" Mesmer squealed. "No!' He tossed the gun past Rolly's face out the driver's window. "There! Motherfucker!"

Rolly jerked back to the right at the precise instant the tractor-trailer screamed past, blaring its deafening horn. The dwarfed minivan fishtailed, its brakes screeching, leaving charred rubber zigzags all over the road.

"Close call there, *partner*!" Rolly laughed, dripping with sarcasm. "You look like you've seen a goddam ghost!"

"Pull over," panted Mesmer. "Find a place to pull over. We need to do some thinking."

"I don't mean no disrespect or nothin'," said Rolly, "but you don't somehow think you're still calling the shots now, do you? I mean, after all, we're fifty-fifty, right?"

"Fine!" said Mesmer, clearly annoyed and upset with this new power shift. "What do you think we ought to do?" he asked, patronizingly. "Is that better?"

"Whole bunches," said Rolly. "Fact is, I reckon we ought to pull over and do some thinking."

The huge tanker whizzed by the Voyager.

"They came that close!" said Sal, indicating an inch with his thumb and forefinger; his voice filled with distraught. "What the hell are they trying to do?"

"Sal," said Sharon, "I swear I saw something fly out of the van just before the truck passed. I could see it in the truck's headlights."

Sal shrugged it off.

"I'm serious," she said. "Could've been the gun, Sal. Slow down. See if we can see it."

They were virtually alone on the road, except for the minivan about a mile ahead. Sal turned up the high beams and brought the Voyager to a crawl.

"Help me look," he said. Sharon climbed over into the back seat and opened the driver's side window, straining her eyes on the slowly passing roadway.

"If you're right," said Sal. "Those two guys are one-on-one right now. That changes everything."

"Not only that," said Sharon. "If we find the gun; that means we have the edge."

"Never in my wildest dreams have I ever imagined myself in situations like we've been in today," said Sal. "If this were a movie, nobody would believe it."

"Check it out," Sharon said. "It looks like they're pulling over."

"Us, too," said Sal. He killed the lights and brought the Voyager to a stop on the side of the road. "As long as they're stopped, let's get out and keep looking for the gun. They'll never see us at this distance."

Stetson and Toomey finally returned to the group, after having spent a good ten to fifteen minutes alone.

"Welcome back, you two," said Curtis Lately, with a tone that smacked of suspicion. "What's up with you guys?"

"Nothing's up," said Stetson. "There's no rule that says we have to stay within 15 feet of the rest of you, is there?"

"Yeah, it's not like we have the money or anything," said Toomey.

"Well, we need to stick together," said Sue Min. "No telling when we may have to take off."

"Sal! Sal!" called Sharon in a hushed voice. "I got it!"

Sal quickly dashed up to her. "That's it!" he said. "That's the gun!"

"Mesmer's not armed," said Sharon.

"And we *are*!" said Sal. "Come on. Back to the car."

Mesmer hated losing the upper hand. His mind migrated to an area only a few feet away in the back of the van where seeds of his new life were waiting to germinate. Since they'd pulled over onto the shoulder, Rolly sat thumping his fingers on the top of the steering wheel; Mesmer leaned against the passenger door, lightly stroking his chin.

Again, Rolly was the first to speak. "The way I see it," he began, " is we have twelve suitcases – that's six apiece. We have one vehicle, which happens to be rented. So, what we need to do is have me drive you someplace – within reason, mind you - you make off with your six suitcases, and we're done."

"Sounds reasonable," said Mesmer, "except for one thing."

"What's that?"

"My car. It's still back there. If we go back to get it, we have to fuck with all those people again."

"I can fix that," said Rolly smiling. "All I gotta do is call'em on my radio here, tell'em to meet me someplace, and they'll take off. We go in. You get in your car with your six suitcases – bingo, case closed."

"I like it," said Mesmer.

"I'll tell 'em to wait for me at the original distribution point – behind Sam's Club."

Mesmer nodded. "Sounds good. Do it."

Amid a spurt of static, "Nappa, this is Rolly."

"Hey, it's Rollo!" said Nappa, pulling the radio from his holster. "Yeah, Rollo, talk to me!"

"It's all good," said Rolly. The group mumbled their approval.

"Man, you have no idea how motherfuckin' excited we are," said Nappa, grinning that full-toothed grin. "How'd you do it, man?"

"I'll explain later. Right now, I want all of you to load up and meet me at the original distribution point. Remember where that is?" asked Rolly.

"Yeah, man," said Nappa, eagerly.

"Now, if I'm not there when you guys arrive, hang loose for me. I've got something to take care of, if you know what I mean," said Rolly.

"Got it, my man," said Nappa. Click. "You heard the man," said Nappa, "let's load up!"

Chapter Thirty-one

First, he needed to turn his six suitcases into twelve. That wasn't going to be easy.

"Oh, shit," said Sal. "They're turning around and heading this way! Get down, quick!"

He and Sharon slid down in the front seat of the Voyager. It was too late to even consider hiding the car. They prayed the blanket of darkness would conceal them. Both wondered why the sudden retreat.

"Where do you think they're headed?" asked Sharon.

"Lord knows," said Sal. "I just hope they don't see us."

"Maybe they're looking for the gun," proposed Sharon.

"Naw, they're moving too fast."

They listened as the minivan soared past them in the opposite direction. What they failed to see was Rolly's smirk as he noted their position.

"All right," said Sal. "Let's get ready to follow."

"We're gonna need to pull into that tavern down the road," said Rolly. "We gotta be out of the way when that lights and sound truck comes by."

"Good thinking," said Mesmer. He looked at his watch. It was four-forty AM. The sun would begin to rise on the other side of town in about twenty minutes, and their dark accomplice would be gone. Exhaustion was scratching at the door. This had been an incredibly long, perplexing day. Mesmer's body ached from the ravages of the stress, strain, and physical exertion of the past twenty-four hours. Coupled with the agony of his already beaten body, the wear and tear of COF had sucked just about every ounce of his strength. He knew, too, he was eons from deliverance. He needed to check in at the airport by seven-fifteen, less than three hours from now. But, more imminently, he had bridges to cross and mountains to climb.

First, he needed to turn his six suitcases into twelve. That wasn't going to be easy. He suspected Hutchins was thinking along the same lines. Then, one way, or another, he had to take possession of the van to transport those dozen bags to the airport. They'd never fit in the Viper. He knew he'd need to ship them cargo. No way he'd attempt checking twelve bags on his seat ticket. That would arouse so much suspicion and attention, they'd name a law after him.

Once he shipped the bags, he could park Hutchin's van in the garage with his Australia itinerary tucked in the visor. That paperwork was still safely tucked in his inside pocket. At least that part of the plan endured.

Two concerns remained: disposing of the Viper and disposing of Hutchins. His thoughts turned to a two-for-one—cremating Hutchins in the Viper. Barring solid reasons to test for DNA, it was just possible they'd think it was Mesmer! *Charred Remains of Casino Executive Found in Auto Inferno!* This fabulous notion fascinated Mesmer. In this scenario, even *he* would be out of the picture—dead to the world, and free to resurrect anywhere else as anyone else.

Rolly slowed the van, turning left into the parking lot of the tavern. Ironically, he pulled up along side the identical eighteen-wheeler that had kept Mesmer company some five hours earlier. He killed the engine and yawned. They would wait for the lights and sound truck to pass by.

Collusion on the Felt

Sal and Sharon were back on the side of the road, about a half-mile from the tavern.

"I don't believe it," said Sal. "They're stopping to have a drink!"

"I'm not so sure," said Sharon. "I saw their headlights shining onto the road when they parked. They're facing the highway."

"At this hour, they surely could have parked closer to the building. Something's up."

"Here comes something," said Sharon.

They watched as the headlights of the large vehicle steaming toward them in the other lane, grew larger. As it darted passed them, they were aghast!

"That's the COF truck!" exclaimed Sal.

"Why would they all be heading east?" asked Sharon.

"Damned if I can figure this out," said Sal. "There's one good thing, though."

"What's that?"

"Our eyes are on the money."

The minivan pulled back out onto the highway, heading west.

"There they go, again," said Sal. "Is it me, or does it seem an awful lot like they were just waiting for the truck to pass?"

"Maybe you weren't so wrong about Rolly after all," she said, fearfully.

"But I *want* to be wrong about Rolly!"

Sharon watched as Sal first lowered his head, then slowly looked away. "We should go," she said, softly.

He merely nodded. The Voyager resumed its chase of the blue Ford minivan.

At five-oh-five AM., darkness had begun the passage to dawn on the eastern horizon. The minivan pulled into the rendezvous area, up alongside the Viper. Rolly shut off the ignition and breathed a huge sigh of relief. "Okay, partner. Here's where we part ways," he said.

"Give me a hand, would you please?" asked Mesmer, opening his door. "Those damn things look awful heavy."

"You sure got your nerve." smiled Rolly, shaking his head. "I'll give ya that."

Mesmer ignored the comment.

Rolly opened the driver's door and hopped out. Mesmer headed directly for the rear of the Viper, fishing in his pocket for the keys. Rolly walked around to the rear of the van and unlocked the hatchback, letting the hydraulics hoist it to its upright position.

"Check this out," grinned Rolly. "You can almost smell the green ink back here!" With that, Rolly climbed up into the rear compartment to fetch the first of six satchels. Mesmer reached into the Viper's trunk and grabbed the shovel he'd stowed there for a somewhat different, but related purpose. As Rolly backed himself to the edge of the rear compartment, dragging one of the bags, Mesmer was waiting.

With an iron grip choked up four inches on the shovel's handle, Mesmer drew upon every stored molecule of energy he could summon. He flung the heavy steel end of the shovel into a 180-degree backswing, and as Rolly descended the van with his back to him, Mesmer mightily swung forward, sending the weighty concave apex crashing against Rolly's skull, creating a massive tolling resonance that perforated the early morning calm.

"What the hell was that?" asked Sal, parked with Sharon on the highway, not far from the clearing.

"Sounded like a muffled church bell," said Sharon.

"I don't like the sound of that at all."

Mesmer dragged Rolly's limp, dead-weight body to the driver's side of the Viper, unlocked, and opened the door. He proceeded with the difficult chore of lifting and positioning him behind the wheel.

Quietly, Sal opened the door to the Voyager. "Stay here," he whispered.

"Please, Sal, be careful," begged Sharon.

He showed her the gun. "Don't worry, I've got this," he said smiling.

Sal edged along the extreme right side of the road's shoulder, carefully placing his feet on small clumps of vegetation wherever he could. Until he'd arrive at the clearing, five-foot high wild bushes concealed him from view. Following each cautious step, he paused to listen. As he neared the opening, he could make out sounds of heavy breathing.

Mesmer had Rolly secured behind the wheel of the Viper, strapped in place with the seat belt and shoulder harness. He removed Rolly's watch, ring, and wallet, placing them in his jacket's side pocket and, panting furiously, felt he was finally ready. But he needed to move the van to a safe distance.

Just as Sal reached the clearing's opening, he peeked up over the final bush, as Mesmer made his way to the rear of the minivan, where he pulled down and slammed the hatchback. The driver's door of the Viper was still open, but the parked angle and raised trunk lid obscured Rolly's presence from Sal. He watched as Mesmer started the van and began pulling away. Where's Rolly, Sal wondered? Where's Mesmer going? Concerned he may be pulling out onto the road, Sal hurried back to the Voyager.

It was dawn now, and they and their car were clearly visible. He opened the door and got in.

"What did you see?" asked Sharon.

"Couldn't see Rolly. Mesmer just got in the van and started driving – but he hasn't pulled out yet."

"Was the Viper still there?"

"Yeah, and the front door and trunk were open, so I couldn't tell if anyone was in there. I'm going back."

Mesmer had moved the van and walked back to the Viper. He reached into the open trunk and lifted the five-gallon red and yellow gasoline can used to refuel his power mower, setting it down beside him.

Meanwhile, Sal was back in position at the clearing's opening. Peering over the bush, his eye immediately caught the gasoline can. He also noticed the shovel leaning against the viper. The church bell sound now made sense. Mesmer had hit Rolly over the head with the shovel, put him in the car and was now preparing to torch it. He prayed his friend was still alive. And he needed to act fast.

Mesmer reached down and began uncapping the gas can. Sal rushed into the clearing. "Hold it, Mesmer," he ordered, double gripping the pointed gun. "Move away from the car, now!"

Sal's presence and voice terrified Mesmer who gasped at the unexpected intrusion. As the gun came into focus, Mesmer slowly released his grip on the gas can cap and raised his hands. This little son-of-a-bitch came out of nowhere, he thought. Another foil was one more than he was willing to accept. As he moved slowly away from the car, his devious mind, once again, chugged into action.

The two men were facing each other, some forty yards apart. Mesmer recognized Sal and knew him by name through discussions with Rolly.

Though it was very difficult to tell for sure, to Mesmer, the gun appeared to reflect a shade of copper. It could be the gun he tossed out the window, he thought. He also remembered there were five bullets remaining in the gun, after he'd fired those two into the air. And at this distance, it was highly unlikely that anyone but a skilled sharpshooter could even get close to hitting him.

"I know you," called out Mesmer. "You worked for me in the casino, didn't you?"

"Keep moving away from the car," Sal replied. "I'm not afraid to use this!"

"No need to," said Mesmer with a crooked grin. "We can negotiate this."

"Where's Rolly?"

"I left him off down the road," lied Mesmer.

"Horseshit," said Sal. "You are such a fucking low-life idiot."

"I swear," said Mesmer. "We stopped at a tavern down the road and he wanted out there. We worked out our differences."

"I'll ask you one more time," threatened Sal, "then I'll let this gun do the talking. Now where's Rolly?"

"He's not here! Come see for yourself."

Slowly, Sal began to move in, training the gun barrel on Mesmer from a fully extended arms position. He needed to see inside the Viper. If Rolly were anywhere, that's where he'd be.

Wanting to maintain the safer distance between them, Mesmer, little by little, backed up as Sal crept nearer. He anticipated the point where Sal would see Rolly strapped in the front seat. Once that happened, Mesmer's minutes would be numbered. *Unless*, he could outlast five shots.

Sal's heart pounded fiercely as he inched his way closer to the Viper, trying to maintain aim amidst quivering hands. Mesmer continued his own backward retreat, hands raised, his eyes riveted to Sal's. As Sal arced slowly to his left, the cockpit of the Viper began to emerge. First the edge of the padded dash; then the fringe of the steering wheel. With the next side step, a dangling arm. One more produced the eerie sight of Rolly, head bowed, body wrapped in webbed strapping.

"Rolly?" Sal's voice shuddered. "Rolly!"

Mesmer made his break, turning and running away from the Viper and minivan.

"You bastard!" Sal pulled the trigger. He missed.

"That's one," muttered Mesmer to himself, continuing his clumsy run.

Sal sprinted after him, firing a stray second shot.

Mesmer ducked, panting. "That's two," he breathed, shifting directions.

Having heard the shots, Sharon, hurried, terrified, into the clearing. From behind the Viper, she watched in horror as Sal fired wildly the third and fourth shots in rapid succession. Her eyes caught Rolly propped in the Viper. She ran to him.

"Three, four," chuckled Mesmer, as he turned again, catching a glimpse of Sharon running to the Viper. Immediately, he took off toward her with Sal following.

"Come on! Shoot me again, you creep," Mesmer hissed to himself.

Just as Sal was about to fire shot number five, he became aware of Sharon at the Viper, directly in the line of fire. Damn! Another shot was out of the question. He opted for a different tactic. Able to forego aiming, he dug in, ratcheted up his speed, and lunged at the aging lowlife's back just as Mesmer reached within five feet of the Viper. In mid air, Sal tossed the gun toward Sharon who screeched a high pitched squeal, but caught the weapon with both hands.

Mesmer and Sal crashed to the ground with a resounding thump. It was all adrenaline now, and the youthful Mooring's supply was abundant. He clutched the hair on the back of Mesmer's head and repeatedly smashed his battered face against the hard, dry desert floor. Mesmer bellowed with shrieks of anguish, blood gushing from his shattered nose and mangled forehead. Veins in Sal's face and neck bulged with vengeance, seethed with hatred. He ached to squeeze the life out of this human blunder.

"You're a dead man, you fuck!" he screamed, clasping his muscular hands around Mesmer's neck. "I'll squash you like an insect!"

"No, Sal!" Sharon pleaded, still pointing the gun loosely in their direction. "Don't do it!"

Mesmer choked and gurgled as Sal's crushing pressure intensified.

"Die, you miserable bastard. Have the fuckin' decency for once in your loser life!"

"Sal stop! Please!" implored Sharon, tears streaming. "The bastard's not worth it!"

"Your wife...!" choked out Mesmer.

"What?" barked Sal, his teeth gritting.

"Your wife...!" he repeated. "She *fucked* the *cop*!"

Stunned, Sharon froze. Trepidation sheathed her entire body. Her eyes flashed to her husband's instantly distressed face.

The words had clobbered Sal between the eyes like an errant two-by-four causing a reflexive loosening of his vice-like grip on Mesmer's neck. Mesmer choked and wheezed. Locked in a numbing slow motion, Sal turned his head toward Sharon, his eyes pleading for a sign of denial, a signal that what he just heard was spurious. But the horror in her eyes, the pain in her face, the quiver in her bottom lip revealed the grimmest of realities. His eyes bulged with bewilderment. A rush of thick, heavy silence filled his head deadening his consciousness.

Mesmer turned his broken, bloodied face toward Sharon. Her look of dismay and Sal's alleviated pressure bestowed opportunity. With Sal and Sharon locked in trance-like stares, Mesmer summoned a final reserve of strength and belted Sal full-fist to the jaw, tumbling him backwards into a crumpled heap.

Sharon screamed. Raising the gun toward Mesmer as he rolled to his side, she cried, "Don't you fucking move!"

Mesmer slowly lifted himself to his feet. "Give me the gun, bitch," he moaned. "Don't be stupid."

"I swear I'll kill you!" she said quivering.

His face hideously rearranged, he limped toward her with his mouth hanging open, covered in bloodied dirt.

"One more step!" she warned. "Sal! Sal!"

Mesmer defiantly reached toward her. She squeezed her eyes shut and pulled the trigger. The blast struck him in the chest, knocking him backwards. Struggling, he regained his balance. He reached for her with one hand and clutched his chest with the other. Blood oozed between his grasping fingers.

Sharon pulled the trigger again, this time a click. The bullets were gone. She backed up, screaming, "Sal! Sal! Help me!"

Sal, weak, pained, and in shock attempted to get up. As he struggled to his knees, Sharon threw the gun at Mesmer, striking him in the temple. He cried out with a piercing, painful yell, but gripping his chest, continued limping toward her. His movement showed definite signs of weakness, but he refused to die on any but his own terms.

Sharon ran around the rear of the Viper, circling toward Sal. Mesmer dragged himself in the same direction, stopping at the back of the car. Uttering vocalized pain, he picked up the gas can and headed slowly, but with determination toward the minivan.

With Sal still on his knees, Sharon grabbed his face with both hands. "Sal! Sal! Darling! Please!"

He looked into her eyes. His face was pleading. "Did ... you?" he asked, his voice barely audible.

Sharon's face erupted in tears. She began to hyperventilate, her own pain strikingly evident. "I am so sorry," she cried. "I am so sorry!" She buried her face in his chest and bawled uncontrollably.

Sal looked up. Mesmer had arrived at the minivan. He opened the hatchback.

"Oh shit!" Sal exclaimed. "No!"

Immediately Sharon turned toward the minivan.

With his one free hand, Mesmer removed the cap on the gas can. He lifted the can and pushed it over, spewing the volatile liquid all over the inside compartment where it scurried beneath and between the dozen suitcases.

"Jesus Christ" Sal shouted. "Stop him!" He and Sharon scrambled to their feet and ran toward the van.

Mesmer lifted the gas can and with grunts, groans and painful squeals, doused himself with the petrol. As gasoline made contact with his bloodied, open wounds, he screamed and yelped in excruciating agony.

Just before Sal could overtake him, Mesmer reached into his pocket and pulled out his lighter. "If not me," he cried out, "*no one*!"

Sal slid to a stop, hesitated, and then leaped toward Mesmer just as he flicked the lighter. Seeing the flame appear, Sal veered his body to the right, landing in a roll on the ground. Instantly Mesmer erupted in flames. He let out a blood curdling scream, bent his knees, and launched himself into the back of the minivan, igniting the fuel soaked carpet, the suitcases and the van, itself. Sal continued rolling out of the way. Sharon ran toward the Viper, screaming. Mesmer's piercing yells were barely audible amid the fire's ravaging rumbles.

The explosion was thunderous. The bright orange ball of flames quickly devoured the van and its contents, sending thick, black smoke pummeling the morning sky.

Sharon ran toward Sal. He was lying facedown about twenty yards from the blaze. "Sal!" she yelled. "Sal, are you all right?"

He lifted his head and slowly nodded. "You?" he asked.

"I'm okay," she said.

"It's gone, Sharon," Sal said, sadly. "That son-of-a-bitch took it with him."

"But, we're alive, Sal. We still have each other."

"Do we, Sharon?"

"What he said, darling…"

"Don't," Sal said, pressing his finger against her lips. "Not now."

Sharon laid her head against his chest. "Please know that I love you. And I want you more than anything."

"We came so close," said Sal. "We actually pulled it off! It was in the palms of our hands! We were fucking millionaires."

"It's obscene," said Sharon. "How one nasty person can single-handedly squeeze joy out of so many. I hope he burns in hell."

Meanwhile, out of their earshot, Sue Min's voice spurted through a burst of radio static.

"Rolly? Sue Min. Can you hear me? I don't think he's got it turned on," she said. "Keep tryin'," came Nappa's voice.

"All right. Rolly? Rolly, this is Sue Min. Come in, Rolly."

"Yeah, Sue Min. This is Rolly. Go ahead – but do me a favor, don't talk so loud, huh? My head's killing me."

Chapter Thirty-two
Epilogue

Rolly felt around for the seatbelt buckle, careful to avoid unnecessary bending at the neck. He slowly and methodically attempted to piece together a status based on his limited observations. He was strapped in the Viper. The minivan was ablaze. Mesmer was nowhere to be seen. Obviously, Mesmer had hit him over the head with something. But how could Mesmer have left with the twelve suitcases, leaving the only two vehicles available behind? And why would he set the van on fire? He needed more dots before he could attempt to connect them.

He had just told Sue Min to bring the COF team to the rendezvous point. He refrained from mentioning the blazing van; no sense jumping to needless conclusions. Perhaps by the time they arrived, he will have assessed the situation more clearly.

Groggy and painfully sore, he squeezed out of the cramped front seat of the low-set Viper. Scouting the immediate area, he spotted the gun on the ground amid a trail of fresh blood sprinklings. As he broadened his view of the area, he noticed two people, apparently a man and a woman, lying prone not far from the burning vehicle. They appeared to be in passionate embrace. More confusing dots.

Rubbing the back of his head, he slowly made his way toward the couple. After a few steps, he recognized Sharon and Sal. A few paces from them, he politely cleared his throat.

"Did you hear something?" asked Sal, breaking off their kiss.

"Hey, you two," said Rolly.

Shocked, they scrambled to their feet.

"Rolly! You're alive!" screamed Sharon.

"Man, are you a sight for sore eyes," said Sal. "Are you okay?"

"Well, I won't be doing sit-ups anytime soon," said Rolly, holding the back of his neck, "but, yeah, I am alive. What are you two doing here? And what the hell happened?"

"We took off after you and Mesmer," said Rolly. "When you guys had that close call with the tractor-trailer, Sharon thought she saw something fall out of the window. We stopped and searched the highway...."

"And I found the gun," said Sharon, smiling.

"Yeah, she did," said Sal. "Then we followed you back here. We heard Mesmer hit you, it turns out, with that shovel." Sal pointed toward the rear of the Viper.

"Rolly, Mesmer set himself and the van on fire," Sharon said. "There was nothing we could do."

"That was after I beat the shit out of him and Sharon shot him," added Sal. "The bastard turned himself into a human torch. He actually took it with him. Can you believe it?"

"I've got the rest of the team coming to join us," said Rolly. "They don't know about the van."

"Those poor guys," said Sal. "They're going to be absolutely crushed."

"I suspect there's going to be fire engines and police out here before too long," said Rolly. "Surely somebody's spotted this fire and reported it."

"We're in deep shit," said Sal. "No money and deep shit."

"We've got to think of a way out of this," said Sharon. "I *did* shoot the man, but he was coming after me. He wanted to kill me! You should have seen him, Rolly. He was a monster."

"First thing we do is get rid of the gun," said Rolly. "Sal, grab that shovel and take the gun somewhere down the road and bury it out in the desert. They'll never find it. But, just in case, give it a good wiping."

"Got it." Sal trotted over to the Viper, grabbed the shovel, and spotting the gun on the ground, picked it up. "Be back in a few," he said, and he darted out of the clearing to the Voyager.

"Rolly?" said Sharon.

"Yeah?"

"Before he blew himself up, Mesmer told Sal about me and Harve Dedman. With one of his last breaths, he screamed 'Your wife fucked the cop!'"

Rolly closed his eyes and looked at the ground. "Oh,00000 my God," he said, shaking his head. "Oh my God."

"Why would you do that to me?" asked Sharon. "And why would you do that to Sal?"

"I swear I never meant for that to happen, Sharon."

"Meant it or not, you need to know you've changed our lives forever, you bastard. One lousy, drunken interlude may cost me the only man I've ever loved. And all because your slimy fingerprints are all over it. Here's a down payment of what I owe you." Sharon reached back and slugged Rolly in the mouth.

Sal, heading due west in the Voyager, had covered about two miles since leaving the rendezvous area. Now in the mountainous region of the western Las Vegas valley, he pulled the Voyager into an off-road crevice and parked out of highway sight, behind a huge ridge of rock. He slid the gun into his belt and, carrying the shovel, trekked into the adjacent canyon, searching for a burial spot.

Several hundred paces from the car, he settled on a nondescript plot, not unlike a million others. His entire body shook with the first clang of the shovel against the concrete-like ground, causing him to shift to a blade scraping approach. That proved to be equally tedious, but eventually, he scraped and dug a one-foot hole. He removed the gun from his belt, wiped it clean with his handkerchief, and laid it in the hole. Then he wiped the perspiration from his face and returned the handkerchief to his pocket. He re-filled the hole, doing his best to blend the new with the surrounding sand and soils.

He walked several paces away and turned to inspect his work. Satisfied that even he couldn't detect any deviations in the landscape, he returned to the car. After wiping off the loose dirt with his damp handkerchief, he slid the shovel onto the back seat floor, and tossed in the damp, soiled hanky.

He turned the key and backed the Voyager out of the crevice and onto the road, for his return trip to the rendezvous point. His watch showed it was five-forty-nine AM.

Missy Mangen reached over and felt for the snooze button on the beckoning alarm clock. She lay there for a second before realizing the other half of the bed was empty. Indeed it hadn't even been slept in. Harve never made it back! She shot up in bed. Nervously, she searched for the TV remote control. Finding it, she pressed the power button. As the picture warmed to life, she focused her eyes on a most eerie image – a distant shot of what appeared to be the World Trade Center with black smoke billowing near the top of the one of the towers.

"Repeating now," the announcer said, his voice quivering, "the north tower of the World Trade Center in New York City has been struck by a commercial airliner. Details are sketchy, but sources say the plane crashed into the tower, just moments ago, at eight-forty-five AM., Eastern time, hitting it at around twenty stories below the top."

"My God!" gasped Missy. "Those poor, pathetic souls!"

"NBC News has confirmed the jetliner was an American Airlines Boeing 767, Flight Eleven, enroute from Boston's Logan International Airport to Los Angeles. There were ninety-two people on board. Flight eleven had been airborne for some forty-six minutes before the plane, clearly off course, exploded into the Trade Center, likely killing everyone onboard, and taking countless others, already at work in the Trade Center, along with them. Hundreds of New York police and fire department personnel have been dispatched to the disaster area. Attempts are underway now to evacuate tower number one, while a temporary command post is being set-up a few blocks away for city officials, including Mayor Rudy Giuliani. At this time, spokespersons for American Airlines and the National Transportation Safety Board can offer no explanation for this unprecedented tragedy."

Like millions of Americans throughout the country at that very moment, Missy sat on the edge of the bed horrified and dumbfounded.

The lights and sound truck pulled in to the rendezvous area.

"I hope to God he got those suitcases out!" exclaimed Nappa, zeroing in on the flaming van. "What the hell happened?"

"There's Rolly sitting on the trunk of the Viper," said Sue Min. "He's with that woman."

Nappa pulled the truck up alongside the Viper, and the COF team quickly exited the truck. Both anticipating and seeing the horror on their faces, Rolly calmly raised his arms. "Take it easy," he called out to everyone. "Come on, gather around here."

Several of the team couldn't help from running over to the van and peering through the blaze. "Christ, they're still in there!" someone yelled. "The money's up in flames!" screamed another.

"Everybody over here!" called out Rolly.

"Fuck this!" hollered Francisco Mercado. "Fuck all this!"

"We need an explanation, Rolly," said Sue Min. "And we need it now!"

"Hold on," said Rolly. "Just give me a chance, here, huh?"

"Hey, pal," said Harve Dedman, "No more bullshit – just pass out the money!"

The group was visibly and audibly enraged. Their anger fed off each other's vicious comments. Rolly observed the threatening looks on their faces. This was not going to be easy. Patiently, he waited for the group's temperature to stabilize.

While brushing her teeth, Missy listened to the unfolding World Trade Center story on a portable radio. "Word is coming in at this moment that the second plane crash was United Airlines Flight 175, also a Boeing 767, also enroute from Boston's Logan International and also heading for Los Angeles. There were sixty-five people on board. For those of you just joining us at this early hour, five minutes after six, this Tuesday morning, September 11th—it just occurred to me, the date is 9-1-1—two commercial airliners, both headed for Los Angeles have…"

Sal reached the rendezvous area and pulled in next to the Lights and Sound truck. Flames still engulfed the van. Rolly appeared to have the group somewhat under control. Sal had the feeling they were all waiting for him. He shut off the engine and let his feet carry him to the other side of the Viper. Sharon was there to greet him. They kissed and turned to face Rolly, wondering, as they all were, what he could possibly have to say.

Only the rumbling of fire coming from the burning van could be heard as Rolly completed his mental preparations for what he was about to say.

"Rolly," Harve Dedman said, pointing to the burning minivan. "We're going to need to get out of here. It won't be long before this place is swarming in badges."

"I know. You're right," said Rolly. "Tell you what. Load up in the truck. Sal, I'll ride with you and Sharon. The truck can follow us. We're headed down the road apiece," he said. "This'll be COF's last stop. I promise."

"What's the point," Stan Reno was heard to say.

"We ought to just go home," said Francisco Mercado.

"Bear with me," said Rolly, over his shoulder. "There's something I need to say and you need to hear. But, we can't do it here."

Craig Stetson and Paul Toomey caught each other's eyes and smiled.

Within a minute, the fully loaded truck was shadowing the Voyager, headed east on Blue Diamond Road.

Three miles from the rendezvous area, Nappa and Sue Min saw the left-turn blinker come to life on the Voyager. "Where the hell they turnin' to?" asked Nappa. "Ain't no road here!"

"Just follow," said Sue Min.

The Voyager cut across the virtually vacant four-lane highway, onto and across the shoulder and beyond. The truck followed, offering its passengers a far bumpier version of the ride.

Collusion on the Felt

The two vehicles converged behind a cluster of bushes and trees, concealing them from the highway. Rolly was the first to exit. He approached the truck, carrying the shovel from the back seat of the Voyager. Rolly motioned to Nappa and Sue Min to join him in the rear of the truck. Sal and Sharon followed.

Rolly opened the truck's back doors, lifted himself up, with assistance from the shovel, and sat on the truck's bed, sideways, so he could address both the interior and exterior of the truck. He leaned back against the side of the truck and let out a monstrous sigh.

"There's a reason for this shovel," he began. "But before I get to that, there are some things I need to tell you."

All eyes were on him. His voice and lips were quivering. It was obvious to them that this speech is one that Rolly had not been looking forward to giving.

"First, let me say how absolutely proud I am to have been associated with this outstanding group. Even though that van is being incinerated back there," he said, "we still pulled off one for the record book. And you need to be proud of that."

Some of the group members made sarcastic noises like yawning, throat clearing, and low mumbles, like "big fuckin' deal."

"Now I need to come clean," continued Rolly. "So here goes. The man burning in that van back there–Nathan Mesmer–was the actual creator of COF. In fact this whole thing was his idea; his plan."

The group was dumbfounded, their eyes wide and mouths opened.

"He recruited me last spring, a month or so after he came to town. Long story short, he put his business card under my windshield wiper one night with a note asking me to have a drink with him. He complimented me on my work, poured liquor into me, and told me he wanted to make me a millionaire. He gave me the gist of the plan and asked me to command the operation. Drunk, hungry, and basically discontent, I agreed. My job was to put together a team of equally discontent people who were tired of living payday to payday and working for a horse's ass. His job was to *be* a horse's ass. He figured by making life at the Desert Empire a living hell, people would be chomping at the bit to rip it off."

"How right he was!" said Francisco Mercado. The group chuckled.

"Yeah, he was very good at that," said Sue Min.

"Here comes the hardest part for me." said Rolly. He paused, searching for the just the right words, looking each of the COF members in the eye, one by one. The pain of what he was about to say shown on his face; in his trembling lower lip. He breathed deeply and expelled a long resigning sigh. "I was supposed to tell all of you that you would get an equal share. And, of course, that's what I told you. But Mesmer made me agree with him that he and I would split the entire take fifty-fifty. In other words, you'd get nothing."

"Son-of-a-bitch!" said Harve Dedman.

"May he burn in hell!" said Curtis Lately.

"All along, I let him believe that's how it would go down." said Rolly. "But, I swear to you, in my heart, there was no way I'd ever have allowed that to happen."

"I believe that," said Stan Reno.

"So do I," said Sue Min.

"If anybody has any doubt," said Sal, "just think about what Rolly went through for us over night."

"Your life was constantly on the line," said Stan Reno.

"Don't you worry none, Rollo. Ain't no one here believes you'd have stiffed us," said Nappa.

"Thank you, guys," said Rolly. "That means a hell of a lot to me. Anyway, come to find out just yesterday that Mesmer had purchased a one-way ticket to Australia, on a flight leaving in a few hours...." Rolly looked at his wrist and realized his watch was missing. He smiled. "The bastard even took my watch...and my ring!" He felt for his wallet. "He took my wallet, too!" He shook his head. "Anyway, this flight to Australia is leaving this morning and the ticket had *my* name on it as the passenger. He neither told me about it, nor let me have the ticket. Mr. Frederick accidentally found it in the office and showed it to me. Poor guy. I think that's why he's dead now. And I have no doubt-that's how I'd be, too, if Mesmer had had his way. That brings me to this shovel."

Rolly jumped off the truck. "I'd like you all to follow me," he said.

"Here we go," Stetson whispered to Toomey.

"You guys know something about this?" asked Stan Reno, quietly.

"You'll find out in a couple of minutes," said Toomey. "Hang loose."

The group of COF team members followed their shovel wielding leader out into the desert. From a distance it looked like a twenty-first century version of Moses.

Along the way, Rolly continued with his story. "The way the plan was laid out, when it came time to pick up the money from the whales, Mesmer was supposed to ride with me. I would drop him off back there where we just parked, then go on alone to the rendezvous point. I'd pick up the money from the whales and meet Mesmer back here where he and I would divvy the take fifty-fifty."

"Then why are we walking out into the desert?" asked Sue Min.

"I'll finish the story up ahead," said Rolly. "Then you'll understand."

When they'd spanned a distance of three football fields, Rolly slowed his pace and carefully scanned the landscape. Noticing the plastic water bottle half-filled with dirt, he held up his left hand, bringing the march to a halt.

"Gather 'round," he said. And they did.

"Now continuing," he cleared his throat. "I never trusted Mesmer, not for one single solitary second. No way would he'd *ever* allow me to go on living if I had something on him. And I knew that from the beginning. So ... Craig, why don't you and Paul clue the team in from this point?"

Craig Stetson moved to the center of the group. "Rolly called me about an hour before COF kicked off yesterday and told me not to ask any questions, but that there was something he wanted me and Paul to do while driving the limousines to the rendezvous area. Paul?"

Paul Toomey joined his friend, center-circle. "Last night, as soon as we left the casino, we drove the limos here, whales and all–right here–using that water bottle as our sign-post. The Chinese guys waited in the limos while Craig and me dug up two huge footlockers that Rolly told us had been buried here. We emptied all the money from the twelve suitcases into those footlockers and re-buried them right here."

"All that was in those twelve suitcases in the van was some of the dirt from around here to give the bags some weight," said Stetson. "Thanks to Rolly, Mesmer set himself and a bunch of dirt on fire. Our money is safe right here!"

"You gotta be shittin' me," said Stan Reno, grinning from ear to ear.

"There *is* a God," said Nappa. "And I bet He's black! I'm rich again!"

Before anyone else could say anything, the team members fell to their knees and began frantically digging with their hands.

"My God, I can't believe this!" said the one known as Jesse.

"Rolly, you're a genius!" yelled Francisco Mercado.

"Here, let me help," said Rolly, moving in with the shovel. They dug through the soft soil, piling the mounds along the perimeter. It wasn't long before they could feel the smooth, solid surface of one of the footlockers; and then the other.

"Pay dirt!" yelled Harve.

"No, that's what Mesmer got," joked Stetson. Everyone laughed.

Working as the team they were, they pulled the two huge footlockers, one by one, out of the chasm and onto the ground.

"In my heart of hearts," said Rolly, "I believe once Mesmer and I divvied up the money, he was going to shoot me dead and bury me in this hole."

Both footlockers were now sitting on the side of the hole.

"Let's check 'em out, man!" said Nappa, flipping up the latches and flaps. One after the other, each footlocker's lid rested in the raised position. They were filled to the brims with freshly wrapped and labeled hundred dollar bills. Thirty-five million dollars, in all. It was a reverent moment. Eyeballs stretched to their physical limits. Jaws hung open. Hearts pounded intensely.

"Have you ever seen this much money in your life?" asked Curtis Lately.

"Not close-up and personal," said Nappa. "This gives me chills, man."

"Okay," said Rolly. "You've earned it. It's one point three apiece, and don't forget, we've got a few team members who aren't here, so their shares go with me. I'll see they get them. Let's divvy!"

While the COF team members secured their futures by reaping the rewards of their all night toil, a third hijacked airliner exploded in flames as it hit the Pentagon in Washington D.C. Shortly thereafter, a fourth plane, also hijacked and believed headed to the nation's capital, was overtaken by a group of courageous passengers who, upon learning via cellular calls to loved ones that other hijacked planes had turned into devastating missiles, decided they weren't going to sit back and do nothing. Responding to one passenger's call to "Let's roll!" they overpowered their brazen captors, forcing the plane to crash in an unpopulated, wooded area near western Pennsylvania, outside Pittsburgh, truly giving their lives for their country.

The FAA, for the first time in history, closed all U.S. airports and cancelled all incoming and outgoing flights. The skies would be stilled for nearly a week.

When the Las Vegas Review Journal hit the driveways and newsstands on Wednesday morning, the headline read: *Terror Strike!* and was followed by page after page of horrific photos and stories of the previous day's terrorist attack on America.

On page six, however, in the lower right hand corner was a rather obscure article following an equally obscure headline: *Charred Remains of Casino Executive Found in Auto Inferno!*

Printed in the United States
130350LV00011B/91-93/P